RHODY JONES

C.J. PETIT

Copyright © 2020 by C.J. Petit
All rights reserved. This book or any portion thereof may not be reproduced or used in any manner whatsoever without the express written permission of the publisher except for the use of brief quotations in a book review.

Printed in the United States of America

First Printing, 2020

ISBN: 9798623767257

TABLE OF CONTENTS

RHODY JONES 1
PROLOGUE...3
CHAPTER 1...12
CHAPTER 2...29
CHAPTER 3...54
CHAPTER 4...75
CHAPTER 5...147
CHAPTER 6...183
CHAPTER 7...216
CHAPTER 8...239
CHAPTER 9...289
CHAPTER 10...372
CHAPTER 11...409
EPILOGUE...488

C.J. PETIT

RHODY JONES

PROLOGUE

**September 4, 1874
The Gulf of Mexico
160 Miles East-Southeast of New Orleans**

The *Vivienne's* bow plunged into twelve-foot wave at forty-degree angle and as the bowsprit emerged from the angry water, the masts tilted dangerously close to the lee.

The first mate shouted to the steersman, "Get her closer to the wind!"

The steersman didn't acknowledge the order as he and able seaman Will Ryan strained to move the wheel to the port side to get the ship turned. But even with the help of the crew's biggest able seaman, he was already fighting just to keep the *Vivienne* on its current course.

The first mate glanced at the foremast and was worried that the lonely gallant might be carrying too much sail in this wind, but it was all that was keeping them from foundering. The barometer had warned them of the pending storm, but the last time he'd checked the instrument, it was still dropping. This was no ordinary gale, the *Vivienne* was being driven by a hurricane, and it hadn't even reached its peak.

He turned to the only other hand on deck and yelled over the roaring wind, "Parker, where's the captain?"

George Parker hung onto the mizzenmast as he shouted, "In his cabin!"

The first mate cursed loudly enough for the three crewmembers who weren't belowdecks to hear then waited until the ship dropped into a trough between the monstrous waves, untied the rope from his waist, let it drop then stumbled across the deck until he reached the cabin door. He wrestled it open as the wind was determined to keep it closed then squeezed through the gap before it slammed shut.

Once inside the creaking, but windless space, he placed his hand on the tilting wall and quickly strode to the captain's cabin. He knew why the captain was in his cabin and not on deck as he should be, and it wasn't out of fear. He had spent most of his life on the sea and had probably been in worst storms than this one, but he wasn't young anymore and while the *Vivienne* wasn't an ideal command, it was probably his last.

He threw open the cabin's door and wasn't surprised to find Captain Dent in his bunk with his eyes closed. There was an empty bottle of Scotch whiskey rolling across the deck as the ship wallowed in the heavy seas.

"Captain! We need to set the sea anchor before it gets even worse!"

RHODY JONES

The captain's eyes slowly opened just before the ship shuddered as it plunged into another wave then rolled dangerously close to its tipping point.

"Captain! Can you hear me?" the first mate shouted.

The captain looked at him through watery, glazed eyes and asked in a slurred voice, "What did you say? Sea anchor?"

"Yes! We need to deploy a sea anchor now. The gallant looks like it's about to rip apart in this wind. Where is the sea anchor? It's not where it should be."

The captain lazily shook his head as he replied, "No sea anchor no more. Gone."

There was no time to question the captain why it was gone, but now that last refuge to ensure that the ship faced into the wind wasn't available and may have been too late to deploy it anyway. It should have been set into the sea when the barometer dropped so precipitously. When he'd told the captain that they should have the crew set the sea anchor an hour ago, the captain had told him it wasn't time then gone to his cabin.

At least now he understood why the captain had left his post. Without the sea anchor, the *Vivienne* was in real danger of being swamped by the tall waves and the captain had simply given up to find his personal refuge in the bottle.

The first mate took one last look at the captain who had already closed his eyes then hurried out of the cabin and reached the exit door. He put his shoulder to the door, leaned forward and then pushed with his legs to force it open. But the ship was on the back side of the last wave and as it rammed its bow into the trough the wind was blocked, and the door flew open.

He flew onto the main deck as the crashing flood of seawater grabbed him and slid him across the heavy oak before he slammed into the pin rail. He was momentarily stunned before he got to his hands and knees and crawled to the mizzenmast where Seaman Parker had now lashed himself.

He grabbed Parker's pants and used them for support as he stood then as the seaman stared at him, he looked at the top gallant and saw that it now had a large tear in its canvas but was still giving them some headway. If it failed, then the *Vivienne* would be lost.

He waited until the ship crested the next wave then as it slid on the back side, he rushed to the quarterdeck, snatched his rope and wrapped it around his waist just as the *Vivienne* crashed into the trough. He braced himself against the deck railing in time to watch the bow dip below the gray water then as it surfaced, the wave raced along the main deck and crashed into the quarterdeck before returning to the sea.

RHODY JONES

He released his grip, knotted the rope then staggered to the wheel.

"The captain is ill. Let's do what we can to keep her close to the wind. When the rudder clears the water on the next wave, give me four spokes to port then tie it off!"

"Aye, aye, sir!" shouted the steersman as he looked at the ocean ahead to wait for the right moment.

The first mate knew it was a dangerous move, but if the top gallant failed, it really didn't matter anyway. He couldn't send a man aloft in this wind to replace their only square-rigged sail, but as he looked at the foremast, he knew he had to come up with some way to maintain some level of steerage if they lost the gallant.

As the ship climbed the front of the next wave, he grabbed the deck rail with both hands and waited for the plunge after they reached the crest.

In the few seconds that the *Vivienne* was suspended and level, he watched the steersman comply with his orders and once the wheel was lashed into position, he shouted, "Get below with the rest of the crew and take Parker with you!"

Seaman Ryan and the steersman needed no encouragement as they stumbled past him and slid down the steps from the quarterdeck before disappearing into the crew cabin. When George Parker saw that they had made it safely below deck, he untied his lashing then chased after them, but he had waited too long.

Just as he let the line go, the ship began her fall into the trough between the waves, and as he reached for the door, the bow dug into the angry water of the gulf and soon swept across the deck taking Seaman Parker with it.

There was no point in looking for him, so the after the ship stabilized, the first mate quickly untied his lifeline then walked as quickly as possible from the quarterdeck and then headed for the bow.

He reached the foremast and wrapped his arms around it as the ship slammed into the next wave then as it twisted and rolled, the *Vivienne* began its next climb.

He released his grip on the mast long enough to reach and unlash the line for the staysail. He didn't have time to grip anything before the next plunge into the trough which would sweep him to his death just as it had taken Parker, but he had no other choice. He yanked his knife from its sheath, cut the sail's ties then after returning his knife to the sheath, he pulled the rope and the canvas quickly filled with wind, but he didn't raise the stay beyond three feet before he hurriedly tied the rope off on its cleat and grabbed hold of the mast just two heartbeats before the bow plunged below the water's surface.

He felt the power of the sea as it ripped past him and he needed every bit of his strength to keep hold of the foremast as the water fought to break his grip on life. As the water receded, he knew that he had won this battle but wasn't sure if the *Vivienne* would win its war with the hurricane.

The staysail didn't look like a real sail as it bulged almost to the bowsprit, but it was doing the job. He looked straight overhead and saw that the gallant's rip had extended to both spars and knew it wouldn't last much longer.

He had done all he could, so after the ship steadied, he raced back to the quarterdeck and as soon as he reached the wheel, he lashed himself to its spokes and prayed.

Eight days later, the *Vivienne* sailed into the mouth of the Mississippi River, but had to drop anchor while she waited for a steam tug to pull her to New Orleans' docks. The hurricane had blown the ship far to the west, so after making enough repairs to make sail, she had spent three days making her way east to New Orleans.

Nothing had been said about the captain's failure during the most critical part of the storm, nor had the first mate received any accolades for his actions. It was just the way of the sea.

When they finally reached the dock the next day, they were surprised that there was such little damage as the city was almost below sea level. It seemed that the hurricane had unleashed most of its fury on Texas.

After their cargo had been unloaded, the crew collected their pay and descended on New Orleans' numerous saloons and brothels, leaving the first mate and the captain alone on board.

Captain Lucius Dent had his first mate standing before him as he sat behind his desk.

"Roland, I won't be signing you up as first mate for the return voyage. If you want to join us as an able seaman, then you're free to do that. However, I will pay you as a first mate for this trip."

Roland looked at the captain, but even as he felt the almost overwhelming need to lash out at the man, he knew it would serve no purpose. He was the captain and it was his decision.

The captain counted out his pay on the desktop, then slipped the cash into an envelope and handed it to him.

"Will you be returning on the *Vivienne*?"

"No," he replied, intentionally not including the almost automatic 'sir'.

He turned and left the captain's cabin, entered his much smaller berth donned his gunbelt and collected his heavy duffle before stepping out onto the main deck.

RHODY JONES

He stopped and scanned what had been his workplace for most of his life then hung his duffle bag over his left shoulder, crossed the gangplank and stepped onto the deck.

He could have taken another ship back home, but he hadn't planned to return after this voyage anyway. He had already told his uncle that he'd be taking a long journey across the western half of the country and might be gone for years. He'd ride to Texas and see if it was anything like the land that had filled his imagination after reading all the stories of the frontier. He wanted to try a new way of life while he was still young. He knew that he'd miss the ocean and his uncle, but the hurricane had solidified his determination to head west.

CHAPTER 1

June 2, 1879
Comanche, Kiowa and Apache Reservation
Indian Territory

Harold Toomey pulled up in a cloud of dust and shouted, "Hey, Rhody, the boss wants to talk to you. He's havin' trouble with the Comanches."

Rhody asked, "What about?"

"He's dealin' with 'em to get the herd movin', but they're squawkin', and he ain't sure what it's about."

"Let's go an find out," he replied before setting his horse to a fast trot to reach the front of the massive herd.

It took him almost five minutes to reach the trail boss, but before he arrived, he could see that it was already a dangerous situation.

The last two drives through the Nations had been growing touchier as the tribes began to demand more than just a few head of cattle as payment for crossing their land. They wanted cash money to spend at the Indian store to buy the iron pots and other things that they couldn't make themselves. The last

RHODY JONES

time the negotiations had almost broken into a shooting battle and he wasn't sure that this was already close to that level as he looked at the line of Comanche warriors facing the smaller, but better armed group of cowhands. If he hadn't been riding drag that day, he probably would have already been with them.

He pulled his tan Morgan gelding to a stop beside the trail boss, and asked, "What's the trouble, boss?"

"I might be misreadin' what that Injun's askin' for, but he's holdin' up ten fingers and I figure he's askin' for a dime a head for lettin' us drive our cattle over his land. I can't see payin' him almost three hundred dollars for just passin' through, but I wanna be sure."

Rhody didn't ask why he hadn't summoned him earlier but walked his horse closer to the Comanche warrior who was sitting astride his light gray animal a few feet before the others.

When he was just ten feet away, he pulled the Morgan to a stop, and asked in basic Comanche, "What do you want?"

The warrior wasn't startled that the white man knew his language, but paused before replying, "You will pay ten cents for each animal in your herd and leave twenty fat cattle with us."

Rhody shouted over his shoulder to the trail boss and loudly asked, "Do you want me to negotiate?"

Stan Brown yelled back, "Go ahead, but you make sure that he don't ask for too much."

Rhody had been watching the warrior's eyes when Stan replied then smiled and said, "You speak English."

Long Eyes smiled and asked, "How did you know this?"

"Your eyes told me that you seemed to understand what my trail boss said. It wasn't much, but I noticed."

"So, will you do as he says and offer less?"

"I will offer you half of what you ask because you know that we have more and better guns than your warriors. I can see the anger on their faces as well as ours, and I don't wish to see any of them die for so little."

"This is not enough. My chief has told me to return with the cattle and the money."

"Is Blue Wolf so stubborn that you cannot convince him that it was wiser to return with half of the money but with all your warriors still alive? I can part with thirty cattle, but to give you ten cents for each animal would not leave us with enough money to pay the Cherokee when we reach their lands."

Rhody could see him thinking and even though the extra hundred and fifty dollars would hardly have as big an impact as he'd claimed, he suspected that he might accept the new offer.

RHODY JONES

After almost a minute of silence, Long Eyes said, "We will accept five cents for each of your cattle, but we will need forty animals. We will choose which ones we will take with us."

Rhody nodded then twisted to look at Stan and asked loudly, "Is that alright, boss? Forty head and five cents for each critter?"

Stan had been listening to them and was a bit miffed that the Indian had been able to speak English knowing he had used his apparent ignorance as a bargaining advantage, but still knew it was an acceptable trade.

"Alright, Rhody. Let's get this done."

Rhody nodded then turned back to Long Eyes and said, "You can deal with my boss now. I'm going to go back to the back of the herd."

Long Eyes nodded then turned to order his men to start selecting the cattle while he received the cash payment from the trail boss.

As Rhody walked the gelding past the other drovers, he smiled at Jack Mason, winked then nudged the horse to a medium trot. He could never figure out why the trail bosses seemed willing to give up cattle more than the cash. Those forty animals would sell for more than eight hundred dollars when they reached the railhead at Dodge City, so it would have been cheaper to give him the ten cents per head and only a dozen critters. It didn't matter to him because he was just a cowhand and would get the same pay when they delivered the herd anyway.

The massive herd, minus the forty cattle they left with the Comanche and the dozen they gave to the Cherokee who were far less demanding entered the plains of Kansas two weeks later.

It had been a good drive so far and they'd only lost another sixty cattle to river crossings, accidents and just by wandering away.

What made it somewhat rare was that they hadn't had any deaths or even serious injuries on the drive. At last night's chow, some of the older hands had said that their good fortune was really bad luck as the odds would soon catch up to them in one really bad day. Most of the others, including Rhody, had laughed at the notion, but there were more than a few who took it to heart including his good friend, Jack Mason.

He was on the far west of the herd riding a taller deep brown gelding today when Jack trotted up beside him.

Rhody grinned at him and asked, "You aren't worried, are you, Jack?"

Jack didn't even smile as he replied, "You don't mess with things like that, Rhody. I'm kinda worried about it, and you outta be too."

"Why would all those good days we had since we left San Antone have anything to do with what happens today or tomorrow?"

"That's just it! We've been too lucky so far and it's gonna catch up with us."

"So, what did you want to see me about?"

Jack pulled a folded sheet of paper from his shirt pocket, leaned across the gap and handed it to him.

Rhody took the paper then let his reins drop, read Jack's scrawl before folding it again and holding it out to his friend.

"Jack, this is downright silly. You're not going to die before we reach Dodge City. You might die in one of those whore houses, but that will be your own fault."

"Just keep it, Rhody, will ya? It'll make me feel better."

Rhody nodded then slid what was a crude last will and testament into his shirt pocket. He wished there was some way of getting that dangerous notion out of Jack's mind but knew there was nothing he could say to change what he believed. The only cure would be when they reached the end of the trail and drove the herd into the holding pens.

Jack finally grinned at him as he said, "Thanks, Rhody, you're a real pal," then wheeled his horse away to return to his assigned slot.

Rhody was smiling as he watched him leave and shook his head. What he had found amusing in Jack's crude will was that he left any pay that was due him to Miss Pauline Gordon, who was a working girl in the Alamo Saloon and Billiard Parlor in San Antonio. He'd ridden with Jack for four long drives now, and it seemed that he was in love with one whore or another on each of them.

He wasn't worried about the will or having to find Miss Pauline Gordon, but he'd remind Jack about it when he fell in love with some whore in Dodge City.

For the next three days, the herd continued north without any major issues and Jack seemed to be less tightly wound when no one had died, but Rhody was smart enough to let the subject sleep.

It was on the morning of the fourth day when the odds finally caught up with them.

After morning chow, Rhody headed for the front left slot, one of the preferable positions with a minimal amount of dust. He reached his designated area and began waking the longhorns that were still asleep by shouting and slapping his Stetson on his right thigh that was protected by his thick leather chaps.

It took another thirty minutes to get the herd rousted and moving as they continued north and Rhody had the tan

RHODY JONES

Morgan dancing along the outside of the herd making sure that none of them decided to go west. The Morgan was his favorite mount from the large remuda, and he rode the small horse as often as he could, and as each of the other drovers had their own preferred mounts, he knew that when he used the Morgan, he'd be well-rested. His other favorite was another Morgan, a handsome black filly, but he rode the tan gelding more often.

They soon reached the fairly wide Crooked Creek, but it didn't pose much of a problem. They'd crossed real rivers and larger creeks on the long drive and by now, the cattle should be used to the crossings.

The creek was about thirty feet across where they'd be crossing and Rhody was at the front of the herd, so he was one of the first to start moving the critters into the water.

The enormous herd stretched more than eight hundred yards across by the time they began the crossing. The two chow wagons and their four supply wagons had already crossed and were back out front where they belonged, and he could see the large remuda of horses being driven across on the other side of the herd by the three wranglers. This was the largest cattle drive he'd been on and it was an impressive sight.

Jack was on the left side as well, but about two hundred yards behind Rhody when his Morgan stepped down into the water.

Rhody and the Morgan crossed easily, and the cattle were moving smoothly as they returned to dry ground where he resumed his job of keep them heading north.

He hadn't looked behind him because he was busy with the cattle, but after he'd ridden for just a few seconds on dry land, he heard a loud commotion behind him to the right followed by two rapid gunshots.

He swiveled in the saddle to look at the source of the problem and saw chaos in the herd along the southern bank. Lou Taylor was in the middle of the tumult with his pistol and Rhody watched as he fired twice more almost straight down while he fought to keep his horse under control.

The cattle around him were panicking and Rhody knew that it might infect the entire herd if those animals weren't calmed down, so he wheeled the Morgan around to head back to the creek and spotted Jack heading that way as well.

The Morgan used his deft footwork to maneuver around the jostling longhorns to avoid having his rider or himself stabbed by those deadly natural spears that each of them wore on their heads.

Other drovers were heading to the commotion from the other side as the terror from the first panicked cattle continued to affect the others. It was only when Rhody reached the creek that he saw what had started the uproar. The cattle's hooves had disturbed two large cottonmouths and the snakes had retaliated. If there weren't so many animals around them, they probably would have just escaped into the creek, but they were trapped, and Lou Taylor had failed to shoot either of them and had probably made it worse when he began unloading .44s into the ground.

He began to shout to the animals to draw their attention away from the slithering and biting snakes, and the others soon joined in but ignored the snakes as each of them understood that their gunfire would only spook the cattle even more than they already were.

The cattle that had been in the stream when the snakes had launched their defensive attack soon clambered up the other bank, leaving space for the snakes to make their wriggling escape into the water. It was still touch and go for another few minutes before the drovers finally managed to get the mewling critters settled down.

Rhody then turned the Morgan back to the northwest to return to his position pleased that the danger was over. He suspected that the others would leave a gap in the herd to avoid a second run-in with the snakes which was unlikely anyway. He hadn't seen two water moccasins in one place before, especially of that size, and wondered if they were both male snakes trying to impress a lady cottonmouth who had then rejected them both and gone on her merry, slithering way.

He was snickering to himself as he let the Morgan find the path through the steers wondering why the big beasts would get so riled about snakes anyway. Even the biggest viper couldn't kill them. It would hurt for a while, but it seemed as if the fear of snakes was just ingrained into their nature as it was in his. He knew his own fear and disgust wasn't really warranted as they were less dangerous than the Comanches or even the coyotes that seemed to be everywhere.

He'd just reached his position when he heard shouting from well behind him that he hadn't noticed over the constant noise from the cattle, so he wheeled the Morgan around again and spotted Al Jeffries waving his hat over his head as he shouted for help.

Al was on the other side of the creek, so Rhody just watched for a minute before he noticed that Jack wasn't riding to Al's assistance. He suddenly had a sinking feeling when he saw Al dismount beside a riderless horse that looked like the one Jack had chosen earlier.

He ignored the cattle, urged the Morgan back to the creek and had to ride along the northern bank to pass the last of the longhorns coming in his direction before he turned the small horse into the water and soon climbed up the southern bank.

Al was only another twenty yards away when he reached level ground, so he quickly dismounted and trotted to the scene, already seeing Jack sprawled on the ground with his chaps lying on the ground beside him and his right thigh bloody and the muscle ripped open. Four more drovers were already standing behind Al as he tried to staunch the flow of blood, but every one of them including Rhody, knew it was hopeless.

Rhody took a knee near Jack but didn't need to ask what had happened. He just removed his hat then lifted Jack's head and slid it underneath before lowering it so he would be more comfortable.

"Thanks, Rhody," Jack said as he managed a grim smile at his friend.

"You're welcome, Jack," he replied then said, "Those were some mighty big cottonmouths. I don't think I've seen any that big before and there were two of them. I reckon they were a couple of randy boy snakes courting a lady snake, but I didn't take time to look too closely."

Jack snickered then replied, "Thanks for not tellin' me that I'm gonna be okay. I ain't gonna make it, Rhody."

Rhody didn't reply as he didn't believe that Jack expected an argument.

As Stan Brown joined the crowd of drovers, Jack asked, "You still got my writin', don't you, Rhody?"

"It's in my pocket, Jack."

"That's good. When you see Pauline, be nice to her. I know she's a whore, but she's a nice gal."

Rhody smiled at his friend and replied, "All of the whores you fell in love with were nice gals, Jack. I reckon it's because you treated them like queens and not whores."

"Always pays to be nice to a lady, Rhody. It makes those two dollars go a long way."

Jack's voice had been fading as more of his life's blood drained from his leg onto the Kansas prairie, but none of the cowhands left and Rhody remained on his knee as they waited for the inevitable.

Jack didn't speak again but let his eyes scan the faces of the men who had shared the last days of his life, watching as each of them removed his hat before he finally focused on his best friend. He never wept, nor did he even moan from the horrendous pain that the horrific gouge must be causing.

No one said any prayers or passed any hopeful comments as Jack breathed his last.

Rhody reverently lifted Jack's head removed his hat then stood and pulled it back on.

He turned to the trail boss and asked, "Do we bury him here or take him to Dodge City?"

RHODY JONES

"It's still another three days to Dodge City, so we'll bury him here. It won't matter where he's put into the ground. He's not with us anymore."

Rhody nodded then Stan asked, "What did he mean when he asked about you havin' his writin'?"

Rhody pulled the folded sheet out of his pocket and handed it to the trail boss.

Stan was looking at Jack as he unfolded the single page then shifted his eyes to the paper and read Jack's scrawled last will.

"Are you gonna take his pay and give it to that whore?"

"I have to, boss. It's Jack's last request."

"Well, it's your choice. He said to give all of his belongings to you, so if I were in your shoes, I'd just keep the cash."

"No, you wouldn't, boss. You would do exactly what I need to do."

"Maybe. Let's get a few shovels and pickaxes and get this done. We still have a herd to move."

―――

Jack's burial only took twenty minutes as none of the men who worked to dig the hole and then return the dirt to where it belonged spent more than five minutes of hurried digging while most of the men had the herd moving.

There had been no ceremony and no marker planted above the ground. It was the way of life on the trail and none of them expected anything different if he had been the one who had gone to meet his maker.

Rhody moved Jack's things to the same supply wagon that he used. It consisted of his saddle and the rest of his gear, his gun rig with a Colt '73 with its sheathed eight-inch knife and his Winchester '66.

―――――

It was around mid-day when the first critters entered the enormous holding pens outside of Dodge City, and it took until almost dark to get the last of them enclosed and counted. The large remuda was herded into a separate corral by the wranglers, and after the day's work was done, the two cooks had a huge spread ready for the hungry men to demolish. Each man attacked his food with gusto in anticipation of heading into town to blow off his two months' worth of contained steam.

Just twenty minutes after sitting down to eat, Rhody and the other drovers headed into the wild streets of Dodge City. As he walked with the crowd of laughing, excited men, Rhody had already decided to move on. It would be too late in the year to catch on with another drive, and he wasn't attached to a particular brand like many of the other cowhands. He'd make the seven-hundred-mile ride back to San Antonio to give Jack's pay to Pauline Gordon at the Alamo Saloon and Billiard Parlor then he'd head west. He wanted to see the Rocky Mountains, the Grand Canyon, and the deserts of the southwest. After that, he'd head to California and then see the world's largest ocean. He knew that despite its size, it didn't have the ferocity of the Atlantic, but he did miss the ocean. Then he'd probably sign on with a ship heading to the East Coast and return to Rhode Island and his former life.

He joined the boys at the Prairie Saloon for an hour or so before leaving with Al Jeffries, who was a teetotaler, to get a room at one of the six hotels in the busy town.

When they had unloaded their gear and were down to their skivvies and laying on their beds in the still overly warm room, Al looked across the small dark space and asked, "So, you're really gonna give Jack's pay to that whore?"

"Yes, sir. Every dime."

"Are you at least gonna get a poke out of it?"

Rhody smiled at Al as he replied, "Maybe one or two."

Al laughed then asked, "Are you ridin' on your own or comin' with the wagons and remuda?"

"I'll talk to Stan in the morning when they pay us off, but I'm leaning on just heading back by myself. I can move a lot faster than having to travel with the wagons."

"I might do that too. Mind if I come along?"

"Not at all."

Al closed his eyes and smiled. He had his own reasons for wanting to return to San Antonio as quickly as possible.

CHAPTER 2

The next morning, the men lined up in the large offices of the purchasing agent for their pay now that the cattle had been sold, and as each man received his due, he would either wave it at those still in line as he passed or just walk past grinning as he stared at the greenbacks in his hand.

When Rhody reached the table, Stan looked up at him, then counted out twelve ten-dollar notes, slid them across the table and Rhody stuffed them into his right pocket but didn't leave.

Stan then counted out ten ten-dollar bills and said, "Here's Jack's pay, Rhody, and don't go askin' why he didn't get the full amount."

"I wasn't about to ask, boss," he replied, "I'll be heading back to San Antonio directly, so I'll be needing a horse. Is that alright with you?"

Stan nodded then said, "Go see Hap and tell him I said it's okay. You got might want to take two of 'em 'cause you've got two saddles now."

"Thanks, boss," Rhody said as he pushed Jack's pay in his other pocket before turning and walking past the eight men still in line.

He stopped near the end and said to Al, "I'm heading out to the remuda to talk to Hap and then I'll saddle the tan Morgan gelding and the black Morgan mare. Ask the boss if you can have one, too. I'm sure he's already figured out that some of us aren't waiting for the wagons."

"Okay, Rhody. I'll see you out there."

Rhody nodded then left the purchasing agent's building and headed for the remuda's corral where he spotted Hap Trotter, a great name for a wrangler, sitting on one of the rails.

"Morning, Hap," he said loudly as he approached, "the boss said I could take two horses with me when I head south."

Hap dropped to the ground grinned and said, "I reckon one of 'em will be the tan Morgan and the other will be that black mare. Go ahead and pick 'em out."

Rhody grabbed one of the rope leads from the pole near the gate then slid between two of the rails as Hap followed to find his tan Morgan while Rhody searched for the black mare.

He found the black Morgan mare toward the far end of the corral. She had four white stockings and a star on her forehead. She was a handsome animal and only five years old. He was sure that this had been her first trail drive after foaling, and probably the first she had ever made, but it would be her last.

RHODY JONES

When he reached her, he smiled rubbed her neck before slipping the lead over her head and saying, "Let's go for a nice jaunt, ma'am."

He led the mare to the gate where Hap was holding the tan Morgan gelding. Hap grinned then opened the gate and each of them led his small horse out before he closed the gate behind him.

Hap handed the lead to Rhody and asked, "You gonna get movin' already, Rhody?"

"I'll see how long it takes to get ready, but I reckon I won't be hitting the trail until tomorrow. I'll get them shoed before I leave, then I need to buy some supplies."

"I reckon Harry and Joe will load you up with some food, Rhody. They're gonna have to fill those chuck wagons for the ride back anyway."

"I'll go talk to Harry in a bit. Al is going to stop by for a horse, too. He'll be joining me on the ride to San Antone."

"I reckon that a few of the other boys will come along, too."

"I'm glad I got here soon enough to pick out these two."

Hap chuckled then said, "Those other boys will most likely be spendin' their pay on liquor and whores for a while."

"That's their loss, Hap. I'm going to head over to the wagons and get my saddles and gear."

"Have a good ride, Rhody."

Rhody nodded before leading the two Morgans to the supply wagon that held his saddles, weapons and personal belongings and tied them off on the rear wheel.

He saddled the gelding first then hung his loaded saddlebags in place and tied them down before strapping on his slicker and bedroll. After sliding his Winchester '73 into its scabbard and hanging his coil of rope and canteen in place, he tied the gelding to the supply wagon's left rear wheel.

Before he started on the mare, Al arrived leading a tall, dark gray gelding then waved as he passed to go to a different supply wagon for his saddle.

He then saddled the mare with Jack's saddle before adding all of Jack's gear. By the time he was finished, Al returned with his saddled gray and asked, "Where are you goin' now?"

"I'm going to talk to Harry about picking up some food before I take the horses into town to get them reshod and maybe pick up a pack saddle. Then I'll go to the general store to pick up supplies."

"I checked the shoes on this one and they seem okay."

Rhody nodded, but said, "It's still a long ride, Al."

"I guess you're right. I'll have them replaced, too."

RHODY JONES

After Harry told them that he would have no problem setting them up with enough food for their journey, Rhody mounted the tan Morgan then led the mare back into Dodge City with Al trotting alongside.

When they dropped the horses off at the livery, Rhody bought a used pack saddle with two large panniers for a good price but didn't accept the liveryman's offer to trade for the extra riding saddle. He'd just store it on top of the pack saddle.

He and Al then did some shopping at Murphy's Dry Goods and Sundries then lugged their purchases to the livery where they moved them into the two panniers before Al moved his personal items to his saddlebags. The liveryman had already started shoeing the mare and said they'd all be done in an a little more than an hour, so after paying for the job, Al and Rhody headed to the chuck wagon to join the men who weren't drinking themselves into oblivion.

As they walked, Al asked, "Are we gonna get a room again?"

"I didn't figure that we'd have the horses shod so quickly, so I think we can head out right after we fill our bellies and pick up the food from Harry."

"You don't wanna wait for the other fellers?"

"Nope. I want to move fast, Al. After we get to San Antone, I'll visit Jack's whore then I'm riding west."

"West? There ain't much out there until you get to Santa Fe. Hell, you're runnin' into Apache territory, too. Why don't you just take the damned train outta Dodge City instead of tryin' to get yourself killed or get lost wanderin' in that empty country?"

Rhody grinned at Al as he replied, "I'll be okay, Al. I'll never get lost and I doubt if anyone will even pay attention to me."

"You ain't ever been there, Rhody. How come you reckon you won't suddenly find yourself in Mexico?"

"Back in San Antone, I have a set of maps of the entire western half of our nation, a sextant and my naval compass. In my pocket, I have my certified chronographic pocket watch. As long as I keep it wound, then I'll always know exactly where I am and which direction to go to reach my destination."

"What's a sextant?"

"It's what sailors use help them navigate the oceans."

"Oh. I forgot that you used to be a Yankee sailor."

"Sometimes, I forget myself, Al," he replied as they reached the chow wagon.

―――

It was just about two hours later when Rhody led the mare pack horse out of Dodge City with Al riding alongside.

RHODY JONES

With the summer sun bearing down on them, they were already sweating before the outline of the growing town disappeared over the horizon, but that same sun would be in the sky for another six hours, so Rhody estimated that they could put thirty miles behind them before making camp.

He didn't need to use his navigation tools for the long journey back to San Antonio as they'd just follow the well-used Chisholm trail and probably have to bypass another northbound herd or two on the way.

They camped for the first night, and then late on the second day's ride, they reached the bank of Crooked Creek, crossed then after climbing up the southern edge soon found Jack's grave.

"At least no critters got at him," Al said as they sat astride their horses peering down at the dry mound of earth.

"We did it right, Al," Rhody replied.

Al nodded then nudged his gelding away while Rhody stayed put.

"I'll give that whore your pay, Jack. Maybe it'll help her out of that life."

He then saluted his friend's gravesite before he set the Morgan to a medium trot to catch up to Al.

―――

They made good time the first two days and soon crossed onto the Comanche reservation that they shared with the Apaches and Kiowa.

"You reckon we're gonna have any problems with them Comanches?" Al asked.

"I don't think so. They don't bother the outlaws that pass through, so I don't think they really care about a pair of cowhands. They make their money off of cattle drives. I sometimes wonder what would happen if they started turning in those outlaws for the prices on their heads. I reckon that would keep outlaws from using their territory for a refuge, but then again, I imagine that no one would pay those rewards to an Indian."

"I reckon not," Al replied then asked, "How'd you learn to talk Comanche? You ain't lived in Texas that long."

"I just have an ear for languages. I don't know a lot of it, but I understand enough to carry on a rudimentary conversation."

Al snickered, then said, "You sure do talk funny, even for a Yankee."

Rhody grinned and answered, "You should have heard the sailors that I worked with on those ships. You probably wouldn't understand a word they said."

RHODY JONES

"I reckon that's so, but how come you don't sound like one of 'em. If you didn't use such big words, then you could almost sound like a homeborn Texan."

"For the same reason I can pick up languages so quickly. If I wanted to blend in even more, I could talk like a regular cowhand, but I thought it might be insulting to all of the boys. When I first arrived in Texas from New Orleans, I thought about changing to keep from being ostracized or worse, but I didn't want to sound phony."

Al laughed then said, "Well, it got you your handle, Rhody. You shouldn't have told the boys you were from Rhode Island. If you said you was from New York, they'd probably just call you Yank or so Yorkie."

"I'll stick with Rhody, Al. I like it better than Roland anyway. I'd cringe when folks called me Rollie, and never did figure out an acceptable nickname."

"What's your middle name?"

"Horatio. My father's name was Roland and he was an admirer of Horatio Nelson, the British naval hero."

Al laughed again then said, "Lordy! You are cursed. Ain't ya? Even R.H. sounds goofy. Maybe you should just go by Jones."

"We can't all have good names like yours, Al."

They never even saw any Comanche, Apache or Kiowa before they crossed the Red River into Texas three days later.

Once in Texas, they could make better time using roads of varying levels of completion but despite the expected faster riding, they still had four hundred miles before reaching San Antonio.

It was after Al had made that observation when he asked, "Just how small is Rhode Island, anyway?"

"About the size of Bexar County."

"You're kiddin!" Al exclaimed, "How did it ever get to be a state in the first place?"

"They didn't like the restrictive religious laws that Massachusetts had, so a man named Roger Williams left that colony and formed the colony of Rhode Island where folks could practice any religion. Did you know that the smallest state in the union has the longest name?"

"How do you reckon that way? It ain't even as long as Massachusetts."

"Its official name is The State of Rhode Island and Providence Plantations."

"You had plantations up there with slaves and all?" Al asked, "I thought you was all dead set against slavery."

RHODY JONES

"They passed a law in the seventeenth century banning slaves, but there were still quite a few around a hundred years later. I think it's odd that they never bothered to change the name. I reckon it was because they had so many seals and documents with the name and thought it cost too much."

"It sure sounds queer to me. You Yankees do all sorts of crazy things."

Rhody let the subject drop because he didn't want to stir Al up with any disparaging remarks about Texas. Besides, he'd chosen to live here since leaving New Orleans and it had been a good choice at the time.

Before he left New Orleans, he'd purchased the large, waterproof satchel of maps at a large bookstore then a new Western wardrobe, including a Stetson and a good pair of boots. He didn't need a pistol as he'd worn one since he became a first mate. He did buy a Winchester and a mule rather than a horse.

When he arrived in San Antonio two weeks later, he was reasonably familiar with the shifting Texas accents as he had proceeded west, but spent another month settling in and learning more about everyday life in the enormous state. Its size had impressed him then and it still did. That four-hundred miles from the Red River to San Antonio didn't even cross the state. If he'd ridden out of his home in Providence and headed west, he would have crossed all of Connecticut then cut across the bottom of New York and reached almost halfway across Pennsylvania, but at least there would be bridges and better roads.

After he reached San Antonio, he'd worked without pay at the Hennessey ranch southwest of the town to learn how to handle cattle. The skills he'd learned with ropes over his years under sail had impressed the other ranch hands, and once they'd learned his background, it was the foreman who had given him the Rhody moniker. As he'd just explained to Al, he had readily accepted the nickname. He was accepted as another cowhand before he joined his first long cattle drive the following spring.

He had never ridden for a brand after leaving the Hennessey ranch, but it wasn't important to him. He had boarded his mule in Hector Lopez' livery on the southwest end of San Antonio and Hector let him store his large crate with his duffle and large leather satchel which contained his sextant, maps and compass while he was gone.

Rhody also improved his Spanish from Hector and the other Mexicans who comprised a large part of the town's population, if not the majority. He'd already learned the language from Cuban sailors on his ship's crew, but he found that Mexican Spanish was different, just like Texas English varies from New England English, and the difference was probably a lot less.

After that first cattle drive, he'd been on six more, going on two drives in '77. When he returned to San Antonio after each of them, he'd sign on with one outfit or another, but each one was different. This drive had been the largest by far, but it would be his last. It was time to start his journey west to the Pacific.

———

They spotted San Antonio around mid-day on the first day of July having had no major incidents on the long ride.

Al had been growing more excited each waking hour over the past two days and Rhody understood the reason for his eager anticipation.

He looked over at Al and asked, "Are you going to come with me to meet Jack's whore or are you heading straight to the Double Bar M?"

Al grinned back at him as he replied, "Are you okay if I leave you behind, Rhody? You've got that packhorse and I want to let Cody run."

Rhody laughed then said, "I think if you got out of that saddle, you'd outrun your horse to get to Mabel. Get going, Al. I don't want to hold you back."

Al was still grinning as he replied, "Thanks, Rhody. Are you gonna come to the weddin'?"

"I reckon not, Al. I appreciate the offer, though. I'll be a hundred miles west of here by the time you and Mabel tie the knot. I wish you both nothing but the best. You're a good man, Al."

"Thanks, Rhody. You take care now and avoid them rattlers."

After his snake warning, Al kicked his gelding into a fast trot as Rhody watched with a smile on his face. When not asking him about his past, Al's favorite subject was Mabel Mooney, the daughter of the Double Bar M's owner. She'd agreed to marry him when he returned from the drive. He'd only gone on the drive because two hundred and forty of her father's critters were in the giant herd. He had been the only ranch hand from the Double Bar M to go on the drive, and Rhody hoped that in his absence, Mabel didn't change her mind.

After learning that none of the other dozen Double Bar M boys had been on the drive, Rhody suspected that Mabel's father might be hoping that Al would have an accident on the trail, or he might be able to convince his daughter to find another beau in his absence. There was a possibility that it was just a coincidence, but it sure sounded as if daddy wasn't happy about his only daughter marrying a regular cowhand.

But that wasn't his business. He had his tan Morgan that he'd christened Jack at a slow trot. The black mare he'd named Morgana for obvious reasons. He'd toyed with naming her after his last ship, but that name still conjured bad memories. He had named his mule after the captain, and almost felt as if he was insulting the mule. He still vividly remembered that day when the ship had been so close to disaster.

After he'd lashed himself to the wheel, the ship had spent more than sixteen hours in a shuddering, dangerous dance with the angry water of the Gulf of Mexico while being battered by the pulsing, powerful winds. His makeshift sail had snapped the spar holding it in place about four hours after he'd set it, but the flapping canvas had provided just enough headway to keep the ship from capsizing.

When the storm had finally lost most of its power, he'd untied himself then managed to make it below deck to get a much-needed drink of water and a stale piece of bread before getting the crew together to start regaining control of the ship.

By the time that the captain finally left his cabin and returned to the quarterdeck, the *Vivienne* had been mostly repaired and was fighting the still strong winds and heavy seas as it made its way north. The captain never said a word about his condition during the storm but acted as if he'd been in control of the situation.

Rhody never was able to examine the captain's entries in the ship's log but was sure that the captain portrayed himself as the heroic savior of his ship. He knew that none of the crew would dare speak a word of what had happened in those critical hours, but that his first mate might.

It was why he'd made the demeaning offer to Rhody to return to Providence as an able seaman, knowing that he would refuse. Rhody also suspected that the captain's log described his behavior during the storm in unflattering terms, and the captain's word was final. He could have waited for one of his ships to arrive and explained the events to the captain, but he hadn't seen the point.

He hadn't explained it in his letter to his uncle other than to talk about the hurricane's power and his decision to head west.

What had really puzzled him about Captain Dent's decision was that the captain knew that Rhody was a half owner of the R. Jones Shipping Company and that if he chose to return on one of his ships to Providence, it would be his word that would carry the most weight among the seafaring men in New England.

His only theory was that the captain had already decided that this was his last voyage and didn't really care that much what happened on his return. He'd collect his share of the voyage's profit then walk away. The only reason for his actions must be personal. Maybe he saw Rhody as a young upstart who had achieved his status because the good fortune of his birth or that he was simply jealous that his career was ending on a second-class vessel and felt that his first mate had flaunted his superiority.

RHODY JONES

Rhody had never even mentioned his uncle on the voyage and let his skills prove that he was worthy of the position, but the captain never had seemed to accept him. Whatever the reason, Rhody didn't really care any longer. He only knew that the captain didn't want him on the ship when it sailed.

He'd received a reply letter from his uncle just before he left New Orleans and still wrote to him often since he'd been driving cattle. He hadn't been surprised to find a draft in that first letter for a thousand dollars and a warm expression of love and respect for his decision. His uncle made it clear that when and if he decided to return, he would be welcomed with open arms, but to be sure to keep him informed of his whereabouts. The draft had been drawn on the company account rather than his personal account as he considered it a company expense. His uncle was a born businessman while his father was more sailor than bookkeeper.

His mother had died when he was born, and he had been taken in by his father's brother, his Uncle Richard. Richard M. Jones and his father, Robert, owned a fleet of eleven ships, mostly schooners, and *The Kingston* was their biggest and newest vessel, just three years old. Rhody's father had always captained the newest ship while Richard stayed in Providence to run the company, which is why Roland lived with his uncle.

His father had been lost when *The Kingston* had struck an uncharted reef in the night near the Florida Keys. When the ship was lost, his uncle became his de facto father.

When the young Roland was twelve, he was sent to sea as a midshipman on one of the schooners and had worked his way to first mate on his merits alone by the time he was eighteen.

His decision to sign on with the *Vivienne* had surprised his uncle because one of their new steam-powered vessels was departing for Charleston the same day, but Rhody had explained that he wanted to sail on a second-class ship with a second-rate crew to learn how to handle bigger problems than those he'd encountered on his uncle's first-class fleet.

Despite the final result, he never regretted that decision and had learned more about men and handling an ill-fitted ship on that one voyage than he'd learned in any of the others.

———

Al had long since disappeared by the time Rhody reached the western end of San Antonio and headed for Hector's livery.

When he reached the large barn, he dismounted and led Jack and Morgana through the wide doors, finding Hector shoeing a tall red gelding.

He stopped, then waited until his hammer slammed the nail home and Hector looked his way.

"Rhody! You're back! I see you have two Morgans with you, too."

RHODY JONES

Rhody grinned as he led the two small horses inside, then replied, "After we reached Dodge City, I asked the boss if I could have them. I'll need to board them for a couple of days and have their shoes changed, too. How's Dent doing?"

"He's in the corral and is getting a bit too fat. How was the drive?"

Rhody tied off his reins as he replied, "It went pretty well, although we did lose Jack Mason to a longhorn after the herd panicked."

"I liked him. He was a good man."

"He was my best friend, Hector. I'm going to add some things to my crate for a little while. Then I'll visit the barber and get a haircut, shave and a hot bath before I to go to the Alamo Saloon and Billiard Parlor."

"After that long drive, you deserve to enjoy the whiskey and women, Rhody."

"That's not why I have to stop there, Hector. Just a few days before he died, Jack gave me his last will. He wanted me to give his pay to one of the whores who works there."

"And you're gonna do it?" he asked with raised eyebrows.

"It's what Jack wanted, Hector, so I don't have any say in the matter."

"Where will you work next?"

"I'm leaving San Antonio and then Texas. I want to see the rest of the West and hopefully the Pacific Ocean. Do you have any panniers?"

"Four, but one is ripped pretty bad."

"I only need two anyway. I'll ride Jack, that's the tan Morgan, but I'll leave the mare with you to have her reshod. I'll be back in a couple of hours to leave Jack with you, too."

Rhody untied the trail rope then handed it to Hector before leading Jack out into the hot Texas sun and mounting.

He rode to Frobisher's Barbershop four blocks east then dismounted and after tying his gelding's reins, stepped inside.

An hour later, Rhody emerged feeling human again then untied Jack, stepped up and turned east again to deliver the hundred dollars to Miss Pauline Gordon.

The Alamo Saloon and Billiard Parlor was a run-of-the-mill place, but was less boisterous than most, especially when compared to any of the eight saloons in Dodge City. Unlike most saloons that included working women, the Alamo's whore house wasn't on the second floor. It was in a separate building behind the saloon, which was attached with a covered porch, but the painted ladies still cruised the big barroom for customers.

RHODY JONES

Rhody pulled up before the saloon, stepped down and tied off Jack before hopping onto the wide boardwalk then striding to the batwing doors.

When he entered, he had to let his eyes adjust to the shadows for a few seconds before stepping across the floor. He saw four women working the room already, but assumed most were still in the other house, either working or sleeping. He didn't know what Pauline looked like because he didn't frequent the establishment, but wanted a cold beer before he went looking, so he headed for the long, polished oak bar.

After the bartender set his beer on the bar, he asked, "Is Pauline around?"

As the barman picked up Rhody's nickel, he replied, "That's her over near the poker table."

"Thanks," Rhody said before picking up his glass and turning to find her.

He spotted Pauline quickly enough as she flirted with one of the card players, but the beer was cold, and he wasn't about to waste his nickel.

She was fairly tall for a woman, probably just an inch or so shorter than his five feet and ten inches. She had black hair and a pleasant face, and he guessed her age to be in the mid-twenties. As with most women in her profession, she was exposing her wares to impress potential customers, and he had to admit they were impressive selling points.

He soon finished his beer, set the glass on the bar then walked toward the poker table just as Pauline recognized that she wasn't going to pry any of the players from their game and swayed her way toward another table where two men were just drinking and laughing.

Rhody walked a bit faster to intercept her before she could convince one of the other men to take her up on her offer, and just before she could start her sales pitch, he stopped beside her.

Pauline turned, smiled at the new arrival who obviously didn't need a lot of convincing then said, "Well, hello."

"Hello, ma'am. Are you Pauline Gordon?"

The use of her last name made her wary, so she asked, "Are you a lawman?"

"No, ma'am. I just returned from a cattle drive. My name's Rhody Jones."

She laughed then said, "Well, Rhody, you may sound funny, but I'll take your word that you're not a lawman. Will you buy me a drink before we talk business?"

"Sure, let's sit over there where it's quieter."

She smiled, waved to the bartender then hooked her arm through his and walked him to the empty table.

RHODY JONES

After they sat, the bartender arrived, set a glass of amber liquid before her then Rhody handed him fifteen cents.

Pauline downed her drink in one quick swallow, popped the empty glass on the table and said, "Now, Rhody Jones, are you going to part with three dollars to take me to my room?"

Rhody actually thought about it, but said, "No, ma'am. I have something to give you."

He pulled Jack's pay from his left pocket and set the notes on the tabletop near her empty glass.

Pauline stared at the pile of bills then looked at Rhody and asked, "Is this some kind of trick? Are they real?"

"Yes, ma'am, they're real. My good friend, Jack Mason, died on the trail to Dodge City, but before he died, he said to give his pay to you."

"Oh," she said as she scooped up the cash and stuffed them into her cleavage before the bartender could see it.

She smiled at him and said, "I guess I owe you some time in my room now."

Rhody was surprised when he found himself a bit irritated because she hadn't expressed the least bit of remorse for Jack's death or even bothered to ask how it had happened.

"Don't you want to know how he died?"

"It doesn't matter now, does it? I mean, I can't change it at all. Let's go in back so I can thank you for the money."

He let out a long breath before asking, "Don't you even remember him at all?"

Pauline seemed offended by his question and snapped, "I've had more than forty customers in the past week alone and you expect me to remember any of them?"

Rhody stood and said, "I reckon not," then turned and left the saloon not bothering to look back.

When he returned to the still bright sun of the late afternoon, he stopped on the boardwalk wondering if he should feel sorry for Jack. It seemed as if he was always in love with one woman or another and most were whores, but at least he enjoyed their company.

"Wherever you are now, Jack," he said aloud, "you know that I've done what you asked. I hope you aren't disappointed."

He then stepped down, untied his Morgan mounted and headed back to Hector's to drop him off.

———

That night, he was in his room at the Lonestar Hotel and began planning for the ride west. He'd pick up more supplies in the morning, pack his things from his crate, pick up his horses and mule then leave San Antonio. Among the purchases he'd make in the morning would be a longer-range rifle and maybe a shotgun. He wasn't under any illusions that the long solo ride across Texas then New Mexico and Arizona Territories would be pleasant, but that didn't detract from the almost magnetic pull forcing him to make the journey despite having no real destination.

CHAPTER 3

After having breakfast, Rhody walked down the boardwalk heading east for three blocks before turning north to visit R. Whitfield, Gunsmith. He'd visited the shop a few times and it was where he'd bought his Winchester and his Colt, so he knew he had a good selection. He was planning on buying a Sharps but would be willing to listen to any suggestions by the gunsmith.

When he entered the shop, he waved to the gunsmith who was listening to a customer who seemed to be having difficulties with his new pistol then walked to the aisle where the long reach guns were on display.

He didn't want anything fancy like a scoped rifle, as he felt that the range advantage itself was all that mattered. If he had a confrontation on the trail, if he could lob a few rounds over the heads of his adversaries at a few hundred yards which should be sufficient to make them change their minds.

He stopped in front of the rack with the Sharps and Spencers, and even a couple of rifles that he couldn't identify, when the gunsmith approached him

RHODY JONES

Rhody turned and said, "Howdy. Rob. I'm looking for a long-range rifle, and I'm leaning toward the Sharps carbine. What do you think?"

"That all depends. What are you hunting, Rhody?"

Rhody smiled that he remembered him after his last visit to the shop over a year ago, but reckoned it was because of his odd moniker that he had explained to him after they'd introduced themselves on his first visit.

"I'm not hunting anything in particular, but that's not the reason I'm looking. I wanted a rifle that had more range than my Winchester because I'll be riding to California and want the advantage."

"Well, a Sharps would surely give you the range, but you'd have the disadvantage of a single shot. Now, I can reload a Sharps in about five seconds or so, but it usually takes most fellers a bit longer, especially if the brass doesn't want to leave the breech."

"What do you recommend?"

"Come with me," he said before he turned and walked back to the front of his shop.

Rhody scanned the aisle's shelves as he stepped behind him, but when he looked back at the gunsmith, he noticed him pulling a Winchester from the wall rack behind the counter.

When he reached the front of the shop, he said, "I already have two Winchesters. One's a '66 and the other's a '73."

Rob Whitfield set the repeater on the counter and said, "And both of them shoot pistol bullets. This is Winchester's first repeater that shoots a rifle round. It's more robust to handle the extra power and is chambered for the .45-75 cartridge. This one is the rifle version and has the twenty-eight-inch barrel. It has more than double the effective range of earlier versions."

Rhody looked at the rifle and could see the differences, but asked, "If it's so much better, why I haven't met anyone who has one?"

"There are two reasons, and both are because of the cartridge. It can't be used in a pistol, so you'd lose that advantage. It's also almost twice the cost of the .44 rimfires."

"Can I use a .45 long Colt? I have an extra Colt that's chambered for a .45."

"I wish you could, but if I'll show you the reason shortly if you're interested in the Winchester. If you want to trade in the Colt, I'll allow you eight dollars credit."

"No, I can't do that. It was my friend's pistol and he died on the trail."

"Sorry to hear that," he said as he reached below the counter and pulled out a box of the Winchester.45s.

RHODY JONES

He opened the box and handed him one of the long cartridges.

As Rhody examined it, he said, "Why does it have this narrowing near the bullet?"

"They needed the extra powder and still keep the same internal design. That's one of the reasons it's pricier than the .44s."

He set the bullet on the counter and picked up the Winchester. The balance was still good, despite the extra eight inches of barrel. He cycled the lever and it felt a bit stiffer, but not too bad.

"How many of those big cartridges does it hold?"

"A dozen in the tube and one in the chamber, so you lose three rounds."

Rhody set it back down then said, "I do like the added range and power and still keeping the rapid fire and quick reload, but I'm still leaning toward something with even more range."

"Have you ever done any long-range shooting?"

"No, sir. I'm reasonably proficient with the Winchester, but I've never even used a Sharps before."

"Then why do you want one? The new Winchester's cartridges may be higher-priced than the older models', but the Sharps cartridges cost even more."

"I'll be riding alone, and I'd like to be able to put a round over the head of some threat at long range to give him second thoughts."

"I'd still recommend the Winchester, but if that's all you're going to use it for then you can buy a Sharps."

"I'll buy the Winchester, but let's go and look at the Sharps and you can show me how to load it."

Rob smiled then walked around the counter and walked with Rhody back to the long rifles.

When they arrived before the display, Rhody asked, "What is that rifle below the Sharps. It looks like a giant Henry."

"That's a Sharps-Borshadt and I only have the one left. It's the last design that the Sharps company made before it went out of business. It's the .50 caliber version and can use any of the long cartridges. It looks like a Henry because the hammer is no longer outside. It's quite an impressive gun, and I think it's the best that Sharps has ever made. I ordered three when their drummer showed up, but I've only sold one. I kept one for my personal use. I don't go hunting anymore, but I do like to shoot the beast. If you think that Winchester was heavy, try this."

RHODY JONES

He lifted the rifle from the rack and handed it to Rhody, who hefted it in his hands then said, "It's not that bad. I've used muzzle loaders that were probably heavier. What's the range?"

"Farther than you can probably pick out a target. Bring it with you to the counter and I'll show you why."

Again, they walked back to the counter and when they arrived, Rhody laid the Sharps-Borshadt beside the Winchester. It was longer than the repeater, but not as much as he'd expected. He couldn't get over how much it resembled a Henry and wondered if that was an advantage.

As he compared the two rifles, the gunsmith set another box of cartridges on the counter, pulled one out and set it on its end beside the Winchester .45 for effect.

Rhody stared at the two and a half-inch long and half-inch thick cartridge that was more than a half an inch longer than the already impressive Winchester round and already imagined the power it held bottled inside the brass.

"This is the .50-100 cartridge. I even ordered some from a different company that are even more powerful and an inch longer."

Rhody slowly raised his head and looked at the gunsmith before asking, "Do you still have any?"

"Not out front. I have two boxes of new cartridges, but two more reloads in back. I tend to get carried away in target practice. I'll be right back."

Rhody watched him leave and was still undecided about the Sharps-Borshadt. It was an impressive weapon, but the Winchester had several advantages.

By the time the gunsmith returned, he concluded that he may as well buy them both. Money wasn't a problem and he did want that long range.

Mister Whitfield returned with two boxes of the huge cartridges, set them on the counter, pulled one free and stood it in line with the other two.

"I didn't believe anyone would make a cartridge that was as large as my middle finger. Do you think a wedding band would fit?"

Rob laughed then replied, "I sometimes wonder if my missus thinks I married my guns. So, Rhody, what do you think?"

"I'll take both of them. How many boxes of the Winchester cartridges do you have?"

"I think it's a dozen, but just to let you know, you probably won't find the Winchester .45-75s in most towns on your way. The Sharps .50 caliber cartridges are even harder to find."

"I figured that. Give me six of the Winchester .45s and two of the .50-100s and would you part with both of the factory loaded .50-140s?"

"Sure. I have my reloads and can order more from my supplier. That's still a lot of .45s, Rhody. How many rounds do you have for your other Winchesters?"

"Six boxes. I have one spare box of the .45 long Colts, but I don't reckon I'll be using them at all. I figure it's better to have too much ammunition than not enough and I have a long way to travel."

Richard nodded before he took five more boxes of Winchester cartridges from under the counter and then added another box of the Sharps .50-100s.

"Will that be all, Rhody? Are you sure you don't want a Gatling?" the gunsmith asked followed by a chuckle.

"No, but I do want a twelve-gauge shotgun and two boxes of birdshot and two of buckshot. I will need to do some hunting on my way."

"At least the shotgun and shells will be cheaper," Rob replied as he walked to the other end of the counter and retrieved a shotgun. He laid it on the crowded counter then added even more clutter when he set the shells beside the boxes of cartridges.

After adding two scabbards and the cleaning kits for the new additions, Rob spend a few minutes showing Rhody how to use the Sharps-Borshadt. He then brought out the two boxes of .50-140s and added them to the stack of boxes.

Rhody had him keep his purchases until he brought his horses around, so after paying for the massive order, he left the shop to return to the livery.

As he walked in the bright sunshine, he wondered if he had gone overboard but in the end, he knew it really didn't matter much. He had no idea what to expect on his long journey across the Southwest, and if that wasn't enough firepower to keep him safe, then it was going to be a lot worse than he expected.

Hector had his two Morgans and the mule saddled when he arrived, so after paying him for the new shoes and boarding, he began moving his crate's contents into the panniers. It took almost twenty minutes to get everything where he wanted, then he shook Hector's hand and led his animals out of the barn and once outside, he mounted Jack and headed west.

After a short stop at the bank to withdraw four hundred dollars to restore his depleted cash reserves that he'd left at the gunsmith, he continued to Wilcox & Sons General Store and Sundries.

He filled two panniers with the supplies and other trail necessities that he would need on the trip then lugged them out to the mule and hung them on the pack saddle. After strapping them down, he mounted Jack again then wheeled him around to revisit the gunsmith.

It was past noon when he was ready to ride out of San Antonio to begin his land voyage across the country but stopped at Angelina's Café one last time for a well-cooked meal. He didn't disparage his own cooking abilities because he'd learned how to prepare meals when he was just a boy, but he still preferred someone else to do the cooking if he could.

As he rode west out of town, he checked his accurate pocket watch and marked the time as 1:43. He let Jack make his own way as he pulled a pencil and his small log from his shirt pocket and annotated the time and location before sliding them back into his pocket and taking the reins again.

He never bothered with his personal logbook on cattle drives, only when he was the one who was doing the navigating. He knew that it wasn't necessary, but he enjoyed marking his progress then calculating his rate of speed and distance traveled.

He soon left San Antonio behind him and began his adventurous journey, not really anticipating anything except an unending series of discoveries but was prepared for the bad times that he might experience. He surely had the means to defend himself.

Rhody didn't need to consult his maps or use his navigational tools for the first few days as he planned to follow the road to Mason before turning due west and start riding cross country. He could have followed the overland mail route, but he suspected that any highwaymen would be lurking in wait for stagecoaches or other travelers along the established routes across the empty country. He'd make his own path after leaving Mason, about a hundred miles north-northwest.

He made his first camp that night, even though he could have stopped in Bourne. Instead he rode through the town just before sunset and put another five miles behind him because he wanted to see how long it would take to make his camp and then load the animals in the morning.

It took him almost thirty minutes to unsaddle the horses and unload the mule before he let them graze and water. He didn't get carried away and set up a full camp that first night on the trail because he didn't believe it was necessary. He just spread one of his bedrolls on the ground and laid his second on top for added cushioning before he covered all of his new weapons with Jack's slicker. He doubted if there would be any dew, but he wasn't about to be surprised by an unexpected thunderstorm.

RHODY JONES

He left his gunbelt near his head before he slid into the bedroll. It was more comfortable than the nights he'd spent on the cattle drives, and as he lay looking at bright band of the Milky Way stretched overhead, he began to name the different stars and constellations. It was a vital thing to know for mariners, and each was burned into his memory, but he also used it as a tool to help him sleep. He'd rarely reached the minor constellations before he drifted away, and tonight was no different.

———

He was on the road just after sunrise the next morning, after having bathed and shaved in the small pond that had provided drinking water for his animals. He was determined not to find himself in such a poor level of hygiene as he'd reached when he had returned from the cattle drive. It was just a matter of finding the water which he knew would become a problem as he rode further west.

But for the past two hours, he was heading more north than west. He was riding the Morgan mare to give Jack relief from bearing his hundred-and-eighty-pound load. Both of the small horses had similar, smooth gaits, and he almost wished that Jack hadn't been deprived of his stallion status. But then again, if he still was a randy stallion, Rhody expected that his trip would suffer frequent interruptions.

He was still grinning at the thought when he spotted traffic coming south on the road, about two miles away. It was making a large dust cloud, so he wondered what it was.

He had his answer just second later when he recognized the boxy shape and knew that he would soon have to clear the road to let the coach pass.

So, as the stagecoach raced to within four hundred yards, he turned off the roadway and pulled up when he was about twenty yards outside of the edge of the road then sat in the saddle and watched.

As the West Texas Line coach drew closer, he noticed that the shotgun rider had his coach gun pointed at him and almost reached for his Winchester but instead, put his hands in the air beside his shoulders and hoped the man didn't have an itchy trigger finger.

The man still held the shotgun level as the coach rolled past, and all Rhody could do was to follow it as it thundered by. He lowered his hands then twisted in his saddle to look back at the stage wondering if the shotgun rider did that to all of the traffic he passed on the route but couldn't imagine that it was the policy of the company.

As he nudged Morgana into a slow trot and regained the road, he was curious about whatever had created the level of concern by the shotgun rider. When he stopped in Fredericksburg for lunch, he'd ask if there was a reason.

RHODY JONES

After pulling up in front of Gertrude's Diner in Fredericksburg, he dismounted and tied off Morgana before entering then finding an empty table. The place was already about half-full, and most of the other diners were men, which wasn't unusual because married men ate at home.

When the waitress arrived to take his order, he asked, "Excuse me, miss, but when I was riding from Bourne this morning, I had to pull off the road to let the stagecoach pass and the shotgun rider pointed his gun at me for no reason that I could fathom. Do you know why he seemed so worried?"

"They had a holdup just north of here two days ago. Three men robbed the stage and took a shot at the driver. They were dressed like Klan and even had their horses in white sheets, so nobody knows who they are."

"Didn't the sheriff form a posse and track them down?"

"No, sir. Sheriff Bettendorf sent two deputies to where the stage had been robbed, but they didn't track the outlaws."

"Well that explains it. I'll just have the special."

"I'll bring it right out," she replied then smiled before walking away.

Rhody didn't see a problem after he left Fredericksburg as he assumed that the three men would have made a rushed escape to put as much distance between them and the lawmen that they expected to arrive within a few hours. At least it explained why the shotgun rider had been so nervous, but it also made him realize that he had to be more aware of his surroundings.

His afternoon ride didn't have any difficulties, and he only passed two riders and three freight wagons heading south to Fredericksburg.

When he pulled off to the west of the road shortly before sunset, he knew that tomorrow, he'd reach Mason and then his ride into the open country would begin. He could ride a few more miles north to Menardville, but he didn't want to keep going north.

Two days after he'd topped off his supplies in Mason, he was soon out of sight of any signs of his fellow human beings. He was no longer concerned about highwaymen but had shifted his focus to Indians. While many of the tribes had been given land in the Indian Nations that he had crossed just days ago on the cattle drive, he knew that many more still lived in his path and were much more hostile than those who had chosen to live on the meager scraps doled out by the Indian agents on those reservations. He didn't blame them, either. If he was a Comanche or Apache, he knew that he'd rather choose where to live. He wasn't even that happy with some of the unfathomable laws and rules that he'd encountered as he'd visited each of the states from Rhode Island to Texas.

He'd loaded all of his new weapons but hadn't put a single bullet through their bores. He had been waiting until he was away from towns or road traffic and was planning to stop early to finally get in some target practice.

He hadn't checked his maps yet either, but he had checked his compass regularly, so he was at least confident he hadn't drifted north or south.

―――

It was late in the afternoon when he pulled up near a decent-sized creek that flowed northeast and probably eventually emptied into the Red River.

After unsaddling the Morgans and unloading Dent, he arranged his packs and just let the animals wander to the creek as he followed with the water bag and canteens. The water wasn't the sweetest he'd ever tasted, but it wasn't as bitter as some of the others and almost had the taste of weak, stale beer. He wondered if he should name it Beer Creek.

He returned to his campsite with his filled water containers, set them near the packs then slid the new Winchester from its scabbard and walked toward from the animals, who were now grazing on the sparse grass. He had a bag of oats with him but was only going to let them enjoy the grain when he felt it was necessary.

There was a cartridge in the chamber, so after he stopped just ten feet behind the Morgans and his mule, he cocked the repeater, put it to his shoulder, aimed it high above their heads and squeezed the trigger.

The heavier round's loud report and kick surprised him, but his eyes were on his animals to see how they would react. All of them jerked their heads away from the grass at the unexpected blast, but after looking at him, they lowered them again to resume grazing.

"Well, that answers my first question," he said aloud as he cycled the lever.

He knew that both Morgans had been around gunfire before, but he wasn't sure about Dent. Satisfied that he wouldn't have any issues with his animals if he had to fire from the saddle, he picked up the spent brass and slid it into his pocket before releasing the hammer.

Now that he'd experienced the impact of the bigger round, he walked away from his four-legged companions and followed the creek for about a hundred yards, stopped and found an acceptable target.

He knew his limitations with firearms and was almost embarrassed to admit it. He'd fired pistols and muzzleloaders when he had served aboard ships and used his Winchester enough to feel competent, but he hadn't done much target practice. He figured that he'd only be shooting mad cattle or dying horses at close range, but now he needed to be better.

His one advantage over most shooters was that his nautical training included ballistics for the small pivot cannons that were mounted on all of his uncle's ships. That knowledge was the same regardless of the size of the projectile.

Rhody picked out a shriveled bush about fifty yards away on the other side of Beer Creek. It was about two feet tall, so he should be able to hit it with his first shot.

He cocked the hammer, shouldered the repeater and set the sights on the bush. He didn't bother with the rear ladder sight at this range.

He held his breath, steadied his sight and squeezed the trigger. The Winchester punched into his shoulder and the bush exploded. He didn't know where the bullet had hit the bush, but at least he'd hit it.

He then scanned for a second target a little further out, but one that was smaller and would at least tell him how far off he was. He found a dark rock that sat in stark contrast to the surrounding gray-brown dirt and grass that was about eighty yards away.

He cycled his Winchester then popped the repeater to his shoulder and barely let the sights settle before he fired. The ground four feet behind the rock erupted in a dirt volcano a fraction of a second later before he lowered the muzzle.

"Well, that's better than I expected," he said aloud before picking up the brass.

He missed on his next two shots, but on his next one, the rock was almost vaporized. He was satisfied with the rifle and his performance.

After cleaning his spent cartridges from the ground, he returned to the campsite and leaned the Winchester on his saddle before removing the Sharps-Borshadt from its scabbard.

After glancing at the critters to make sure that they hadn't wandered, he just turned to the south then set the ladder sight to six hundred yards almost as a joke to himself. He really only intended to get a feel for the big gun but figured the cost of the long cartridges demanded that he at least aim it at something.

He had one of the .50-100 cartridges in the chamber, so he expected the range and drop to be less than the .50-140s. As the purpose for even having the rifle was to scare any threats more than hit them, it wasn't that important.

As he searched for a distant target, he recalled Rob Whitfield saying that it would shoot further than he could see and now, he understood what he had meant as he looked downrange. Six hundred yards was more than a third of a mile away and as he scanned for a target, it seemed like a full mile.

RHODY JONES

He finally chose what looked like a broken wagon wheel, but he wasn't sure what it was at this distance.

After cocking the hammer, he brought the heavy rifle level, set his sights on whatever it was then held his breath and squeezed the trigger.

He'd been expecting a bigger punch from the Sharps-Borshadt than he'd felt from the Winchester but was surprised that it was about the same. Then even though he was expecting it, he had to wait for more than a second before the heavy slug of lead slammed into the target. As the dust cleared in the distance, he wasn't even sure where it had hit, but was in awe of the weapon's power. He was about to turn back to his camp, but decided he had to know how far off he'd been.

Rhody hopped across the creek without getting his feet wet, then trotted across the rough ground and after a few minutes, reached his target which turned out to be a shattered wagon wheel after all. What did shock him was that the broken wagon wheel had the top portion of the rim ripped off by his shot…at six hundred yards!

He didn't attribute it to his skill but more to simple coincidence and luck as he turned and headed back to the camp. Even if it had been just a lucky shot, he felt a growing respect for the Sharps-Borshadt.

———

By the time he was enjoying his hot supper, he'd cleaned and reloaded both of the new rifles. He didn't bother firing the shotgun because he'd used them often and accuracy with a scattergun wasn't necessary.

As he slid into his bedroll, he felt that he had just improved his chances that he would live to see the Pacific Ocean.

CHAPTER 4

Before he resumed his journey the next morning, he wound his watch and set the alarm for 11:30, so he'd have time to get a noon reading to mark his position.

He knew he was in sparsely populated Bexar Territory, not to be confused with Bexar County with its relatively large number of folks. There were a few ranches and even some farms in the area ahead, but towns were few and far between, and some barely qualified to be called a settlement.

Rhody still hadn't seen another soul by the time he'd stopped for a break, taken his noon sighting and marked his map. He was pleased with his progress when he mounted Morgana and continued west.

He had the mare moving at a slow trot as he approached a wide hill and debated about going around it or riding over the crest. He decided to make the climb because he believed it would take less time and he'd be able to get a better view of the terrain from the top of the hill. His maps were a bit vague about the landscape ahead and only showed rivers and large creeks.

It didn't take long for him to reach the top and before Morgana's hooves even reached the level ground, he spotted a small ranch house about a mile to the southwest.

He pulled the mare to a halt at the start of the decline and studied the house. There was a harnessed wagon parked in front of the house and people moving things from the house onto the wagon. He assumed that their ranch had failed, and they were tossing in their hand and moving on but twisted and removed his nautical telescope from his right saddlebag.

After pulling off the lens caps, he extended the tube and put the lens to his right eye and instantly realized that he had been as wrong as he could be in his assumption.

The figures that were removing items from the house weren't the one who built it. They looked like Comanches and were looting the place. As he studied them, he noticed that they staggered as they carried their loads from the porch, even if they were small. They seemed to be laughing as well, which meant that they had probably discovered the rancher's jug of corn mash, or whatever else he may have used to make his home brewed liquor.

He was sure that the original inhabitants of the ranch house were dead and probably mutilated, and the smart thing to do was to turn around and swing wide of the hill using it as cover. But there were two reason why he didn't head back. He had only seen four Indians and was sure that there were many more in the war party that had attacked the ranch. Those four had been assigned to clear the house before they rejoined the rest of the band. That meant that the others had gone to raid another ranch or farm, but Rhody didn't want to run afoul of that many angry Comanches.

The other reason was less logical, but more imperative. His vision of those people lying dead and mutilated inside the house for simply trying to make something of their lives drove his need to extract justice.

After returning his telescope to the saddlebag, he nudged Morgana down the long slope and pulled his Winchester '76 from his right-hand scabbard. The Sharps-Borshadt was on his left side, and he hadn't even thought about trying to scare them away from the house with the impressive rifle. He wanted to get as close as he could and make each of them as dead as their victims.

The Comanches still hadn't noticed him by the time the mare stepped onto level ground, and he wasn't sure if it was because he was coming from an unexpected direction or they were confident in the absence of any threats. What was more likely was that they were in a state of alcohol-induced euphoria. He knew that most home distillers tended to make very strong liquor and that Indians did suffer from a lack of defense against its effects. He didn't know why, but it was the only one of the many myths about them that he found to be true.

He had his Winchester cocked as he drew within five hundred yards without being detected and about that point, he was close enough to realize that there were no rifles of any sort on the short porch or the wagon. The larger group that had ridden off must have taken all the guns with them because the four left behind wouldn't need them because any white people in the area were already dead.

It would be nothing short of murder when they saw him, but that wasn't his concern. His only difficulty would be if they ran back into the house and he had to flush them out. If they did that, then they'd have the advantage even in their current state. But he was so sure that they had left no one alive on the ranch, that he'd already decided to burn the house down if they used it for a refuge. That would bring their friends back when they saw the smoke, but they'd miss them sooner or later anyway.

Morgana was moving at a fast walk, and the closer she was to the house, the more nervous he found himself despite his advantages. He didn't rue his decision to attack the house, but he still found his heart pounding against his ribs. He tried to calm his mind as he passed four hundred yards, knowing his nerves would affect his accuracy.

He sucked in a long breath then slowly let it out as he focused on the Comanches whose voices and laughter had begun to reach his ears. They seemed to be enjoying themselves, and those sounds did what no amount of deep breathing could accomplish as his anger and hate pushed aside his jitters.

It was just a few seconds later that one of them finally noticed Rhody's approach and shouted a warning to his fellow warriors. They may have been drunk, but when they turned their faces toward him, Rhody could see the anger in their eyes as they reached for their war tomahawks or knives.

There was a brief pause when one of them said something that Rhody thought meant dwelling, and he expected that they'd make the smart move and rush through the open door, but the warrior who must have been in charge shook his head, raised his tomahawk over his head and screamed his war cry. The other three did the same and then the leader shouted and all four scrambled away from the house charging across the open ground toward Rhody.

He didn't know what had driven the leader to make his attack whether it was the mind-numbing effect of the liquor, his personal pride, or his hatred and disdain for white people. Whatever the reason, it was a bad one.

Rhody let Morgana walk for another ten seconds then pulled her to a stop, dismounted and took a few steps toward the onrushing Comanches. They were still running, and he was surprised that they didn't stumble at all, but it didn't matter.

He remained standing as he leveled his Winchester settled his sights on the leader and squeezed the trigger.

As the Comanche awkwardly tumbled face first into the ground, he quickly levered in a second round, expecting the other three to start shifting their direction and separating to make themselves more difficult targets, but they didn't. They continued in a straight line, now about a hundred yards away, and still screaming their war cries.

He may not have felt any remorse for killing them, but he was ashamed for the ease in which he was doing it.

One after the other, the remaining three Comanches were pummeled by the powerful .45 caliber rounds and as the gunsmoke of his fourth shot wafted away, he slowly lowered his muzzle and looked at the carnage. He could see one of them still breathing before he returned to his animals and mounted but kept his cocked Winchester in his hands as he nudged Morgana forward.

When he reached the one who was still alive, he knew that the warrior wouldn't live much longer after seeing the pool of blood pouring from his stomach wound. He didn't say anything or even bother looking down at the man on the ground as he walked his mare past. He didn't glance down at the other three either but headed for the house to verify his belief that the rancher and his family were all dead. It wasn't going to be a pretty sight but knew he had to check in case one of them was still alive.

RHODY JONES

He pulled up next to the loaded wagon, released his Winchester's hammer and slid it home before he dismounted, then tied off his reins on the back wheel. He then removed his Stetson, hung it on his saddle horn and pulled his Colt in case there was another Comanche still inside, which was highly unlikely, but he wasn't about to make that fatal assumption.

He stepped into the front room felt his stomach rebel and hurriedly rushed back onto the porch and vomited. He'd seen a lot of death and horrible injuries in his years on the seas, but nothing could match what his eyes had just revealed. He knew he couldn't go back inside, so he left the foul porch, walked to his black mare and removed his canteen to rinse the rancid taste from his mouth.

After spitting out the first mouthful, he swallowed a second, then as he was lowering the canteen, he spotted movement from the north and was ready to grab his Winchester again when he realized that it wasn't another Comanche.

He capped his canteen, hung it over his shoulder then took his hat from the saddle horn pulled it on and waited for the boy to reach him. Rhody guessed that he was around ten to twelve and he could already see the fear and sadness in his eyes as the blonde headed and blue-eyed boy approached him warily.

When he was close, Rhody asked, "Are you all right, son?"

He didn't answer until he stopped just four feet away and looked up at him.

"They killed everyone. Didn't they?"

"I'm sorry, son. Are you okay?"

He shook his head violently and exclaimed, "I hid! I watched them do that and I didn't help! I'm a big baby and I should be dead too!"

Rhody took a long stride to the boy then wrapped him in his arms as he exploded in tears and began to shake.

"You did the right thing, son. What good would it do if you were dead in the house? Do you think your mama and papa would want that? You're just a boy and you couldn't have helped."

The boy didn't reply as he continued to sob, soaking Rhody's shirt with his tears.

As the boy cried, Rhody scanned the area, expecting to see more Comanches soon after they heard his gunfire. They would know that there were no firearms back at the ranch and would have to send help soon. His only hope was that they were already far enough away or busy enough not to have heard his shots.

He then put his hand on the boy's blonde head and said, "Son, I know you probably don't want to talk about it, but I need to know what happened. Can you be brave and tell me?"

He felt the head nod then stepped back as the boy sniffed, wiped his nose on his shirt sleeve and looked up at him with his mournful blue eyes.

"There were about twelve of them and they came from the south early in the morning. I already left to hunt jackrabbits for supper when they showed up. I...I stopped and just stared. I was so afraid I just stood there like a statue."

He then paused almost as if he was in a trance as his mind replayed the horrible memory.

"The rest of my family was still in the house having breakfast. I shoulda run to warn them, but I was too afraid and too far away. Then I laid on the ground so they wouldn't see me. I didn't do anything! I just laid there all scared and all I cared about was not dying. I closed my eyes a few times, but I still watched when they went inside and I...I heard my mama scream."

The tears began again, but he managed to continue.

"It was like a nightmare that wouldn't go away. There were Indian yells and my father and brother shouting while my mama and sister screamed. They were all being killed, and I stayed hiding like a coward on the ground just watching. When all I heard was the Indians, I closed my eyes and waited for the Comanches to come and get me, but they didn't. I heard them leaving but was too scared to look up."

"When did you start looking again?" Rhody asked.

"When it got quiet. I thought they were all gone, but when I looked, there were some left, and they had our wagon in front of the house. I kept watching them and I was getting mad when I saw them taking all of our things."

"How long ago did the others leave?"

"I don't know. It was like a bad dream," he replied then glanced at his shadow and said, "I reckon it was right after they killed everyone, so it was a few hours ago. I needed to pee and was almost gonna go in my pants when I saw you ride in, then shoot them all."

"Do you know where they went?"

"They rode west, so I'm pretty sure they went to the Brandt ranch. It's that way."

Rhody hadn't seen another ranch when he was on the top of the hill nor had he seen any other Comanches, so the Brandt ranch had to be a good five miles west.

Then Willie softly asked, "Did you see my mama and papa in the house?"

Rhody nodded then replied, "I'm sorry, son. You don't want to go in thoro. I found your mama, papa and your big brother," then realized that the boy had said he'd heard his mother and sister scream and quickly asked, "You said you have a sister?"

RHODY JONES

He nodded as he replied, "Marta, but I call her Marty. She's seven."

"I didn't find her with the rest of your family, so I'll go back inside and check in a minute. What's your name, son?"

"Willie Ernst, but my real name is Wilhelm."

"I'm Rhody Jones, but my real name is Roland. You can call me Rhody because I like it better. How old are you, Willie?"

"I'm eleven. Can you find Marty now?"

"I'll do that," Rhody replied then handed his canteen to Willie before stepping back to the house dreading what he would soon have to witness for a second time.

As much as it had sickened him to find the mutilated bodies of the boy's parents and brother the thought of seeing the horribly mangled body of a little girl was almost overwhelming.

He stepped through the door and averted his eyes from the three bodies he'd already seen then scanned the rest of the room before entering the only bedroom in the small house. It didn't take him long to realize that Marty's body wasn't there, so he left the bedroom and checked the small kitchen before leaving the house through the back door and scanning the ground.

He didn't return to the house but walked around the outside until he reached Willie who was staring at the bed of the wagon with his family's possessions.

Just before he reached the front of the wagon, Willie jerked, then looked at him and asked, "Did you find her?"

"No. I don't think they killed her, Willie. I think they took her with them."

"*They took her?*" Willie exclaimed as his eyes expanded into small white saucers, "*Why would they do that?*"

"Because she was young and had blonde hair. Lots of the tribes seem to place great value on blonde or redheaded girls and women."

"Mama had blonde hair and blue eyes, but they killed her," Willie said with closed fists.

"Your mama probably fought them just as your papa and brother did. If she'd just stayed standing in the corner, she probably would have been taken captive."

"Would they have taken me, too?" he asked as he ran his hand through his blonde locks.

"I don't think so, Willie. You're too old. If you were Marty's age, they might have, but let's not talk about that now. I'm worried that the others might come back soon, and we wouldn't stand a chance against them. I have to decide what to do, but I'm unfamiliar with this part of Texas. Isn't there an army fort about twenty miles north?"

"They call it a fort, but there aren't any soldiers anymore. There's still a trading post and a blacksmith, though. Once a month, papa would take the wagon there to get supplies."

His answer quashed his option of gaining army help but soon, another factor was added to the mix of the more pressing issues now.

Willie was looking at him when he pointed west and shouted, "Smoke!"

Rhody quickly turned and spotted a black cloud rising into the Texas sky about five or six miles west and there was no question what was providing the fuel. The Comanches had finished their deadly work on the Brandt's ranch. He suspected that the four that they'd left behind were supposed to set fire to the Ernst home before they left and thought that if he did their work for them, the others might not return even if they'd heard the gunshots. But it wasn't his call because it wasn't his home or his family's bodies on the floor inside.

He turned around, looked down and said, "Willie, we need to get out of here quickly and I don't have time to bury your family properly."

Willie surprised him when he turned to look at the ranch house and replied, "Burn it just like they did to the Brandt's house."

"Alright, Willie. I'll do that. Do you need me to get anything out of the house first?"

"No. My clothes are in that small chest on the wagon."

"I'm really sorry for having to do this, Willie."

"It's okay," he said quietly before turning away so Rhody couldn't see his tears again.

Rhody then took Morgana's reins, tied them to the back of the wagon and climbed aboard. He drove the wagon to the edge of the corral, stepped down and tied the harness leads to one of the posts in case the mules were spooked by the fire.

He didn't have any kerosene, so he needed to take another trip into the house, but luckily their can of coal oil was in the kitchen, so he could avoid returning to the horrible scene in the front room.

Ten minutes after finding the can, the Ernst house was already an inferno as the dry wood fed the flames.

As Willie stood beside the wagon and watched his life burn, Rhody was still thinking about what he should do next. He had thought that it was just as likely that the Comanches had killed Willie's sister somewhere else. She might have run and hidden as Willie had done, but unlike her brother, she had been caught. He hadn't done a thorough search for her body but wasn't about to do it with Willie. He'd already undergone a horrible experience and Rhody wasn't sure if he could bear seeing his sister's body in that same, revolting condition.

He hadn't lied about the tribes' blonde and redhead fascination, but a lot depended on the individual groups.

He was still thinking when Willie looked at him and asked, "Are we going to find Marty?"

If a man had asked him that question, Rhody would have probably told him that there was no way that it was even possible, but as he looked into the sorrowful eyes of a boy who had lost all of his family except his little sister, there was no other answer he could give but the one he did.

"Of course, we're going to find her, Willie. We just need to get things ready. Okay?"

Willie didn't smile, but his eyes lost some of their sorrow and pain as he replied, "Okay. What are we going to do?"

"We can't take the wagon with us, so I need you to tell me what you want out of the wagon. We'll leave the rest here and we can pick it up after we find Marty. We'll move your things onto my pack mule, then you can ride Jack, he's the tan horse. I'll let your mules loose, so they can take care of themselves."

"Alright."

Rhody knew that the boy's hands were too small to use a pistol, so he asked, "Can you shoot a Winchester, Willie?"

"I shot my papa's Henry. Is it the same?"

"Pretty much. You'll have one on each side of the saddle."

"When we leave, where will we go?"

"We'll head for the smoke. If they set fire to the other ranch, then that means they're already gone. If they were coming this way, we should have seen their dust cloud by now. We'll see which direction they went and follow, but we don't want to get too close until we see their village."

"Then what do we do?"

"We trade for Marty."

"*Trade?*" he asked sharply.

"If it's one thing I've learned when dealing with Indians, it's that they're always willing to part with something they don't value for something that they do. I can see some of your cattle south of here, so that means they didn't take them all. They might have just had some of their men that you didn't see drive them away."

"They took our horses, though."

"They'll take every horse they can get because they value horses more than anything else."

"Won't they want the mules more than the cattle?"

RHODY JONES

Rhody smiled then answered, "I believe you're right, sir. I'll tell you what we'll do. I'll tie off your mules behind my pack mule and when we get to the Brandt place, if there are any cattle left, I'll add one to each of the mules. You're a smart boy, Willie."

Willie finally managed a weak smile as he nodded then climbed into the wagon bed and began to rummage.

Rhody unharnessed the mules and used the long reins as trail lines rather than wasting any more of his rope. After they were linked to Dent, he took the last two harness straps, wrapped them tightly into a disk and put them into one of his panniers.

When he returned to the wagon, Willie had stacked his clothes on the edge of the wagon's bed along with Marty's then when Rhody was close, he hopped down from the wagon.

Rhody looked at the small pile of dresses and felt a knot in his throat aware of the small chance of finding Marty still alive.

"Let's get the clothes into one of Dent's panniers and we'll start riding. I'll adjust Jack's stirrups before we mount."

"Okay."

———

Ten minutes later, Rhody and Willie rode away from the still burning remains of the Ernst home and its grizzly contents. Neither of them had mentioned the four Comanche bodies that lay behind them in the hot sun.

As they rode west, Willie asked, "Rhody, why are you here?"

"I figured on seeing California and was heading that way."

"Why didn't you take the train? It's a lot faster, but I've never been on one."

"I wanted to explore, Willie. You can't do that from inside a train's passenger car."

"You have a lot of guns."

"I reckoned it's better to have too many than not enough."

"Are you a cowhand?"

"I was for the past five years, but before that I was the first mate on a sailing ship."

"You were a sailor? Why did you stop? Did your ship sink?"

"In order, I was a sailor since I was your age. I stopped because the captain on my last ship was a weak man and didn't want me around anymore. That ship didn't sink, but it was close when we were caught in a hurricane."

RHODY JONES

"Was it scary?"

"More than you can imagine. Most of the crew stayed below decks, even the captain. We rode out the storm and then had to spend another week or so just repairing the damage. Once we reached New Orleans, I wasn't surprised when the captain didn't want to sail with me again."

"Are you going to be a sailor again?"

Rhody looked at him and replied, "You know, I'm not really sure anymore. I do miss the ocean, and the sea gets in a man's blood, but I'm not sure if I want to work on a ship anymore."

Then he asked, "Willie, what can you tell me about the Brandt ranch and family?"

"Well, Mr. and Mrs. Brandt aren't as old as my papa and mama, but they had Mr. Brandt's brothers living with him to help work the ranch and had two boys, too, but they were younger than me. One of his brothers, Carl, was married, but they didn't have any kids yet."

"Was it a bigger ranch than yours?"

"Yes, sir. It had a bigger house and even a barn. They had more cattle than we did, too."

Rhody wondered if that was why they'd hit the Ernst ranch first. If the Brandt spread had three men then they'd be out with the cattle and he couldn't imagine how the Comanches could have gotten so close to the ranch without being detected. They left the Ernst ranch long before he arrived, yet he hadn't heard any gunfire. Surely, the Brandt men would have had time to prepare.

He kept their pace to a walk to avoid any surprises and still had to come up with some sort of plan. He hadn't lied to Willie about using the mules and cattle as a trade for Marty if she was being held captive in their village. But he knew that even if they agreed to the trade, all bets were off once he and Marty were at a distance far enough from their village that satisfied their honor. He was certain that if they were fortunate enough to find and retrieve Marty, he'd have to be prepared to fight for their lives after they left.

It was another thirty minutes before Rhody finally spotted the remnants of the Ernst ranch house. The Comanches had set fire to the barn as well, so the smoke was still thick. There were no horses in sight, but there were cattle, so he began to believe that cattle would no longer be of value to the Comanches in a trade.

His concern now shifted to Jack, who was a fine horse and knew that once he started bargaining, if it got that far, they would demand his second horse, probably in addition to the two mules.

Willie startled him when he exclaimed, "They burned their barn, too!"

RHODY JONES

"I can see that. They took all their horses but left a lot of their cattle. They must not have enough men to move that many critters."

"That means we can take more than just two."

"Nope. It means just the opposite. If they just took a dozen or so cattle, then offering them two more won't be enough. They'll want the mules, but I think they'll want even more."

"What will they want?"

"The horse you're sitting on, but they'll never see him or you. I'll explain after we find where they went."

"Okay."

Rhody knew what they cherished almost as much as horses, and even though they probably just added to their village arsenal with the weapons from the two ranches, he was sure that one of the Winchesters would be a good bargaining chip. He didn't want to give up his new '76, as it had already proven its value, and he wasn't about to give them Jack's Yellow Boy, so that left his '73. He wished he didn't have to trade any of his weapons but knew that if it was necessary to make the deal for Willie's sister, he'd do it without hesitation. He was just annoyed about giving the well-maintained carbine to the Comanche renegades who'd murdered two families.

They reached the smoldering piles of cinders that used to be the Brandt home in late afternoon and didn't bother dismounting to inspect the house but rode past the devastation and headed south. If he had taken the time to examine the devastation, he might have spotted the remains of the two Comanche warriors who had died in the assault. Their bodies had been laid out on stacks of hay on the porch and been burned as if they'd been in their village. Unlike the whites who were dead in the house, the two Comanches had received honors from their fellow warriors, but that ceremony had added another hour to their departure time.

Once the mess was behind them, Rhody pulled up and said, "It looks like they went back the way they came, Willie. They took their wagon, too. Your father probably would have known if their village was close, so they probably won't reach it today. They'll have to set up camp."

"What will we do?"

"We'll follow their trail and I'll figure it out as we ride. One thing I've already decided is that when I think we're close, I'll want you to wait there with the pack mule. I'll ride to their village or their camp with the mules, but I'll inspect it with my telescope to see if I can spot Marty. If I see her, then I'll ride in and have a talk with them."

"Won't they kill you?" Willie quickly asked.

"I don't think so. It'll depend on how they act when they see me. If they have their guns pointed at me, then I'll deal with that problem. They may be curious enough to wait for me to get close enough so I can talk. I'll just have to play it by ear."

"What do I do if I hear gunshots?"

"You turn tail and ride to that trading post. Do you have any other relatives nearby?"

"No, sir."

Rhody reached into his pocket, pulled out some currency and handed it to Willie before saying, "When you get to the trading post, take the stagecoach to San Antonio and ask for Hector Lopez. He runs a livery. He'll find a family to take you in. Okay?"

Willie stared at the money then slid it into his pocket before he said, "Mister Jones, I don't think it's right. You don't even know me or Marty."

"I know that, Willie, but after seeing what those Comanches did to your family, I want to help you as much as I can. I've dealt with Comanches before, and I'll admit that they were reservation Comanches and not renegades like this bunch, but I know how they think, so I'll have a good chance to get Marty away from them."

"Thank you, Rhody."

"You're welcome, Mister Ernst. Now, let's see how far behind we are."

Just eight miles south, Bear Who Speaks was pleased with the way the mission had gone. He'd lost two of his men when they made that second attack on the larger ranch, but he'd expected worse. His father's people were short on food and ammunition for their four rifles, but in addition to the twelve beef animals he was bringing, the other group had driven eight animals south. The horses weren't as good as he'd hoped, but the mules that the other four would be bringing from the first ranch were strong. He'd had to use two horses to pull the wagon of food and utensils from the second ranch and thought it was beneath the dignity of even the less impressive horses they'd gotten from both ranches.

The first house had yielded some much-needed flour and other vital supplies, but the wagon behind him held much more from the bigger house.

What made it worth the loss of the two warriors was that they'd almost doubled their number of rifles and added two more pistols. He only regretted not finding more ammunition for the guns. None of his men had found where they had been stored, but as soon as the flames reached the ammunition, it began to send bullets flying everywhere.

The four warriors he left at the first ranch should be miles ahead of him by now and might even have joined the others who were driving the cattle. He was down to just seven men now, but with the cattle and the addition of more guns, his father's people wouldn't have to worry about food or the so-called charity of the whites.

But overall, the mission had been very successful. The discovery of the gold-haired girl and woman was just a bonus. It was too bad the one in the small house had tried to fight them. She would have been a fine addition to his lodge, but he really appreciated the younger one with the silvery yellow hair.

———

They'd been riding at a medium trot for two hours, and there were still four hours of sunlight remaining on the long summer day when Rhody caught a glimpse of a large dust cloud on the horizon which surprised him. It wasn't because the Comanches were stirring up so much dust, it was that they were so close.

"Is that them?" Willie asked.

"I'm sure it is. I thought they'd be a lot further away than that. They're probably only four miles ahead. Stay with me until we get closer, but we need to start looking for someplace to set up for a defense. If it has water nearby then that's a real bonus."

"Why do we have to worry about fighting? I thought you were gonna trade for Marty."

"I am, and if I ride out of their camp with her, I don't trust the Comanches to let us get away. They'll let us go to a point where they believe they've honored their side of our bargain then they'll chase us down."

Willie was about to ask what good it would do to take Marty from them if she was going to be captured again but was afraid to raise the possibility.

As they continued to close the gap, Rhody's mind was still trying to stay one step ahead of the Comanches. It was still possible that Willie's little sister wasn't with them, but the longer they followed the hoofprints and wagon tracks, the more he was convinced that she was.

The dust cloud was noticeably larger after another thirty minutes, and when Rhody picked up the first dots ahead, he said loudly, "Slow down, Willie."

They reduced their speed to a slow trot as Rhody pointed to a lone cottonwood nearby and said, "Let's head over there, but I want you to stay in the saddle."

"Okay," Willie said before he angled Jack to their right.

When they reached the tree, Rhody quickly dismounted, removed his telescope from his saddlebag and trotted to the old tree. There was a dying creek trickling past its roots which kept it alive, so as he began his climb, Willie walked Jack and the mules to the creek while Morgana made her own way.

Once he reached a strong limb about twenty feet above the ground, Rhody stood on the stout branch with his back against the thick trunk, popped off the lens caps and extended the tube.

He had a difficult time seeing the Comanches through the dust created by the herds of cattle and horses, but he took his time. They were moving slowly, or it would have been worse. He began counting human heads and even as he was surprised at the reduced number, he thought his eyes were playing tricks on him when he found a blonde head on one of the horses that was attached to a trail rope behind the wagon.

He blinked, then steadied the telescope on the blonde hair and when the horse shifted slightly, he knew his eyes weren't lying, but he needed to talk to Willie.

He snapped the telescope closed, replaced the lens caps and began to clamber down from his observation post.

After dropping to the ground, he quickly headed to the creek, and after he replaced his telescope, he looked up at Willie and before he could ask his question, Willie asked his.

"Did you see Marty?"

"Yes, I did. She's riding on a horse behind the Brandt's fully loaded wagon."

Willie started giggling with unrestrained relief and joy that his sister was alive, so Rhody used the opportunity to test the water. If it was better than the water he had in his canteens and water bag, and he'd replace it when Willie was past his excitement.

After taking a loud slurp, he found that the water wasn't nearly as bitter as he'd expected then turned back to Willie.

"Marty wasn't alone, Willie. She was with a blonde lady who must be Mrs. Brandt. Is that right?"

"Carl's wife was blonde, but lighter than my mama or Marty's. They took her, too?"

"Yup. Either she didn't fight, or they grabbed her early. It doesn't matter, but it does mean I'll have to change my approach to the Comanches. I thought we'd have to do it tomorrow morning, but we're close enough now that I think I'll do it today after they set up camp. Let's replace the water in the canteens and water bag then keep following until we find someplace to set up on this side of their trail. That creek is barely surviving, but it's good water."

After refilling their six canteens and the water bag, they were soon back on the trail of the Comanches.

It was thirty minutes later when Rhody found a good defensive position where a monstrous flash flood had carved a deep gouge into the eastern bank of the creek's bed where the creek turned. After the rushing water had dug the hole, the creek had eventually returned to its previous bed and left the natural fortress. It was an ideal location, so they turned toward the creek and when they were just on its rim, they dismounted.

"Okay, Willie, here's what I'm going to do. We'll take Jack and the pack mule into that hole where you will wait as close to the edge as we can get them. I'm going to leave all of my guns except my Winchester '73 and my Colt with you, and I'll only take two boxes of .44 cartridges. Don't unsaddle the horses yet in case we need to ride rather than fight."

"Why don't you take another rifle?"

"Now that I have to negotiate for Marty and Mrs. Brandt, then I'm sure that they won't settle for two mules. I'll have to give them a repeater and ammunition to make the deal. Let's get down there."

"Okay."

It took another twenty minutes to get everything rearranged, but when Rhody left Willie, he was riding Morgana and trailing the two Ernst mules. His Winchester '73 was in the only scabbard strapped to his saddle and he felt almost naked as he set Morgana to a medium trot, which would have been amusing considering he'd ridden from New Orleans to San Antonio with just what he had now and had felt well-protected.

He was incredibly nervous as he closed the gap to the Comanches. He was going to get close then slow down and match their speed until they began to set up camp. Then he'd ride in and hopefully get close enough to begin bargaining for the lives of Marty and Mrs. Brandt.

Willie had given him her Christian name, Emma, and then when he asked if she could speak any other languages other than English, Willie said that she spoke German. That had been a real plus for Rhody as he was reasonably sure that some of the Comanches probably understood either English or Spanish, but he could say something in German to Mrs. Brandt that he didn't want the Comanches to understand. He even began to wonder if he should arrive and ask if they could speak German before he asked about Spanish or English. He wasn't worried about a proper accent, because he doubted if any of them had ever heard German.

Just three miles ahead, Emma Brandt clung to Marty as the horse plodded behind the wagon that held what was left of her life. She had no illusions of what would happen to her once they reached their village, if not tonight when they stopped for camp. She'd seen what they'd done to her sister-in-law, Mary, before they killed her, but hadn't seen them murder Carl, Frank, or Peter as they'd been outside trying to defend against the sudden attack. Mary's boys had run from the house at the first sound of gunfire, and she had to restrain Mary when she panicked and tried to chase after them. Emma knew that their presence would only distract the men as they tried to stop the Comanches.

She didn't know why they hadn't killed her or even molested her. All she remembered was that she and Mary were huddled in the middle bedroom without weapons, and she had been holding her weeping sister-in-law when two Comanches broke down the door then ripped Mary from her arms before everything went black.

When she was slapped awake, she saw Mary's naked body lying dead on the floor and expected it would soon happen to her, but they had wrestled her out of the room and led her outside. She had closed her eyes when she had first been lashed to the stirrups of one of the family's horses and let her mind create unspeakable terrors that awaited her while she listened to the Comanches as they began loading their wagon. She was in the depths of her despair when one of the marauding Indians slapped her leg and when she opened her eyes, she saw him with Marta Ernst.

As she stared at the terrified face of the little girl, the Indian lifted her onto the horse in front of her and then walked away.

Marty had quickly wrapped her arms around her and began to shake as she sobbed and cried, "They killed mama and papa! They killed everybody!"

Until that moment, Emma hadn't shed a tear as the shock of the unexpected attack and the vivid memory of seeing Mary's naked body on the floor had put her into a distant state of mind. But once she held the innocent, grief-stricken girl in her arms, Emma could no longer hold back her own flood of emotion and joined Marty in a deluge of tears.

She didn't speak of the horror that she'd seen in the bedroom but instead, as she wept, she said softly, "It'll be all right, Marta. I'm with you now. I'll take care of you."

Marty didn't reply, but Emma's soothing voice had calmed her massive fear and grief, yet she didn't understand how Emma could say that things would be all right.

Even as she tried to comfort Marty, Emma knew that there was nothing she could do to prevent their ultimate fate. She knew what would happen to her but didn't understand what they would do to Marta, who had just turned seven last month. Whatever it was, she hoped that she wouldn't be alive to witness it.

———

Rhody had kept the same distance between him and the Comanches, and with each passing minute, he wondered how long it would be before they set up camp. He didn't think they'd wait until sunset because they had the cattle and horses to corral, so it would take them longer, and they'd probably want to stop and inspect their booty.

His wish was soon granted when he noticed the dust cloud suddenly being to fade in the early evening light. He estimated he'd ridden about two miles since leaving Willie but wasn't worried about it at the moment. With the Comanches another two miles away, he'd have to make his move now before it was too late.

He set Morgana to a fast trot and was trying to steady his nerves as he picked up movement on the ground ahead but didn't even think about turning around. He knew as soon as he was spotted, he was committed to his plan.

As the figures ahead became more discernable, he inexplicably thought of his last voyage when he'd lashed himself to the wheel, knowing that his fate was now in the hands of the hurricane's power. Now he was riding into a different kind of storm, one that was created by man and not by nature. For some reason, that memory soothed his nerves knowing that he was more in control of his fate this time.

Bear Who Speaks was helping down the blonde woman when Quiet Owl trotted up to him, pointed north and said, "A white man is coming."

The war chief turned back to look as he set the woman on the ground and didn't pay her any attention as she took the blonde girl's hand.

"He is only one. Where did he come from? Is he a crazy man?"

"He must be crazy. Do we shoot him when he is close?"

"No. But get our rifles and we will wait to see why he is crazy. If he has his gun out, we will kill him."

Quiet Owl nodded then jogged away to tell the others while his war chief still stared at the approaching crazy man.

Emma didn't understand what they were talking about but had turned to look north when the Comanche had pointed that way and seen the lone rider approaching and had the same question. *Was he insane for riding into the Comanche camp?*

Marty looked up at her and asked, "Who is he, Aunt Emma?"

Emma was staring at the rider as she replied, "I don't know, Marta. I didn't think anyone was close enough to know what happened, but I don't know what he's thinking or if he's thinking at all. He must know that they'll kill him when he gets within range."

"Is he going to take us away?"

Emma almost laughed at the idea but didn't want to frighten Marta who had just begun to act rationally, so she replied, "I hope so, sweetheart."

Marty looked north again, and soon every human face in the encampment was staring at the incredible sight of a lone white man riding toward them as if they weren't even there. He must have seen them with their rifles and that made it even more ludicrous.

RHODY JONES

Rhody's mouth was as dry as the Texas ground Morgana trotted across, so when he was eight hundred yards out, he pulled his canteen took a quick drink then capped it and returned it to his saddle. He didn't want to make any sudden movements when he was closer that might be interpreted as an attempt to pull his Winchester.

The closer he was, the clearer he was able to do assess the situation and began to plan for a different reaction by the Comanches. It they began firing, he'd have to release the mules, which wouldn't be difficult because they were attached to Morgana with a slip knot. Then he'd charge at them with his Winchester and hoped he could get close enough to start picking off the ones who were closest to their hostages. He had sixteen rounds in his fully charged Winchester and another six in his Colt. There were seven targets who would be firing at him and he hoped none were proficient. Hopefully, it wouldn't come to a shootout, at least not here. If he could get the woman and girl out of the camp and reach Willie and his other weapons, then he'd be in control.

As he passed the two-hundred-yard mark without any of the Comanches bringing his rifle to his shoulder, his hopes that he'd at least be able to talk to them rose.

His mouth was getting dry again as he passed the Winchester's effective range, but he wasn't about to reach for his canteen again. He began to make out individual faces and tried to find the warrior who was in charge of the raid.

Rhody was fifty yards out when he saw Emma Brandt's blue eyes looking back at him as she clutched onto Marty, but quickly resumed his search for the Indian chieftain.

Bear Who Speaks had noticed the two mules that the man was trailing, but neither had a saddle and he wondered why he had them with him. It was one more piece of evidence that the man was mad.

When the rider was just twenty yards away, he pulled up and held out his hand in a sign of peace then surprised the war chief when he spoke in his own language, saying just one word…trade.

Bear Who Speaks was beyond curious as he stepped forward with his repeating rifle and approached the mounted white man.

When Rhody saw him leave the others, he knew that he wasn't just a spokesman. He could see the confidence and power in the man's demeanor that only a natural leader possessed.

He then asked loudly in German, "Do you speak German?"

Bear Who Speaks had never heard the language the white man used, so he turned to his warriors, and after each of them shrugged, he looked back at Rhody without replying.

RHODY JONES

Rhody spoke in German again, saying, "That is bad because my friend Willie is waiting four miles away," then he asked in Spanish, "Do you speak Spanish?"

Bear Who Speaks then replied, "I know the tongue."

Rhody nodded then said, "I came to visit my sister, but found her home on fire. She is standing with your warriors and I have come to bargain for her release and for the girl's as well."

"They are my captives and not for trade."

"All things are for trade, even our lives. I know that you have no mules, or you would not have been pulling the wagon with horses. I will trade you the two strong mules for the woman and the girl."

Bear Who Speaks stared at Rhody for thirty seconds before replying, "It is not enough. We have many horses and another wagon and two mules already."

"You do not have another wagon or mules. The four warriors you left behind found a jug of whiskey and were drunk when I arrived. They are drunk no longer."

"You killed them and yet dare to ride into my camp!" he exclaimed.

"They disobeyed your orders when they drank the whiskey. If they hadn't, they would have been gone before I arrived.

They are to blame for their disobedience, not me. I acted as any man who had discovered what they had done."

"That may be so, but two mules are not enough even for the girl."

"I will also give you my only rifle and two boxes of ammunition. It will leave me with only my pistol and the bullets I have on my belt."

"That is still not enough for both of them. You may take the girl. You do not have anything to trade that is enough for the woman, not even your horse."

Rhody glanced at Emma then twisted in his saddle, opened the flap to his right saddlebag and removed his precious nautical telescope.

He then held it before him and said, "This is a special telescope that is better than others. It was given to me by my uncle when I was a boy."

Bear Who Speaks stared at the instrument in his hands as he asked, "Why is it special? We have white man's glasses for two eyes and do not need one like that."

"This is more powerful than field glasses, so you can see further away and much clearer. With this telescope, you can see the face of the moon and distant stars. I will let you use it so you can believe my words."

RHODY JONES

Rhody pulled the lens caps off then snapped it open and demonstrated its use by pointing it at Emma Brandt's face. He was startled to see her blue eyes as if he was just inches from her instead of fifty feet but could see the hope and fear that lay beneath them. He shifted the view to Marty and saw even more hope in her bright blue eyes then dropped it from his eye, leaned down and handed it to the Comanche leader.

The war chief set his Winchester against his leg then quickly pointed the telescope at one of the horses at the far end of the campsite, put the lens to his eye and was stunned when he found the dark brown gelding staring back at him. He then slowly swung the telescope across the landscape amazed at the clarity of the distant objects. This looking glass would be worth even more than six rifles, and he would have probably given up both the woman and the girl in trade if the stupid white man had realized its true value.

Rhody watched his expression and knew that he was impressed with the telescope but knew that he'd never admit it. But seeing his face gave him the idea that he'd raise his own demands because he was sure that the war chief had to have the telescope now.

Bear Who Speaks finally lowered the telescope but didn't offer it back to the white man.

Instead, he looked up at Rhody and said, "I will make the trade."

Rhody then said, "I will need the horse that they were riding. I have a long way to go and my small horse will not be able to carry all of us."

The war chief glanced back at the horse and then looked back at Rhody as he thought about the new demand. He knew that the horse and saddle were not even as valuable as his blonde-headed hostages, but it irritated him that the white man had made the request. He was about to refuse, but the weight of the telescope in his hand coupled with his plan to chase down the white man after he left with his captives made it unnecessary. Let him think that he is safe with his one pistol against seven Comanche warriors all armed with rifles.

Rhody was expecting a counteroffer, but when the Comanche leader said, "They can ride the horse," he was surprised but understood the reason for his sudden agreement.

He dismounted, stepped around Morgana, yanked the slip knot on the trail rope and let it drop before he slid his Winchester from its scabbard then removed the two boxes of cartridges from his saddlebags.

He then waited by his mare as he watched one of the warriors give Emma Brandt the reins to the horse and gestured for her to mount. When she was in the saddle, the same Comanche lifted Marty onto the saddle in front of Emma then waved her toward Rhody.

RHODY JONES

As Emma steered the gelding away from the wagon, Rhody stepped closer to the Comanche war chief and held out the Winchester. After he grabbed the carbine, Rhody handed another warrior the two boxes of cartridges then stepped backwards to Morgana. He may have just made the bargain, but that didn't mean he had to trust them.

He mounted Morgana just as Emma and Marty reached him, so he said to her in German, "Keep going north, and I'll join you when you're out of rifle range. If you hear a shot just ride away as fast as you can. Willie is waiting about four miles away near the creek. Don't answer, just go."

Emma stared at him for a few seconds in disbelief, but then nudged the tired gelding into a medium trot as Marty continued to look at Rhody.

As they rode away, Rhody wheeled Morgana to the north, then pulled his canteen and took his time unscrewing the cap and then taking a few long swallows before capping it then returning it to his saddle. He didn't hear any hammers being snapped back behind him, but he had another hundred yards to go before he would feel remotely safe.

Emma had the gelding more than a hundred yards away now, so Rhody set Morgana to a fast trot to catch up. His nerves were still taut, and his adrenalin was still pulsing through his system as he rode away from the camp without turning around. He wasn't sure if the Comanches viewed it as an act of courage or one of foolishness, but it really didn't matter as long as they didn't open fire.

By the time he caught up with Emma, they were more than four hundred yards from the campsite. When he had Morgana trotting alongside, he glanced at Emma who kept her eyes focused ahead, but even as Marty looked at him curiously, she too remained silent.

Rhody could understand her need for silence, or at least believed that he did, so he didn't disturb her thoughts.

Emma was a boiling stew of emotions driven by horrible images and deep worries and was still trying to comprehend all that had happened to her on what had started as a normal summer day.

She felt an intense guilt for surviving when everyone else on the ranch had suffered a horrible death and an inexplicable shame for feeling the joy of relief when the stranger had rescued her and Marta.

They rode for another five minutes in silence before Marty asked, "Aren't you happy, Aunt Emma?"

Emma shook her head to shake away her selfish thoughts knowing that she had to care for Marta now.

"Yes, Marta, I'm happy that we're safe."

"Will you stay with me now?"

RHODY JONES

Emma looked into her innocent eyes and smiled, something she thought she'd never do again.

"Yes, sweetheart, I'll take care of you now."

Once she was out of her shell, she turned to look at their rescuer and asked in German, "Who are you?"

Rhody was almost startled to hear her voice for the first time but turned, smiled at her and replied in English, "My name's Rhody Jones, ma'am. Willie told me that you spoke German, so I only spoke German to you to make sure that none of the Comanches would know what I was saying. Are you and Marty all right?"

"Physically, we're unharmed, but I don't know if I'll ever get past what happened."

He then smiled at Marty and said, "Howdy, Marty. Willie said you were a pretty girl and he was right."

"Is Willie really waiting for us?" she asked with big eyes.

"Yes, ma'am. We need to get to him as quickly as possible. I don't trust the Comanches to let us just ride away."

"But why would they chase us? They made a bargain; didn't they?" Emma asked sharply as her demons threatened to return with a vengeance.

"They made a bargain, but I've traded with Comanches and other tribes, and the way each of them interprets the trade is different. Those Comanches were renegades, and I was grateful that they even let me talk, so I don't trust them to honor a bargain. I just want to find Willie before they find us."

"But you don't have anything more than a pistol."

"I have two more repeaters, a long-range rifle and another pistol with Willie. I have my pack mule of supplies there as well. If we can get there, then we'll be safe."

"I know you told me your name, but why did you come for us? You aren't one of the Ernst's relatives, are you?"

"No, ma'am. I was just passing through.""

"But why did you help us, especially knowing how dangerous it was?"

"Because Willie asked me to find Marty."

"That's all? Just because a boy you've never met asked you to find his sister who may have been taken by a war party of Comanches, you agreed to go?"

"Pretty much, but I walked into the Ernst house before Willie returned and if there was a chance of preventing that from happening to her, I had to try to stop it. I wasn't sure that Marty had been taken or had just run away until I spotted her through my telescope. You can imagine my surprise when I saw you with her."

RHODY JONES

Emma then glanced behind them saw the Comanches still in their camp then looked back at Rhody and asked, "Why were you even there? It's not on a road and I was even surprised that the Comanches knew we were there."

"Most likely the Comanches recently moved their village into the area then sent scouts out to search for game and found your ranches. I was just riding west from San Antonio on my way to California, but I didn't want to ride a train or even take the roads. I wanted to see the land."

As they talked, Marty listened but stared behind them terrified that those Indians would try to take her away again. She had heard her mother's screams, but never saw what had happened to her. She thought that her father and brothers had all been killed, but when the stranger had said that he had Willie with him, she had no idea how it was even possible. Now she was close to seeing Willie again and the idea that those horrible Indians could take her back again was almost making her start crying again. The only reason she didn't was that she was still holding Emma closely and she said that she would take care of her now.

After the spare horses were hobbled and the cattle bound together in pairs by the horns, Bear Who Speaks brought his warriors together. He wasn't worried that they were angry because he had made the trade but knew that, to a man, they expected him to go after the white man and return with his two horses and the captives. The arrogant white man had trumpeted how he had killed the four warriors he had left behind to clear out the first ranch, and he must be made to pay for his actions.

When they were together, he said, "He cannot travel far with the woman and girl on that tired horse. They must set up camp soon, but we must move now before we lose the trail. It is difficult enough as their sign is mixed with our own, so we need the light. Get your rifles and we will go."

"Do we leave someone here to watch over the horses?" asked Hunting Puma.

"No. They will not run, and we should return soon."

Five minutes later, the seven Comanches were on their horses and riding at a fast trot away from their camp.

―――

By the time they left camp, Rhody, Emma and Marty were two miles away, but their gelding was losing wind and they had to reduce their speed to a slow trot.

Marty then shouted, "The Indians are coming!"

Rhody and Emma both turned to look and knew they were too far back to catch them before they reached Willie, even at their current speed.

RHODY JONES

Rhody then looked at Marty's terrified face and said, "They won't catch us, Marty. By the time we reach Willie, they'll still be more than a mile away. Okay?"

"But there are so many of them!"

"Willie is waiting in a very safe place and I have more guns there that can shoot farther than the ones they have. I promise that they'll never come near you."

"Really?"

"Really."

Rhody fought back the urge to get their gelding moving a little faster because they still had another fifteen minutes before they would reach Willie then he'd have to hurry to prepare for the Comanches. The fading light meant that he'd have to end this quickly or drive them away. Maybe they'd realize the futility of their effort after he sent a .50 caliber round their way at six hundred yards, but after what he'd witnessed from the four drunk Comanches at the Ernst ranch, he doubted if they'd be impressed.

———

Willie had spotted the two horses saw the blonde heads on one of them and began to bounce around the ground in front of carved-out bend in the creek bed in anticipation of seeing Marty again.

After he settled down, he just smiled as he stood with his arms folded and watched the two horses grow bigger in his eyes. Then he spotted the dust cloud about another mile behind them and remembered what Rhody had said about the renegades chasing them after agreeing to let them go.

He quickly slid down the embankment into the hole, stepped over to the pack mule and tried to think what he could do before Rhody reached him. He finally decided that all he could do was to wait and keep an eye on the Comanches.

———

Rhody was already scanning off to the left as they rode, searching for Willie. He didn't doubt that Willie had already seen them, but he didn't want him to shout, even though the Comanches were still more than a mile behind them.

He spotted Willie's head then waved to let Willie know that he'd seen him.

After Willie waved back, Rhody turned to Emma and said, "Willie's just ahead about four hundred yards, so start angling to the left."

"I saw him wave," Emma replied as she shifted the exhausted horse toward Willie.

Rhody matched her change in direction and just two minutes later, they pulled up near the edge of the hole, and he quickly dropped to the ground.

RHODY JONES

He stepped to Emma's horse, lifted Marty to the ground then turned and said, "Ma'am, I need you to lead your horse down the bank."

Emma didn't reply, but dismounted, took the reins then quickly stepped to the shallower slope and led the horse to the creek where he lowered his head and dipped his muzzle into the water.

As Willie and Marty embraced in a flood of tears, Rhody let Morgana join the gelding at the creek then hurried to Jack and Dent where he had tied them to a root sticking out of the dirt wall from some long-gone tree.

Emma walked up next to him and asked, "What can I do?"

Rhody looked at her then removed his hat and handed it to her.

"Ma'am, your hair is like a lighthouse on a clear night. Put this on."

She folded her silver blonde hair over her head then pulled on the Stetson which fit surprisingly well.

As she was pulling it on, he slid the '66 from its scabbard then when her hair was hidden, he handed it to her.

"Ma'am, can you handle a pistol or a Winchester?"

"I can use both."

He nodded then walked to his saddlebags, pulled out Jack's gunbelt and handed it to her.

There wasn't much time for talk as she wrapped it around her waist and tightened the belt onto her hips.

He then slid the '76 from Jack's scabbard and pulled the Sharps-Borshadt from Dent's before he returned to the edge where he set the two rifles down and walked back to Emma.

"Ma'am, I'm not sure if the Comanches spotted the pack horse, but what I'm going to ask you to do for the time being is to stay close to the front of the hole with the children. I'll watch to see what the Comanches will do and I need you close so I can talk to you without shouting."

"Alright."

He then walked to Jack and pulled a box of .50-140 cartridges, removed three and slid them into his right pocket before returning the box to the saddlebags. He then took a box of .45-75s for the Winchester and returned to the edge of the hole. After setting the box of Winchester ammunition on the ground, he picked up the Sharps-Borshadt opened the breech then removed the .50-100 cartridge and inserted the longer .50-140 before slipping the removed cartridge into his left pocket. He wanted the extra range to impress the Comanches and maybe convince them that coming closer would be a mistake.

RHODY JONES

By the time he'd finished, Emma had gathered Willie and Marty and was sitting with them four feet to his right while the horses and the mule were to his left.

He looked south and counted the number of riders and was surprised that they had left no one behind. It worried him somewhat because it might mean that the others who had driven the Ernst's cattle away may have joined them already.

Emma had seen him look and asked, "How far away are they?"

Without looking down at her, he replied, "They're moving cautiously now and are about a thousand yards out."

"How much longer before they attack?"

"If they do, it'll be in less than ten minutes. I'll be taking one shot with the big rifle in a minute or two to let them know that I have more than just a pistol."

"Do you really think they might leave?"

"I don't know. It depends on a lot of things. Does their leader risk losing more men to seek vengeance or soothe his pride? We'll find out soon enough."

"We don't have much daylight left."

"I know. They'll have an advantage in the dark because the moon won't rise for another hour after sunset, but I'm already working on that problem."

As Rhody stared at the Comanches, Emma asked, "What do you do for a living? You don't sound like a Texan."

"I spent the last five years working as a drover and a cowhand, but I was a sailor for most of my life. I was born and raised in Providence, Rhode Island. It's why the boys christened me with Rhody."

"You were a sailor?"

"Yes, ma'am. I'll be happy to explain how I wound up in west Texas later."

"If there is a later," she whispered.

Rhody had heard her whisper and understood her reason for saying it. He may have two rifles ready to fire, but there were seven armed Comanche warriors about eight hundred yards away, and they were sober.

Bear Who Speaks pulled his horse to a stop and waited for his six warriors to gather.

"He has taken the woman and girl into the gully ahead. We will make a wide half circle around them, then you will wait for my war cry, and we will attack. Do not shoot until we are close."

White Hawk asked, "Why not a full circle?"

"We do not have enough men to surround them and even a half circle will be leave wide gaps, but it should be enough."

He assigned each warrior to a position with himself in the center, then they began to separate staying about five hundred yards from the hole. In the dying light, none of them had spotted the pack mule or the two dark sticks on the ground at the edge.

"They're moving again," Rhody said as he watched the Comanches, "but they're beginning to spread apart so they can surround us."

"What can we do if they get behind us?"

"If they try to surround us with seven of them, then they'd either have to be very close or leave wide gaps between each of them. I'll let them know in a minute that it won't be a good idea to get that close. I want the west clear after the sun goes down."

"Why?"

"We're going to make our escape in that direction. If I can keep them pinned down then as soon as it's dark, you take Willie and Marty and lead the animals west as quietly as possible. I'll keep firing to let them believe that nothing's changed, and after a couple of minutes, I'll chase after you."

She didn't reply, but Willie who had felt as if he'd been pushed aside, asked, "What can I do, Rhody?"

"When I say 'go', you untie the horses' reins while Mrs. Brandt gets Marty in the saddle. You make sure those critters walk quietly when you get them moving."

"Okay."

Rhody then stepped behind the Sharps-Borshadt, slipped his hands under the big gun and slowly lifted it from the ground, then cocked the hammer. He wanted to keep its presence a surprise until it loudly made its debut.

———

Bear Who Speaks faced a dilemma as he sat on his horse with his warriors spread in its wide semicircle. He thought he'd seen the white man with a rifle in his hands but wasn't sure with the setting sun in his eyes. He was concerned about losing the four men at the first ranch and was debating the same question that Rhody had already speculated that he might be asking himself. *Was it worth it now?*

There was the wagonload of supplies, the cattle, horses and mules, and the guns that his father's people needed, but it had now come down to what was practical and what his pride allowed. He'd told his warriors that they would attack, and if he called it off now, then they might question his leadership and even worse, his father might be ashamed of him.

RHODY JONES

He glanced to the left and then to the right at his men who were poised for the attack before looking back at the white man in the distance, who was little more than a dark bump as he stared at them. He still was unsure if he had a rifle, but even then, it was still one against seven. The question of whether or not he had a rifle was soon answered when he saw the long flash of fire appear in front of the white man.

Rhody had kept his sights on the Comanche in the center position of their semicircle for more than thirty seconds and didn't expect to hit him but wanted his massive bullet to be at least close enough for him to realize that he was within range. He had compensated for the added powder in the bigger cartridge but wasn't sure just how much it would change the bullet's drop at five hundred yards. He did have the light advantage with the setting sun at his back which illuminated his target.

When he squeezed his trigger, he felt the big rifle slam back into his shoulder more noticeably than it had when he'd fired the .50-100 round, but as soon as the bullet left the muzzle, he set the Sharps-Borshadt down and grabbed his Winchester, keeping his eyes focused on the Comanche.

Bear Who Speaks had been stunned by the size of the muzzle flash, but in the second and a half that the bullet took to reach him, he believed that the white man was being foolish in wasting his ammunition. He was about to shout his war cry when the rolling thunder from the Sharps-Borshadt arrived just a tiny fraction of a second before the half-inch-thick slug of lead slammed into his chin.

He didn't have a chance to shout his attack order or do anything other than fall backwards over his horse's rump after the powerful bullet almost severed his head from his neck.

As he tumbled to the ground, his second-in-command, Quiet Owl who was three hundred yards to his left, was stunned at the distance and as much as he wanted to continue the attack to avenge the loss of their leader, he knew that they still had a long distance to go before they reached the white man. Even if they reached him, there would probably be fewer of them left.

Unlike his dead leader, Quiet Owl knew that the smart thing to do was to return to their camp with Bear Who Speak's body. He would send a warrior ahead to tell the chief of his son's death and was sure that he would send more warriors to find the white man and have his revenge.

He then shouted in Spanish, "White man! We will take our leader's body and go! Do not fire again!"

Rhody was still stunned that he'd hit the Comanche and even more surprised that he had been their leader, but soon replied, "I will hold my fire, but do not follow or I will kill each of you!"

RHODY JONES

As the Comanches began to ride toward the empty horse, Rhody said, "I killed their leader, so they're going to collect his body and leave."

Emma felt a rush of relief and closed her eyes before asking, "Are they really leaving or is it a trick?"

"I'll watch them, but as soon as they're out of sight, we're heading west. I don't trust them that much."

"Neither do I, but why would we go west? There's nothing there."

"I know, but so do they. They'll be expecting us to head north, and we'll do that until our tracks are mixed in with the mess that they made with the horses and cattle, then we'll turn west."

"Won't we get lost in the night?"

"It won't matter, Mrs. Brandt. I'll be able to plot our exact position at noon tomorrow and set a course to wherever we want to go. I used to be a sailor, remember? I have all my navigational tools with me and a good set of maps."

"You can do that?"

"Yes, ma'am. I've been doing it for most of my life."

"When can we have supper?" Marty asked, "They didn't give us any food."

Rhody looked down, smiled at her and replied, "As soon as the Indians are gone, I'll fix you something before we leave. Okay?"

"Thank you. Can I call you Rhody, too?"

"Yes, ma'am. I've already called you Marty, so it's only fair."

Emma then stood, brushed the dirt from the back of her dress, handed Rhody his hat, letting her long blonde hair flow onto her back like a waterfall then stepped beside him and looked at the Comanches.

He looked at her and said, "You can keep wearing the pistol if you wish."

"I will for a while at least," she replied then asked, "Are you that good with that gun?"

He pulled his Stetson back on and replied "No, ma'am. It was more luck than anything else. I only wanted to put the bullet as close to him as I could to let him know that he wasn't safe. I probably couldn't make that shot again if I'd fired another fifty rounds."

"Well, thank God you were lucky this time!"

"Amen to that, Mrs. Brandt."

She then quietly asked, "Did you find any bodies on our ranch?"

"No. I didn't even look, but I'm pretty sure they were all inside the house when the Comanches set it afire. We didn't see any bodies on the grounds outside."

"Can we go back and look? Maybe someone escaped like Willie did and was hiding until they left."

"We can swing by, ma'am, but you have to be honest with yourself. If someone had been hiding, then they would have seen me and Willie ride past. We weren't exactly quiet."

Emma closed her eyes sighed then asked, "But can we at least check? Please?"

"Alright. We should get there by tomorrow afternoon, but we can't stay long because the Comanches may send more warriors after the six who just left to return to their village. I just don't know how big the village is. They're renegades, so it could only have a dozen or so warriors, but if it had thirty or forty, then they'll probably send a few after us."

"Why would they do that when the six who were already here are leaving?"

"The reason they made the raid was to take as much as they could get from your ranches. That was all left behind, and they were in a bad situation after I showed them that I could hit them from long range. They'll probably send one back to the village with the news and if they have the men, then they'll organize another war party to avenge the death of their leader.

If those supplies and critters weren't back there, they probably would have attacked tonight."

"How do you know all this if you've only been in Texas for five years?"

"It's just what I would do if I was in their moccasins."

As he explained his thoughts to Emma, Rhody was watching as the Comanches lifted their war chief's body and hung it over his horse then tied it down before mounting and riding away.

Rhody and Emma continued to watch as they disappeared into the growing darkness. Once they were confident that they weren't about to return, Rhody picked up his Sharps-Borshadt then with his hands full of rifles, he walked to Morgana and slid his unused Winchester home.

"Let's go, Willie and Marty," he said as he walked to Dent, opened the Sharp-Borshadt's breech and extracted the brass, then inserted the .50-100 cartridge from his pocket before slipping the rifle into Dent's scabbard.

As the children popped to their feet and then dusted off their behinds, Rhody strode to the edge again, retrieved his box of .45-75 cartridges and returned to Morgana where he dropped it into his saddlebags before returning the .50-140 cartridges to their box.

RHODY JONES

He had just buckled his saddlebag's straps when Marty walked close and asked, "Can we have something to eat now?"

"I promised you that I'd get you something; didn't I?"

Marty nodded, then Rhody smiled at her before walking back to Dent. He untied the lashes from the food pannier then lifted it from its hooks and set it on the ground.

After opening the flap, he said, "Now you have to understand that I bought food that I liked and still could be eaten after sitting in the Texas summer heat for a few days. I can't promise that you'll like it."

"I'll like it, Rhody," Marty said as she stared at the pannier.

Rhody grinned at her then looked at Willie and asked, "Could you get us a couple of canteens, Willie?"

"Yes, sir," he replied then quickly walked to Jack for the canteens.

He lifted a leather pouch from the large pack, set it on the ground then removed three large jars before he took out a single soup spoon.

"You won't need any knives or forks, but this is filling."

Even Emma was watching as he opened each of the jars, then flipped open the leather pouch's flap. He slid a flour tortilla from the sack then used the spoon to spread a swath of refried beans across the center before adding some shredded smoked beef and then covering it with a salsa mix.

After folding it into a roll, he handed it to Marty who quickly took a big bite and grinned as she chewed.

He made a second, gave it to Emma then gave the third to Willie who had set the canteens on the ground. He made his own burrito then stood to have his late lunch and supper. He knew that his charges hadn't eaten since breakfast either and as he ate, he watched them devour his creations.

They had been so focused on making their escape from the Comanches, that the subject of where Mrs. Brandt or the children would go now that their houses were gone hadn't been broached. It wasn't a critical question yet, but it would be by the time they reached what used to be her home.

Willie swallowed and said, "This is really good, Rhody."

"I'm glad you like it, Willie. I found Mexican food to be better on the trail than jerky or just smoked beef and crackers. But do you know what I really miss?"

Willie had a mouthful of burrito, but Marty asked, "What?"

"Quahogs and lobster."

Willie laughed, then said, "I never heard of them before. What are they?"

RHODY JONES

Rhody smiled then replied, "A quahog is what the folks where I grew up called a clam."

"What's a clam?"

"Well, if you took the two top halves of a turtle shell and put them together to make a bigger shell, that's what it looks like. Inside is the clam's meat, but it's locked inside that double shell. It lives a few inches under the bottom of the ocean, and men take small boats out with really long rakes that look like bent pitchforks and dig them out.

"When I was a boy, we used to go to the beach and wade into the water until it was knee-high, then when we found small holes on the bottom, we'd just dig out the quahog with our feet by simply wiggling it into the sand."

"And you ate them?" Marty asked with big eyes.

"Yes, ma'am. They didn't want to come out of their shells to be eaten, and I wouldn't want to eat one raw anyway, but some folks did. What we'd do is stick them in a pot of water and set it to boil. The two shells would open wide almost saying, 'eat me', then we'd stick a fork into the meat, dip it in butter and then malt vinegar."

"What's a lobster?" Willie asked.

"A lobster is like a crawdad, only a lot larger."

"I don't know what a crawdad is, either."

"A lobster, or lobstah as they say back home because they don't seem to like the letter R, lives underwater like the quahog, but he crawls around on the ocean floor with eight legs, like a giant spider. He also has two enormous claws that he uses to fight and catch food."

"And you eat them, too?" asked an astonished Marty as she grimaced.

"Yes ma'am. You cook them like clams then crack open their hard shells and eat the meat with melted butter."

"I wouldn't eat them," Marty said as she shook her head.

Rhody just laughed lightly then began making seconds for each of them as they quenched their thirst, but after everyone was fed, he put his makings away while Willie refilled the canteens then hung the pannier back on Dent and lashed it down.

Before they mounted, another necessity arrived when Marty whispered to Emma that she needed to pee, so Emma looked at Rhody and said, "We need some privacy."

"Go back to the creek and walk a few yards downstream. We'll stay here."

"Thank you," she replied and led an anxious Marty out of their fort and disappeared into the night.

RHODY JONES

While the ladies were gone, Rhody and Willie took care of their own bladders' demands.

After they fastened their britches, Willie asked, "Where can we go now, Rhody?"

"We'll ride north for a mile or so, then we'll head west and make a wide loop until we're heading east. We'll need to get some sleep before we make the turn east, too."

"I meant where will me and Marty go after?"

"We'll talk to Mrs. Brandt about that once we're riding. Okay?"

"Okay," he replied, but Rhody could sense that he was worried that he and his little sister would wind up in an orphanage if they were lucky.

Rhody looked down at Willie and remembered how he was at that age and understood how fortunate he'd been. Although he'd lost his mother before he even knew her and barely remembered his father, he'd been raised by his uncle who had loved him as his own son. He had ensured that he had a good education before letting him go to sea, which had been his own choice without a hint from his uncle. When he was Willie's age, he knew what he wanted to do and where he was going to go. He did love his time at sea and hadn't ruled out returning to New England. He enjoyed his time in the saddle as well but felt as if he was shortchanging himself. He was almost thirty now and until today, he'd had five years with no real responsibilities.

But as he looked at Willie, he felt what must have been the same sense of obligation that his uncle had felt for him. Willie may not be family, but he needed someone to give him direction and purpose. Once he had that then Willie could make his own choice about what to do with his life.

Rhody then put his hand on Willie's shoulder, smiled and said, "I'll make sure that you and Marty will be okay."

Willie smiled back and was about to reply when Emma and Marty returned.

Rhody tapped Willie on the head then said, "Let's get mounted and leave our fortress behind. I'll still ride Morgana, she's the dark brown mare. Mrs. Brandt, you and Marty can ride Jack, my tan Morgan, and Willie you can ride the gelding. Give me a minute to adjust the stirrups."

Emma quickly said, "I can do Jack's."

"Thank you, ma'am," Rhody replied then walked to the gelding.

Ten minutes later, they were riding north when the moon appeared on the horizon.

RHODY JONES

After another ten minutes, they turned west and headed into the unknown.

Rhody was riding in the center, trailing Dent while Willie rode on his left and Emma and Marty rode on his right.

Now that they felt relatively safe, Rhody asked, "Mrs. Brandt, do you have any family nearby?"

"My parents live in New Braunfels, and I have a sister living in Seguin with her husband and three children."

"If we don't find anyone left on your ranch, do you want to return to New Braunfels?"

Emma took a deep breath then exhaled before she replied, "I suppose so."

Rhody wasn't sure if she was annoyed that he had mentioned the likelihood that her husband was dead, or she wasn't overly happy with the prospect of returning to her parents. Whatever her reason for the disappointed tone in her answer, at least it gave him a destination. It was less than thirty miles north of San Antonio and he'd been to the town a few times. It was a heavily German population as it had been founded by Germans and then immigrants from Austria and Germany were funneled into the rapidly growing town.

Marty then asked, "Are we coming with you, Aunt Emma?"

Rhody looked at Mrs. Brandt in the moonlight to listen to her answer wondering if she would reply with the same sense of disappointment.

Emma smiled at Marty and replied, "Of course, you are. I promised you, didn't I?"

"Yes, but you didn't promise Willie. Is Willie coming, too?"

"Of course, he will. I'd never separate you."

Rhody assumed that it had been the mention of her husband's likely death that had made her respond as she had to his question and not that she was disappointed at the prospect of returning to New Braunfels.

He wasn't sure if Willie had heard Marty's question and Mrs. Brandt's answer, but that mystery was solved when Willie asked loudly, "We're going with you, Mrs. Brandt?"

Emma looked past Rhody and replied just as loudly, "I promise, Willie."

Willie then looked at Rhody and asked, "Are you going to take us there, Rhody?"

"Did you think I was going to make everyone walk a hundred and fifty miles?"

"I was just wondering if you were just gonna take us to a town and put us on a stagecoach."

"No, sir. I'll take you all to New Braunfels. Okay?"

"Okay. Are you going to stay there, too?"

"Let's not worry about that right now, Willie. We're going to be stopping to set up camp pretty soon so everyone, including the animals, can get some sleep."

"Alright."

Rhody's recently conceived plans for helping Willie had evaporated when Mrs. Brandt had said she'd take the children with her to live with her parents, but he knew that it was probably better for them both.

―――

While they had been eating, the warrior sent by Quiet Owl had reached the village leading the horse bearing Bear Who Speaks' body. After the chief, Howling Wolf, looked at his son's body, he had two warriors take it from the horse then demanded to know what had happened.

Tall Pony initially described the successful raids to offset the tragic loss of their leader and six other warriors, but it didn't matter to Howling Wolf. The white man who had killed his son must die, but he would have to wait for the others to return. He would dispatch eight warriors, and two would be armed with their only long-range rifles that could hold seven rounds while the others would have repeaters.

Rhody knew everyone was in danger of falling from their saddles from exhaustion, so he finally had everyone dismount and began setting up a cold camp. It took twenty minutes to unsaddle the three horses and unload Dent, and by the time Rhody had removed Dent's pack saddle, Emma had tucked Willie and Marty into one of the two bedrolls, and they were already asleep.

Lee was hobbling the horses when Emma approached and said, "There's only one bedroll left."

"I know. You go ahead and use it. I still need to clean my rifle and I'm used to sleeping in the open anyway."

Emma then said, "I never did thank you for saving us. I can't begin to describe how terrified I was from the moment I first saw those Comanches. I didn't believe that I would live to see the sun rise. If I didn't have Marta with me, I would have gone mad."

Rhody finished hobbling the gelding, then stood and replied, "I only saw the aftermath of what they had done, and I can't imagine how horrible it was for you or Marty. All any of us can do now is to go on with our lives."

"Have you ever watched someone die horribly, Rhody?"

"A few times, once when I was just twelve. Life aboard a sailing ship is a dangerous place, and it was a rare voyage when we arrived with the same crew that had boarded the vessel."

"I don't know if I can find sleep as easily as the children have. It's all too vivid in my mind."

"Just go ahead and get into the bedroll and close your eyes. You're probably exhausted, and sleep will come."

"Will you be nearby?"

"I'll be near you and the children. You'll be able to smell my gun cleaning fluid."

Emma smiled then nodded, turned and walked away with her silver blonde hair reflecting the moonlight.

Rhody had seen many men die, and some were horrible deaths, but none had been remotely as bad as those who had died at the hands of the Comanches. If it hadn't been for Mrs. Brandt and the children, he'd ride south and shoot every one of those warriors who had been part of the raid.

After Emma was in her bedroll, she didn't close her eyes but watched Rhody as he slid his big rifle from its scabbard, then removed a box from his saddlebags. When he'd asked about her family, she hadn't been prepared for the question. If she had, she might have even lied and claimed that she was an orphan because in her mind, she was made an orphan a year ago when she had been told to marry Carl Brandt and then gone with him to his brothers' ranch Then she had been punished by God when she lost the baby. She knew that if she showed up on her parents' doorstep, that solid oak door would open and then would be slammed in her face in a heartbeat.

When the smell of gun cleaning fluid wafted over her, she finally closed her eyes and without understanding why, she smiled.

After cleaning and reloading the Sharps-Borshadt, Rhody slipped it into its scabbard, returned the cleaning kit to his saddlebags then took out one of his two blankets and spread it out six feet above the sleeping children and Mrs. Brandt. He took off his hat but left his boots on before unbuckling his gunbelt and setting it on the blanket.

As he looked down at the woman and two children he hadn't even known to exist until this morning, he was pleased to see them sleeping peacefully after witnessing the day's horror. He expected that it was because they were physically and emotionally drained but didn't expect them to sleep peacefully tomorrow night.

He stretched out beside the gunbelt and began to name the constellations, even though he was so tired that he probably didn't need his mind-relaxing aid. He hadn't even reached Cassiopeia before he fell into a deep sleep.

CHAPTER 5

Rhody's eyes snapped open, and he realized that the sun must have been up for over an hour. He threw back the blanket, stood and scanned the horizons but calmed down when he found them empty of Comanches.

He strapped his gunbelt in place then pulled on his hat and while everyone else slept, he walked away a few yards to a nearby group of bushes and answered nature's call.

He then began collecting deadwood and anything else combustible and when he had enough to burn for thirty minutes, he returned to the camp and set the pile down beside a natural fire pit.

He was rubbing the heavy stubble on his face as he walked to the food pannier where he removed two cans of beans, some coffee he'd already ground, and the jars of shredded beef and salsa. After leaving them near the fire pit, he returned for his skillet and coffeepot.

Rhody started the kindling then began layering on the larger pieces of wood.

Willie was the next to awaken and as he tried to extract himself from the bedroll he shared with his sister, Marty was obliged to exit as well.

Fifteen minutes later, everyone was gathered around the fire watching the simmering mix.

"I only have two cups and plates, so we'll have to share," Rhody said as he stirred their breakfast.

"Do you still think that they'll be back?" Emma asked.

"I don't know what they'll do. It depends on their chief and if he's willing to risk more men with very little reward. He lost five yesterday that I know of, and some might have been wounded in the attack on your ranch and died later. I don't know how many warriors he has in his band, but if it had been one of the bigger bands before most of them moved to the reservation, I'd guarantee that they'd come back with a vengeance."

"When will they come if he does send some?"

"I don't know how far away their village is, but if they were setting up camp, it had to be a good ride south. They do have one other advantage. They know that we'll have to go east to reach a town. If I were their chief and was angry enough to send some warriors, I'd have them lay in wait a few miles east of the Ernst place and station a man on the highest point to watch for us. But that would only work if he dispatched them at night."

"How can we get past them?"

"I have enough supplies to last us for another week or so. After we stop at your ranch to make sure that we didn't miss anyone, we'll head north for a few hours then make our turn east. Even if they were on a high hill, their line of sight would be limited to about ten to twelve miles."

Emma paused before she said, "We don't have to go to the ranch. I know that no one is there."

Rhody replied, "I'm sorry, ma'am," then began scooping the mix into two plates and handed one to Emma and the second to Willie.

"Willie, share with Marty," he said as he handed him a spoon before giving the second to Emma and saying, "I'll just have some coffee and a tortilla."

"But you need all your strength," she protested.

"I'll make up for it when we stop for lunch, ma'am," he replied as he poured two cups of coffee then set one near Emma took the second and walked to the food pannier for the tortilla.

He really wasn't that hungry, which surprised him as the morning chow on the trail drives was usually enormous and he always cleaned his plate.

As he chewed the tortilla, he looked south and wondered if the Comanches would wait until the warriors returned with their cattle, horses and wagons, or would their chief send them as soon as he received word of the death of his war chief and the other four he had killed on the Ernst ranch. He may not have known that he'd killed the chief's only son, but he knew them well enough to believe that the chief would still want him dead. He didn't want to alarm Mrs. Brandt and the children, but he had been honest in his expectation of their strategy to hunt them down. Following their trail wouldn't be very smart because they might never get close enough to mount an attack. He was convinced that if they had ridden east from the Ernst ranch, the Comanches would be waiting. He had to pass well north of the ranch.

He finished his coffee then set the cup on the ground and walked to the pannier that contained his navigation tools and his maps. He wasn't going to take a reading yet but wanted to plot a course to the nearest town.

Five minutes later, he had the large map of Texas spread out on the ground and looked at the scale on the bottom. If it hadn't been for their precarious situation, he would have laughed. He put one finger on his best estimation for where they were then looked east and the closest town was Menardville, about a hundred and twenty miles east-northeast. If they made good time and didn't run afoul of Comanches, it would take them four days to reach it, but he'd take a noon reading to get their exact position. Before he folded the map, he wound his pocket chronometer then checked the time before sliding it back into his pocket. It was already after eight o'clock, so they had to get moving.

When he returned to the camp, the fire had burned itself down to embers, so he poured himself another cup of coffee, then topped off Mrs. Brandt's cup before dumping what was left in the coffeepot onto the glowing remnants, creating a cloud of coffee-scented steam.

As the steam disappeared, Rhody knew that from now on, they'd have to conserve water, even if they found another creek. They had three horses and a mule, and they would need more water than the humans on their backs required.

"Do you know where we are?" Emma asked.

"Pretty close. I'll know exactly when the sun is directly overhead, and I take a reading. Once I do that, then we'll just follow the compass to Menardville."

"I keep forgetting that you were a sailor, even after you talked about clams."

He smiled at her as he replied, "It's hard to imagine when we're standing in this open, dry country. Isn't it?"

Rhody was pleasantly surprised when she returned his smile before saying, "It is, but I've never seen the ocean."

"It's an awesome sight to behold when you're out on the sea but at times, it can send the bravest men scurrying for the safety of the belowdecks."

"You'll have to tell me about that sometime."

"We'll have four days, ma'am."

"Would you mind calling me Emma, Rhody?"

"I'd be honored, Emma," he replied then said, "Let's get the horses saddled and begin our ride to Menardville."

It was another twenty minutes before they were mounted and moving. Rhody had his compass with him and was guiding them north and would continue heading in that direction for another two hours before turning northeast, then after he took his noon sighting, they should be directly east of Menardville.

―――――

The chief had sent some of his older warriors out of the village at daybreak to relieve the young one who were returning with the wagon and hoofed animals. By the time that the four whites were leaving their campsite, he'd assembled his eight warriors, but was so short of men now that he had to include four of those who had just returned. He appointed Quiet Owl as his new war chief and after packing their supplies and water, two were issued Spencer rifles, but their supply of the unique .56-50 cartridges was limited to the rounds in the magazines and even at that, neither was full. One had five rounds and the other only four, but their range was necessary after Howling Wolf had listened to the report of how the white man had shot his son at five hundred yards.

Quiet Owl also had Rhody's telescope in his leather pouch of supplies, which he believed would add to their advantage in firepower. He considered it his personal property after Bear Who Speaks died.

When the eight warriors rode out of their village with the chief's instructions to block the whites' path back to their towns, they were twenty-nine miles south of their prey.

———

Rhody had them moving at a fast walk to conserve their horses' energy and each of them, even Marty, were scanning the horizons for the Comanches. The landscape, while mostly bare, level ground with a scattering of bushes, cacti, trees and patches of grass did have a number of hills and dry creek beds, along with some deep gullies, so there were places that could become either an ambush location or a defensive position, depending on who arrived there first.

It was the hills that attracted Rhody's attention, knowing that they provided a good vantage point to scan for the Comanches. He wished he still had his telescope but knew that there had been no other way to make the trade. There were still Kiowa in the area as well, but they probably wouldn't do anything more than watch the white people pass.

Other than the search for the Comanches, he was on the lookout for water in any form. He'd let the horses drink no matter how brackish it was, so they could keep the sweet water in the canteens and the water bag for themselves.

When the sun was almost directly overhead, and it was time for his noon reading, he spotted a bare rivulet of a creek to the east and said, "Let's take a break and let the horses drink whatever water they can get out of that creek."

After they dismounted and let the horses and Dent head for the creek, Rhody walked with the mule, then as he dipped his muzzle into the water, he opened a pannier and lifted the walnut box containing his sextant then set the box down, released the catch an opened the lid.

As the others watched, Rhody took an early sighting to adjust the azimuth. When it reached noon, he took a second sighting and made the slight adjustment then read the angle, and returned the sextant to its case before putting it back into the pannier. He then checked his timepiece, and after slipping it into his pocket, he pulled out his small personal log and began to write.

"What are you doing, Rhody?" Willie asked.

Rhody didn't look away from his notebook as he replied, "I measure the angle between the sun and the horizon, and that tells me where we are between the equator and north pole. Then because I know the sun is directly over our heads, so it's twelve o'clock here, I can look at my watch that tells me what time it is in Greenwich, England. Between those two readings, I can go to the map and mark exactly where we are, then set a course for Menardville."

Emma asked, "Is it hard to do?"

"It took a while to learn to do it right, especially on a ship that's constantly rocking and rolling in the seas. Doing it on land is a lot easier, but most of the sailors didn't have the understanding or the lessons in math to figure it out. Even some of the officers who should have been able to do the math didn't get it right. On the ocean, that can lead to disaster."

He then carried his notebook to the pannier, pulled out the map case and extracted the map of Texas. As he marked their current position, he smiled. They weren't as far from Menardville as he'd originally thought. They were just under a hundred miles and almost exactly due east of the town. It wasn't even as big as Mason, but it probably had a stagecoach line, so Emma and the children wouldn't have to ride all the way to New Braunfels.

He folded the map, slid it into the leather pouch and after returning it to its pannier, he stood then turned to face the three sets of curious eyes.

"I won't need to do another sighting. Menardville is due east and is less than a hundred miles away. We should reach it in three days."

As he watched them, he saw Willie and Marty both grin at him and then at each other, but Emma wore the same expression that she had when he had asked her if she wished to return to New Braunfels. He may have been curious, but unless she explained why she wasn't pleased with the notion, it wasn't his business.

"I'll make us some more burritos to celebrate," he said, then looked at Willie and asked, "Who wants to be the brave boy who will taste the water in the creek?"

Willie was still grinning as he trotted to the foot-wide stream of water and scooped out a cupped handful. He slurped it then grimaced and spit it out.

"I guess that's our answer," Rhody said as he walked to Dent to get the fixings for their burritos.

"We'll be back in a few minutes," Emma said as she took Marty's hand and led her downstream to some low bushes.

After they semi-disappeared from view, Willie walked to where Rhody was making their noon meal and asked, "Why wasn't Mrs. Brandt happy that we were going to reach the town in three days?"

RHODY JONES

Rhody was surprised that he'd noticed then replied, "I don't know. For people who have been through that horror just yesterday, I was very impressed with how well you're doing. Maybe it's because each of you is so relieved about escaping from that hideous situation, I don't know. She seemed fairly normal and even smiled this morning, but she acted the same way when I asked her if she wanted to go back to her parents' home. Do you know anything about her family back in New Braunfels?"

"Mama said that when she and Carl got here right after they got married, she was gonna have a baby, but then she lost it."

"Didn't she and her husband arrive with the other brothers?"

"No, sir. They only got here about a year ago, and mama said that she was sad about something, but didn't say what it was."

Rhody handed him a burrito then began making the second beginning to understand why she hadn't been enthusiastic about returning to her parents' house. It was a common tale, especially in the ports where sailors left pregnant daughters behind after the ship sailed.

Parents would sometimes evict the girl for her sinful ways and let her fend for herself. With sailors, it was difficult for the parents to have the man marry her whether either of the couple wished it or not. He guessed that Emma hadn't been married when she became pregnant and her parents had insisted that she marry Carl. That would explain his late arrival at the ranch as well as her reluctance to see her parents again. But he assumed that she still loved Carl because she'd asked him to take her to the ranch to search for him.

Even if that was the case, it still wasn't his business, and if she didn't object to getting on a stage to New Braunfels then there was nothing that he could do about it.

By the time Emma and Marty returned, he had their lunch ready and piled on one of the plates while he worked on his own burrito.

Willie trotted away to use the bushes as Emma and Marty each took one of the burritos from the plate.

He folded his tortilla then stood and asked, "How sore are you?"

Emma held out a finger as she swallowed then replied, "I'm fine. I've spent a lot of time in the saddle over the past year."

He then looked at Marty and asked, "How about you, young lady? Are you all right?"

She had a mouthful of burrito, so she simply nodded.

Willie jogged back from his necessary break then scooped up a second burrito.

RHODY JONES

As he ate his lunch, Rhody walked to Jack and took one of the full canteens from his saddle then returned, unscrewed the cap and handed it to Emma.

After she took a long swallow, she gave it to Marty then glanced down at the last burrito on the plate before looking at Rhody.

"Go ahead," he said before she asked, "I made mine larger than the others."

"Are you sure? It didn't seem any bigger."

"It had more inside."

"Alright," she said before picking up the last one.

Marty then asked, "Do you have anything besides Mexican food in there?"

"Yes, ma'am. I have all sorts of things inside, but these were the fastest way to get food into your belly. I'll change the menu when we set up camp tonight."

She had her mouth around today's menu as she nodded, and Rhody smiled at the cute blonde girl as Willie handed him the canteen.

Rhody took one swallow then capped it and returned it to Jack's saddle. He then looked east and identified some landscape changes that he could use a rough guide for their travel so he wouldn't have to keep checking his compass.

He'd check it once each hour, but dead reckoning would be good enough to keep going in the right direction during the time in between compass checks.

Quiet Owl was tired but led his warriors northeast at a fast trot to get ahead of the white man and the two captives he'd freed. He wasn't sure that they could get there in time, so he pressed the animals at a rate that he wouldn't have used on a raid.

He and the other three with the war party who had witnessed Bear Who Speak's hideous death at such a long distance weren't anxious to find the white man, but the other four warriors' blood lust was aroused and each of them was excited in anticipation of finding him. The four who were more reticent didn't dare to express that sense of caution as it would mark them as cowards.

They had enough food and water for four days or maybe five if they stretched it, but it was their level of ammunition that bothered Quiet Owl. Even though they had traded for two more boxes of cartridges for their repeaters, Howling Wolf had only allowed them enough to fill their guns, telling them that if the bullets that they had in their eight guns wasn't enough to kill one white man, then they deserved their fate and should die with honor.

RHODY JONES

They were almost twenty miles southeast of where the white people had stopped to have their lunch, and Quiet Owl wasn't going to stop for lunch or anything else as he rushed his men to cut off their escape.

If each group kept their current headings, their paths would cross in another thirty-six miles, and the Comanches would arrive at that point four hours earlier.

After they'd been riding east for ten minutes, Emma asked, "Rhody, why did you become a sailor?"

"It's a family tradition. My great grandfather served in the Continental navy during the Revolutionary war and every other succeeding generation on the male side of the family went to sea."

"Then why did you leave that life? Why did you decide to become a cowhand?"

"When my ship docked in New Orleans in '73, the captain didn't want me on the crew for the return voyage, so I decided to try something different."

"That's a big change. Isn't it?"

"Not really as much as you might think. I knew how to handle rope better than any of the others, and I'd been riding since I was nine, so all I really needed to learn was about the cattle. I've always been fascinated with the West, just as I'm sure many boys growing up in the middle of the country are intrigued by the oceans."

He then asked, "How about your family? What did your father do?"

"He owns a bakery in New Braunfels, and I worked there whenever I wasn't in school."

He was about to ask if she was going to return to work at the bakery, but the discomfort she exhibited in answering his first question about her family made him change his mind.

After almost a minute of silence, Emma suddenly blurted, "I don't want to go back to New Braunfels."

Rhody turned to look at her and thought she was about to seriously weep as her eyes were already watery.

"I already had that impression, Emma. Why don't you want to go back home?"

She inhaled sharply as she looked straight ahead without seeing, then replied, "My parents wouldn't want me back, and by now I'm sure that the entire Lutheran community feels the same way."

With the subject broached, Rhody asked, "Why wouldn't they want to see you again?"

RHODY JONES

"My father was an important man in the community, and I caused them shame when I sinned with Carl Brandt, who my father thought wasn't respectable. So, when I married him, my parents told me that I wasn't their daughter any longer. Carl was forced to leave New Braunfels when no one would hire him, so we had to leave town and come here to join his brothers. He never forgave me for that," she replied before the tears arrived in massive sheets.

Rhody didn't say anything else as they continued riding into the sun. Guessing her situation and knowing it were two totally different things. He began to understand why she had asked to search their ranch for her husband, and it wasn't because she hoped he was alive or that she even loved him. She must feel an enormous amount of guilt for many things and might even blame herself for his death. If she hadn't become pregnant, then Carl wouldn't have had to leave New Braunfels. It was still just a guess, but he wasn't about to ask her.

Three minutes later, she looked across at Rhody and said, "Now you know why I can't go back home. I don't know where I can go or what I can do, and I promised Marta that I'd take care of her and Willie."

Rhody hadn't taken his eyes from her since she lapsed into her tearful silence, and as he looked at her sorrowful and lost face, he said, "Don't worry about the future, Emma. It'll be all right. I promise."

Emma was about to protest, but when she looked at his sincere face, she somehow believed him. *How could she not?* He had risked his life to rescue her and Marty from a fate worse than simple death without ever having met either of them. A man who would do such a selfless, heroic act was beyond reproach or challenge.

"Thank you, Rhody. I'm sorry about the tears."

"You're entitled to even more, Emma, and so are the children. You've all been through a lot."

"I just hope those Comanches stayed in their village."

"So, do I."

She wiped her eyes with the sleeve of her dress then asked, "Why didn't your captain want you back?"

Rhody glanced at Willie who obviously wanted to hear the full story as well, then replied, "I was the first mate on a schooner named *Vivienne*. We sailed out of Providence with a cargo of furniture, manufactured goods, clothing and bolts of cloth. We ran afoul of a hurricane in early September…"

As his oft told narrative continued, it left out any references to his uncle or R. Jones Brothers Shipping as he always did. The only one who knew his position and location lived on Eddy Street, just west of the extensive docks. His uncle's letters had kept him updated on the rapidly evolving state of the firm as they shifted from their sailing ships to steam powered vessels.

They still had four large sail-rigged ships, but now had fourteen screw-driven cargo ships. They'd skipped over the paddle wheelers just by virtue of timing. He also had his personal yawl, the *Bluefin.*

When he finished, Emma asked, "Why didn't you just tell the shipowners what had happened?"

"On a ship, the captain's word is final and if he writes it in the log, it is very rare for it to be questioned. It didn't matter that much to me anyway. I had toyed with the notion of going west after my last voyage to Galveston."

Marty then asked, "Are the Indians still after us?"

"I don't know, sweetheart. Let's not worry about them until we see them. Okay?"

"Okay, but I hope I never see them again. Did they have Indians where you grew up?"

"Not anymore. There was a tribe called the Narragansetts in Rhode Island before I was born, and they were mostly friendly, but there was a war about two hundred years ago."

Emma then asked, "Are you still planning to go to California?"

"It was almost a pipe dream when I left, so I may head back to Providence or even stay in Texas. Whatever I decide, I will keep my promise to take care of each of you."

Emma found it difficult to understand how he could keep his promise if he did go back to Rhode Island and even had difficulty imagining the place, but she didn't ask him how he could be so sure that he would be able to do it without having a job.

As she looked at him, she saw the man she should have waited for rather than that mistake with Carl. His bravery was secondary to his kindness and compassion, but she knew that he would probably never even consider her as anything more than what she was, a widow and a sinner.

Quiet Owl knew he was pushing their horses despite having taken two breaks to let them water and rest, so he reluctantly slowed their pace to a medium trot, not knowing that the slower speed actually would increase their likelihood of finding the white man and the two blonde-headed hostages. If he'd managed to maintain his higher rate of speed, they would have crossed Rhody's path hours earlier and never seen them. They would still arrive at that point before the whites did, but instead of being hours early, they would be just minutes ahead and well within sight of their targets.

It was late afternoon when Rhody spotted the reflection of water to the northeast and hoped it wasn't a mirage from the heat waves rising from the roasting earth.

He looked over at Willie. Then pointed and asked, "Is that a pond over there?"

Willie looked and replied, "I think so."

"It won't hurt to check," Rhody replied then turned Morgana toward the reflection.

Five minutes later, he was pleased to discover that it wasn't an optical illusion, but a small pond that spawned a creek which then flowed to the northeast. That meant it was spring-fed and was probably much sweeter water than they'd found earlier.

After reaching the pond, he quickly dismounted then let Morgana trot to the water while he helped Marty to the ground. Soon all four animals were at the pond's edge quenching their thirst with Willie off to their right tasting the water and Rhody decided that they may as well camp here for the night. There were no signs of anyone having visited the pond recently, so that meant that there were no Kiowa or Comanches in the area, except for the ones that he was sure were either trailing them or trying to cut them off.

He looked at Emma and said, "We'll set up camp here tonight. I want to take advantage of the good water as long as we can."

"That's a good idea. I'll even cook if you think it's alright for us to make a fire."

"That's another reason I want to stop early. If we build the fire during the day, it won't be very noticeable but at night, we could be found easily."

She nodded then took Marty's hand and walked with her to the pond to wash the dust from their faces. As he watched her walk away, he wasn't surprised that she hadn't taken off the gunbelt. He had been impressed with her rapid recovery from yesterday's horror and then the terror of knowing what would probably happen to her while she rode with the Comanches. He knew that he hadn't really met the normal Emma Brandt yet, but figured he never would get the opportunity. He just didn't know what he would do for her and the children other than to ensure that they were safe.

She was a handsome young woman, so she could probably find a new husband quickly, but he wondered if she would want to go through that again. If she did, he began to think he should stay in Texas for a while to get to know her better. He still didn't know if she had loved her husband because he hadn't gotten a good read on her yet which wasn't unusual for him. He could read men easily enough, but he'd always had difficulty understanding women.

That lesson had hit him hard when he was eighteen and was returning on a relatively short voyage to Charleston anxious to spend some time with his girlfriend, Rowena Bedard. He thought that he'd surprise her and instead of returning to his home that he shared with his uncle, he'd swung by her house and found her with the son of a fabric mill owner. She'd told him that he was just a family friend, and he had foolishly believed her. But when he mentioned it to his uncle, he learned that she'd been seeing him even before he left on the voyage. When he asked her about it the next day, she denied it and he'd accepted her excuse a second time.

When he returned to Providence after his next trip to New Orleans, he found that she'd married and moved to Boston. He never saw her again but realized his shortcomings when dealing with the gentle sex. He'd visited other women until he made the fateful decision to join the *Vivienne* on his last voyage but didn't trust any of them. His brief interlude with Jack's whore, Pauline Gordon had only reinforced that distrust.

Willie soon returned with a head of wet hair and a grin, saying, "It's really good water, Rhody, and it's cool, too."

Rhody smiled at him then said, "We're staying here for the night, Willie. Help me get the horses unsaddled and the mule unloaded."

"Okay."

Forty minutes later, their new campsite was ready and Rhody had the campfire built, but not lit. The dry wood wouldn't last long, so there was no need to set it aflame until Emma was ready to start cooking. They surely didn't need it for heat.

Rhody took advantage of the pond to finally scrape the stubble from his face then he and Willie removed their shirts and washed off the accumulated grime while Emma and Marty sat near the saddles talking.

As he washed, Rhody was thinking about the Comanches that may be lying in wait over the horizon. He glanced at the horses and knew that the gelding that Emma and Marty had been riding wasn't nearly as young or strong as the Morgans, so he decided that starting tomorrow, they would ride Morgana and he'd ride the gelding. That way, in case it became necessary to run, he could stay back and set up a defense while they rode to Menardville. He knew that he'd need Willie's help to make that happen.

So, as he and Willie made their way back to the camp, he said, "I'm going to show you how to use my compass."

"Okay. Is it hard?"

"No, sir. It's pretty easy."

"I don't have to use arithmetic. Do I?"

"Nope. It just points your way."

Willie was pleased with the idea, so when they reached the camp, he said, "Rhody is gonna show me how to use his compass, Marty."

"Can you show me, too?" she asked.

"Sure. It's really easy," Rhody replied as he removed his compass and flipped open the cover.

Emma joined Marty and Willie as they watched the dial.

Rhody said, "See how the needle's moving? It will always point north, so when it steadies, all you need to do is to rotate the compass until the letter N is where the needle is pointing. Then you know which way is east, which is where Menardville is."

"That's easy!" Willie exclaimed.

"I'll tell you what, Willie. Why don't you hang onto the compass for me? My pockets are full of other things anyway," Rhody replied as he snapped the cover closed and offered it to him.

Willie took the compass then smiled at him and said, "I'll take good care of it, Rhody."

"I know you will. Now, let's have supper before the sun sets."

As Emma walked to the food pannier to start rummaging, she wondered why Rhody had given the compass to Willie. She suspected that he might have another reason because his left pocket was empty but didn't know what it could be.

After Emma made her selections, Rhody struck a match and the campfire sprang to life. He had a short pile of wood nearby to keep it going, so there wasn't a real rush.

While Emma prepared their dinner, Rhody was making emergency plans if they ran into the Comanches tomorrow and things began to go badly. Now that Willie knew how find Menardville, he needed to make sure that they had enough money to afford to take a stage to San Antonio. Willie still had the cash that he'd given to him yesterday, but he'd need more, and he'd also need to know what to do once they arrived in San Antonio.

He took out his notebook and pencil then flipped to the back page and began to write. He hoped that he'd never have to give the sheet to Willie or Emma, but it was the only way he could fulfill his promise to take care of them if he didn't make it to Menardville with them.

As he wrote, he almost snickered when he thought of his original plan to ride to California. He hadn't even made it out of Texas, and now it looked as if he'd never see the Pacific Ocean.

He closed the notebook and slipped it back into his shirt pocket with the stub of a pencil then walked back to the campfire to observe Emma as she cooked, curious about her menu and enjoying just watching her.

RHODY JONES

Emma had seen him writing, and it only added to her suspicion that he was planning something that he didn't want her to know about. She doubted if he was going to abandon them, not after having faced the Comanches to rescue her and Marty. It must have something to do with the possibility that they might face them again soon. She didn't want to ask him in front of the children, but she was determined to find out later when the youngsters were asleep.

"That smells really good, Emma. What is it?"

"It's just a stew. I used a tin of your sliced potatoes and one of carrots, then added some onion and some of your shredded beef before adding salt and pepper."

"I wish I had more cups and plates. We'll have to share again."

"And you'll eat more than you did at lunch, Rhody."

He smiled at her and said, "Yes, ma'am."

As they ate, Willie asked, "Do you still reckon those Comanches are east of here?"

"Well, they're not behind us, so if they aren't there, then we'll have a pleasant ride to Menardville. We'll take every drop of water we can carry from the pond before we leave, too."

"How far is it to Menardville?" Marty asked before she accepted the spoon from Willie and dipped it into the plate of stew.

"I won't know exactly until noon tomorrow, but I'd guess it's about seventy miles away. We should get there in two more days."

"And we can use the compass, so we don't go the wrong way," Willie said as he grinned.

"Exactly. Just make sure that you keep checking it to make sure that you don't drift," Rhody replied as Emma handed him their spoon.

As he took the spoon, he looked at her blue eyes and saw something different but wasn't sure of what it was. If she'd been a man, he would have believed it was curiosity, but she was far as distantly removed from his own sex as possible and he didn't know her that well either. She could just be waiting for a comment about her stew.

He took a bite, handed the spoon back to her then after he chewed and swallowed, he said, "This is much better than I could make, Emma."

She smiled and replied, "It isn't that great, Rhody, but thank you for the compliment."

"You're welcome, ma'am," he said as he picked up his cup of coffee.

RHODY JONES

The sun was setting, so Rhody set out the bedrolls and his blanket keeping his Winchester '76 nearby. He didn't expect any nighttime visitors, at least not human ones, but the pond's sweet water was likely to attract critters while they slept but was counting on the horses to identify any of them that posed a threat.

Two hours later, he was sitting on his blanket and looking east in the moonlight but listening for intruders when he heard Emma's footsteps, which surprised him because he thought that she was sleeping.

He looked up at her and almost thought her hair was glowing as she sat down next to him and he knew he'd been wrong when he'd guessed that she was curious about his evaluation of her stew.

"I thought you were asleep, Emma."

"I couldn't sleep. Last night I was exhausted, but I'm not that tired now and to be honest, I'm a bit worried about falling asleep."

"I can understand that. I often had nightmares after some of the bad days at sea or on the trail."

"What happened on the trail?"

"On my last drive, my good friend, Jack Mason, was gored by a longhorn while we were trying to stop a stampede. You wear his gunbelt and that's his Winchester '66 and his saddle on Morgana."

"I was wondering why you traded the newer rifle rather than that one."

"Just a few days before he died, he gave me his last will and wanted me to have them. He also asked me to give his pay to a woman in San Antonio."

"Was she his fiancée?"

"No. She was a whore at the Alamo Saloon and Billiard Parlor. After I gave her the money, I asked her if she even remembered Jack, and she told me that she didn't. To her, he was just another customer. I don't blame her really, but it still bothered me that Jack sent her the money."

"Why didn't you ask her before you gave her the money? Then you wouldn't have to give it to her."

"I would have anyway because I promised Jack that I would. I just hoped that he was looking down and thanked me for keeping my promise."

Emma then asked, "Why did you show us how to use the compass and then give it to Willie?"

"Because I wanted him to know how to find Menardville in case anything happened to me."

"Is that the same reason that you wrote something in your notebook?"

Rhody sighed then replied, "Yes. I promised to take care of you and the children, and I wanted to make sure that I could keep my word no matter what. I wasn't going to give it to you until it became necessary, and I hope that it doesn't come to that."

"May I ask what it is?"

"It's a way of contacting my uncle in a way that lets him know that you are who you say you are."

"You've already made plans in case we run into the Comanches tomorrow, haven't you?"

"It would be foolish not to be prepared, Emma. I can fend off quite a few with my rifles but I'd want you and the children to stay safe. If we run afoul of them tomorrow and the way east is clear, I'll send all of you east with my pack mule. I'll give you or Willie the rest of my cash and you can take the stage from Menardville to San Antonio. After I take care of the Comanches, I'll follow you."

Emma stared at him for twenty seconds before asking, "Why are you doing this? You risk your life to save two people you've never met, now you're planning on sacrificing yourself for us again? Why?"

"I wasn't planning on sacrificing myself, Emma. I plan on mounting a strong defense against the Comanches. They probably won't have more than ten warriors and I can at least shoot their horses before I follow you. Even if I only take two or three down, that may be enough to make them return to their village. Look what happened after I shot one of them yesterday."

"That was different, and you know it. They still had the cattle, horses and a wagonload of our things to get back to their village. If they're waiting for us, then the only reason that they would be there is to kill you before they captured us again."

"That may be, but I can still shoot their horses before they get within range of their Winchesters. My '76 can reach another hundred yards over their .44 shooters."

Emma closed her eyes briefly then asked, "What exactly did you write in your notebook?"

"I wrote my uncle's address, 121 Eddy Street, Providence, Rhode Island. Then I wrote to tell him that I had asked him to provide whatever support you requested."

"How will he know that you were the one who was asking?"

"I used the nickname that only he used when I was in the house. He called me Roho."

"Roho? What does it mean?"

"He knew I wasn't fond of either of my given names, Roland and Horatio, so he combined them and came up with Roho. He thought it was funny, so even though I thought it was worse than Rollie, I let him use it."

"Rhody," she asked, "you said you were a sailor, but it sounds as if your uncle is a powerful man. Is that true?"

"He is. Remember I told you that my great grandfather was in the Continental Navy during the Revolutionary War? Well, after the war, he bought a brig at a bargain price and started a shipping company. His name was Rudolph, so he named it the R. Jones Shipping Company, probably because he wasn't fond of his name either. My grandfather was named Roland, so he wouldn't have to change the company's name after he took over. He had three sons, the oldest was also a Roland, but he died when he was just ten, then came my father, Robert, and the youngest was my uncle, Richard.

"My father died when I was four, and I was adopted by my uncle. He never went to sea but preferred to run the company. He was very good at business and was always ahead of most of the other shipping firms when it came to innovation. He didn't bother with clippers that made the run to the Far East, despite the enormous profits if they successfully made the long voyage. He preferred coastal operations because the risks were lower and if the cargo was right, the profits were almost as good."

"Does that mean that you own part of the company?"

"Yes, ma'am. I inherited my father's half and as my uncle is still a bachelor with no intentions of marrying, then I'll eventually be the sole owner."

"Then why, in God's name, did you leave that all behind to be a cowboy?"

"I really did want to see the West and for the reasons that I told you. I felt it was my last chance to do what I really wanted to do. My uncle is fifty-three now and I'm not looking forward to having to run the company. I spent a lot of time with him learning the ins and outs of business, but I found it boring to say the least. I was on board one of our ships for most of the time since I was eleven, but my last voyage wasn't on one of ours. It was on a second-rate ship because I wanted to see how I did with the second-class crew."

Emma was still distracted after hearing his story, so she didn't reply when he finished, but simply stared at him.

Rhody then said, "After it almost sank, and the captain dismissed me, I took it as a sign that I should make the ride west into Texas."

RHODY JONES

Emma slipped from her trance and said, "But that was years ago. Why did you spend so long on the trail before you continued west? Surely, it wasn't because you needed the money."

"No, it was never about the money. It was just that I found that I enjoyed the life on the cattle drives. It was hard but honest work, and the boys who rode with me were all honest as well. The best part is that I was able to just be one of them and not the part owner of a shipping company. It was only after Jack died that I realized it was time for me to make the long ride."

She then quietly asked, "What will you do when you get to San Antonio?"

Rhody looked into those bright blue eyes in the moonlight, then hesitated before replying, "Let's figure that out when we get to San Antonio."

"Alright," she said then stood and looked down at Rhody before she added, "In spite of everything that happened in New Braunfels and afterward, I did love my husband."

Rhody just nodded then watched her turn and walk back to her bedroll then wrapped her skirt around her legs and slid inside without looking back.

Rhody watched her for a while wondering why she seemed to feel obligated to tell him that she loved her husband. It was almost as if she knew that he was curious about her motives for wanting to return to the burned-out shell of their ranch and was worried that he might be attracted to her and she wasn't ready for any man's attention. He was definitely attracted to her but accepted her declaration and felt both disappointed and relieved. He sat and thought about their conversation for a while, but never could come up with a reason before he finally stretched out and drifted off to sleep.

Quiet Owl had finally halted their ride when their horses were almost to the point of total exhaustion and they had reached a creek.

When they made their quick camp, he sat with the other warriors while they talked about how far they'd have to ride to get ahead of the white man and the captives and what they would do when they found them. None of them believed that the whites could have ridden far enough to get ahead of them.

They were thirteen miles south-southeast of where Rhody and his charges slept when they finally fell asleep on their blankets.

CHAPTER 6

Even though the Comanches had stopped for the night much later than Rhody had, they were mounted and riding before the whites were even awake.

Rhody did wake up five minutes later and in the light of the predawn, he took advantage of the privacy to prepare himself for the day.

He was already anxious as he began saddling the horses, putting his on the back of the old gelding before saddling Morgana with Emma's. Jack was the only one of the three horses to wear the same saddle that he'd worn the day before.

Rhody hung two of the newly-filled canteens on his saddle then attached the scabbards with his Sharps-Borshadt and his '76 before moving all of their ammunition into his saddlebags. Other than those critical items, all he added was a pouch of beef jerky. If he didn't have to act as a rear guard then it wouldn't matter where his other things were.

By the time, Emma, Willie and Marty slid out of their bedrolls, he was already saddling Dent.

"Are we gonna make another fire?" Willie asked.

"No, sir. I want to get on the move as soon as possible. Why don't you let Marty and Mrs. Brandt have some privacy?"

"Okay."

Emma had Marty's hand as they quickly walked past and headed for the pond's heavy rushes and bushes while Willie walked in the other direction.

When Emma and Marty returned five minutes later, she noticed the switch and was about to comment, but quickly understood why he'd moved her and Marty to the young Morgan mare.

"I'll make some burritos in a minute," Rhody said as he tightened the last strap holding the fourth pannier in place.

"I think I can handle it now," Emma said as she walked around Dent and flipped open the food pannier's flap.

"Yes, ma'am," Rhody said with a grin.

Despite the grin, he was growing more nervous in anticipation of the expected confrontation. He kept trying to convince himself that the Comanches had learned their lesson after witnessing their leader being shot off his horse at five hundred yards. They probably believed he was a sharpshooter after that lucky shot and if their chief was rational, he would have kept his warriors in the village even if some wanted to exact revenge. He was sure that it was just his own irrational worry that had persuaded him that the Comanches were waiting for them past the eastern horizon.

———

After Emma's burritos were gone and the canteens and water bag were topped off, they mounted and began riding with the bright morning sun in their eyes.

The horses were moving at a medium trot and Rhody was doing his best to scan the landscape ahead for any signs of the Comanches, but the sun was making it difficult.

He may not have spotted the Indians, but he did note the various locations that they could use for a defensive position. He was concerned about the hills to his southeast that could mask the Comanches, so he spent more time on the hills than anything else. If they were there, then one would probably appear on the summit to use its height to find them and thought it might be smart to climb one himself to see if they were even there. The hills were a few miles away, so he'd have time to make up his mind.

———

Quiet Owl's group was just six miles southeast of the hills that had attracted Rhody's attention and as they had resumed their fast pace the hill soon came into view, and Quiet Owl thought it was an ideal time to try out his new telescope.

———

Rhody had decided against climbing the hills for two reasons: it would make him visible to the Comanches when he reached the summit and he didn't want to leave Emma and the children alone for the time it took him to make the climb and then return. But he did decide to make a wider curve around the hills so that they wouldn't be close to any surprises on the other side when they passed. It turned out to be a fortuitous decision.

After passing the first set of hills, Willie asked, "Are you gonna climb up the hill to look for them Comanches?"

"No, sir. I'd stick out like a big old tree on the top and if they're close, they'd see me. Just keep your eyes open."

"Okay," he replied as he began scanning the horizons more diligently.

Rhody and Willie weren't the only ones whose heads were swiveling back and forth as both Emma and Marty were also searching for the unwanted visitors.

Quiet Owl had his warriors wait as he climbed the hill with his telescope. It wasn't that tall, maybe a hundred feet, but the surface was rocky and the soil was loose enough to force him to go more slowly than he wished.

He reached the top and immediately looked west hoping to see the white man and the two yellow-haired captives. When he didn't, he made the mistake of using the telescope just to be amazed by its power. He turned the telescope to the south and slowly panned across to the west and after he had it pointed north, he lowered it and smiled.

Only then did he turn and look east then swore as he thought he spotted riders almost four miles away riding east. He quickly returned the telescope to his eye and had to shift it in circles to get the riders into view.

―――

As Quiet Owl was searching, it was Marty as she sat facing south on the saddle who pointed at a flash of light behind them on the top of a hill and shouted, "What's that?"

Everyone's eyes then turned and when Rhody saw another flash, he immediately knew what had caused the reflection.

"Let's ride to the next hill as fast as we can!" he exclaimed, then waited until Emma and Willie nudged their mounts to a fast trot before he matched their speed with the old gelding.

―――

Quiet Owl had them in view as they raced away and kept the telescope focused on them for another minute after seeing a fourth rider he hadn't expected. It was another short one with yellow hair, but he looked like a boy. It didn't matter what he was. Now he and his men had them and they were running.

He quickly closed the telescope and even put the lens caps back on as he began his hasty descent down the hillside.

He shouted that he'd seen the whites before he was halfway down and soon slid to the flat ground and bolted to his horse. He put his telescope away then mounted and accepted his Winchester from Yellow Sky.

The eight Comanche warriors then accelerated around the hill to catch the escaping whites.

Once past the next hill they rode for another four hundred yards before Rhody had everyone pull up.

"Stay in the saddles," he ordered as he dismounted then quickly walked to Emma.

"This is what I told you last night, Emma," he said then he pulled his notebook from his pocket, ripped out the last page and handed it to her.

Then he reached into his pocket yanked out almost all of his remaining cash and gave it to her before he looked at Willie.

"Willie, make sure you keep going east. Don't ride too fast. Keep a measured pace and stop when the horses need a break. And make sure you check that compass often, no less than once an hour. Do not argue with me."

RHODY JONES

Willie nodded then said, "Yes, sir."

Rhody smiled at him then turned to Emma and said, "You need to take care of the children, Emma. I'll catch up to you in San Antonio if not sooner. Okay?"

Emma was feeling ashamed again knowing that she must abandon Rhody and that she would probably live while he might die.

"Alright. I'm not happy about this, but I'll as you ask."

"Okay, make sure you keep the hill between you and the Comanches. I'm going to set up now so I can delay them as best I can. When you get to Menardville, leave the horses and the pack mule at a livery and pay for a week before you get on the stage. Go!"

Emma looked at him once more before she wheeled Morgana to the east and set her to a medium trot as Willie saluted Rhody then swung Jack to follow her and Marty with Dent trailing behind.

Rhody watched them ride away for a minute before he mounted the gelding again. He had briefly thought of climbing the hill to gain the high ground, but that would allow some of the Comanches to swing wide and go after Emma and the children. He needed to cover them better but didn't know how much time he had.

He was already four hundred yards behind them when he set the gelding to the east and began looking for someplace to mount a defense.

He rode for another four hundred yards when he spotted a shallow gully just to the southeast. It wasn't much, but it would give him some cover and a wide field of fire when the Comanches arrived.

A minute later, Rhody dismounted then took one last look at Emma and the children as they continued to ride east. They were already a half a mile away, and he was pleased that they hadn't even looked back.

But they had looked several times before he checked on them. Each of them even Marty, wanted to return, but knew it would only cause Rhody problems. That knowledge did little to assuage their feelings of guilt for abandoning him.

He quickly removed his canteens and set them into the gully before he unstrapped his saddlebags and dropped them alongside. Finally, he removed his two rifles along with their scabbards to keep them clean and set them on the ground near the canteens.

He scanned the horizons to the south and west then took the geldings reins and led him to the other side of the gully where he could graze on some dry grass then hobbled him before returning to the gully.

RHODY JONES

He removed the box of .50-140 cartridges then set them on the western edge of the gully before putting the box of .45-75s beside them. He slid each of the rifles from its scabbard and laid them on top of the leather. He was as ready as he could be, and after another scan of the empty horizons to the south and west, he took one last glance at his disappearing charges. He was pleased to have made the emergency plan and hoped that they made it to San Antonio safely. Now he had to give them more time and hope that he made it to Menardville alive.

Yet as he settled in for his defense, he felt a sense of loss knowing that there was a good chance that he'd never see them again. In less than three days of feeling responsible for each of them, he'd come to think of them as family. As much as he had shared the love and respect with his uncle, he'd never felt a part of a real family who were his responsibility. Now he was doing his duty as their protector and hoped that he'd meet them again in San Antonio.

But first he had to stop the Comanches.

After their initial charge, Quiet Owl had slowed to a medium trot and dispersed his men, sending four around the other side of the hill where he'd lost sight of the white people. He didn't want to be surprised by that white man. He had been stunned as much by the accuracy of his shot that had killed Bear Who Speaks as he was by its power. They may have two Spencer rifles, but he knew that the two warriors who had them weren't nearly as good as that white man had already demonstrated.

Yellow Sky was with him and had one of the Spencers and Barking Coyote had the other, but he'd send him with the four to ride around to the other side of the hill. He'd slowed to give them time to mirror his own position on this side.

When they passed the curve of the hill, Quiet Owl spotted the white man dismounted and waiting for them about eight hundred yards away, He had his warriors pull up to await the other four who should appear soon. He could see the three yellow heads riding off in the distance, but they would have to get past the white man before chasing them down. They were almost two miles away, but without the white man's protection, they would be easy to track and this time, they wouldn't be captured. They had been traded away, so they were fair game.

Rhody spotted the four warriors on the south side of the hill and was relieved that the chief hadn't sent more. He could handle four Comanches and one of them had his telescope.

He dropped to the ground between his rifles then picked up the Sharps-Borshadt and pulled six of the three-and-a-half-inch cartridges from the box and laid them atop the scabbard.

As he set up, he saw movement on the north side of the hill and had to recompute the odds of his survival when he counted four more warriors and that was before he discovered that two of them had Spencers.

―――

When Quiet Owl spotted his other four warriors, he turned his horse north to meet them at the middle of the hillside to tell them of his plan for attack which revolved around the two Spencers.

After they joined, Quiet Owl detailed his plan, which wasn't very complex. They would form a line abreast leaving just twenty yards between them. They would start their horses at a slow trot toward the white man, and when they were about five hundred yards out, the two warriors with the Spencers would open fire with their rifles to keep the white man's head down or at least spoil his aim. But there was one more thing he wanted them to do. He instructed them to shoot the gelding that was standing behind him just cropping grass. Without a horse, the man would be unable to make an escape.

He expected the shooter to quickly mount now that he'd seen all eight warriors begin to move, so as soon as he finished talking, he had them form their line and wait for his command to begin the attack.

―――

At eight hundred yards, Rhody still hadn't noticed the difference in their rifles, and assumed they all had .44 caliber repeaters and not the older Spencer repeater with its longer range and enormous .56 caliber round. He had briefly removed his hat, but the afternoon sun made him change his mind. He needed the brim to block the glare when he aimed. He set his ladder sight to six hundred yards, ignoring the difference between the amount of gunpowder in the non-standard cartridges he was using. At the Sharps factory, they'd set the marks on the gunsight for .50-90 cartridges and the one he had in his chamber had almost double the amount of powder. It probably only added another twenty percent in range, but when dealing with over a thousand yards, that twenty percent is pretty impressive.

He knew he couldn't be as lucky as he'd been when he'd shot the Comanche leader, but he could hit their horses and put them on foot. This wasn't a game where there were rules; this was either going to be his death or theirs. He had the range advantage and would use it as best he could. He hoped to eliminate half of them before he switched to his Winchester. At least he knew he was reasonably accurate with the repeater, so he'd still have an advantage, but didn't expect to come out of the fight unscathed. This group wasn't going to leave after losing one or two warriors. He would have to kill them all.

He had his sights set on the warrior on the end of their line, knowing that he and the one on the other end were the most dangerous. They were already in range and he needed to let them know that they weren't safe.

RHODY JONES

He slowed his breathing then at more than a half a mile, he squeezed his trigger. The bullet would take more than two seconds to reach its target, so as soon as the big rifle slammed into his shoulder, he opened the breech and extracted the brass.

Quiet Owl hadn't expected the white man to fire at such a long range even after having witnessed Bear Who Speaks' death. When the sound of the shot reached his ears, there was a moment of derisive belief that the white man was wasting ammunition before the big slug of lead arrived.

Red Fox was on the far right of the line, holding his Winchester and looking at Quiet Owl for the sign to move when he heard the roar then as he turned, he felt a hammer slam into his inner thigh just below his groin, then the slug of lead passed through the tissue and buried itself into his horse's back. He felt his warm blood pouring from the wound as the horse bucked and writhed in pain throwing him to the ground. He was already dizzy from blood loss and would die after another thirty seconds in the hot Texas sun.

Rhody saw him fall and didn't take time to pat himself on the back but slid a second round into the Sharps-Borshadt's breech and snapped it close. He was shifting his aim to the other end of their line when Quiet Owl yelled but instead of a slow walk, he ordered them to charge at a full gallop. There was no longer a reason to approach slowly.

More than two miles away, the distant report reached Emma and the children and each of them looked west, knowing that Rhody had engaged the Comanches.

Willie wanted to return to help, but knew he had a responsibility now and kept riding.

Emma was despondent knowing that there was nothing she could do, but just as Willie understood his responsibility, she knew she had to protect the children and get them to San Antonio.

―――

Rhody was startled by their sudden charge but had to keep firing, so he led the warrior on the left end of the line knowing that the bullet would take time to reach the target then fired. He had the rifle's breech open when his second shot hit the warrior's horse in the neck. The horse plowed into the ground and the warrior flew over its head and as he landed face-first into the hard ground, his head snapped back crushing his second and third cervical vertebrae, so he didn't feel his left forearm snap in half sending the sharp ends through his skin. He wouldn't die for another ten minutes, but he wasn't capable of moving, and his horse wouldn't last that long.

Yellow Sky and Barking Coyote knew that they had to start firing their Spencers earlier to spoil the white man's aim, so without coordination, each of them leveled their rifles and fired within two seconds of each other.

RHODY JONES

Initially, Rhody thought that two of the Comanches were panic firing as they were still six hundred yards out and moving fast. It was only when he heard the sound of their Spencers that he realized he had a problem even before the thick bullets arrived a fraction of a second later. One of the heavy slugs slammed into the gully bed just to his left before the second exploded into the ground just eight feet in front of him.

He shifted his sights to one of the Spencer shooters and fired but missed. He cursed himself for even missing a horse, but quickly opened the breech, extracted the brass, then inserted a fresh cartridge.

They were well within Spencer range as he fired another shot at the same warrior and watched as the man flipped off the back of his horse as if he'd hit a low-lying branch.

He reloaded once more as the other Spencer-shooter fired and wasn't concerned about where the bullet went until he heard rather than saw its destination when the hobbled gelding screamed in pain and he heard the horse collapse to the ground. He couldn't take the time to see if he had to end the horse's suffering, but aimed at the last Spencer shooter, taking an extra two seconds to be sure. This was going to be his last shot with the Sharps-Borshadt.

They were less than four hundred yards out and as he squeezed his trigger, he could see the Spencer shooter levering in another round but in less than a second, he knew that he'd never get the chance to cock the hammer when his .50 caliber bullet slammed into the man's chest. Now he needed the rapid-firing capability of the Winchester.

Quiet Owl knew that he was down to four warriors but remembered what Howling Wolf had told him before they'd left the village; either kill the white man or be branded cowards. He was not a coward nor were any of his men, and he knew that the white man wouldn't survive now that his horse was dead but wanted to be the one who killed him, not the hot sun.

As they passed three hundred yards, each of the remaining Comanches began to fire their Winchesters to distract the white man before they got within range.

Rhody held his Winchester's sights on the nearest Comanche when they began firing. He knew that they were out of effective range and on the backs of running horses, so even if their bullets reached him, they'd be spent and probably off target.

As the ground fifteen to twenty feet before him began erupting in dirt geysers, he kept his sights on the one warrior, waiting for him to come within range. The nearest Comanche was Quiet Owl.

He squeezed his trigger and felt the Winchester's brass plate pop against his shoulder before he quickly cycled another round into the chamber. The spent brass was still in the air when the bullet glanced off of Quiet Owl's horse's head, making him rear and throwing his rider into the air.

The horse veered away as Quiet Owl slammed into the ground then rolled twenty feet before stopping. He hadn't broken any bones but was disoriented as he managed to scramble to his feet.

As he watched, the white man continued to exchange fire with his last three warriors.

Rhody picked off another Comanche with his fourth shot from his Winchester and thought he might make it out of this mess without a scratch when one of the two shooters' .44s drilled into the left edge of his chest and ricocheted off a rib before popping into the dirt.

He grunted in pain as the fusillade of .44s began creeping closer. His Winchester had been cocked when he took the hit, so he didn't need to lever in a new round before he sighted on the Comanche who was getting ready to fire while his companion was cycling his repeater. He squeezed his trigger just as the Comanche fired his rifle. The Indian missed, but he didn't and as the warrior fell from his horse, he painfully levered in a new round and fired at the last rider before he could fire again. When the man dropped his Winchester, Rhody slowly stood and cycled his '76. He spotted one Comanche about two hundred yards away just standing there looking at him among the carnage.

As he watched, the Comanche walked a few feet then picked up his rifle, and Rhody expected that they'd have a one-on-one shooting match but then, the last Comanche surprised him.

He walked to one of the four standing horses and leapt onto its back, then instead of charging at him, Rhody watched him wheel the horse around and thought he was going to return to his village with news of the disaster. He then made the mistake of releasing his Winchester's hammer to let him go.

After the Comanche began to ride west, Rhody turned and looked at his dead horse and apologized for not removing his hobble before the shooting started then leaned his Winchester against his knee to examine his wound. He ripped open the bloody shirt and saw the dark blood, but the damage wasn't as bad as he'd expected, so he began walking toward his canteens.

He picked up one of the canteens then turned to make sure that the Comanche was still riding away and wasn't surprised to see that he'd gathered the remaining horses, and immediately realized his enormous error in not shooting the last one when he had the chance. He was going to strand him out here in the middle of nowhere without a horse.

The man was still within range of the Sharps-Borshadt, so he quickly capped and dropped the canteen then trotted to where the long rifle lay on its scabbard. He had just picked up a new cartridge when he heard a distant gunshot and jerked his head up, expecting to see the Comanche riding toward him but what he witnessed was even worse.

Quiet Owl had realized that his only advantage now was that he was on horseback and the white man wasn't. He was surprised that the white man was foolish enough not to understand but was grateful. After mounting, he gathered the three other healthy horses then rode far enough away to be out of range then once he was satisfied, he tied the three horses' rope bridles together.

He glanced at the white man who wasn't even paying attention then brought his Winchester level, aimed at the first horse and fired. He quickly shot the other two before he turned his horse, the only horse still alive for miles around and began to ride northeast, keeping the safe distance from the white man. He knew that the white man would die within three or four days, but even he would know that the golden-haired woman and the two children would die before he did.

Rhody had watched in disbelief as the Comanche shot each of the horses because he knew how much they valued them, but he also realized why he'd done it but even then, he misjudged the man. He'd expected him to ride west and then disappear, but he had turned northeast and was going to circle him. Initially, he thought that the Comanche was looking for a better firing location, but that didn't make any sense because no matter where he was, he'd always be at a disadvantage. Then he realized the surviving warrior's intent and felt sick. He was going to chase down Emma and the children.

He had to ignore his wound as he quickly reloaded the Sharps-Borshadt, put two of the cartridges into his pocket then picked up his Winchester and returned to the gully. With a rifle in each hand, he began jogging northeast while the Comanche was now almost due north. He wanted to cut the gap as much as possible. The Comanche was six hundred yards away, so he might be able to get off two long-range shots, but that would be all. After that, he wouldn't have a chance to stop him.

Quiet Owl watched him as he jogged along with his two rifles and almost laughed but losing seven warriors wasn't a laughing matter. He'd make the white man pay for what he'd done and knew that there was nothing he could do about it. He wasn't stupid enough to push his horse as he knew he'd need it to be strong for a few hours as he ran down the woman and children. He knew that they had two better horses and a pack mule, so the chase was much more than just vengeance.

Rhody was losing wind and knew that his heavy breathing would take its toll on his accuracy, so he slowed to a walk to catch his breath knowing that he'd be giving up distance.

When he was confident that he would be able to keep the heavy rifle steady, he stopped lowered the Winchester to the ground then brought the Sharps-Borshadt level and set his sights on the distant Comanche, leading him by ten feet. He squeezed the trigger and quickly lowered the rifle and opened the breech, knowing that if he missed then the Comanche would probably increase his horse's speed and the next shot would be more difficult with each passing second.

Wherever his first shot went didn't matter as he put the rifle's butt to his shoulder and aimed at the faster moving target. He prayed that he didn't miss and squeezed the trigger.

Quiet Owl had watched the white man fire his first shot and was gratified when he didn't even hear the bullet pass. He'd missed by a significant amount and he thought that he was now even safer as he'd kicked the horse into a fast trot and ducked down.

When he heard the second loud report just seconds later, there was another moment where he thought the white man had missed again before the massive bullet slammed into his horse's gut, just behind his right knee.

The horse leapt into the air as it writhed like a rattlesnake and screamed like a banshee. He was able to hold onto the horse's mane as the horse entered his death throes, but when he had the chance, he leapt from the horse with his Winchester still in his hand then hit the ground in a controlled roll and scrambled away from the thrashing hooves.

Rhody had seen the result of his second shot then picked up his Winchester and left the heavier Sharps-Borshadt on the ground before he began walking toward the Comanche who had regained his feet and was looking his way.

Quiet Owl stared at the white man then cycled his Winchester and strode toward him. His sharp eyes had seen him leave the big gun on the ground, and he knew it was now an even fight between them and he would not flinch.

Rhody levered in a fresh round as he kept his eyes focused on the Comanche who was still more than three hundred yards away. His side was throbbing, but he had to ignore it until he finished this. Even as the gap closed, he found himself thinking about Emma, Willie and Marty. They were safe now because even if the Comanche won, he was on foot and could never catch them. He'd fulfilled his promise and all that remained was to be able to walk away.

Both men continued walking and soon passed the two-hundred-yard mark, but even though Rhody knew his Winchester had the range and power for a killing shot at this range, he kept walking. He didn't want to miss.

The afternoon Texas sun was baking the top of his head under his Stetson and sweat was beginning to drip down his forehead and into his eyes, so Rhody quickly tossed the hat aside and wiped his forehead and eyes with his shirtsleeve as he continued to stride toward the Comanche.

He was only a hundred and twenty yards away now and each could see the other man's face. Rhody's heart was pounding against his ribs as the concentrated on his target and watched the Comanche's dark eyes studying him for any sign of weakness or fear. He couldn't see any measure of concern in the warrior's eyes and hoped that his weren't displaying his own nervousness.

RHODY JONES

    Suddenly, Quiet Owl stopped and whipped his Winchester to his shoulder and quickly fired.

    Rhody didn't have time to react, and felt the bullet tug at his heavy flannel shirt just below his right armpit then froze, brought his Winchester's butt to his shoulder and as the Comanche was quickly levering in a new round, he held his breath and let his sights settle before squeezing the trigger.

    The '76 kicked and sent its .45 caliber round spinning across the dry Texas ground at over eleven hundred feet per second. It crossed the three hundred and forty-eight feet in just over a third of a second and found its mark when it blasted into Quiet Owl's chest, shattering his breastbone before exploding his aortic arch.

    The last Comanche dropped to his knees, letting his cocked Winchester drop to the ground as he stared at the white man with fading vision before he fell face forward to the ground.

    Rhody lowered his repeater and kept his eyes on the dead warrior. He didn't believe that he was playing possum after he'd seen the flood of blood appear on his bare chest.

    He finally turned walked back a few yards and picked up his hat before he walked back to where he'd set down the Sharps-Borshadt and picked it up as well. He then returned to his gully, set the rifles down picked up a canteen and was tempted to empty it, but only took two long swallows before putting the cap back on.

He then looped the canteen around his shoulder then did the same for his full canteen before picking up his saddlebags and hung them over his left shoulder.

After he picked up his rifles he began walking back to the last Comanche's body and when he reached the man, he looked down at him, but didn't bother picking up his Winchester. He was already overloaded and was going to have to walk, but he did want to find their water and maybe some food, so he left the body and headed for the man's horse.

He found a water bag and a leather pouch with some salted beef and hung both over his shoulder before he turned west to add to his supplies. At least he wouldn't have to find water for a horse.

The other dead horses had more water and food, so he began consolidating his finds until he had a full water bag and a pouch with a good amount of food. He finally reached the last dead animal and discovered what he was really hoping to find. It had to be there because he'd seen the flash on the hill. He pulled his telescope from a leather pouch and slipped it into his saddlebags. He then guzzled the water in the last leather sack and tossed it aside.

Rhody then turned east and began walking. As he passed each of the dead Comanches and their horses, he suddenly realized that none of their pouches held any spare ammunition. All they had was what was in their rifles. If he'd known that, he would have ridden with Emma and the children then held back a few hundred yards and fought a moving retreat to force them to use their ammunition. They would have had to return to their village, and he wouldn't be on foot.

But he was on foot and knew he'd have to treat his wound somehow, so before he passed the last dead horse, he picked up the empty water bag and tucked it under his gunbelt. He'd cut it up and form a leather bandage when he stopped for a break. His nerves were still wound tightly after the fight and knew he would soon drop into exhaustion. But now he'd walk as far as he could and was curious if Emma, Willie and Marty had heard all the gunfire.

They were probably more than five miles away by now and the sound might not have reached them. He knew that they'd be stopping to set up camp around sunset but by then, they'd probably be ten to twelve miles ahead of him if not more. They could be in Menardville by tomorrow night if they made good time. If he was able to keep walking, then he could get to the town in four or five days. He would sleep during the hot days and walk during the cooler nights, but he had to manage his water.

———

Emma and the children were actually just four miles away when the shooting stopped because they had slowed their pace to listen to the distant gunfire, but the echoes had faded away before they stopped. They were now almost eight miles away.

Willie then asked, "Do you think Rhody is okay?"

"We'll find out when we get to Menardville. He should arrive just a few hours after we do."

"Shouldn't we wait for him?"

"No, Willie. Rhody was right when he said we shouldn't stop. What if they sent some Comanches around him to chase after us? We'd ride right into them and I'm not that good a shot."

Willie nodded but still looked at their backtrail hoping to see Rhody. He understood the real reason why Mrs. Brandt knew that they shouldn't wait for Rhody. It was because Rhody might have died and the Comanches would be coming. He wished that he was older then he could just go back on his own but even then, he had the compass that would guide them to Menardville. He'd already checked it twice and was sure that they were still riding east.

Emma glanced west herself and didn't see anyone on the three miles of empty Texas. She hated to think that Rhody was dead but knew that he was facing eight Comanches and even though he said he had the advantage with his guns, she remembered him saying that it had been sheer luck when he'd killed the first one right after rescuing them. As guilty as she had felt for almost forcing Carl to leave New Braunfels, she felt much worse for leaving Rhody behind. If he died, then she would be responsible for two men's deaths and as much as she hated to admit it, Rhody's would hurt much more. She had first believed that it was just gratitude she had felt for him, but soon realized that it was something different…much different. She'd never felt this way before especially not with her husband.

Carl was the youngest of the Brandt brothers and when the older two had decided to build their own ranch out west where the land was free for the taking, Carl had turned them down because he considered himself a towner, not a rancher.

He was a handsome boy and Emma had been infatuated with him enough to become intimate, believing that he would marry her. When she discovered her pregnancy, she had told Carl, but he denied it was his child and accused her of dallying with another man. She knew she wouldn't be able to hide her condition and after she had confided in her mother, her father had demanded to know the name of the baby's father, and she had honestly told him who the father was.

Carl had married her but had been stunned when he had been fired from his job at the lumber mill. For two weeks, he hunted for another job but was denied even though he knew that they needed more workers. It was only when he was turned down at the stockyards that he learned that Emma's father had put out the word that he was an immoral man and not to be trusted.

Carl's only choice was to join his brothers at their ranch, so he thought he could just go without Emma, but her father had threatened to write a letter to his oldest brother, so he had reluctantly brought her with him. He may have resented her, but he still behaved as a husband should and didn't beat her or even shout at her very much. Aside from bedding her, he treated her more like a housekeeper.

By the time they reached the ranch and moved into their room, Carl had become a quiet and almost morose man with none of the zest for life that he'd shown in New Braunfels. He was a beaten man and believed that he was no longer in control of his own fate.

When Emma lost the baby just a month after they arrived, Carl even began to lose interest in her as a woman which she blamed on herself. The longer she had spent with Rhody who was as selfless a man as she'd ever met, she found herself wishing she had married him instead of Carl, and that desire made her feel as if she was being unfaithful which is why she had the urge to tell Rhody that she loved her husband.

But as soon as she'd said it, she realized how phony and just plain stupid it was. She felt as if she was cursed ever since she'd given herself to Carl. All she could do now to atone was to follow Rhody's instructions and take care of Willie and Marty. She just hoped that it wasn't the last time she heard his voice.

RHODY JONES

Rhody finally stopped under a lone Texas ash tree where he leaned his rifles against the trunk before letting his loads slip from his shoulders and plopping down.

He wanted to sleep but needed to take care of his wound. He had enough water, so he could clean it before wrapping it in leather and now that he was in the shade, he pulled off his bloody shirt then poured some water from the bag into his cupped hand and began to wash the clotted dry blood from the wound.

It was about an inch long and not too deep, but he could feel bone and hoped that it hadn't been fractured. His breathing wasn't as bad as he'd experienced when he'd pulled chest muscles on the trail, and he couldn't figure out why it didn't but suspected it would hurt worse later.

After washing the wound, he took the empty water bag then used his big knife to cut the seams to make a long leather square which he folded until it was a half an inch thick. He used the straps of the water bag to hold it in place before he donned his shirt again. If it had been the winter, he would have gone shirtless, but he knew how badly he'd burn if he went bare-chested in the Texas summer.

He ate some of the Indian's salted beef then drank more water before he looked at the Sharps-Borshadt. It was a good ten pounds of metal and wood and he wondered if it was necessary to take with him any longer. He doubted if he'd need the long range and he still had two boxes of ammunition for the Winchester and one more for his Colt.

He finally decided that the gun was too good to leave behind and used the last strips of the water bag's leather to fashion a strap for the rifle. It would add to his load but as he drank the water, it should balance out. He could always leave it behind later, but it wasn't that bad now.

He rested for another ten minutes and thought about Emma. He had been surprised that she hadn't had any nightmares the second night and wondered how she had managed to keep a rational mind after undergoing all of her turmoil. Marty hadn't seen what had happened to her family, and neither had Willie, but Emma had seen what the Comanches had done to her sister-in-law and knew what they probably had done to her husband as well.

He knew that she would be grieving for a long time and that she may never want to marry again but began to wish that she didn't. He knew that he hadn't really met the real Emma yet because she had so much on her mind and too much grief in her heart, but he hoped that she didn't marry someone else before he had the opportunity to know her. He'd already been more impressed with her in the brief time he'd known her and suspected that the more he understood Emma, the more he'd like what he discovered.

Rhody wanted to move as much as he could before he got some much-needed sleep, so he stood then reassembled his load and left the lonely ash tree and began walking east, following the trail left by Jack, Morgana and Dent.

It was well after seven o'clock when Emma said, "Willie, let's set up camp near that cottonwood."

"Yes, ma'am," Willie replied before he turned Jack to the right.

"Are we gonna have a fire, Aunt Emma?" Marty asked.

Emma looked down at her and knew that there was a danger but decided it was worth the risk.

An hour and a half later, she was stirring another stew in the skillet while Willie stared west into the dying sun hoping to see a rider on the horizon.

"He's not coming," he said softly before turning and walking back to the campfire.

"He'll meet us in Menardville, Willie," Emma replied even though she was beginning to believe otherwise.

Marty said, "I hope so. I like Rhody."

"We all do, Marty. We all owe him so much."

Willie sat beside his sister and asked, "What if he doesn't get there tomorrow? Will we wait in Menardville until he does?"

"No, Willie," Emma replied, "He said he'd meet us in San Antonio. He may have had to ride a different direction after fighting off the Comanches."

"I suppose."

Emma's excuses for Rhody's absence were growing weaker. She knew that if he hadn't reached them yet, especially with the campfire acting as a signal then it was likely that he wasn't coming at all. She continued stirring and as that thought echoed in her mind, she felt tears streaming down her face, so she turned away so the children wouldn't see her. She wiped her tears away then took a deep breath and added some pepper to the stew without tasting it first.

———

By the time Rhody stopped walking, he was almost fifteen miles behind Emma and the children. It took him ten minutes to set up his small cold camp and tried to make himself comfortable in a bed of sand.

He still wore his gunbelt, but had his rifles leaning on top of his saddlebags to keep dirt out. He knew they both needed cleaning, but that wasn't his top priority. He needed to stay alive.

He soon fell asleep hoping that no critters would come to visit him while he slept. He no longer had any horse alarms to warn him, so he hoped that the plentiful amount of horsemeat he'd left a few miles behind him would attract all of them and let him sleep in peace.

Before they slid into their bedrolls, Emma led the children in prayer for Rhody's safety. As their eyes closed, each of them had tears dripping onto the ground. Emma may have been making excuses, but even Marty now believed that Rhody was in heaven and they were alone.

Emma had her gunbelt on the ground to her right and the Winchester '66 was near Willie. She remembered that Rhody had told her that the horses would let them know if any dangerous animals showed up, and she smiled. Rhody had done so much more than just save them. He had given them a future when he'd handed her that small piece of paper. She just wished it wasn't a future without him.

CHAPTER 7

Rhody awakened with a start as his chronograph began chiming and he quickly sat up feeling a sharp pain on his side from his damaged chest.

He took in as deep a breath as his wound would allow then slowly stood and walked a few feet away to answer nature's call. It wasn't much as most of his body's moisture had been evaporated as sweat, but he soon replenished the loss with the sweet water from the water bag before he began to prepare for his night walk. He was chewing on some of the salted beef as he began walking in the night. If he'd been on horseback, he wouldn't have been able to see the hoofprints, but he wouldn't need them during the night as he was guided by the stars that he knew so well

He felt surprisingly spry in the cooler air even though it was probably close to eighty degrees. He didn't push himself as he knew he had a long way to go but would continue after daybreak until it became too hot. He wished it would rain to cool things off for a while but if they came, it wouldn't be in the form of a refreshing shower. It would be a nasty thunderstorm probably accompanied by hail or even a twister. He'd seen one of the swirling monsters before and didn't want to see one up close.

RHODY JONES

He didn't have his sextant with him but estimated his distance to Menardville to be around thirty-eight miles when he set out. If he was able to keep this pace, then he might be able to reach it in two days rather than three. It would all come down to his stamina, the weather, and if he ran afoul of any more Comanches or Kiowa.

When the thought of encountering more Indians entered his mind, he picked up his pace. He hoped that Emma and the children didn't encounter any of them, but even though they were probably within twenty-five miles of Menardville, it was still possible.

———

Rhody had been walking for more than two hours yet was still nine miles behind Emma and the children, who were stirring from their bedrolls.

Emma didn't rekindle the fire but prepared some of Rhody's burritos and set them on a plate before she began saddling Morgana.

Willie and Marty joined her after taking care of their personal needs, and soon wolfed down the burritos and followed them with cups of water.

After she'd had her breakfast, Emma and Willie saddled and loaded Dent's packs and in less than an hour after leaving their bedrolls, they were mounted again while Willie checked the compass.

Once in the saddle, each of them looked west at the empty horizon then turned Morgana and Jack east and set out for Menardville.

Rhody had closed to within eight miles before they left, so he didn't see them, but he was pleased to see that their path had held true. Willie was doing a good job navigating.

He was walking into the rising sun, so his eyes were downcast as he trudged along. The temperatures were still moderate, but he knew that they'd rise quickly now that the sun's power controlled the atmosphere. Being a mariner, he understood that anything that happened to the weather, from snowstorms to hurricanes was because of the sun. It gave the planet life, but it could snuff out whole towns when it generated a powerful storm.

For now, all he knew that it would soon send the temperatures skyrocketing and he'd have to find a shady spot to get more sleep so he could resume his journey after sunset.

He managed to keep walking for another three hours before the sun became overbearing and he was losing too much sweat, so he began hunting for some relief from the heat.

Ten minutes later, he stopped under a rocky shelf that only gave him three feet of clearance, but the ground beneath it was dark and much cooler.

After unloading, he drank some water then stretched out on the ground and promptly returned to sleep.

———

Willie had his hat, and Marty had found a bonnet among her clothes that Willie had rescued from their wagon, so Emma had taken a towel from one of Rhody's panniers and draped it over her head to keep out the sun.

They were riding at a steady, medium trot since they'd left camp and Emma estimated that they would arrive in Menardville before sunset. She was a bit nervous because she'd never been in charge of anything before, but knew she had to follow Rhody's last instructions and take care of Willie and Marty. Once they arrived, she'd check on the coach scheduled, get a room at the hotel then take the horses and mule to the livery and give the liveryman Rhody's instructions. Then she'd take the children to dinner before turning in for the night.

If she had time in the morning, they'd each take a bath and she'd see about buying some more clothes and other necessities before the stage left. It would be a long ride to San Antonio, over a hundred miles, but the stage would be much faster and would only take two days, including an overnight stay in Fredericksburg. In three days, they'd arrive in San Antonio and she'd send the telegram to his uncle. She was already tortured with the thought that she might have to include that Rhody had died but decided that she wouldn't make that terrible assumption. The less she thought about the possibility of never seeing Rhody again, the more functional she was.

―――

They stopped for a quick lunch and a break for the animals shortly before noon when they reached a good-sized creek but were back in the saddle just twenty minutes after stopping.

Just three hours later, Willie shouted, "Is that Menardville?"

Emma put her hand over her eyes then smiled when she spotted the spire of a church on the horizon to the northeast. They were safe and hadn't been more than two miles off in their path.

"Yes, sir! That's Menardville," she replied as she whipped the towel from her head and wiped her face before stuffing it into Morgana's saddlebag.

Marty was beaming under her bonnet as she said, "Can we have a big supper now, Aunt Emma?"

"Of course, we can, Marty."

RHODY JONES

Their spirits were lifted knowing that the dangers were behind them as they shifted their direction to the left toward Menardville.

———

Rhody was awake under his rock after a disappointingly short nap. He knew it was too hot to leave the overhang's protective shade but having only three feet of clearance meant he couldn't even sit up. He was planning on resuming his hike after sunset, but as he lay under the rock shelf, he was getting twitchy and anxious to be moving again.

So, twenty minutes later, he was loaded down and moving again. He'd finished the last of the water in the pouch, but he kept the bag for the leather in case he needed it.

He had the sun on his back as he stepped along following the trail left by his horses and pack mule. He was already planning on what to do when he reached Menardville, and the first thing would be to fill his stomach with something other than dried beef. Then he'd check with the liveryman for Morgana, Jack and Dent. He didn't expect to find Emma and the children still in town because he'd told them to take the next stage to San Antonio, but he also was sure that they believed that he was dead by now. Even if he'd managed to kill all of the Comanches, he would have caught up with them before they set up camp. As he walked, he wondered how long it would be before he spotted their campsite.

It was mid-afternoon when he'd left his stone shelter, and he wasn't planning on stopping until he was too tired to continue. He wanted to find his adopted family as soon as he could, so when he reached Menardville and found Jack and Morgana, he'd negotiate with the liveryman for the sale of his pack mule and most of his supplies. He needed the money anyway. He'd kept only five dollars of his two hundred and sixty that he still had with him when found Willie. That was more than enough to get him some dinner, a shave and a bath, but he would need more for the ride to San Antonio. Part of his negotiation with the liveryman would be to get his Morgans reshod.

Planning for what he would do when he reached the town kept him occupied and made the tiring, boring journey not as bad as it could have been. The longer he walked, the more he thought about Emma and wanted desperately to talk to her again.

Emma, Willie and Marty rode into the town of Menardville late in the afternoon and even as small as it was with fewer than a hundred residents, each of them felt as if it was as palatial as St. Louis.

They rode to the hotel, then dismounted out front and stretched before stepping onto the boardwalk and walking through the open doors. Emma knew that she must look a fright in her soiled dress and dirty hair with a Colt at her hip, but she didn't care as she walked to the window holding Marty's hand.

"May I help you, ma'am?" the woman behind the wide window asked.

"Yes, I'd like a room for the night please."

"Of course. That'll be a dollar and fifty cents."

Willie had given all of his cash to Emma before they started the day's ride, so she handed her two one-dollar bills and accepted her change.

"Your room is number two, just down the hallway on the right. The bath is at the end of the hallway and the privy is out back."

"Thank you," Emma said then asked, "Can you tell me where I could buy stagecoach tickets to San Antonio?"

"We handle the ticketing for the West Texas Line, ma'am. The stage runs every other day. It arrives on Monday Wednesday and Friday, then departs on Tuesday, Thursday and Saturday."

"Oh. I hate to sound ignorant, but we just rode in from out west and I can't recall the day."

"Today is Tuesday, so the stage left this morning. Did you wish to purchase your tickets now for Thursday's stage?"

Emma replied, "Yes, I may as well take care of that now, and I'll need to pay for another night's stay as well."

She looked at a chart and said, "Your tickets for you and your son will be twenty-eight dollars, but your daughter's fare will only be seven dollars."

"And that's all the way to San Antonio?"

"Yes, and it includes a night's stay in a hotel in Fredericksburg."

"Wonderful," Emma said as she paid for the tickets and accepted their room key along with the paper tickets.

She then looked down at Marty and said, "Let's drop off the horses at the livery and then go and get a real dinner."

Marty smiled and exclaimed, "I'm hungry!"

They left the hotel and rather than mounting just led the horses and mule down the street to the livery just a block away.

When they entered, they found the liveryman sleeping on a row of burlap bags full of oats, but he soon sat up and yawned before grinning at them.

"Afternoon, ma'am. What can I do for ya?"

"I need to leave our horses and pack mule with you for a few days."

RHODY JONES

"That's what I'm here for. It'll run you sixty cents a day for all of 'em. Want me to check their shoes?"

Emma paused then replied, "Yes, please. We need to take some things out of one of the panniers, but don't want to lug the big thing around. Do you have an empty burlap sack?"

"Yes, ma'am," he answered then hopped to his feet, walked to a small room and soon emerged with the burlap sack.

While Emma was moving all of the necessities that she thought that they'd need before they left Thursday morning, the liveryman checked the Morgans' and the mule's shoes.

"Yep, it looks like they'll all need new shoes, ma'am. They sure are a couple of pretty horses, too."

"They're very nice," Emma said, then asked, "How much for the shoes?"

"That'll run you another nine dollars, ma'am."

She peeled off a twenty-dollar bill and handed it to the liveryman.

"We'll be leaving on the Saturday stage, but a man named Rhody Jones will be stopping by to claim his horses and pack mule. He said to pay for a week, but he should be here sooner."

"Is he your husband, ma'am?"

Emma stared at him for a few seconds before she replied, "Yes, he is. We had to leave our ranch and were chased by Comanches. He held back to hold them off and give us a chance to escape."

The liveryman's eyebrows rose as he said, "Your husband is one brave feller, Mrs. Jones."

"Yes. Yes, he is. He's a wonderful man, too," Emma replied before Willie tossed the burlap bag over his shoulder and they left the big barn.

As they walked to the small diner across from the hotel, Willie asked, "Why did you say that Rhody was your husband, Aunt Emma?"

"Because he's been like a husband to me and a father to you and Marty."

"I hope he's okay," Marty said as she squeezed Emma's hand.

"We all do, sweetheart," she replied.

―――――

Rhody had taken a break from the long walk and was sitting on a boulder with his rifles laying atop his saddlebags. He had one of his two canteens in his hand and swished it around to estimate how much water he had remaining. He hadn't come across any creeks and didn't know the country, so he couldn't predict when he'd find water, especially at this time of the year.

He finally allowed himself one swallow before he capped the canteen, hung it over his shoulder then removed his hat.

He ran his hand through his sweaty hair and continued his damp hand across his neck to cool it down. He estimated his walking speed at around two and a half miles per hour, so he'd walked another ten miles after his nap, which should mean he only had another twenty-five miles or so to go. If he pushed it, he could reach Menardville by tomorrow night, but wasn't sure that it was possible. He needed to rest, and he needed to find more water.

After a filling supper, Emma and the children returned to their hotel room and after unpacking the burlap sack, Emma and Marty walked down the hallway to take a bath.

Willie sat on the bed with Rhody's Winchester '66 on his lap and tried not to imagine what had happened to him. He knew that if Rhody had killed all of the Comanches, he should have arrived by now. He then pulled out Rhody's compass, opened the cover and watched as the needle swung to the north.

"The bed is pointing south to San Antonio, Rhody," he whispered as he stared at the dial.

He closed the cover slid the compass back into his pocket then leaned the Winchester against the wall and lifted the gunbelt from the footpost of the bed. He released the hammer loop and slid the Colt from its holster. He had never shot a pistol before and had hoped that Rhody would show him how when he returned but now, he didn't care if he ever learned how to shoot a pistol.

When Emma and Marty returned looking much nicer, the gunbelt had been returned to the bedpost and Willie quietly left the room with his clean clothes to take a bath.

Emma was still wearing her miserable excuse for a dress, so after Willie had gone, she went to the clothes she had packed and changed into a pair of Rhody's britches and one of his clean shirts.

"Aren't you gonna buy a new dress tomorrow, Aunt Emma?" Marty asked as Emma buttoned the shirt.

"I am, but I think my dress is beyond salvation, Marty. The shirt and pants are a bit too large, but they'll do until we do some shopping in the morning."

"I think you look nice in Rhody's clothes."

Emma smiled and replied, "Thank you, Marty. I hope Rhody doesn't mind that I borrowed them."

Marty's smile evaporated before she asked, "Is Rhody still coming back?"

Emma sat on the bed beside her then stroked Marty's long blonde hair as she replied, "Of course, he will. We prayed for him last night, didn't we?"

Marty nodded, then said, "I hope God was listening."

"I'm sure He is, sweetheart."

Emma then put her arm around Marty and looked at the ceiling so the little girl couldn't see the tears in her eyes.

———

Rhody spotted their campsite just before sunset and took a few minutes to examine the ground to make sure that they were all still healthy. Once he found Emma's footprints and two smaller sets he smiled and resumed walking.

He knew he was still a long way from Menardville, but just seeing their footprints gave him a shot of additional strength and a stronger incentive to finish the journey. He knew that they'd probably already be in San Antonio by the time he arrived, but once he was astride Jack or Morgana, he'd make that hundred-mile ride in a day and a half.

The moon was up, and he enjoyed a surprisingly cool night, but he understood that the sudden change in temperature meant that it was likely that a thunderstorm was in his near future.

He turned to look to his west and noticed the stars no longer shone along the lower edge of the sky and could see distant flashes of lightning, but no thunder yet. He couldn't see any of the clouds, but he was sure that he'd soon be soaked. As long as the wind wasn't too strong or he wasn't pelted with hail, then he'd let the water give him a shower. He may not have any soap, but once he felt the first drops, he'd take off his shirt. He'd have to flip his rifles upside down to keep water out of their barrels, but even if they did get wet, they'd dry out in the morning before they could rust. When he reached Menardville, he'd find his gun cleaning kits and clean and oil both of his long guns before he made his fast ride to San Antonio.

Until the rains arrived, he took advantage of the cooler air and picked up his pace. He was in a good mood and was glad he'd kept the water bag. If the rain arrived in the downpour that he expected, he could probably fill it in just a few minutes.

He kept checking behind him as the stars began winking out announcing the growing clouds. The first indication he had of the storm's true power was the sudden increase in the wind that raced in from the northwest even as the thunder grew louder with the advancing lightning. The wind itself wasn't the problem as much as it was the sand that it picked up and pelted into his face and neck. He dipped his Stetson into the wind to give him some protection and wished the rains would come to keep the dirt where it belonged.

RHODY JONES

The first heavy drops began to plop onto the ground ten minutes later and by then, Rhody had already overturned his rifles, pulled his hat's chin strap into place and readied his water bag to catch Mother Nature's bounty. But after feeling the stings of the flying sand, he decided to keep his shirt on.

The wind soon began pushing him aside with powerful gusts as the rain fell in earnest. He struggled to hold his water bag level as the rain pounded his Stetson into a soggy, drooping piece of headgear. He could feel the water bag gaining weight as he struggled to stay upright while the wind shoved him across the slippery mud.

A nearby crack of lightning and an almost instant earth-shaking boom made him realize that he was a walking lightning rod with his two steel rifles. He looked for someplace nearby to at least stash his guns, but there wasn't even a good-sized boulder within sight.

He almost fell when a vicious gust blew him four feet to his right, sliding him into a muddy, rainwater-filled hole. He stumbled out of the hole and leaned into the wind as he strained to stay on his feet. He'd become almost fatalistic about the possibility of being struck by a bolt of lightning as the sky flashed all around him and a long streak of blinding light shattered the sky before his eyes followed by the violent crash it created when it disturbed the wet air. The storm grew even more intense as the thunder continued almost without pause. He'd stopped walking and just faced into the wind with his head down.

Suddenly, the rain stopped as if a spigot valve had been twisted closed and Rhody almost laughed as the gusts diminished to a steady strong breeze. He was giddy knowing that he wasn't about to become a conduit for a lightning bolt's journey to mother earth. He felt the added weight of the water bag and thought it was worth the ten minutes of nature's fury.

He was grinning as he turned to start walking east again, but within seconds, he realized that the worst may not be over after all when he felt a stinging jab on his right shoulder. Without any moonlight, he wasn't sure of what had caused the pain until he felt another one on the back of his neck and then a third on his right shoulder again. He quickly lifted his empty canteen above his head and stopped walking as the hail increased in volume and size.

They were just annoyances at first and no worse than mosquito bites, even Texas mosquito bites. But soon, as the storm continued east, the size of the balls of ice began to grow well beyond insect sized.

His tin canteen was being pummeled by pea-sized hail, but it didn't protect his arms or his back. He had his saddlebags over his left shoulder, and it was providing some protection, but he knew he'd be in big trouble if the hail continued to grow larger.

Seconds later, the first of the walnut-sized hail arrived, and when one of them slammed into his left pinky finger, he jerked the hand away in reaction and the protective metal shield dropped away. He didn't bother to put it back over his head but dropped to the ground on his right side and quickly stretched his saddlebags over his torso before curling up in a ball. The hail was hurtling all around him and striking his left leg, but he had the canteen over his head again with his hands curled beneath his head holding onto the canteen's strap to keep the wind from blowing it away.

The hail continued to pound him for what seemed like hours but was probably no longer than three minutes. He wasn't sure when the hail began shrinking, but when it finally stopped, the sudden cessation of the drumming seemed eerie. He slid the canteen from his head pulled the saddlebags away then laid on his side in the thick mud for another five minutes as he assessed the damage the hail had done to his body. He stretched his legs and knew he wouldn't be able to walk at his previous pace, but he could still walk.

Rhody slowly stood, but before he picked up his saddlebags, he checked his pistol, which had been rammed into the mud when he'd laid down on his right side. The outside of the grip was filthy, but the rest of the revolver was just wet from water. He'd clean it with some of the rainwater until he could do a proper job in Menardville. His Sharps-Borshadt was much worse as it had slipped from his sling into the mud. His Winchester had stayed in his arms, so it was the cleanest of the three guns.

After he picked up his saddlebags and tossed them over his shoulder, he hung his filthy Sharps-Borshadt over his shoulder and looked at the almost empty water bag.

"Well," he said aloud, "I think I can fill it before the heat arrives tomorrow."

Then just as he resumed walking the moon reappeared overhead and the wet landscape suddenly was bathed in what seemed like sunlight.

He stopped, looked up at the mocking face of the Man in the Moon then shouted, "Where the hell is the damned tornado? You missed that one, didn't you?"

He started walking again in the thick mud but knew he wouldn't be making much headway until it dried, so he looked for someplace where he could clean the mud from his guns and maybe add some of that frozen water to the water bag and his empty, dented canteen.

―――

The violent storm that had almost beaten Rhody to minced meat arrived in Menardville just minutes later, but the clouds that produced the hail swung south of the town. Nonetheless, the powerful winds, heavy, driving rains and impressive displays of lightning and thunder kept Emma and the children awake as the windows shook with each rolling roar of thunder.

RHODY JONES

Willie was in his own bed while Emma and Marty shared the second.

Marty was snuggled in close with her head on Emma's shoulder as she asked, "Is Rhody gonna be okay?"

Emma had her hand behind Marty's head when she replied, "A man who stopped all those Comanches isn't going to be hurt by some rain, Marty. He probably just took off his clothes and danced around to take a shower bath."

"Wouldn't the lightning hurt him?"

Emma kissed her forehead and said, "It wouldn't dare."

Marty sighed then smiled as a nearby boom shook the hotel's walls.

Emma glanced over at Willie who was staring at her and wondered if he believed what she had just told Marty. He'd been growing quieter with each passing hour that Rhody had remained missing. They had another full day in Menardville, and she knew it would only get harder to deny the obvious.

As that thought resurfaced, she turned her eyes away from Willie and let the tears fall.

———

Rhody had only walked a couple of hundred yards when he found what he'd needed so desperately when the hail had arrived. It was a cluster of misshapen boulders that even had enough space for him to use as a refuge. It may have been too late to protect him now, but it would serve his current needs.

He dropped his canteens, empty water bag and saddlebags to the almost dry ground at the base of one of the large boulders then set the Winchester on a flatter rock before swinging the Sharps-Borshadt from his shoulder and laying it alongside the repeater.

Finally, he removed his gunbelt and set it down before picking up the empty canteen and water bag. He walked around the front of the flat boulder then dipped the canteen into a large gouge in the rock. After it was filled, he screwed the cap on and set it aside before filling the water bag with the cold water complete with chunks of hail. He hung the water bag over a nearby bush which had been stripped of most of its leaves then began to clean his guns. He removed the cartridges from his pistol, then dipped it into the water and vigorously shook the gun. It wasn't the best thing to do with the weapon, but it needed to be clear of the mud. After he removed the pistol, he blew the barrel clear of the water then set it aside to let it dry.

He had to spend more time with the Sharps-Borshadt because it didn't fit into the gouge, so he had to almost hand bathe the rifle. The Winchester just needed a quick shower, but when he finished its makeshift cleaning, he set it aside to dry with the others.

He then dipped his gunbelt into the water to rinse off the mud before setting it aside to dry. He'd have to reload the guns later, but now that the guns were clean, he needed to remove the mud that coated him. He didn't care about the cartridges that were still snug in their leather loops.

He stripped off everything including his boots, socks and the leather bandage then took a deep breath and began taking scoops of water from the gouge and scrubbing himself with the chilly water. If it had been earlier in the day, he would have been enjoying every moment, but the cooler air and the damaged skin and muscle made the cold water far from pleasant. Despite the discomfort, Rhody made sure to clean every bit of skin he could reach then washed his hair as well as he could without soap.

It may have been cooler, but it wasn't exactly frigid, so after he was reasonably clean, he began to wash his clothes. He wasn't sure what the water looked like by the time he first dipped his bloody shirt into the water, but he doubted if it was as clean as it had been when he'd filled the canteen.

He laid each of his cleaner clothing items onto the flat rock, then sat down on the small amount of free space.

He looked at the clothes then down at his naked legs and chuckled.

"What would Emma think if she saw me like this?" he asked aloud.

Yet as he sat there without a stitch of clothing, he began to think about Emma again. She was such a mystery to him, and he wished they'd met under different circumstances. When that concept reached his mind, he recalled that she had only married Carl about a year ago, so he could have seen her on one of his visits to New Braunfels. *What if he'd stopped in her father's bakery and she'd been behind the counter? Would that have changed everything? Would they have struck up a conversation? Would he have made her laugh with some of his stories of his boyhood growing up in Rhode Island?*

He then realized that he'd never heard Emma laugh. He'd heard Willie and Marty laugh, but never Emma. He could understand why she hadn't but now, more than anything else, he wanted to hear her laugh.

An hour later, Rhody was dressed and his guns were reloaded. He even fired a round through each of them before he was satisfied that they were safe to use. They'd all still need a good cleaning and lots of oil to keep them from rusting, but he should still reach Menardville in time to take care of his weapons.

He didn't bother walking any longer that night but managed to find a reasonably dry spot under the boulders and after winding his chronograph, he laid down and quickly fell asleep.

CHAPTER 8

When Rhody awakened in the morning, he felt every one of those hailstones that had struck his legs, mostly the left. He sat up then slowly stood and left his boulder cover.

The ground was already dry, so he returned some of the moisture before walking to his things and opening his saddlebag. He took out three large sticks of jerky and began chewing while he examined the trail. He wasn't surprised to find it gone after the punishing downpour followed by the pounding hail, but he didn't need the trail or even a compass to keep heading east for Menardville.

He knew the latitude and the time of year, so as he looked at the early morning sun, he knew it would be rising in the northeast, so he'd just work off of that. It wasn't as accurate as a compass by any means, but he only needed to find a town that was about twenty-five miles away. If he missed it south, he'd find the roadway.

Rhody finally loaded himself down and began a slower, more painful walk toward Menardville. His hopes for reaching the town today had been more realistically been pushed back until early tomorrow, assuming he didn't run into any more natural or human problems.

"What are we gonna do after breakfast?" Marty asked as she cut into her flapjack.

"We're going to go shopping. I think you should have a nice new dress, Marty."

"I can? That would be so nice!" she exclaimed as she beamed at Emma.

She then looked at Willie who was poking at his eggs and asked, "Would you like something at the store, Willie?"

"No, ma'am. I'm okay," he replied as he finally pushed some scrambled eggs onto his fork and slid them into his mouth.

"Are you sure? I think you could use a better shirt."

"I like this one fine."

Emma nodded and took a bite of ham wondering how much worse Willie would get before they reached San Antonio. She'd been working so hard to keep a bright outlook for him and Marty despite her own feelings of despair and hopelessness. It was difficult enough to pretend everything was all right, but to try to cheer up Willie was threatening to shatter her own façade. The last thing that Willie, or especially Marty, needed right now is for her to break down into a sobbing wreck. She needed to be strong for the children because Rhody would expect nothing less.

———

After breakfast, they strolled along the boardwalk to A.J. Smith & Sons General Store and soon entered the open doors.

It wasn't exactly a large, well-stocked mercantile, but neither of the children had even seen such a large selection before as they'd only visited the trading post north of their ranch.

Willie may have been in a foul mood, but he still walked the aisles with wide eyes. Marty wasn't bashful about pointing to the dresses and asking Emma which one she should buy.

Emma eventually walked to the counter with two dresses and new underclothing, socks and shoes for Marty, and despite his earlier refusal, two new shirts, a pair of britches that were the correct size after his recent growth spurt, underpants, socks and a pair of boots for Willie. She bought three dresses, a nightdress, socks, and undergarments for herself then added a comb and hairbrush set, three toothbrushes and a tin of tooth powder.

When she made her last trip to the counter, she looked at Marty and asked, "How about some penny candy?"

"We can have some candy?" Marty asked with wide eyes.

"You and Willie just tell the gentleman what you'd like."

Even Willie managed a smile as he and Marty pointed to various colors and flavors of the unexpected treats.

As she paid for the order, the proprietor smiled at her and said, "I don't recall seeing you around here before, ma'am. Did you and your young'uns just arrive?"

"Yes, we rode in last night, but we'll be taking the stage tomorrow."

"Well, I appreciate your business and wish you Godspeed on your journey."

"Thank you," Emma replied.

She took one heavy sack while Willie took the other and both followed Marty out of the store. It was still early, but Emma didn't know what else they could do to fill their day, so they returned to the hotel room and once inside, Emma opened the window to let some air into the stuffy room.

"Can I brush my hair now?" Marty asked.

"Let's unpack our things and I'll brush it for you. Okay?"

"Alright."

Willie then said, "I'm gonna walk around for a while."

"Don't you want to have some penny candy?"

"No, ma'am. I'll have some when I get back."

"Okay. Be careful, Willie."

"Yes, ma'am," he replied before leaving the room.

Marty watched her brother depart and asked, "Why is Willie sad?"

"I think he's worried about Rhody."

"I'm worried too, but I know that he'll find us. He killed all those Comanches and he'll find us no matter where we are."

Emma smiled at her as she rummaged through one of the sacks, found the hairbrush and joined her on the bed to begin untangling their hair.

As she brushed out Marty's snaggles, she wished she could be as optimistic as the little blonde girls by her side. It was one of the joys of being a child, even one who witnessed terrors that no one, adult or child, should ever have to see.

―――

Rhody was shuffling more than walking as the cool air was replaced by steadily rising heat. It wasn't because he didn't want to walk faster, it was just that his muscles refused to cooperate as well as they had earlier. His chest still reminded him of the bullet wound every time he made a sudden move or took a deep breath, so that contributed to his lethargic pace.

But for more than four hours that morning, he had kept his feet moving as he headed east. He knew that he'd have to stop soon because of the overbearing heat, but he wanted to get as close to Menardville as he could before he rested. He guessed he was less than twenty miles away by now, and even if he couldn't increase his speed at all, he'd reach the town by this time tomorrow.

His perfect light brown Stetson had been pummeled and soaked and become a milliner's nightmare. He'd see about buying one in Menardville and doubted if they'd have what he wanted, but knew it had to be replaced. He'd still take it with him to San Antonio to see if the local milliner could restore it using some magic tricks that regular folks couldn't be allowed to know.

―――

After leaving the hotel, Willie walked to the livery to see Jack and Morgana. He wanted to take Jack for a ride west for a few miles and hopefully spot Rhody. His horse might have gone lame after killing all the Comanches, and that would account for the delay. That horse wasn't in great condition, so his new explanation for Rhody's absence seemed more than reasonable.

He entered the big doors and spotted the liveryman changing Morgana's shoes then stopped when he was ten feet away to let him finish the job.

RHODY JONES

After one last whack with his hammer, the liveryman let Morgana's hoof return to the ground then looked at Willie and said, "Mornin', son. What can I do for ya?"

"Can I ride Jack for a little while? He's the tan Morgan."

"I reckon that'd be okay as long as your ma don't mind."

"She's not my mother. She's my aunt but my parents were killed by Comanches a few days ago, so she'll be my mother now."

"That so? Comanches done that? Musta been that bunch of renegades I've been hearin' about. Your pa stopped 'em?"

"He's my uncle. He shot one of them from over five hundred yards with his Sharps rifle and the rest ran away. They sent more after us, but he stayed behind to drive them away again. We heard the gunfire, but we were too far ahead to hear all of it. We only kept riding because he told us to come here and then go to San Antonio to wait for him."

"You reckon he killed all of them Injuns?"

"Yes, sir. But I think the old horse that he had left must have gone lame because he should be here by now. I'm going to ride west for a few miles to see if I can find him."

"You ain't got a gun, son. That's not a smart thing to do."

"I left my Winchester in the hotel, but I'm not going that far, and Jack is a good horse."

"Both of those Morgans are mighty fine critters. I'll help you get him saddled."

Ten minutes later, Willie left the livery on Jack and headed south until he reached the spot where they had entered the town then headed west.

He rode for more than twenty minutes, scanning the horizons for any sign of Rhody, but only spotted a lone coyote. He finally wheeled Jack back to the east to return to Menardville.

He would have had to ride another four hours before he spotted Rhody who was already asleep under a stubby oak.

———

Rhody slept most of the day until he finally stirred in the late afternoon. He was even stiffer now than he'd been when he started out that morning, but he'd have to wait until the temperature moderated a little before he resumed his long march.

He leaned on the oak's trunk and scratched his stubbled chin as he planned what should be the last leg of his journey. He probably could make it in another fourteen to sixteen hours but knew that he'd still need some sleep sometime during the night. He'd walk as far as he could today and hopefully would see Menardville's magnificent skyline sometime tomorrow morning.

RHODY JONES

He slowly rose to his feet, stretched and twisted his aching body then began heading for some nearby boulders. He wanted to climb on top to scan the entire horizon and would have used the oak, but the branches didn't seem stout enough to bear his weight.

He had just set his right boot onto the lowest rock when he froze at the chilling sound of a rattlesnake's buzz just to his right. He slowly turned to look at the angry snake and winced, wondering if his luck would ever change.

He knew he could probably carefully move to his left, but he decided to go on the offense and loosened his hammer loop and gradually slid his Colt from its holster.

The rattler hadn't changed his tune as Rhody cocked the pistol's hammer and very, very slowly brought the sights in line with the snake's flicking tongue just five feet away.

The two very different creatures stared at each other until the one with the bigger bite struck. The Colt's muzzle blasted out a .44 that reached the snake's head almost instantly.

The snake's body writhed for almost a minute while Rhody holstered his pistol and pulled the hammer loop into place.

When the snake finally ceased its motion, Rhody stepped over to the four-foot-long reptile, grabbed it by the body just behind what used to be its head and carried it back to his camp. He'd do his reconnaissance later but now, he'd build a fire and have a filling lunch of roast rattler. He didn't have any salt, but it didn't matter.

After he'd skinned then cut up the snake meat into chunks, he roasted three of them over his fire then dropped the cooked meat onto a flat rock before roasting the rest. He stuffed the long rattle into his pocket as a gift for Willie when he caught up with them in San Antonio.

When he finally made his climb to the boulder's peak, he didn't discover anything that posed a threat, but didn't see anyone or anything that could make the next twenty miles any easier. At least he'd do it on a full stomach and had enough snake meat to carry him through until he enjoyed a real, sit-down dinner.

By the time Willie returned, Emma's silvery blonde hair shone, and Marty's golden yellow hair was straight and tangle-free. All of their things were stacked on the dresser, so they'd be easy to pack before they left.

Emma had thought about buying a travel bag at the store, but decided it was just a waste of money…Rhody's money. It seemed everything she did, said or touched reminded her of Rhody, and inspired visions of his lifeless body lying on the broiling Texas ground. She hadn't gone as far as to imagine the vultures and coyotes that would always find food to scavenge, but just the imagined sight of him lying with lifeless, staring eyes looking back at her was enough.

It was now Marty who kept her from growing too despondent and not the other way around. It was almost as if Marty knew that Emma needed to be cheered up despite Emma's positive demeanor.

When Willie entered the hot room, she asked, "So, how was the ride?"

"How did you know I went for a ride and not just a walk?"

"You don't get that dusty from just walking, Mister Ernst."

"Oh. It was okay. Mister Wallace, he's the liveryman, had all the shoes changed when I got back."

"Good. We're going to get some lunch soon then stop at the livery to pick up Rhody's sextant. When we come back, I'll read you both a story. Okay?"

"When did you buy a book?" Marty asked.

"I didn't. I found it in one of Rhody's packs."

"Oh. Is it a good book?"

"I don't know, but it looks interesting. It's about a man who makes a boat that can go underwater."

Willie quickly asked, "Really? How can a boat go underwater? How can people breathe down there?"

Emma smiled at him and replied, "I guess we'll have to read the story to find out. He had other books in the pannier, but they were much thicker and probably weren't as much fun."

Emma knew her objective had been met when she saw Willie's smile. It may only be a small victory, but it was a first step.

―――

Rhody left his oak shelter as the sun was low in the sky. It was still hot, but with the sun setting in another hour or so, the temperatures should drop a little. He was making a little better time after starting out as his muscles seemed to be recovering. His biggest problem now was his chest wound. He hadn't replaced his leather bandage because he thought that taking it off would be more of a problem than a solution. At least it hadn't started bleeding again when he'd removed it before his impromptu bath.

While his speed was faster than it had been that morning, it was still nowhere close to his normal walking speed. He was making about two miles an hour on level ground but much slower when he had to avoid obstacles and climb down and up gullies.

He was only twelve miles away from Menardville when he was simply too tired to continue and had to stop for the night.

RHODY JONES

He wanted to arrive tomorrow and still be fit enough to ride out of town within an hour after he arrived.

With two full canteens and fresh dinner in his saddlebags, he didn't bother looking for water but searched for a reasonably comfortable flat space.

It was just before midnight when he stretched out on the ground using his sad hat for a pillow.

―――

The lamp in their room had burned until nine o'clock as Emma read *Twenty Thousand Leagues Under the Sea* to Willie and Marty. She left the last two chapters for the stagecoach ride tomorrow, and she was just as anxious as her charges were to learn the fate of the *Nautilus* and Captain Nemo.

Rhody's sextant was in its case on the dresser with his pouch of maps. When they had stopped at the livery to go through the panniers one last time, she wondered what would happen to the two Morgans and the mule after they left Menardville. She imagined that the liveryman would just take possession after a week or so. She had already decided to keep the sextant herself but would give the maps to Willie. She still wasn't sure how Rhody's uncle would react to her telegram, but she hadn't changed her mind about not including the news of his nephew's death.

As much as her logical mind told her that it was true, her heart focused on the incredibly slim possibility that Rhody would meet them in San Antonio as he'd promised.

———

Rhody's alarm awakened him with the predawn, which had only given him five hours of sleep, but he felt remarkably refreshed as he began what should be his last day on foot.

He quickly polished off the last of the snake meat followed it with a long swallow of water then rapidly loaded himself with his rifles, saddlebags and canteens. He tossed the empty water bag aside before he stepped away from his crude camp.

His legs were still sore and his side ached, but he didn't let either affect his pace. He'd checked the stars before he left and knew he was heading east.

When the sun rose an hour later at his eleven o'clock position, he knew he was heading in the right direction. He evaluated the landscape before him and knew that in just a few more hours, he'd spot Menardville and as soon as he could, he'd ride south to find Emma, Willie and Marty.

———

"Have either of you ridden on a stagecoach before?" Emma asked as she cut her small steak.

"No, ma'am," Willie replied, "We only rode in the wagon."

"Well, the stagecoach is a lot faster, but a lot dustier, too. There aren't going to be any other passengers on the ride to Fredericksburg, so I'll sit with Marty in the middle of the front seat and you can sit in the middle of the back seat, so you won't get too dusty."

"Are you going to finish the story, Aunt Emma?"

"Of course, I will, Marty. It's a pretty exciting story, isn't it?"

"I can't wait to find out what happens at the end."

Willie took a bite of a butter-coated biscuit then said, "I wonder if Rhody could build a submarine like Captain Nemo."

Emma smiled at him, noticing the lack of sadness in his question then replied, "I'm sure he could."

"I wish we could go sailing with him on one of his boats, too."

"We'll have to ask him when he gets to San Antonio, Willie."

Willie was about to say that Rhody wouldn't be able to answer the question but held his tongue when he looked at Marty's happy face.

Emma then said, "The stage leaves in another hour, so we need to finish eating then go back to the hotel and get our things. Did you see the stagecoach arrive out front as we were leaving?"

"I saw it, Aunt Emma, and it looked really big. It had six horses, too!"

"And we'll have it all to ourselves."

Just before eight o'clock, Emma and Marty stepped into the stage and were followed quickly by Willie. Because they were the only passengers as soon as their burlap sack and two cloth bags were stored in the coach's boot, the driver snapped the reins and the coach lurched once then rolled rapidly out of Menardville.

The shotgun rider set his scattergun in the footwell then leaned back in the seat and watched the road ahead. It was fifty miles to Fredericksburg, and they should arrive by mid-afternoon, so he was looking forward to a good dinner.

As the coach raced south along the road throwing up a large plume of dust in its wake, Emma began reading.

The shotgun rider glanced west as the stage rolled and rocked on the uneven roadway then turned to the driver and said, "I coulda swore I saw some feller walkin' in from the west. Maybe my eyes were playin' tricks on me."

The driver took a quick look then returned his eyes to the front before replying, "You're gettin' old, Ed."

"I know that, but I figured my eyes were still pretty good. They gotta be good if we run into those damned white-cloaked bastards."

"They haven't bothered anybody for a couple of weeks, Ed. They're probably down in San Antone drinkin' away their haul from the last one."

"I shoulda shot those bastards, Joe."

"Nah. You woulda only got one of 'em, but they sure woulda put a .44 in your gut."

"I still shoulda let 'em have both barrels."

"They didn't even get a hundred bucks out of that robbery. They probably rode off to find better pastures. Hell, we ain't exactly Wells Fargo or Overland."

"You're probably right, Joe," Ed said as he reached for his shotgun.

"I'm always right, Ed."

———

Rhody had spotted Menardville just thirty minutes earlier and seen the coach speed across his vision. He grinned knowing that the same stage had probably carried Emma and the children to San Antonio yesterday or the day before.

He found new life in his step as he drew closer to his destination. He knew he must look like the devil with his thick stubble and filthy clothes, but he remembered the days on those cattle drive where he would have fit right in. It was his hat's condition that really irritated him.

The stage was already eight miles south when Rhody finally arrived in town and walked directly to the livery to find his Morgans and make a deal for Dent.

When he walked through the doors, the liveryman grinned at the stranger and said, "I reckon you must be Rhody Jones. Your missus told me you was comin'."

"My missus?" Rhody asked as he walked inside and looked at his two Morgans.

"Yup. She said to put new shoes on all of 'em and that you'd be here in a few days, but you sure got here quicker. Did you really hafta fight off a bunch of Comanches?"

"Yes, sir. There were eight of them, and one put a round too close to my ticker for comfort."

"I see the damage. Too bad you didn't get here an hour ago. Your missus and young'uns just left on the stage. I reckon they weren't expectin' you so soon."

"*They just left on that stage?*" he asked excitedly.

RHODY JONES

"Yup. You gonna chase after 'em? Your horses are ready to go, and the mule is in good shape, too."

Rhody forgot about the big meal, bath or anything else. He was only an hour behind Emma and the kids.

He said, "I'll tell you what. I need to get a few things out of my panniers then I'll load my rifles, saddlebags and canteens on Jack, and leave the rest with you."

"I already owe you some money 'cause your wife paid for more'n a week."

"It doesn't matter. I've got to get riding. I can probably match their speed and I'll get something to eat and clean up in Fredericksburg."

"Well, Mister Jones, I'm right grateful for the mule and pack saddle. The least I can do is help you get your horses saddled while you check your packs for anything else you might want to put in your saddlebags."

Rhody nodded then strode quickly to the packs. The only things he found that he wanted to take with him was his ammunition, a change of clothing, his shaving kit and his cleaning kits. He was smiling as he moved everything into his saddlebags knowing that Emma had taken his sextant and maps even though she probably thought he was dead.

It only took twelve minutes to have both Morgans ready before Rhody mounted Jack and led Morgana out of the livery, waved at the liveryman and headed south at a fast trot.

He felt exhilarated having the wind in his face and not having to move his legs. He was already hungry, so he began chewing on jerky as the tan Morgan gelding devoured the road. He planned on riding Jack for two hours before shifting to Morgana. If they were lucky enough to cross a stream, he'd adjust his schedule.

He couldn't see the coach ahead and doubted if he'd see it before he reached Fredericksburg, but he wasn't about to slow his pace.

He was off in his calculations as the West Texas Line didn't have the resources to keep a large number of spare horses, so they couldn't afford to push the teams as much as the bigger outfits.

Rhody was actually gaining on the stage as he and his Morgans left their own large dust cloud trailing behind them.

As he rode, he took a long drink from his canteen and knew that he'd have to let the horses drink soon because they were doing all the work, so he began scanning the passing landscape for a creek when he spotted a windmill in the distance on his left.

RHODY JONES

When he was closer, he spotted a ranch house down a short access road then turned left and walked his Morgans toward the house.

He pulled up and shouted, "Hello, the house!"

No one opened the door, but he heard someone reply from his right, "What can I do for you, mister?"

He turned to find an older man walking out of the barn wiping his hands on his britches.

"I was just wondering if I could water my horses at your trough."

"Go ahead. I was just a bit nervous 'cause of the firepower you're carryin'."

He walked Jack to the trough then stepped down as the Morgans lowered their heads to the water.

"I can understand that, but they came in handy when I ran afoul of some Comanches out west."

"That explains that hole and blood on your shirt. How many of 'em did you take down?"

"Nine who were sober and four who were deep into the ranch owner's jug of white lightning. They murdered two families and burned their ranch houses. If you have a hankering to add to your herd, there are a bunch of mavericks a couple of days ride west."

"No, thanks. I'm not about to ride into that hornet's nest."

"Well, I appreciate letting me water my horses. We'll be heading south now. I've got to run down the stage."

"You ain't far behind. It only passed by here about an hour ago."

"Really? I figured I was a good hour and a half behind."

"You're probably movin' a lot faster than that old stage. You have a handsome pair of horses there."

"I'm kind of partial to them," Rhody replied as he switched the trail rope.

"Well, I hope you catch up to that coach pretty soon. Why are you chasin' it, anyway?"

Rhody mounted Morgana then looked down and smiled at him before answering, "My wife and children are on that stage. They probably thought I was dead."

The rancher grinned at him and said, "Well, you'd better get ridin' and surprise 'em."

Rhody tipped his misshapen hat then wheeled Morgana around and headed back down the access road.

He soon had Morgana moving at the same fast trot and was still smiling after telling the rancher that Emma was his wife and Willie and Marty were his children. He still wondered why the liveryman thought that Emma was his wife. *Did she tell him that or did the liveryman just assume it?*

As the coach headed south, Joe turned to Ed and asked, "Does number one seem like he's holdin' the rest of 'em back? We're not movin' as fast as we should, and that ain't very fast anyway."

"He seems all right to me. Maybe you're gettin' too old yourself."

Joe snickered then snapped the reins to see if he could inspire number one to pick up the pace just a little.

Inside the cabin, Emma finished the story and closed the book.

"Well, what do you think?"

Wille had the Winchester '66 across his lap as he answered, "I wish the *Nautilus* didn't have to sink at the end. I didn't like Captain Nemo, though."

Emma was wearing Jack's gunbelt as she smiled at him then looked at Marty and asked, "How about you, Marty?"

"I'm glad that the submarine sank. It was sinking all those other ships for no reason," she replied then asked, "Do you have any more books like that, Aunt Emma?"

"Not like this. Maybe when we get to Fredericksburg, we can see if they have any others like it. We'll be staying there overnight, and the store should still be open when we get there."

"Is it a big store like the one in Menardville?"

"Oh, no. Fredericksburg is a much bigger town, so I'm sure that the store will be much larger, too."

"That's good."

Now that she wasn't occupied by reading, she set the book on her right then picked up Rhody's satchel of maps and opened the flap.

After extracting the map of Texas, she unfolded the large sheet and put her finger just south of Menardville.

"This is where we are right now, and this is where we'll be sleeping tonight. See San Antonio down there a little bit?"

"It doesn't seem so far away on the map," Marty said.

"No, it doesn't. Does it?"

Willie then asked, "Is there a map of Rhode Island in there?"

"No, Willie. Rhody said that he only had maps of the southwestern United States."

"Oh. Just wondering," Willie replied as he stared out the right-side window.

Emma sighed then refolded the map and returned it to the pouch.

Eight miles ahead, Potty Williams, Al Frobisher and Chuck McKay were sitting on their horses hidden in a small copse of cottonwoods. If anyone really looked for them, they would be spotted, but they didn't expect anyone to be paying that much attention because it had been a couple of weeks since the last job.

"How much longer do we wait?" asked Al.

Chuck replied, "They should be by in another hour or so. You anxious to put on your robe, Al?"

"Hell, no! That damned thing is hot as blazes. I don't know why we gotta wear 'em anyway. Why don't we just wear regular face coverin' like other guys?"

"'Cause we ain't exactly near any big towns to go off and hide. Besides, wearin' these outfits scare the bejesus outta folks, including the law."

"I suppose. I hope we get more outta this job than we did from that last one."

"We'll do okay. Let's get the horses ready first."

"Alright," Al replied before he dismounted.

They each had a heavy sack hanging from their saddles. They dropped the sacks to the ground and pulled out an enormous white sheet and began to drape it over their horses. There were cutouts for the saddle horn and scabbard, as well as slits for the stirrups and another cutout for the horse's head. After each of their animals was shrouded, they tied them down around the horse's necks with the attached lines before taking their Ku Klux Klan lookalike outfits from their sacks and setting them on the ground. They put their hats into the bag then hung it over their saddle horns.

All they had to do now was to pull on their robes, mount and pull their Winchesters. They'd used the disguises three times before, but never set up in the same spot. Sometimes it was south of Fredericksburg and some were north, but none were more than six miles from the Star Six ranch where they worked. The boss gave them Saturday afternoons off, and they made the most of it.

―――

After leaving the ranch, Rhody was pleased when he had learned that he was gaining on the coach because it wasn't a first-rate outfit, just like the *Vivienne* hadn't been a first-rate ship. He remembered his brief encounter with the stagecoach before he'd left the roadway to head west and how the shotgun rider had kept his scattergun's muzzle pointed at him as the coach rolled past.

RHODY JONES

The waitress in Frederickson had mentioned the reason for his anxiety, but once he'd left the road heading west, he hadn't worried about the oddly garbed holdup men. Now he was riding down that road again, so he renewed his scanning of the landscape. He wasn't leading a pack mule this time, but he did have two very nice horses and some weapons that desperately needed cleaning. He had five dollars in his pocket, too. He grinned when he realized how little he was worth at the moment.

Forty-five minutes later, he spotted the coach's dust cloud and even though he knew he'd been closing the gap, he was surprised that he had caught up so quickly.

He fought the desire to nudge Morgana into a faster speed, knowing that he'd catch up to the stage long before it reached Fredericksburg and he didn't want to spook the nervous shotgun rider into throwing a load of buckshot his way.

"Here it comes!" Al exclaimed with a muffled voice under his pointed white hood.

"We got another ten minutes before we show ourselves, so don't get too anxious. You almost shot the driver the last time," Chuck replied.

"I'm okay."

Their Winchesters were cocked as they waited for the stagecoach to reach the trees.

Rhody spotted the stage in the middle of the dust cloud and slowed Morgana down to match its speed. He was about two miles back and didn't want to get much closer. He wasn't about to try to stop the coach just to let Emma know that he was alive. He was smiling as he imagined her face when she saw him. Willie and Marty would be excited too, but he really wanted to ask her if she'd told the liveryman that she was his wife and whether he should read anything into it. He also wanted to see if he could make her laugh.

He was still watching the coach when he spotted a flash of white coming from some trees to the left of the stagecoach and immediately nudged Morgana into a canter. He didn't pull either rifle yet because he wasn't sure what was happening, but the recently revived memory of the stagecoach holdup two weeks earlier was on his mind.

Joe spotted the white-robed highwaymen before they exited the trees and shouted to Ed, "It's them!"

Ed pulled back his shotgun's hammers as Joe began furiously snapping the reins to get the coach past the threat, but he'd have to shift off the road to the right to give Ed a clear shot.

RHODY JONES

As the stagecoach's front wheels crossed the berm along the roadway, the cabin bounced on its tired springs tossing Emma and the children from their seats.

After they managed to get back onto their wildly rocking seats, Willie had a better view and spotted the outlaws in their recognizable outfits.

"It's the Klan!" he shouted as he cocked the Winchester's hammer.

Emma had seen him pull the hammer back and shouted, "Willie, do not try to be a hero! Let the shotgun rider do his job!"

"Rhody isn't here, Aunt Emma! I'll do what he asked me to do!"

Emma knew her protests would fall on deaf ears, so she just held onto Marty and tried to see what was happening.

———

The three outlaws had been surprised by the driver's maneuver to avoid them and as the coach shot past, Chuck quickly brought his Winchester to his shoulder and fired at the shotgun rider.

Ed saw the muzzle flash and was about to unleash both barrels when the .44 slid across his right forearm then went on its merry way. He jerked his arm back in pain, dropping the shotgun which fell butt first down the front of the stagecoach then slammed into the yoke, setting off both shells of buckshot before it rammed into the dirt. The loud explosion right behind them spooked the already anxious team, so they shifted even more to the right as Joe fought to keep them under control while Ed tried to staunch the bleeding from his arm's gunshot wound.

The three highwaymen then turned and chased after the stagecoach as it bounced and yawed across the rough ground.

Rhody had closed the gap to just over a mile when he saw the three outlaws mount their attack. He didn't change speeds but slid the Sharps-Borshadt from it scabbard. It had a .50-140 cartridge in its chamber, but he didn't expect to hit them. They weren't Comanche warriors or even white soldiers. They were nothing but thieves who were trying to steal from a shoestring stagecoach operation.

Potty, Al and Chuck didn't pay any attention to the north as they chased after the bouncing stagecoach. Even if Chuck didn't know he'd hit the shotgun rider, all of them had heard the shotgun's report and then rode past the fallen scattergun as they chased the stage.

The driver and shotgun rider may have a pistol, but none of them expected any resistance.

RHODY JONES

Joe glanced back and knew it was a losing proposition. Ed couldn't draw his Remington, and Joe knew that he was far from a good shot with his Colt. He began slowing the coach hoping that they wouldn't shoot him.

Willie felt the stage slowing down then dropped to his knees and pointed the Winchester's muzzle at the back window on the left.

Emma watched him then released her hammer loop and extracted the Colt. She'd fired a pistol before but never shot anyone. She already resolved that she wouldn't hesitate if those bastards tried to harm the children. They were all she had now, and she wasn't going to allow herself to be taken hostage again, not now or ever.

"Stay brave, Marty," she said as she pulled back the Colt's hammer.

Marty's voice trembled as she said, "I wish Rhody was here."

"We all do, sweetheart," Emma replied as she aimed her Colt at the back window on the right side.

―――

Rhody was within range of the Sharps-Borshadt, but even though the stage was slowing, it was still moving, and he wanted to get close enough to switch to the Winchester if they decided to make this into a gunfight rather than make a hasty escape. If they chose to run then he wasn't about to follow. His job was to protect Emma and the children and get them to San Antonio.

By the time the stage came to a stop, Rhody was just four hundred yards back and slowed Morgana to a slow trot. He cocked the Sharps-Borshadt's hammer then brought it level as he watched the outlaws approach the coach. He was about to fire when he heard a Winchester's bark from the coach. None of the outlaws were hurt, but he could tell that they were startled when they backed their horses from the coach.

Then he heard a pistol shot and knew that Willie and Emma must have Jack's weapons with them. Now it was time to let those bastards know that they weren't just facing a woman and a boy.

He set his sights right between two of the white hoods and squeezed his trigger.

Chuck, Potty and Al were surprised to hear gunfire erupt from the coach and as soon as they decided to start firing into the cabin, they were shocked when a much louder report echoed from behind them. As they turned, Chuck and Al could hear the large round buzz between them through their cloth-covered ears.

They all turned to look to the north as Rhody set Morgana to a medium trot but kept the empty Sharps-Borshadt in his hands hoping that they believed he had reloaded.

RHODY JONES

"Who the hell is that?" shouted Potty.

With the two shooters in the coach and the man with the big gun heading their way, it wasn't a difficult decision for Chuck.

"Let's get the hell out of here!" he shouted then wheeled his horse to the east and set him to a gallop as he leaned against the draped horse's neck.

Potty and Al both raced right behind him as they headed for the protection of the trees hoping that the rider with the big gun didn't follow. None of them had recognized the stranger's horses, so they had no idea who he was. The only thing that made any sense was that he was a bounty hunter, but none knew that they had rewards on their heads.

Inside the coach, Emma still held her cocked pistol in her hand after taking her one shot, but she didn't even know she was holding the Colt. That sound, that unique deep rifle report was so familiar to her, but she didn't dare hope that it was Rhody who had made the shot. Maybe it was just some sheriff who had a Sharps rifle of his own.

Willie had released his Winchester's hammer then looked at Emma and said, "That sounded like Rhody's big gun."

"I know, but it's probably a lawman who has one of his own."

Marty peeked around Emma and said, "I think it's Rhody."

She finally released the Colt's hammer and slid it home before she replied, "Just stay put until the driver tells us it's safe. Okay?"

"Okay," replied Marty before Willie said, "Yes, ma'am."

Rhody watched the three outlaws race away with their white robes flapping in the wind and their horse's sheets billowing away.

He kept Morgana to a medium trot as he slid the Sharps-Borshadt back into its scabbard and put his right hand in the air to make sure that the shotgun rider didn't get too excited.

When he passed the fallen shotgun, he lowered his hand and soon reached the back of the coach and stepped down.

Joe had watched him approach and was enormously relieved, but soon turned his attention to his wounded shotgun rider.

Rhody dropped Morgana's reins then stepped closer to the back window and was about to tell Willie not to fire when he spotted Emma's silver blonde hair in the shadows and then stopped and looked at her stunned blue eyes before he spotted Marty grinning at him.

"Rhody!" she screamed as she hopped from the seat.

Rhody swung the door open and Marty leapt from the coach into his arms.

RHODY JONES

He kissed her and set her down as Willie exited with Jack's Winchester and a giant smile.

"I heard you fire your Winchester, Willie. You did well."

"Thank you, Rhody. We all thought you were killed by the Comanches."

"It wasn't as close as you might have expected, but I did have problems with the weather and my feet."

"You were shot!" he exclaimed as he stared at Rhody's shirt.

"I'm all right."

He then lifted his eyes back to the stagecoach door as Emma slowly stepped down and wordlessly approached him.

Neither said a word as she put her arms around him then buried her face into his chest and began to shake as her tears began soaking his shirt. He put his arms around her and let her cry. She'd been through so much and now, just when she thought she was safe, those three idiots had to do this.

Emma wasn't crying because she had been frightened because she had found that she had more courage than she'd realized. Nor was she upset because of all of the incredible trauma she'd experienced over the past few days. She was weeping tears of unrelenting joy because Rhody was alive and well after all. Maybe it was their prayers that had brought him back to her and the children, but she suspected it was Rhody's own courage and determination that had made this reunion possible. She was holding him now and vowed to never let him go.

Joe finally finished helping Ed then looked down at the scene and thought that their woman passenger was just grateful to the stranger. He was might appreciative himself but wasn't about to hug the man.

Emma finally lifted her head from Rhody's chest and turned her blue eyes to look into his hazels and asked, "What happened? Why were you so late?"

"I had to walk, but that's a long story and I think the driver wants to get to Fredericksburg."

"Will you ride in the coach with us?" she asked as she wiped her eyes.

"Let me talk to the driver. I'm sure he won't mind, but I only have five dollars if he wants me to pay for the fare."

Emma laughed lightly then said, "I still have most of your money, Rhody. I think you'll be all right."

He smiled at her then said, "You three get in the coach, and I'll join you shortly."

She nodded then said, "Thank you, Rhody," before she ushered Marty and Willie back into the stage.

RHODY JONES

Rhody was still smiling as he turned and walked to the front of the stage then looked up at the driver and noticed the shotgun rider's bloody arm.

"I really appreciate you showin' up when you did, mister. Old Joe here took a .44 in the arm and we were in big trouble."

"Glad I could help. Old Joe needs to see a doctor, so I imagine you need to get rolling again. Mind if I tie off my horses in back and climb inside?"

'I'd be grateful to have you along. You sure scared those bastards. I just wish we coulda figured out who they were."

"When you get to Fredericksburg, tell the sheriff that one of them was riding a dark gray horse with two white boots in back and another one was on a black. The last one was riding a dark brown with a black tail. That should narrow down his search. I don't think they were Klan, either. I've actually run into a few of those crazy bastards and those outfits they wore weren't right."

"Well, I'll be damned! I'll sure as hell tell the sheriff when we get in."

Rhody waved, returned to his Morgans, tied Jack to the back of the stage then mounted Morgana and trotted her to where he'd seen the shotgun.

After returning the scattergun to the driver, he tied Morgana to the other side of the coach then climbed inside and took a seat beside Willie. He'd barely put butt to leather before the coach lurched then rocked and rolled its way back onto the roadway.

Once they were moving normally again, Emma asked, "What happened after we left, Rhody? We heard gunfire, but it faded away."

"I was waiting in a shallow gully when I spotted four of the Comanches come around the south side of that hill. Then I saw another four come from around the north. I waited until they were within range of my Sharps-Borshadt hoping that they'd run when I let loose, but they had a couple of Spencers and…"

Rhody didn't skip any details about the encounter as Willie sat beside him with his mouth open.

"…after the last warrior shot the horses, I knew he was planning on leaving me to chase you down, so I cut him off and wound up shooting his horse. After I killed him, I had to walk to Menardville which is why I couldn't make it in time."

"You said that you had problems with the weather. Is that what happened to your hat?"

Rhody removed his flattened, droopy Stetson, looked at it and grinned before replying, "The wind and rain was bad enough, but it was the hail that really beat it down to this disaster."

"That was a powerful storm, but we didn't get any hail. How big were they?"

"They were mostly pea-sized, but there was a minute or so where they were about the size of walnuts. I had covered myself with my canteen to protect my head and my saddlebags were laid across my torso, so only my left leg took the beating. Do you know what really spooked me about the storm?"

"I imagine that none of it was very pleasant."

"It was when a lightning bolt struck nearby, and I realized I was a walking lightning rod with my rifles. I had nowhere to hide them, so I only could hope that I'd get lucky. Then when I was lying on my side when the hails began hammering into me, I began to worry that one of the big stones might punch into one of the cartridges that were in the saddlebags. That would have been a mess, but it was too late to change anything, so I spent those few minutes wondering if either of the boxes of cartridges were lying inside the saddlebags with the percussion end facing up."

"What would have happened if one hit it?" Willie asked.

"Probably nothing because the hailstones were round and the saddlebag's leather and the box's cardboard would have absorbed most of the impact, but it did give me something to think about it."

Emma asked, "When did you get to Menardville? It had to be soon after we left."

"I actually watched your stagecoach roll out of town, but I didn't know you were on board until I talked to the liveryman. I'm glad that I didn't stop to have the big breakfast I was looking forward to, or take the time to have the bath and shave that I still need. I thought you were already in San Antonio."

"I could have seen you if I'd look west then, wouldn't I?"

"Probably. None of that matters now, Emma. We're going to be arriving in Fredericksburg in a few hours and I'll be happy to treat everyone to a big late lunch."

Emma smiled then reached into her pocket, pulled out the remaining cash and held it out to him as she said, "You should keep your five dollars, sir. Here's what's left of the money you gave us."

Rhody accepted the bills stuffed them into his pocket then spotted his map pouch and sextant case beside her.

"I see that you remembered to take my sextant with you, Emma. Why did you bother if you didn't think I'd survived the fight with the Comanches?"

Emma picked up the case slid her fingers across the polished maple surface and said, "I wanted to keep it because I knew that you treasured it."

RHODY JONES

"Thank you for bringing it, Emma, but I'm much more grateful for the reason why you did."

She dropped her eyes to the case and softly said, "I thought…I thought it was all I would ever have of you."

"Well, I'm with you now, Emma."

She lifted her eyes to look across the dust-filled air of the coach's cabin then smiled.

"Yes, you are here now, and looking as if you'd just returned from a long cattle drive."

Rhody laughed then pulled his battered hat back onto his head and replied, "That's what I thought when I reached Menardville. I'll get all cleaned up when we get to Fredericksburg. I have a spare shirt in my saddlebags."

"I have another one with me and a pair of your britches, too. My dress was beyond repair when we arrived in town, so I changed into your clothes before we went shopping."

"That makes them special, I guess."

"So, what do we do when we get to Fredericksburg?"

"After I drop off Jack and Morgana at a livery, we'll get something to eat then we'll get a couple of hotel rooms before I head over to the barbershop. When I return, we'll see what we need to do next. I do have to seriously clean all my guns, and I'll have to clean your Colt and Willie's Winchester, too."

"Can I help?" Willie quickly asked.

Rhody turned to his seatmate and replied, "You'd better, mister. You're the one who made it dirty."

Willie grinned at Rhody before he looked down at the Winchester on his lap.

The rest of the ride was filled with normal conversation that didn't touch on what would happen when they arrived in San Antonio tomorrow.

Rhody knew that he wanted to keep Emma, Willie and Marty with him as his family, but didn't want to make Emma uncomfortable with the idea while she still grieved over the loss of the husband whom she had loved. Even though he knew he still didn't understand the real Emma, he wanted to discover as much as he could about her. He didn't know her maiden name or even her age. She looked to be in the early twenties, but he'd never asked.

She was a remarkably pretty woman and her light blonde hair accented those piercing blue eyes. Many men would stop there, but he wanted to learn more about her. Hearing her laugh was just the first step. Now that they were out of danger, he'd let her get past the last week of almost constant terror before he even mentioned the idea of really becoming the most important person in their new family.

———

RHODY JONES

When the stage pulled into Fredericksburg, the driver first stopped at the sheriff's office where he explained what had happened, including Rhody's description of the outlaws' horses then dropped his shotgun rider at the doctor's office before pulling up before the Walcott Hotel.

Rhody stepped out first and was followed by Willie. He then helped Marty to the ground before he took Emma's hand to assist her exit. When he had taken her hand, he realized that he had never even touched her before.

Emma knew it as well because when she did take his hand, she felt a sudden flush run through her that she hadn't anticipated.

Once she was standing on the street, Rhody released her hand and said, "The driver will bring your bags into the hotel. I'll just tie off Jack and Morgana on the hitchrail and accompany you inside."

Emma took Marty's hand and was still feeling flushed before she replied, "Alright."

Rhody smiled at her then walked to the back of the stage and untied his two Morgans before tying them to the hitchrail four feet away.

———

Twenty minutes later after leaving their things in their rooms and with Rhody wearing his spare shirt, they entered Mabel's Diner and found a table near the window.

After giving their orders to the waitress, Rhody smiled across the table at Emma then looked at Willie and Marty in turn as he recalled the last time he'd seen them before he met the Comanches.

He then asked Emma, "Did you know what I was thinking as I watched you, Willie and Marty ride away?"

"That we were deserting you?"

Rhody shook his head and replied, "Hardly that, ma'am. I felt as if I was losing my family. I've never had anyone but my Uncle Richard, so I never knew what it was like to have a family. Yet when I watched all of you riding away, I didn't think about the Comanches. All I could think of was that I was protecting my family."

Emma then asked, "Speaking of family, are we going to tell the Brandt family what happened? No one else knows, and I think they should be told."

"We'll take a carriage up to New Braunfels on Monday."

"Can you tell them? I wasn't well-regarded by their family either."

"I'll handle it, Emma."

"Thank you."

Willie then asked, "Will you tell our grandma and grandpa too, Rhody?"

Rhody quickly shifted his eyes to Willie and replied, "You didn't tell me you had family in New Braunfels, Willie. When was the last time you saw them?"

"I was six, but Marty was only two, so she doesn't remember them at all."

"Do you remember where they live?"

"I think so."

"Okay, Willie, we'll visit your grandparents, too."

Willie grinned as he said, "Thank you, Rhody."

Rhody nodded then glanced at Emma wondering if she had known about their grandparents or what the potential impact would be. When he told them about the loss of most of their family, it was likely that they would want Willie and Marty to live with them. He knew that he couldn't deny them their right to raise their grandchildren, so unless they were rock-hearted people, he would most likely lose two members of his new family. He just didn't know how Willie and Marty would react to that change. He imagined that they would both be happy to stay with their grandparents, and that was what mattered.

Emma hadn't been on the ranch long enough to know the Ernst family well enough to discuss extended family. When Willie had mentioned grandparents, she made the same leap that Rhody had made. But there was something else that had sprung into her mind when Rhody had talked about family.

Although she was rejected by her father, she missed her sister who lived in nearby Seguin. She knew that her mother had remained silent when her father had interrogated her and then had Carl marry her before he banned her from the house but could understand why she had. Her father, like many German men, was a strict disciplinarian and absolute ruler in his home. Her mother wouldn't dare challenge him even if it meant she might never see her younger daughter again.

She then looked at Rhody and asked, "After we leave New Braunfels, can we swing by Seguin so I can visit with my sister?"

"Of course, we can. We'll probably have to stay there overnight before returning to San Antonio anyway."

"That would be even better. I'd like you to meet my sister's family."

"You never talked about her very much. Was she upset when you were leaving?"

"She was very upset, but there was nothing she could do about it. I haven't written to her in months and I only received one letter and that was in December, just before Christmas.

RHODY JONES

She said she was pregnant again, so this would be her fourth child. She has a boy and two girls, and I'm pretty sure that her husband wants another son to balance the scale."

Rhody chuckled then replied, "I'm sure he'll be happy even if she's a girl."

Emma just smiled at the thought of seeing her sister again but wasn't pleased with the prospect of meeting her husband again.

Their food arrived, and Rhody attacked his thick steak with a vengeance. He barely noticed the side dishes as his knife and fork demolished the defenseless cut of beef.

Forty minutes later, they returned to the hotel where Rhody said, "I'll set my watch's alarm for six o'clock then I'll tap on your door when Willie and I make our way down to the washroom."

"Then you'll treat us all to a big breakfast?" Emma asked with a smile.

"Yes, ma'am, and I'll make short work of that, too."

Emma and Marty then entered their room before Willie and Rhody took a short walk down the hallway to the adjoining room and went inside.

After Rhody tossed his dilapidated hat onto the dresser, he unbuckled his gunbelt and hung it over the bedpost. Then he walked to where his saddlebags were sitting in the corner and opened the flap while Willie sat on the bed watching.

"I thought you might like this, Willie," he said as he removed the rattlesnake's warning tail then walked to the bed and handed it to him.

"This is really big, Rhody. How'd you get it?"

"I was climbing a rock when the owner of that rattle let me know I wasn't a welcome guest. Normally, I'd take him at his word and just back away, but I was hungry, so I shot him. After skinning him for the meat, I figured that you might want the rattle."

"How big was he?"

"I'd say around four feet."

"I never saw one that big before."

"I've seen longer ones, but not this close."

Willie was shaking the rattle when Rhody said, "So, tell me about your grandpa and grandma."

He set the rattle down on the bed then replied, "Grandpa looked like my father, only older and fatter. Grandma is a lot skinnier, but she's funnier than grandpa and used to bake me cookies."

"It sounds like you like your grandparents, Willie."

Willie nodded as he said, "I do, but I haven't seen them in a long time."

"Well, you'll be visiting them in a couple of days."

Willie grinned then picked up his gift and made it buzz while Rhody finally began to clean and oil his guns but left the '66 for Willie to clean. It was probably the only thing that would have had more appeal than the rattle.

―――

Next door, Emma couldn't ask Marty those kinds of questions because she'd been so young when she'd last seen her grandparents, but she could tell that Marty was excited at the prospect of meeting them for the first time as a child with a memory.

As Marty paged through *Twenty Thousand Leagues Under the Sea*, looking at the pictures and some of the words, Emma looked at the blonde girl and already felt a sense of loss, knowing that she and Willie would probably stay with their grandparents. She'd never had a child and the loss of her baby weighed heavily on her.

She had bonded with Marty almost from the instant the Comanche had set her on the horse with her. It was because of Marty that she was able to push away those nightmarish hours with the Comanches. She had focused all of her attention on the frightened little girl and now that she could feel as if Marty was her daughter, she was going to lose her.

If that happened, she and Rhody would return to San Antonio after she visited her sister and Rhody hadn't explained what they would do after that. She wanted to stay with him but wasn't sure that he wanted to keep her with him. He had just said that he would provide for her, but that could mean nothing more than leaving her with some money.

With the likelihood of Marty's loss and the uncertainty of Rhody's plans, Emma slid into a depressing sense of loneliness knowing that within a week, she could be alone.

CHAPTER 9

The stage pulled out of Fredericksburg just after eight o'clock the next morning with Jack and Morgana trotting behind.

The driver had told them before they left that the sheriff had already arrested the three outlaws based on Rhody's description of their horses, especially the gray with the white stockings because they were regulars in town and worked at a nearby ranch. He also had sent a telegram to the army notifying them of the renegade Comanches.

They had a replacement shotgun rider who was just a local who wanted to visit San Antonio without buying a ticket.

In the coach's cabin, Emma was brushing Marty's hair, something she hadn't had time to do in the rush to get on the stage. In addition to the temporary shotgun rider, there was one other passenger, a drummer for Remington firearms, which was a welcome distraction for Rhody and Willie.

He had a heavy display case with him and tried to convince Rhody of the advantages of the Remington Model 1875 New Army over the Colt 1873 or the Smith & Wesson Model 3, but Rhody wasn't about to change. He was interested in the Remington derringer, but didn't see any reason to buy one.

Having the drummer aboard kept his mind occupied and mostly away from the changes that would be coming tomorrow when they drove to New Braunfels. It was about a three to four-hour drive then another hour to Seguin, but it wasn't the length of the journey that bothered him.

As the drummer droned on about the added strength of his primary product, Rhody glanced at Emma as she stroked Marty's hair. Since she'd asked about visiting her sister, his mind naturally blended the likelihood of losing Willie and Marty with the possibility of Emma deciding to stay with her sister in Seguin. After all, she was family and she'd only known him for a week or so. People needed comfort and he would always remind her of those terrible days when she lost her husband and almost lost her life.

By the time the stage approached San Antonio, he had almost convinced himself that Emma would tell him that she wanted to stay with her sister. He'd seen the look of anticipation in her face when she talked about seeing her sister's family again and could understand why she would want to stay.

———

The coach rolled to a stop at the depot in San Antonio and Rhody hopped onto the street before turning and helping Marty to the ground. While he took Emma's hand to assist her exit, Willie climbed out of the other side.

RHODY JONES

It was almost like a repeat of the stop at Fredericksburg, but Rhody was much more familiar with San Antonio, so he untied Morgana and Jack then hung their bags over Morgana's saddle and tossed his saddlebags over Jack.

He led them to the Royster House Hotel nearby and after getting two rooms and dropping off their things, he let them get settled while he brought his Morgans to visit Hector Lopez.

Rhody spent more time with Hector than he had expected because Hector had asked him what had happened to the mule. He then arranged to rent Hector's carriage for a couple of days before returning to the hotel.

As they ate their late lunch, Rhody said, "I've rented a carriage for tomorrow's trip to New Braunfels. Did you want to leave right after breakfast, Emma?"

"That's fine. Are we checking out of the hotel before we leave?"

Rhody looked at her wondering if she'd already made up her mind to stay with her sister then replied, "I think that's probably a good idea. We're probably staying overnight in Seguin anyway."

Emma nodded as she cut a slice of meat from her roast chicken.

Willie then asked, "Are we bringing your guns tomorrow, Rhody?"

"I'll wear my pistol, but the only rifle we'll have is the '66. The rest are with Hector at the livery."

"Okay."

After leaving the diner, they walked to Wilcox & Sons General Store and Sundries to pick up some items that they'd forgotten in Menardville, which included a replacement Stetson. The cream color wasn't exactly the shade he'd wanted, but it had a dark brown band, so it was acceptable. He discarded the idea of having his old hat repaired when he discovered a small rip along the seam which must have been caused by a particularly large hailstone.

He acquiesced to Marty's request to buy another book like the one about the submarine and purchased another one of Verne's works, *From the Earth to the Moon,* and Emma promised to read it to them after dinner and then on the ride to New Braunfels.

After they returned to the hotel, Willie and Marty went to his and Rhody's room so he could show her what Rhody had given him, but not telling her what it was in advance.

With the children gone, Rhody and Emma stayed in the lobby set their bag on the floor then took seats on the couch as Rhody removed his new hat.

Emma smiled and asked, "Do you think Willie is going to try to scare her with that gift you gave him?"

"How did you know about it?"

"I heard it through the wall. I couldn't figure out what was causing the buzzing at first and even looked out the window. Then I heard you and Willie talking and picked up the word 'rattlesnake'. It's probably the best gift he's ever received."

Rhody smiled as he said, "The only way I could get him to stop shaking that thing was to let him clean the '66."

Emma then asked, "Do you think his grandparents will want them to stay?"

"I'd be surprised if they didn't. I asked Willie about them, and it sounded as if he was fond of them. Did you know he had grandparents in New Braunfels?"

"No. I didn't even know the Ernst family was from there until I met them."

"I guess we'll just have to wait to see how that turns out."

As Emma nodded, Rhody then asked, "What about you, Emma?"

"What do you mean?" she replied.

"Are you thinking of staying with your sister? It sounds as if you miss her very much."

"I do miss her, but I don't believe that she'd want me hanging around her house."

"Why not? You're a very pleasant person."

Emma sighed then said, "In case you haven't noticed, sir, I am a fairly attractive young woman. My sister is older than I am and is currently pregnant with her fourth child. Don't you see a potential problem if I lived in her home? Besides, her house isn't that big and with another baby coming soon, I would be much more of a nuisance, not to mention the cost of keeping me around. I could help her as a nanny, but I still think that she'd be uncomfortable having me in the house."

Rhody felt immensely relieved as he said, "As you seem to believe that I've gone blind, I assure you that I have definitely noticed that you are much more than a fairly attractive young woman, Emma. But I will also admit to being ignorant about family things like that. Growing up with just my uncle spared me all of the family intrigues. We were almost like good friends and he even had a signal flag he'd fly in the house whenever he had a woman friend visiting."

Emma laughed then asked, "How about you, Rhody? Did you have your own signal flag?"

"No, ma'am. I've had bad luck with ladies, probably because I was at sea so often, unlike my Uncle Richard who stayed ashore. I was close to getting married when I was eighteen, but my girlfriend trifled with another man when I was at sea and married him before I returned."

"Just the once?"

RHODY JONES

"Just the one time that I got that close. It was difficult because I was gone more than I was at home."

"What's it like when you're on the ocean?"

"It depends on the weather. It can be terrifying, like that hurricane I told you about but most of the time, it's exhilarating. When the ship is really taking hold of the wind and cutting through the dark green water and the ocean spray blows into your face when the bow cuts through a wave it's like nothing else in the world."

"But if you loved it so much, why did you leave it for five years?"

"I really did want to see the Southwest. I may not have planned on spending that much time just going back and forth between Texas and Kansas, but I'm still glad that I did. Aside from giving me greater appreciation for my years on the sea, I learned a lot about other cultures and men."

"And you saved me and the children. I'll never be able to thank you enough, Rhody."

"There's no need, Emma. How could I do anything less?"

"It was almost like divine providence that sent you to that spot at that time."

He smiled and said, "And from a real Providence at that."

She laughed again before saying, "What's Rhode Island like, Rhody?"

"Sea water and trees, Emma. I could probably draw you a map if I wanted to waste the time but basically, the state is almost all on the west with a smaller part on the east that are split by Narragansett Bay that makes up about a quarter of the state. Providence itself is quite large, around a hundred thousand people, but the rest of the state is mostly woodlands."

"That many?" she asked with wide eyes.

"It's just that they're concentrated mostly in one city. Texas had about five times as many people as Rhode Island, but they're just spread out more because it's so big. It may have five times as many people, but it has more than a hundred times as much space to fill. Of course, that doesn't include cattle."

"I can't imagine a city that big."

"New York is much bigger. It has as many people as the entire state of Texas. I'm not fond of the city, though."

"Why not?"

"Well for one thing, they make terrible clam chowder."

"What's clam chowder?"

RHODY JONES

"In Rhode Island, where we make it correctly, it's a thick, creamy soup with chopped clams and potatoes with just the right amount of spices. Those New York folks make it with a thin tomato broth instead of cream. They don't pronounce it right, either. They call it chowder when everyone knows it's called chowdah."

Emma laughed again before she said, "Do they really talk like that?"

Rhody smiled at her and replied, "Most of them do, and I don't know where it came from, but some still sound like they're from merry old England. Of course, it's still much easier to follow than some of the boys on the cattle drives and ranches. It took me months to figure out some of the stranger terms. It's an odd thing about American English. A word in Boston means something entirely different than it does in Charleston and even something else in New Orleans."

"Like what?" Emma asked thoroughly enjoying the freedom to laugh again.

"What is a cabinet?"

"It's a piece of furniture where you store things."

"Yes, but if you walk into an ice cream parlor in Rhode Island, you can ask for a coffee cabinet and they'll give you a thick, coffee-flavored ice cream drink."

"Really?"

"Yes, ma'am. I asked for one in New York and the man behind the counter thought I'd lost my mind before he told me where I could find the nearest furniture store. At least I didn't ask him for a frappe. That's what they call it in Boston."

"You've seen so much of this country and all I've seen is West Texas."

"Most folks never move more than five miles from where they were born. I just happened to be born into a world of seafarers."

"I shouldn't have moved as far as I did," she said quietly, "or Carl would still be alive."

"Don't do this to yourself, Emma. You can't blame yourself for what the Comanches did. You didn't ask them to come to your ranch and kill your husband. I know that you loved him, but it was his decision to bring you to the ranch, not yours."

Emma almost confessed to her previous lie about how she felt about Carl, but her guilt and her embarrassment for having said it kept her from telling him the truth. She had been so close when she admitted to her feelings of guilt over Carl's death, but she was concerned that Rhody would think less of her if she admitted to the lie.

Rhody may have difficulty understanding women, but he knew that Emma hadn't accepted his advice when she hadn't answered him.

RHODY JONES

After a pregnant pause that lasted almost thirty seconds, Rhody said, "Speaking of my uncle, I need to go to the post office and see if I received any letters from him in my absence."

"Didn't you tell him that you were leaving to go to California?"

"I did, but he may have written and posted it during the week or so that it took for my letter letting him know that I was leaving to get to Providence. I need to write a reply anyway."

"Why don't you check right now?"

"Did you want to tell Willie and Marty and come along? Or would you rather stay with them?"

"I'll stay here. I believe that they're waiting to discover how someone can fly to the moon."

Rhody rose picked up his hat then waited for Emma to stand before saying, "I'll be back in a few minutes."

Emma smiled then nodded before leaving the lobby.

Rhody watched her walk away then pulled on his hat and left the lobby in the other direction.

Once outside, he turned west and strode quickly down the boardwalk. San Antonio's post office was quite large, and he'd always had letters from his uncle addressed to general delivery in case he changed his residence.

He entered the post office three minutes later then had to wait in line while three folks mailed their packages.

Once he'd reached the front, he didn't have to say a word before the clerk said, "I have one for you, Rhody. I'll be right back."

"Thanks, Luke."

Luke handed him his letter, and Rhody quickly turned and walked to the back of the post office to read what his uncle had written. He wasn't expecting any earth-shattering news but was always glad to hear from him.

He used his pocketknife to slide open the envelope then after closing it and slipping it back into his pocket, he extracted the two folded sheets.

When he opened them, he soon discovered that it was far from a routine report of how the business was doing.

He read:

Dear Roho,

Well, the pennant's flying almost every day now!

I know you find it hard to believe, but I'm going to be married. You probably think I'm just an old fool, but I'll admit to being hopelessly and shamelessly smitten by a younger woman.

RHODY JONES

Her name is Elizabeth Wormwood, and she's exquisite and totally charming. We met at the Yachtsman Club last month during a Sunday soiree, and I can't believe how fortunate I am. She's everything that I could want in a woman. I can't do her justice in mere words. I'm just so alive when I'm with her! You'll understand when you meet her.

We set the wedding date for the first day of August to give you time to return for the ceremony. I hope that you haven't gone on one of those long cattle drives.

Captain Randolph is sailing to Galveston tomorrow morning and I told him to have someone drop this letter off at the post office then delay sailing until you met him. If you're not there by the tenth of July, he'll head back. I hope you get this letter first.

I know that you expressed your desire to ride across the Southwest, and I hope that you haven't gone yet. After the wedding, you can sail on the next ship to New Orleans or Galveston and start again. I can't tell you how much I wish to have you at the ceremony. It is the only thing that could make me happier than I already am.

On a much more mundane front, we sold the Argyle and replaced her with another steamer that I named the Sweet Elizabeth. Captain Randolph is taking her on her maiden voyage to bring you home. I thought it was fitting.

I'm having your yawl overhauled and if you don't mind, I plan to use it to take my new bride on a honeymoon to Newport.

I hope this letter finds you well and even more, I hope it finds you in time to make it to the wedding.

Love and Respect,

Richard

Rhody had to read the letter a second time to get a grip on the news. His uncle had never really gotten serious over a woman before. He was married to the business, but he was practically swooning over her in his letter.

As much as he loved and respected his uncle, he never regarded him as a good catch, at least not on the physical side of the equation. He was fifty-two, portly and had a fairly large nose. He did have sharp, intelligent eyes and a boisterous personality that made him popular in the business world and in his circle of friends, but Rhody didn't think that it went over well with the ladies. The women he brought back to the house were usually highly regarded and well-paid prostitutes.

Rhody returned the letter to its envelope then left the post office to return to the hotel. He thought about sending a telegram to his uncle to let him know that he was coming but decided to wait until he got to Galveston and boarded Captain Randolph's new steamer. As much as he was concerned for his uncle, he was excited about seeing the latest addition to their fleet. He'd be able to talk to Myles Randolph about his uncle's fiancée as well.

He stepped along quickly to tell Emma the news and soon entered the hotel. He was taking off his new Stetson as he reached the open door to Emma and Marty's room. He could hear her reading Verne's book before he entered, but she stopped, and her blue eyes turned from the page and looked up at him.

He briefly halted in the doorway and looked back at the scene as Emma sat on a one of the beds while Willie and Marty sat on the other. Just before their eyes had turned toward him, there was just that moment where he had seen the tranquil family image that he'd always imagined; his wife reading to their children as they sat transfixed by the story and by her soft, loving voice.

He smiled then walked into the room and said, "You're not going to believe what I just read in my Uncle Richard's letter."

"So, he did write one. What was so exciting?" Emma asked as she set Verne on the bed beside her.

Rhody carefully placed his hat on the dresser then sat in the straight-backed chair.

"Now you must remember how I described my uncle before I tell you. He's fifty-two and is enjoying the benefits of being wealthy and a bachelor. In other words, he's a bit round. He's not the most handsome fellow, but he's a wonderful man and well-liked."

"And?" Emma asked.

"He's getting married on the first of August."

"So, why are you surprised?"

"My uncle has always been fond of women, but never paid them as much attention as he did to running the business. Let me put it to you this way…when the pennant was hoisted to the yardarm, his bank balance dropped by twenty dollars."

"Oh. You didn't tell me that."

"It wasn't important at the time. Anyway, he never mentioned his betrothed in any of his letters because he'd only met her a few weeks ago. He said she's much younger than he is, but he's totally smitten. What does surprise me is that Uncle Richard was always honest about his lack of physical appeal and now he's enraptured by a younger woman that he describes as exquisite."

"Does it matter why she's marrying him if it makes him happy?"

RHODY JONES

"Not at all unless she's going to make him miserable right after the honeymoon. I don't want him to have his heart broken. He's too good-hearted."

"Are you going to write him a letter?"

"No. He bought a new steamer and named it the *Sweet Elizabeth* after his bride-to-be. He sent it to Galveston and had one of the crew drop this letter off at the post office. He's having the captain hold it in port until the tenth of July to provide me passage back to Providence. He said I could return and start my trip west after the wedding."

Emma paused before saying, "He didn't know that you'd already gone."

Rhody shook his head as he replied, "No, ma'am. I'll send him a telegram when I get to Galveston."

"Then you are leaving," she said quietly.

"I have to go, Emma. We'll talk about it more after we return from New Braunfels and Seguin. Okay?"

"Alright."

Rhody was close to asking her to come with him, but with the children sitting there and looking at him with hopeful eyes, he didn't want to broach the subject of what he expected to happen when they reached New Braunfels tomorrow. Even though Emma had told him that she wouldn't move in with her sister, he didn't know how she would react if Willie and Marty would stay with their grandparents. Emma had become so close to Marty, Rhody began to wonder if she wouldn't offer to stay with the Ernst grandparents as a nanny.

He had already decided to remain in Texas and even move to New Braunfels if that happened, but he needed to return to Rhode Island to meet his uncle's fiancée and talk to his uncle before he walked down that aisle. Maybe she really was attracted to him despite his physical shortcomings. But after the wedding, he'd take the next ship back to Galveston or New Orleans. He just hoped that Emma didn't find a suitor in the month that he'd be gone. She was a very handsome young woman and had the quick mind and good heart that enhanced her outward beauty.

He wasn't sure how long she would have to grieve over her lost husband and seemed to have accepted his loss already, but it was difficult to get past losing someone you loved. He only believed that he'd loved Rowena Bedard and when he found out that she'd been unfaithful, he'd been crushed. He couldn't imagine having a loving spouse snatched from you in such a hideous manner. At least she hadn't witnessed his death and had her sorrow blunted by Marty at the same time it was replaced by hours of stark terror.

He was snapped out of his ruminations when Willie asked, "Are you going to keep reading, Aunt Emma?"

RHODY JONES

Emma had been staring at Rhody and was swimming in her own storm-tossed ocean of thoughts and emotions and didn't hear his question.

After not getting an answer for ten seconds, Willie asked, "Are you all right, Aunt Emma?"

Emma blinked then looked at Willie and replied, "Oh. I'm sorry, Willie. What did you say?"

"I asked if you were gonna read some more."

"Yes, of course."

As Emma resumed reading aloud, Rhody sat and listened, but almost didn't hear the words of the tale. He just listened to her voice and hoped that he didn't return to San Antonio alone.

―――

The next morning, Rhody was driving the rented carriage out of San Antonio just before eight o'clock. They'd checked out of the hotel, had breakfast and then loaded the carriage with their bags before driving into the sun along the well-traveled road to New Braunfels. Nothing more had been said about Rhody's pending departure and Willie and Marty were excited about seeing their grandparents, but neither realized the likelihood that it might be the last time they saw Rhody or Emma.

When he'd picked up the carriage from Hector earlier, Hector had mentioned that a stranger had stopped by and rented a horse late yesterday who had a funny accent, even for a Yankee. Rhody had assumed it was the sailor from the *Sweet Elizabeth*, but figured he'd stayed around to enjoy himself. He just couldn't understand why he'd rented a horse.

As San Antonio's last buildings faded from view, Willie said, "There sure are a lot more wagons and riders on this road than there were on the other one."

"There's a lot of business traffic between San Antonio and New Braunfels."

"The man riding back there is on a Morgan like Jack," Willie said as he looked behind them.

Rhody glanced back and said, "Jack doesn't have that white slash on his forehead, Willie, but I'll admit that he's close."

Willie grinned then said, "But the man has a funny hat, too."

Rhody hadn't paid attention to the rider as he was still thinking about what would happen in three or four hours, so he didn't bother to look back again.

Willie then plopped back down to the leather seat next to Marty who asked, "Do you think grandma and grandpa still look the same now, Willie?"

RHODY JONES

"I don't know. They were pretty old when I saw them, but I was just a little kid even younger than you are now."

"Oh. How old are you, Rhody?"

Rhody kept his eyes on the road as he replied, "I turned twenty-seven in April."

She then asked, "How old are you, Aunt Emma?"

"I turned twenty-one in April."

Rhody did turn to look at Emma before he asked, "What is your birthday?"

"The twenty-second. What's yours? It's not the same day, is it?"

"Sorry, ma'am. I was born eighteen days earlier on the fourth."

"Eighteen days and six years."

Rhody grinned as he said, "Yes, ma'am," then he asked, "Why didn't you get married until you were twenty? Most girls get married before they're eighteen, and surely you had a large number of suitors."

"My father was very strict, and I was very helpful in the bakery."

"I imagine that you attracted quite a few gentleman customers who ordered baked goods that they didn't need. You probably put twenty pounds onto every man in New Braunfels."

Emma laughed then said, "There were a few."

Two hundred yards behind them, Second Mate Jean LeClair trotted along on his rented Morgan. He'd been lucky to spot Jones as he'd stepped down from the stage and almost didn't recognize him after all those years, especially in that cowboy outfit.

He had hoped to find him alone in the night, but the man was always with that young woman and the children except when he'd gone to the livery or the post office this morning. When he'd visited the livery after Jones had returned to the hotel, he pretended to be interested in the two Morgans and the liveryman had told him that they belonged to his friend and that he was renting a carriage to go to New Braunfels in the morning to bring the children and the young woman to their families. Then he'd rented a horse to keep tab on Jones.

The job would be more complicated when Jones was with company, and he wasn't about to kill a woman or children to get the job done. But when he'd learned that Jones was going to be dropping them off in New Braunfels, he saw an opportunity. Out on the road, his body wouldn't be found for days and he'd be on the train to Galveston by the time it was discovered.

When New Braunfels appeared on the horizon, Emma's stomach flipped knowing that her father was close. She wished she could visit her mother but knew her stubborn father wouldn't allow her to enter the yard, much less the house.

"Where do we go first, Emma? Do we head to the Brandt's house or the Ernst place?"

"I think we should let Willie and Marty see their grandparents first."

"That's fine," he replied then turned to Willie and said, "You'll have to give me directions, Mister Ernst."

Willie hopped up from his seat and climbed onto the seat between Emma and Rhody leaving Marty alone in the back seat.

"When you get into town, turn left on the second street. It's a big brown house with a red door. I don't remember the number, though."

"I hope they haven't painted it since you've been gone, Willie, but I suppose we could ask around if they did."

Willie grinned at him before returning to his back seat and setting the Winchester '66 on his lap.

Rhody glanced over at Emma and saw her tense expression but wasn't sure if it was because they might lose Willie and Marty, or she was so near to her parents' home. It was probably a combination of both as she hadn't spoken much on the ride and not at all in the last few minutes until he'd asked her about their first stop.

He soon turned the carriage left after passing the first intersection and soon spotted a brown house with a red door on the right.

Willie exclaimed, "There it is, Rhody!"

"At least it's not yellow now."

Rhody pulled the carriage to a stop before the house then stepped down and helped Marty to the ground as Willie hopped down on the other side. Emma took Rhody's hand as she stepped to the ground then gripped his hand tightly as they headed down the walkway to the house.

After stepping onto the porch, Rhody knocked on the door with his left hand as his right was being strangled by Emma.

Willie was standing on his left and Emma was holding Marty's hand on her right when after a minute's delay, the door swung open and Franz Ernst looked at Rhody then glanced down at Willie.

RHODY JONES

Before he had the chance to ask what they wanted, Willie exclaimed, "Grandpa, it's me, Willie!"

Franz looked back down at his grandson and asked, "What are you doing here, Wilhelm? Where is your papa, mama and brother? Is this Marta?"

Rhody interrupted Willie's answer by quickly saying, "Mister Ernst, I can explain, but I'd rather that I tell you inside so your wife can hear it as well."

Franz nodded then opened the door wider and said, "Please come in."

Rhody let Willie, Marty and Emma enter first then walked into the dark house and closed the door before removing his hat.

―――

Jean had pulled up at the intersection and watched them enter the house. He knew that Jones had probably seen him, but the road was well populated, and he never was close enough to be recognized even if Jones remembered him. He was hoping to see Jones leave the house alone then head back to San Antonio. The road may have had a lot of traffic, but even if he didn't have his opportunity on the ride back, he'd wait until he ventured out of the hotel after dark.

He wasn't planning on using a rifle if he made his attempt during the night. He had his favored weapon for this kind of work; a belaying pin that could easily crush a man's head. Then it was just a matter of leaving him in an awkward position and it would look as if he had fallen and cracked his skull against a stone wall.

Rhody was sitting beside Emma on a setee while Willie and Marty sat in separate chairs across from their grandparents who were seated on the couch.

"Mister and Mrs. Ernst, my name is Rhody Jones and I was riding west and came upon your son's ranch. There were four Comanche warriors looting the place and loading a wagon…"

Franz and Greta Ernst sat quietly as Rhody explained what he had discovered inside after killing the drunk Comanches but avoided graphic details. He could already see the stress on their faces after his second sentence.

He described meeting Willie and then their chase after the Comanches from the Brandt ranch. For ten minutes, Rhody talked non-stop, but just glossed over how he'd reached Menardville and what had happened when he caught up with their stagecoach.

When he finished, he looked at the elder Ernst and said, "I'm sorry that I didn't arrive early enough to stop them."

"No, you saved young Wilhelm and Marta and that was more than most men would have done. They are all that we have left of our family now, and I thank you for what you did to save them."

Rhody nodded then glanced at Emma wondering if he should ask if Willie and Marty were going to stay with them, but decided to let their grandparents bring up the subject.

Franz then stood and slowly walked to Willie and put his gnarled hand over his grandson's shoulder.

"You're a brave young man, Wilhelm. I'm very proud of you. We cannot replace your mother and father, but we will raise you as they would have wished."

Willie smiled at his grandfather then turned his eyes to Rhody.

"I'll miss you, Rhody."

Marty began to quietly cry as she stood and walked to Emma and hugged her. She didn't say anything, but just looked up into Emma's eyes which were shedding tears of their own.

Rhody said, "Mister Ernst, I've only known Willie and Marty for a few days, but I've never met two finer youngsters."

"Will you stay for lunch, Mister Jones?" Greta Ernst asked.

"I wish we could, ma'am. But we have to make two more stops today and the second one is in Seguin."

He then rose and waited for Emma to stand. When she did, Marty turned and walked to Rhody then after she sniffed, quietly said, "Thank you for saving us, Rhody."

Rhody just smiled and nodded unable to reply.

After almost a minute, he turned to Willie and said, "Can you and Marty come out to the carriage to pick up your things?"

"Yes, sir," Willie replied as he stood.

Franz Ernst shook his hand then Greta took his hand in hers and said, "You will always be in our prayers, Mister Jones."

"Thank you, ma'am."

He took Emma's hand before they left the house with Willie and Marty walking behind them.

When they reached the carriage, Willie picked up the big bag with their clothes then set it down on the cobbled walkway.

Rhody smiled at him then shook his hand before saying, "Don't forget your Winchester, Willie."

"I can still have it?" he asked.

"It's yours, Willie. It used to belong to my best friend, and now it belongs to my new best friend."

Marty then looked up at Emma and asked, "Can I have the book about the submarine, Aunt Emma?"

"Of course, you may. You can keep both of them."

"Can you and Rhody sign them?"

Emma looked at Rhody who nodded then pulled his notebook from his pocket, but before he handed the pencil to Emma, he wrote his address on the back page and ripped it out.

He gave the pencil to Emma but handed the small piece of paper to Willie and said, "This is my address in Rhode Island. I expect to find a letter from each of you when I get back. Okay?"

Willie accepted the paper and replied, "Yes, sir."

Emma had signed both books and handed them and the pencil back to Rhody who added his own signature to the cover pages below hers. He noticed that Emma had added "With All My Love" above her autograph.

After he returned the books to Marty, he knew that they couldn't delay their departure without causing each of them more distress, so he took Emma's hand again and guided her to the carriage.

After she was sitting, he climbed aboard and took the reins in hand. He and Emma then both turned, saw Franz and Greta

Ernst on the porch and waited until Willie and Marty joined them before they waved.

The reunited Ernst family waved back then Rhody snapped the reins and the carriage rolled away. He didn't look back but could see Emma staring at them. He felt like a heel for even deciding to take Willie and Marty to their grandparents, but knew it was the right thing to do even if it did break Emma's heart.

He made a turn onto the main street and they lost sight of the Ernst house, so he asked, "Where is the Brandt house?"

"My father's bakery is coming up on the right and my parents' house is right behind it. The Brandts' home is three more blocks, just past Gerda's Haus. That's a restaurant. Take a left there and it's three houses down on the right."

"Okay. Did you want to come with me?"

"No. In fact, can you stop well short of the house so they can't see me?"

Rhody glanced at her then answered, "Would you rather just wait in the restaurant? We need to get something to eat anyway."

"Would you mind?"

"I think that it's better this way."

"Thank you, Rhody. I just don't want to see them again."

"I understand."

He pulled up in front of the restaurant and just waited while Emma quickly stepped out of the carriage.

"I'll wait for you inside. Did you want me to order your lunch?"

"That's fine. I should be back shortly."

"Thank you, Rhody," she replied before quickly walking into the restaurant.

Rhody let out his breath then popped the reins and the two geldings pulled the carriage away from Gerda's Haus.

Just three minutes later, he climbed down from the carriage in front of the Brandt house then strode down the walkway to the porch. He suspected that he wouldn't be getting a warm reception this time. He removed his hat and held it in his left hand.

After knocking on the door, he took in a long, nervous breath in anticipation of meeting Emma's late husband's parents.

The door opened and he found himself looking eye-to-eye with a massive woman who probably outweighed him by thirty pounds and would most likely crush him in a wrestling match. She had broad shoulders and an enormous, almost frightening bosom. If her threatening chest wasn't enough to create fear in his heart, her stern face certainly didn't help to give him any peace of mind.

"Mrs. Brandt? My name is Rhody Jones and I wonder if I could talk to you and your husband for a few minutes. It's about your sons."

"My husband is still at work. What do you need to tell me?"

He noticed that she hadn't asked him to enter the house and he was glad that she hadn't as he had a feeling that he'd need to make a rapid escape.

"I was riding west on my way to California when I found the Ernst ranch, which was four miles east of your son's ranch, being ransacked by renegade Comanches who had already murdered most of the family. After I killed those four, I trailed the others to your son's ranch. The Comanches had set the house and barn ablaze by the time I arrived."

She didn't express a hint of shock or grief, but quickly asked, "None of them survived?"

"When I arrived at the Ernst ranch, I found their young son who had hidden north of the ranch. He told me that the Comanches had taken his seven-year-old sister, so we trailed the Indians. When we found them, I saw that they also had your daughter-in-law, Emma, with them. I managed to free them, and we just returned the Ernst children to their grandparents."

RHODY JONES

"So," she said in a snarl worthy of Satan himself, "that harlot was the only one to live. I should have known. I'll bet she spread her legs fast enough for you on the way back, too."

Rhody was stunned to hear her vehemence and foul language. She was talking like some of those rowdy cowpunchers on the cattle drives.

"Ma'am, Emma is not a wanton woman. She's a fine lady and you should show some consideration for what she's been through."

"I don't care what she's been through. Carl was my favorite and he was going to stay in New Braunfels, but he met that whore and her bastard father made our son marry her and then forced him out of our home. She didn't even like him! Hell isn't hot enough for the likes of her!"

Rhody glared into the woman's fierce blue eyes as he growled, "Lady, I don't care if you have breasts under that cloth or not, you are the foulest creature I've ever met, including the four-foot-long rattlesnake I shot a few days ago. Emma isn't going to hell, but you probably have a whole castle waiting for you."

As Mrs. Brandt unleashed a string of vile insults, Rhody spun on his heels and marched from the porch. He had been so close to pulling his Colt and putting the muzzle into her foul mouth, but he didn't want to have to clean his pistol again.

He leapt into the carriage, snapped the reins and made a U-turn, never looking back at the house.

He was still seething when he stepped down and tied off the horses in front of the restaurant and strode through the open doors.

Rhody spotted Emma at a table near the window, so she must have seen the fierce look on his face.

When he removed his hat and sat down, she said, "I can tell that you must have talked to Olga Brandt and not her husband."

"Her husband was at work. I wouldn't be surprised if he never came home. What a vile woman!"

"That's one of the reasons that I couldn't go there. Her husband isn't a bad man at all, but she dominates the house. What did she say?"

Rhody sighed then replied, "She didn't even seem to care that her sons had all died but wasn't very flattering in her comments about you."

Emma nodded before she said, "I can imagine the words she used to describe me, but I suppose that I deserved most of it."

Rhody had dismissed all of the large woman's disgusting vitriol but had one question about what she had said.

RHODY JONES

"Emma, I know that you told me that you loved your husband, but that poor excuse for a woman said that you didn't even like her son. Why would she say that?"

Emma closed her eyes and exhaled before answering, "I shouldn't have told you that, Rhody. I don't even know why I did. Carl Brandt was a very handsome man, and I'll admit that I'm an attractive woman. There's no excuse for what we did because it was nothing more than rutting, so she was right in a way.

"I thought he was charming at first, but after a while, I found that it was all he had to offer. It was too late by then, so we had to marry, and my father put out the word in the community that Carl was an immoral man and shouldn't be hired. I think he just wanted the shame that I'd brought to the family to go away and the best way to do it was to have Carl take me out to his brothers' ranch."

"Why did his brothers go so far out to build the ranch? There is so much open land out there that he could have found something closer."

"It had to do with the cattle. They rode west gathering mavericks and then when they had enough, they stopped and built the ranch. Willie's father heard about it and decided to start his ranch a few miles east."

The waitress brought them their lunch off roast veal and boiled potatoes then set a mug of beer on the table.

After filling both of their mugs, she smiled and left.

As Rhody cut into his veal, he said, "Everything that happened before doesn't matter anymore, Emma. I wish that I could tell you not to worry about it, but after all you've been through, the best thing you can do is to look forward. You'll be seeing your sister again in a couple of hours."

Emma looked across the table at him, smiled weakly then replied, "It'll be nice to see Anna again. She was quieter than me, but we would share things that we couldn't tell our parents. I guess my rebellious nature got the better of me in the end."

"You don't seem that rebellious, Emma. You are strong willed and independent woman and if you'd been my brother, you'd probably be a captain by now, or at least a first mate."

He'd hoped to see her genuinely smile at his comment, but she just took a sip of her beer and then continued eating in silence.

It was early afternoon when they set out for Seguin, and Rhody felt odd not having Willie and Marty with them. He was certain that Emma felt it as well and that loss only exacerbated her sour mood. He hoped that her sister welcomed her as warmly as Emma seemed to expect. He was curious if she had the same silver blonde hair and bright blue eyes. After having three children and carrying her fourth, he imagined she'd look much older than the two years that separated them.

After Emma and Rhody had entered the restaurant, Jean LeClair had gone to a smaller café just down the street and ate a quick lunch. He'd been pleased that the children were no longer with them but wondered if he was going to keep the woman with him. He was confused when he let her off at the restaurant but followed him to the intersection and watched as he had the confrontation with a big woman at the door.

He was disappointed when Jones returned to the restaurant and even more so when they returned to the carriage and left New Braunfels but didn't head southwest to San Antonio. They were driving southeast, and he wasn't familiar with the area, so he didn't know where they were headed.

He stayed as far back as he could yet still keep the carriage in sight. There wasn't as much road traffic as there had been on the first one, but he didn't think that he'd be noticed.

Twenty minutes out of New Braunfels, Rhody finally broke the silence by asking, "What does your sister's husband do for a living?"

"He's a whip maker and has his own shop near their house."

"What do you think of him?"

"Anna likes him," she replied.

Rhody interpreted her answer to mean that Emma didn't care for him, but didn't want to ask her why, especially after their conversation in the restaurant.

Emma then asked, "When are you leaving for Galveston?"

"Probably in a couple of days."

"Are you going to send him a telegram to let him know that you're coming?"

Rhody had been pondering that very question after reading his uncle's letter, so he replied, "No, I don't think so. He knows that the *Sweet Elizabeth* will be returning no later than the twentieth of the month, and he'll expect me to be on it."

"But wouldn't he have received your letter that said you were leaving Texas?"

"Yes, but if I was already gone, he wouldn't expect a wire either."

"So why don't you send him the telegram?"

"What did you think about his decision to marry sweet Elizabeth after I described the situation?"

"Without knowing either of them, I'd think that it is most likely that she's marrying him for his money."

"I know my uncle better than anyone and that's my opinion as well. I want to talk to the captain about my uncle's fiancée after we sail. Captain Randolph is a friend and he'll be honest with me. I'd rather just arrive and surprise Uncle Richard. That letter that I sent will probably let her believe that I'm not coming, and I want to see sweet Elizabeth's reaction when she sees me, so I can make my own judgement as to her motives."

She turned to look at him before she asked, "Will you come with me when I see my sister?"

"I will, but I would have expected that you would want it to be more private."

It wasn't the reason for her question, but she replied, "I'm not sure if she's been poisoned by my father's anger since I've been gone."

"Haven't you written letters to her?"

"I have, but I haven't gotten a single reply after I received that one letter in December that told me she was pregnant again and that's why I'm concerned that she may not want to see me now."

"Mail isn't exactly consistent out where you lived, Emma. I assume you have to pick it up at the old fort's trading post. Is that right?"

"Yes. Carl would drive the wagon once a month to the post to get supplies. He'd bring a steer with him to trade."

"It was always Carl who made the trip?"

"He was the youngest brother and by the time we arrived, I think he wanted two days free of me each month."

"Surely it wasn't that bad, Emma."

"It wasn't so much bad as it was strange. He didn't hate me or beat me, and he did his husbandly duty. But he always had a simmering anger and disappointment over losing the life that he'd enjoyed as a bachelor in a nice town. I'm sure that when he made his drive to the trading post, he enjoyed the favors of one of the three prostitutes that worked there."

"Maybe Carl picked up letters from your sister then read them and threw them away as a form of punishment."

Emma stared at Rhody for a few seconds then said, "I never thought of that. He'd return with an occasional letter for his brothers or sister-in-law, but none ever came to me after that first one. I wonder if he posted the letters that I wrote to Anna."

"You can ask her in a few minutes. I believe that's Seguin up ahead."

"When you get on the main street, look for P. Schmidt, Whips and Lariats. Their house is right behind it. It's not nearly as large as my parents' house or the Ernsts' place. I don't know how they'll manage with another child on the way."

"Does she have your hair and eyes?"

"Her hair is blonde, but darker, more like Marty's, and she has green eyes rather than blue. We didn't know where they came from because everyone else in the family has blue eyes. When we were girls, she used to joke that she was adopted when she was a baby, but when we were teenagers, it shifted to whispers that our mother had a secret lover."

Rhody laughed, then said, "Now see, Emma? There's an example of what I meant when I told you that I wasn't good at understanding women. I have been around men for most of my years, and I never knew that girls talked about things like that. I always figured all you talked about was crocheting and dances."

Emma echoed his laugh before she replied, "You have to be joking, Rhody! Get a few young women together and the last thing they would talk about is crocheting. If they talk about dances, it's only to gossip about the boy who held her in his arms and the effect she was having on him. You really had no idea that they discussed such immoral subjects?"

"No, ma'am. I figured that was limited to the rowdy boys who I worked with on the sea or on the trail. Now that I know, that explains why they would giggle so often when they were clustered nearby."

Emma was enjoying herself for those brief moments and was able to push aside her concerns about meeting her sister or worse, about meeting her husband and her feelings of loss after leaving Marty and Willie. Yet the giant question that still lingered over both of them had yet to surface. *What would happen after they returned to San Antonio?* He hadn't asked her to accompany him to Galveston, and she didn't know what she would do if he didn't.

That question was still on Rhody's mind as well. He knew he had to go to Galveston to board the *Sweet Elizabeth*, but even with the knowledge that Emma's marriage had been far from the loving union he'd believed, he was still unsure of what she wanted. He had decided to postpone that discussion until after she'd visited her sister and they were on the way back to San Antonio.

Jean LeClair saw the rooftops of Seguin in the distance and hoped that Jones and the blonde woman would be stopping there. He assumed once they left New Braunfels and headed in this direction that the woman's family lived in the town ahead and he would leave her there just as they'd dropped off the children in New Braunfels.

RHODY JONES

If that was Jones' plan, then he'd have his opportunity on the long drive back to San Antonio. He'd still prefer to use his belaying pin in the dark, so if Jones rode alone back to the city, he'd wait until he returned to his hotel room. He wasn't that good with a pistol and he expected that Jones was much better after spending five years in Texas.

Rhody spotted the whip maker's shop and Emma said that he was probably at work, so she could talk openly to her sister.

He pulled up in front of the small house behind the shop, then stepped down and took Emma's hand as much for moral support as for physical assistance.

Just as she had when they walked down the walkaway to the Ernst home, Emma had a vise-like grip on his hand as they strode along the short, dirt path to her sister-in-law's house.

After stepping onto the porch, he let Emma knock then felt her hand tighten even more which surprised him until he realized that if her sister had become tainted by their father's anger then she would have lost all of her family.

The door opened, and despite her darker blonde hair and green eyes, Rhody saw the facial resemblance and was pleasantly surprised to see that Anna wasn't as bedraggled as he'd expected. She was definitely well along in her pregnancy and was standing in front of three blonde-headed children.

"Emma?" she asked with wide eyes.

Emma's concerns evaporated at the sight of her older sister then instead of answering, she instantly released Rhody's hand then wrapped her arms around Anna as tears slid across her cheeks.

Anna began to weep and for more than a minute, Rhody stood beside the hugging sisters and looked down on the small children. He knew their names and ages and it wasn't difficult to match each one to Emma's descriptions.

When Anna and Emma separated, Anna's next question surprised him and probably stunned Emma when she asked, "What took you so long to get here?"

Emma asked with wide eyes, "What do you mean, Anna? We only left a few days ago and it was a long journey."

Anna then glanced at Rhody before asking, "Where's Carl? Who is he?"

Emma said, "Let's go inside and talk, Anna. I have a lot to tell you."

As they entered the front room, Rhody could understand Anna's confusion but didn't know why she seemed to have anticipated Emma's return.

RHODY JONES

After the sisters took a seat on the couch, Rhody removed his hat and sat in one of the chairs, feeling like a spectator or a caged animal in the zoo as the three children all stared at him.

"Why did it take so long for you to return?" Anna asked again.

"What do you mean, Anna? Why did you expect me to come home after father banned me from the house?"

"I wrote you four letters begging you to come home to see papa. I thought you were still so angry with him that you didn't even bother to reply to any of them."

Emma glanced at Rhody before replying, "We were just talking about that on the drive from New Braunfels. I think Carl was destroying any letters that I received and not posting the ones that I wrote."

"You've been to New Braunfels already? So, you know about papa. If you do, then why did you come here so quickly?"

Emma shook her head and replied, "No, Anna. I didn't stop to visit him and mama. We had to stop there for another reason. What should I know about our father?"

Anna closed her eyes briefly then answered, "He's dying, Emma. Doctor Lange says he has cancer in his lungs and won't live much longer. He seems to accept that there is nothing he can do, but he asked me to write to you and tell you that his greatest regret in his life was how he treated you. He knows he will soon stand before God and confess that greatest sin and wants to see you before he dies so he can ask for your forgiveness. You are the only one who can give him that peace, Emma."

Emma stared at her sister as a massive crash of emotions collided inside her mind. The man who had sent her away with a man she didn't love was now begging her to forgive him. And yet he was the same man who had given her the greatest gift of life and had provided for her for until she had carelessly tossed it aside by cavorting with Carl Brandt. *Who had committed the greater sin?*

She quietly asked, "How is mama?"

"Mama is barely holding on. I can't spend more than a day there because I have to take the children with me. When I wrote my letters, I asked if you could help mama until he passed before you returned to the ranch."

"But you didn't want me to come with Carl, did you?"

"No. Besides believing that it would be a bad thing for papa to see Carl again, I knew that you'd be happier to come alone."

"And you wrote that in the letters?"

"Yes. I never expected that Carl would read them. Where is Carl?"

RHODY JONES

"He's dead, Anna. Everyone else on the ranch is dead after the Comanches attacked the ranch and burned the house and barn. They kidnapped me and a young girl from the neighboring ranch, but the extraordinarily brave and wonderful man sitting across from us who didn't even know I had been taken, came to rescue the little girl and saved us both. He then brought us back and had to fight off a band of Comanches to give us a chance to escape."

Anna looked at Rhody then asked, "You did all that?"

"Yes, ma'am."

"What's your name?"

"My real name is Roland Jones, but everyone calls me Rhody."

Anna then turned back to her sister and said, "Are you going to visit papa to give him peace, Emma?"

"I will. Rhody and I will return to New Braunfels shortly and I'll see mama and papa."

"Can you tell me what happened before you go?"

"I'll let Rhody tell the story because only he knows all of it. He told the grandparents of the children he saved, but I was a bit distraught at the time, so I missed parts of it."

"Children?"

Emma nodded then said, "Just listen, Anna."

Rhody took his cue when the sisters turned their faces toward him and began the now familiar narration.

When he finished ten minutes later, Anna stared at him for thirty seconds before asking, "What will you do when you return to San Antonio?"

Her question implied the singular version of the pronoun meaning that Anna must expect Emma to remain in New Braunfels. He had already begun to realize that she would stay after hearing about their father's condition, but the question still unsettled him.

"I'll be leaving to go to Galveston where I'll board a ship for Providence. I need to attend my uncle's wedding," he replied, not expanding on the fact that he was the partial owner of the ship or that he intended to stop the wedding if sweet Elizabeth was a gold digger.

―――

Jean LeClair had ridden the rented horse to the livery near the whip store where he could watch the carriage in front of the small house. While the liveryman inspected the rental's shoes, he asked him if there was a shorter route to San Antonio than the way through New Braunfels.

The liveryman had laughed and said that going through New Braunfels was the long way around and there was a direct route that started south of the town. It didn't take him long to look at the well shod horse, so Jean thanked him for his time and gave him a dime before leading the horse back outside and tying him off at the whip shop and entering the place. He couldn't see the carriage any longer but wanted to stay out of sight. He began inspecting the various whips that were hung on lines and pegs when the whip maker approached him.

"Good afternoon. What are you looking for?"

"I'm not so sure. I thought I'd look around for a while if that's okay?"

"Go ahead. You're not from around here, are you?"

"No, sir. I'm from back East. I'm just here visiting an old friend."

"Well, if you find something you like, bring it over and I'll give you a good price."

Jean grinned at the man and nodded before turning and walking along the front of the store where he could watch the street while he examined the whips. He hadn't intended to buy anything, but as he looked at one of the impressive bull whips, he thought that it might be an impressive thing to have when he returned to Galveston.

Once he'd decided to have one, he began to search for one with a fearsome design on the handle and smiled when he saw one that looked as if the handle was wrapped with snakeskin. It was a bit pricier than the plain ones, but he thought it was worth the extra dollar.

After saying their farewells, Emma and Rhody boarded the carriage. He made another U-turn and the sisters waved to each other as the carriage passed before the house.

As they approached the main road, Emma said, "I don't know how I'll act when we get to New Braunfels, Rhody. My father is dying and wants my forgiveness, and I don't know if I need to give him forgiveness or ask for it."

Rhody kept his eyes on the cross traffic ahead as he replied, "You'll only have your answer when you see him, Emma. Maybe neither of you has to ask for forgiveness, just understanding. We're all human and prone to mistakes, especially when dealing with other people. You made yours with Carl and he made his with you."

"I suppose you're right, but I've felt guilty for many more sins since that first one with Carl."

He pulled the carriage to a stop before entering the busy main road then looked at her and said, "So, forgive yourself before you even think about forgiving your father."

Emma replied, "I'll try, but I don't think it will be easy."

"No, I wouldn't think so," he said as he looked to his right for oncoming traffic and spotted that same tan Morgan with the white slash on his face that Willie had pointed out to him on the ride to New Braunfels.

He turned left onto the main street and wondered why the horse was there. If he had been riding to Seguin from San Antonio, he should have taken the direct route. It would have saved him more than fifteen miles.

Rhody was still thinking about the horse when they left Seguin but couldn't come up with a logical reason for the rider to have taken that unusual path.

Emma had been silent since they made the turn onto the main street, so he was able to concentrate on the puzzle. It was only when he realized that the horse was parked before her brother-in-law's whip shop that he began to suspect that the man was following him. *But why was he following and who was he?*

If Jean LeClair hadn't decided to spend the time looking for the right bull whip, Rhody might not have suspected that he'd been followed. It was just a fortunate coincidence, at least for Rhody.

His concentration was broken a few minutes later when Emma said, "I still find it hard to believe that Carl wouldn't let me know that my father was dying. I would have thought that he'd see that as a reason to get away from the ranch permanently."

"He probably would have if he thought that he'd be accepted when he returned, but you'd only been gone a year and he probably suspected he'd be treated the same if he did return."

"Then why wouldn't he just let me leave? I know that once I was gone, I wouldn't be there to remind him of what he'd lost and he'd feel free again, maybe for a few months."

"I don't know, Emma. Maybe when he read how your sister explained that your father was begging for your forgiveness to bring him peace, the worst punishment he could inflict on him was to deny him your presence. If that is true then once he read a letter from your sister telling you of your father's death, he'd probably let you read that one."

Emma sighed then said, "Maybe I shouldn't feel so guilty about what happened at the ranch anymore."

"No, you shouldn't."

As Emma began examining her soul, Rhody returned to thinking about that Morgan back in Seguin. As he concentrated on the horse rather than the rider, he made another connection. When he'd asked Hector about renting a carriage, Hector had shown him the carriage out back and when he'd looked at the team in the corral, he'd spotted another tan Morgan and briefly thought he was Jack.

RHODY JONES

He hadn't seen the Jack lookalike's face, but that glimpse convinced him that the man who sounded funny to Hector had rented the horse from him. That meant that the rider was probably on the crew of the *Sweet Elizabeth*. He doubted if his uncle would send someone just to spy on him, so whatever the sailor was doing was on his own.

He hadn't been near enough to see the man's face and wasn't sure if he would have recognized him anyway. He'd been gone for five years and there had been more ships added to the fleet and more seamen had signed up and others had been replaced. Still, knowing that he was obviously being followed by one of the members of the crew did set off warning bells.

He took a quick look behind them but didn't see anyone trailing. The road was reasonably straight with only a few obstacles, so he could see at least two miles behind them. He suspected that the follower had missed their departure and would either return to San Antonio via the direct route or ask someone where their carriage had gone and follow them to New Braunfels. Whichever it was, he wasn't about to be surprised but wished he hadn't left his Winchester with Hector. All he had now was his Colt and that would give the man a decided range advantage, assuming he wasn't just following as a spy. He still had no idea as to his motive but had to assume the worst.

They were halfway to New Braunfels when Emma asked, "Will you come with me when we get to my parents' house, Rhody?"

"I'll be wherever you need me, Emma."

She smiled at him before saying, "From the first moment I saw you sitting on Morgana in front of those Comanches, you always have been where I needed you to be."

He smiled back as he replied, "I try, Emma."

An hour later, they turned down the side street beside her father's bakery and stopped before her parents' home.

Rhody looked at Emma's nervous face and asked, "Are you ready, Emma?"

Emma slowly nodded before Rhody stepped down and took Emma's hand to help her exit.

Once on the ground, she grasped his hand even more tightly than she had earlier, if that was possible. Emma's last memories of making this short journey along the bricked walkway was one of the worst moments in her life and hoped that this one would help to heal the pain from that day.

They stepped onto the porch and this time, Rhody knocked as he felt Emma's hand beginning to tremble and knew she was too distraught to handle even that simple task.

RHODY JONES

They stood before the door for almost a minute and Rhody could almost feel Emma's urge to turn and escape to their carriage when the door swung open and he saw her mother. She was much shorter than Emma, and her hair was still blonde, but her blue eyes were tired and red from almost constant worry. But the moment she saw Emma's face, those eyes instantly shifted from exhaustion to unrestricted joy.

"Emma! You've come home after all!" she exclaimed before taking one step forward and embracing her daughter.

Emma hugged her mother back and Rhody experienced a feeling of déjà vu after witnessing Emma's arrival at Anna's house just hours earlier.

This time, after they released each other, Mrs. Ludden simply pulled her daughter inside by the hand without even giving him a glance. Rhody followed then closed the door and removed his hat as Emma's mother almost yanked her into the parlor.

He waited until Emma and her mother sat on the setee before sitting on a nearby chair.

"I'm so happy to see you again, Emma," she said as she held her daughter's hands in hers before she finally looked at Rhody then asked, "Who is the young man who escorted you to New Braunfels?"

She smiled at Rhody as she replied, "His name is Rhody Jones, Mama, and he didn't escort me. He rescued me and two children from the Comanches after they killed everyone else on two ranches. I owe him my life, Mama."

Her mother glanced at Rhody then turned her shocked face to her daughter as she asked, *"Everyone else died?"*

"Yes, Mama."

She sighed, then looked back at Rhody and said, "Thank you for saving my Emma, Mister Jones. You have no idea how much this means to me."

"You're welcome, ma'am."

Rhody kept his response brief as he expected that they had a lot to talk about and the most important subject was Emma's father. He wasn't wrong.

Maria Ludden shifted her focus back to Emma and said, "I didn't think that you would come after all this time, but I'm very grateful that you finally decided to see your father. It will be such a comfort to him."

"And to you too, Mama. I would have come earlier if Carl hadn't been destroying Anna's letters. I didn't know about father's condition until I talked to Anna a couple of hours ago. How is he?"

"He's sleeping now. The laudanum that Doctor Lange gave him for the pain makes him drowsy. He's just wasting away, Emma and it's breaking my heart to see him this way. I feel so hopeless because all I can do is keep him clean while he suffers. I don't sleep very much, so I can't help him as much as I wish I could."

"Anna said that he wants me to see him so I can forgive him for making me marry Carl and then leave."

"Can you do that for him, Emma? It would give him a measure of peace and relieve his soul from torment."

"I'll talk to him when he awakens, Mama, but I don't think I need to forgive him. I need to ask his forgiveness for my behavior that created the problem."

Her mother sighed again then said, "No, sweetheart, you don't need to ask for his forgiveness. He should have helped you and not punished you. I must ask your forgiveness as well for remaining silent when he decided to do all those things that hurt you and Carl both. Can you forgive me for my sins of silence, Emma?"

"Of course, I will, Mama. I understood why you didn't argue with him and I never blamed you for it. How long will father sleep?"

"It varies by how much laudanum he takes and how great his pain is. He coughs a lot, so don't be shocked when you see the bloody towels near his bedside."

"I won't, Mama. I've been through so much these past two weeks that I've almost become immune to the sight of blood."

"What happened, Emma?"

This time, Emma didn't refer to Rhody as she'd just heard the story again and wanted to add her own insights which would include the praise for Rhody's actions that he'd omitted in his narration to Anna.

Rhody listened with his new Stetson in his hands and felt uneasy when she did comment about his bravery and selflessness but understood why she felt it was necessary. As she spoke, he knew that he'd probably soon be hearing her voice for the last time.

After her mother had described her father's condition and how she was having to act as his nurse while watching him die, he knew that she'd have to stay to help her mother. If he didn't have to return to Rhode Island, then he'd just rent a room in New Braunfels, but he couldn't let his uncle marry sweet Elizabeth if she was really a sour Elizabeth.

When Emma finished, her mother looked at Rhody again and said, "You are a remarkable young man, Mister Jones. Thank you again for all you did to save Emma and the children," then before Rhody could reply, they heard a series of violent coughs from the hallway.

"Your father is awake, Emma. Can you come with me now?"

"Yes, Mama," Emma replied before she stood.

RHODY JONES

As her mother rose from the couch Emma glanced at him, and Rhody knew that she had to see her father without him, so he just looked at her without moving.

Maria took her daughter's hand as they left the parlor and entered the hallway before they turned into an open doorway.

Emma may have seen a lot of violence in the past two weeks, but none of those horrors had prepared her for the sight of her emaciated father lying on his sickbed.

The last time she'd seen him just a year ago, he'd been a robust man with an almost fierce countenance. Now he was little more than a skeleton with sallow, sunken cheeks and distant, unseeing watery eyes. He held a towel to his mouth that was already spotted with blood when he looked up and saw Emma.

He hacked a series of spasmodic coughs into the towel before he lowered it to his bed and tried to focus on Emma.

Her mother released her hand and Emma walked slowly to her father then sat in a chair near his head.

He raised his shaking, bony hand to her and she took it into hers.

"I'm home, Papa," she whispered as her own eyes began to tear.

"Emma," he croaked, "I'm…I'm so sorry… for…what I did to you. Will you for…forgive me?"

"I am the one who should be asking for your forgiveness, Papa. I was headstrong and disobeyed you. I know I was an adult but doing what I did was disrespectful. Will you forgive me for what I did to bring you such shame?"

Gustav squeezed his daughter's hand with his diminished strength as he whispered, "I'll forgive…you…if you will…forgive me."

"I forgive you with all my heart, Papa."

Her father closed his eyes and managed a slight smile before he said, "Thank you, Emma. I can see God now and…He will…grant me…entrance…into…into His house."

"I'll stay with you now, Papa, and help mama to care for you."

Gustav didn't reply but was still smiling as he drifted back to sleep.

Emma carefully set his hand on the bed before standing and taking her mother's hand.

"Thank you so much for that, Emma. He's at peace with himself now."

"So, am I, Mama. Let's go back to the parlor. I need to talk to Rhody."

"Is he staying in New Braunfels, Emma?"

"No, Mama. He needs to take a ship soon."

Maria looked into her daughter's eyes as she asked, "You love him, don't you?"

Emma wasn't startled by the question and softly replied, "Yes, Mama. I'm almost ashamed to admit it to myself, but I've felt this way almost from the first day. It's not like anything I've ever felt before."

"Then why is he leaving? Doesn't he care for you at all?"

"I don't know, Mama. I know that he respects me and thinks well of me, but I know he has to leave because of a family problem back home in Rhode Island, and I'm not going to put any pressure on him to stay by telling him."

"I understand, Emma, but once he's gone, you know that he might not return. A lot of bad things could happen on that long journey."

"I know, Mama."

Her mother nodded then she turned, and they walked out of her father's sick room.

Rhody looked at Emma's face as she entered the parlor and could see the marked difference from her brief visit with her father and knew that each of them had found the peace that they so desperately needed.

He smiled at her and Emma's warm returning smile confirmed his belief in her newfound serenity.

Emma and her mother returned to the couch before she said, "We forgave each other, Rhody, and I'm much better now."

"I could tell just by looking at your eyes, Emma."

Maria then said, "I'm going to the kitchen to start cooking dinner. Are you staying, Mister Jones?"

"I'd like to, ma'am, but I need to get back to San Antonio."

"I wish you'd stay, but I understand."

She then stood and walked out of the parlor leaving Emma and Rhody alone.

Emma looked across the room then patted the couch seat beside her.

Rhody rose, crossed the parlor and sat down beside her already knowing what she was going to tell him.

"I have to stay and help my mother, Rhody."

"I know. I need to tell you something before I go. Remember that rider that Willie mentioned on the ride from San Antonio? The one on the Morgan that looked like Jack?"

"Yes."

RHODY JONES

"That same horse was parked in front of your brother-in-law's shop in Seguin and then I remembered seeing it in Hector's corral in San Antonio when I went to rent the carriage. He told me that a man who talked funny rented a horse, and I thought it might be the sailor who dropped off my uncle's letter and he'd decided to spend a few days in San Antonio before he returned to Galveston."

"Why would he follow you?"

"That's what I can't figure out. I'm just letting you know because it's the reason I want to leave right away."

"Will you be all right?"

"I'll be fine. Do you need anything before I go?"

Emma took his hands before she replied, "No. I'll be all right."

"I gave Willie Jack's Winchester and we gave Marty the books to remember us, so what can I give you?"

Emma wanted so badly to tell him how she felt, but instead she quietly replied, "I don't need anything to remember you, Rhody. You'll always be held close in my mind and heart."

Rhody exhaled. reached into his pocket, pulled out his notebook and pencil then wrote his address on the last page and after carefully ripping it free, he handed it to her.

"Will you please write to me, Emma? Visit Willie and Marty and tell them how much I miss them and let me know how they're doing. You know that I'll miss you most of all, don't you?"

"Will you, Rhody? You won't board that ship and forget me by the time you dock in Providence?"

"I'll never forget you, Emma."

"Will you come back, Rhody?" she asked quietly.

"All I can promise is that I'll try. I don't know what will happen when I meet my uncle and Elizabeth, but I'll write to you and let you know. If you ever need anything, send me a telegram. Okay?"

Emma nodded then wiped her eyes to prevent any tears from escaping to her cheeks.

Rhody was about to stand when he looked into those marvelous blue eyes then thought it may be his last chance, so he leaned forward and barely brushed his lips to hers.

He then stood and smiled down at her before he said, "Goodbye, Emma."

Emma whispered, "Goodbye, Rhody."

He turned and was pulling on his Stetson as he reached for the doorknob then soon exited the house.

RHODY JONES

Once he was on the porch, he blew out his breath and quickly hurried down the steps to get to the carriage. He had to fight the urge to return and see Emma again.

Emma was sitting on the couch with her fingertips touching her lips. As much as she understood why he had to leave and hoped that he would return, she believed that the one light kiss would be the only one she would ever receive from him. She began to believe that he would never return as if God was still punishing her by showing her what love was and then taking it away.

After she heard the front door close, her mother walked into the parlor and saw Emma with her fingertips still pressed to her lips.

"Are you all right, Emma?"

Emma slowly turned her eyes from the closed door and looked at her mother before she replied, "I don't know, Mama. I'll help you cook dinner now."

―――

Rhody left New Braunfels behind in the late afternoon and expected to reach San Antonio before sunset. As much as he'd like to spend the ride thinking about Emma, he knew he had to focus on the sailor who had followed him to Seguin. If it had been just a Texan on the Morgan, he would have been worried that he was trailing Emma, but this mariner was following him, and he still had no idea why.

So, even as he kept the carriage moving at a brisk pace, he scanned the road ahead and occasionally glanced behind him but found no one following. If he was being followed then unless the sailor killed Hector's horse by running him at a gallop for ten miles, he'd never catch up. He was still inside the shop when they'd left Seguin, so it was more likely that he'd taken the short route back to San Antonio.

Despite that mental reassurance, he still watched for a possible ambush while he tried to come up with the motive. He then broke it down to the basic reasons for most violence: money, love, power or revenge. He knew that the sailor wouldn't be upset over a woman's lost affection, so that left money, power and revenge. Money didn't make much sense to him because even if he was dead then his uncle would get his half of the business. Then just before that idea was discarded, he made the short jump to sweet Elizabeth.

He forgot about looking for potential ambush sites while he reviewed the timing for everything. His uncle meets sweet Elizabeth a few weeks earlier, and after she accepts his marriage proposal, he writes his letter asking Rhody to return for the ceremony because he hadn't received his letter letting him know that he was riding west. He gives it to Captain Randolph who sails out of Providence on the larger *Sweet Elizabeth*. Once out of port, there was no reason for Uncle Richard to contact the captain, even after he'd received his letter. The ship was carrying cargo to Galveston and needed to finish the voyage anyway.

RHODY JONES

He almost didn't see the road ahead as he tried to imagine the sequence of events. The easy part was coming up with the prize at the end of the plot...the R. Jones Shipping Company. For it to work, the sailor had to kill him then return to Galveston and tell Captain Randolph that he'd dropped off the letter but didn't find Roland Jones. The ship would sail on the tenth and would return with the bad news. His uncle would marry sweet Elizabeth and once she became a widow, she would inherit everything.

There were still many questions, including how the bride had convinced the sailor to assassinate him. It wouldn't be as simple as most people would expect. If she approached the wrong seaman then he'd just turn her in to Uncle Richard and she'd be out on her ear. The second big question was how she could arrange for Uncle Richard's untimely and accidental death. Even then, she'd need proof of his own demise in order to satisfy the probate court.

He then pulled his uncle's letter from his pocket and let the horses find their way when he read it more carefully.

He finally stopped on the line that read: *I'm having your yawl overhauled and, if you don't mind, I plan to use it to take my new bride on a honeymoon to Newport.*

Uncle Richard hadn't sailed in decades and Rhody doubted that he could manage the yawl on his own, so he'd need to have a seaman handle the boat for him. Rhody would have expected his uncle to choose one of his trusted men for the job, but if he was as besotted as he appeared to be then his new wife might be able to get him to change his mind and she could have the same sailor who was probably waiting for him in San Antonio to be the man at the tiller.

He still had no idea how she could have convinced the man to do the job, and he may be totally wrong about everything, but he'd discover his answer soon enough when he returned to San Antonio. He just hoped he didn't get the answer just before he died.

———

Jean LeClair hadn't bothered trying to follow Jones but left the shop with his new bullwhip and mounted his rented horse after hanging the bullwhip over the saddle horn. He didn't know if Jones still had the woman with him or not but didn't care anymore. He knew that Jones wasn't taking the quicker route, so he'd be in San Antonio before Jones could arrive then he'd return the horse and practice with his new whip and wait to see him return the carriage. If he was alone, so much the better.

He had returned to his original plan to use his belaying pin but wasn't sure about the best location. He could just wait until late in the night and enter his hotel room while he slept, but he preferred to find him outside. The train to Galveston left at 8:20, so he'd have to handle the job tonight. The only question was where he'd do it and that depended on Jones' movements.

RHODY JONES

He rode into San Antonio while Rhody was still twenty-two miles away and soon pulled up outside of Hector's barn and dismounted. He led the Morgan into the livery and handed the reins to Hector.

Hector saw the new bullwhip as Jean lifted it from the saddle horn and said, "That's a nice whip, mister."

"I bought it in Seguin. Mind if I try it out back for a while?"

"Nope. Go ahead. It's quieter than gunfire."

Jean laughed then left through the big barn doors and circled around back past the corrals to an open area where he still had a decent view of the road from New Braunfels.

He was practiced in the use of whips but had never had one that was this long. He was almost startled when he heard the first loud crack as the tip of the whip broke the sound barrier.

He grinned and said aloud, "That's louder than my pistol."

———

By the time Rhody spotted San Antonio, the sun was dipping below the horizon and he wished he'd bought that Remington derringer. He'd drop off the carriage and ask Hector about the tan Morgan then after having dinner, he'd return to his room if he hadn't spotted the sailor. When Willie had mentioned his odd hat, Rhody realized he was probably wearing a seaman's cap. They weren't a standard piece of headgear by any means, but many of them favored the flat fisherman's cap.

Jean LeClair had long since stopped cracking his whip and had gone to the café across the street and down a block from the livery so he could watch for Jones' return while he filled his empty stomach.

He'd just had his food delivered when Rhody drove down the street, stopped in front of the livery and stepped out of the carriage. He was alone which pleased Jean immensely.

Rhody stepped into the barn and found Hector standing beside Morgana wearing a grin.

"I heard you drive up, Rhody. Where are the children and the lady?"

"I left them with their families, Hector," Rhody replied as he walked closer to the liveryman.

"Is everything all right?"

"It's fine, Hector. That man who rented your horse may have been following me. Is it that tan Morgan that looks like Jack the one he rented?"

"Yes. Why would he be following you?"

"I don't know, but he followed me all the way to Seguin."

"He said he bought a bull whip in Seguin."

RHODY JONES

"You don't know where he is, do you?"

"He went to have dinner at Juanita's about ten minutes ago."

"That's interesting. Well, that's about all I need right now, Hector. I'll probably be taking the train to Galveston tomorrow, so I'll be leaving Jack and Morgana here. Can you keep my Winchester and Sharps-Borshadt with you?"

"Sure, but when will you be back?"

"As soon as I can, but that might not be for a couple of months. I'll pay you for boarding the horses," he said before pulling out two twenty-dollar bills and handing them to Hector.

"This is too much, Rhody."

"I know you'll take good care of them while I'm gone, but if something prevents me from coming back before the middle of October, can you take the horses to New Braunfels for me? Just leave them at the bakery and tell the baker that they're for the owner's daughter, Emma. Can you remember that?"

"Yes, sir, but I hope I don't have to do it."

"Neither do I, Hector," Rhody said before popping Hector on his shoulder then turning and leaving the barn.

He was hungry anyway, so he decided to have dinner at Juanita's and see if he could find the sailor. He wouldn't be wearing his fisherman's cap, but his eyes should give him away.

Jean watched him leaving the livery and was momentarily surprised to see him heading to the diner, but immediately put aside his concern knowing that Jones was probably just as hungry as he had been.

When Rhody entered the diner, he didn't scan the room but walked to the back of the diner and took a seat that faced the window, assuming that the sailor would be watching for him.

He didn't even glance that way as the waitress approached his table.

He smiled at her when she arrived and said, "Good evening, Yvonne. What's good today?"

"All by yourself tonight, Rhody?"

"Yes, ma'am."

"The cook just took a nice beef roast out of the oven."

"That sounds perfect."

"I'll be back with some coffee in a minute," Yvonne said before she turned to walk back to the kitchen.

Rhody smiled as he watched her walk away, getting a decent look at the only other table that was occupied by a lone male diner. He didn't recognize him, but there was something about the man that tickled the back of his mind as if he'd seen him before but couldn't recall when he had.

Yvonne brought him a small pot of coffee and filled his cup before heading for another table.

He never looked at the stranger again, so after finishing his dinner, he left fifty cents on the table then stood, picked up his hat and walked out of the diner. He didn't turn to look back as he walked to his hotel and soon entered his room.

After hanging his hat on a wall peg, he removed his gunbelt and sat on the bed, trying to remember where he'd seen the man. It had to be at least five years ago, but he had met a lot of sailors before he took to the saddle, and only some of them worked on his and Uncle Richard's ships.

Finally, he gave up trying to recall who he was or even what his connection to sweet Elizabeth was and concentrated on what he might do. He had to assume that the man knew where he was staying and probably even knew his room number. He doubted that the man would attempt anything during the day in front of people, especially in Texas where most of the men packed iron and many of the women carried a pistol or derringer somewhere. He'd have to strike at night and Rhody suspected that he had to act soon because he would know that he was going to be on tomorrow's train to Galveston.

He lit the room's only lamp then worked out a plan for dealing with the stranger if he decided to make his attempt tonight. He had two sets of saddlebags in his room: one with his spare clothes and personal hygiene necessities and the other with his sextant, telescope, map case and a box of ammunition for his Colt. He stood, pulled back the covers and arranged the saddlebags and the pillow to make a reasonable bumpy outline of a sleeping man, but felt a bit silly after it was done. The white pillowcase looked pretty obvious, so he removed his pistol then rolled the gunbelt and set it on the pillow with the pistol's lighter grips behind the dark leather. It looked like a rolled up gunbelt, but after he blew out the lamp, it wasn't that bad. The stranger wouldn't use a pistol, not in a hotel. He'd use a knife and have to plunge the blade in quickly to silence his victim, so he couldn't afford to take his time to look closely. By then, Rhody would have his Colt's muzzle pointed at him.

His only concern was falling asleep. He pulled his watch from his pocket and the hands told him it was 9:32. He would have to stay awake for another four hours or so if the man made his attempt tonight, and that would be difficult.

He moved the room's straight-backed chair into the corner of the room which gave him a clear angle to the door yet would leave him in the shadows when the door opened. The moon was half full and would provide enough illumination in the room for him to take the shot if it became necessary. His hope was that the man would drop the knife after hearing Rhody's warning and then admit who had sent him and the motive behind the plot.

RHODY JONES

―――

Jean had waited for another two minutes and watched Jones enter his hotel before tossing a quarter on the table and leaving the diner. He didn't want to go to the hotel yet but needed to waste some time so Jones could enter his room for the night.

The best place to kill time was obvious, so he headed for the Alamo Saloon and Billiard Parlor.

―――

It was after midnight and Rhody found himself nodding off as he sat on his chair with his Colt on his lap. He was close to the dresser and its pitcher of water and wash basin, so he stuck his fingers into the lukewarm water and rubbed it over his eyes and face before blinking and shaking his head.

He'd stayed up all night more than a few times on the trail and knew the dangers of just sitting idly in the saddle, but he couldn't sing to the sleeping cattle or even hum. He couldn't walk around either and the worst thing he'd done is when he began to think about Emma and those last few minutes they had shared. When he'd done that, he had been seriously close to drifting into a fantasy world and had only snapped out of it when a boisterous guest had stumbled down the hallway.

―――

Jean left his room fifteen minutes later clutching his heavy belaying pin. He checked the quiet hallway before slowly stepping toward room #11. He stopped before the door and listened intently for any signs that Jones was still awake. There wasn't any light coming from under the door, so he was convinced that he'd soon put his belaying pin to good use.

He'd go for the head which should be on the pillow to the left of the door and should only need one hard blow to finish the job. It wouldn't look like an accident, but he didn't care now. Let them find the body late in the morning and by then, he'd be on the train to Galveston.

―――

Rhody was drifting again when he heard the very light sound of the doorknob being turned and was slammed into an adrenalin-fueled state of alertness. He gripped his Colt then slowly rose and pointed his pistol toward the door but didn't cock the hammer yet.

His heart rate accelerated as he watched the door slowly swing open into the dark room and the shadow of a man enter. He was just ten feet away from the stranger and watched him bring his knife back over his head.

In one swift motion, he slammed his weapon down onto the gunbelt and even as Rhody was preparing to shout to have him drop his knife, Jean's belaying pin struck where Jones' head should be but found the gunbelt's spare .44 cartridges.

RHODY JONES

Two of the rimfire primers did their job when the hard oak pounded into them. The belaying pin was still on its downward arc as it ignited the cartridges and in that brief instant as the chemical reaction was taking place, the momentum of the belaying pin pushed the top edge of the gunbelt into the pillow and helped to keep the brass from being shot from their leather loops. Those leather loops, which had been soaked by that vicious thunderstorm and then quickly dried were another reason for keeping the brass part of the cartridge from blasting free in that briefest of moments.

The gunpowder was ignited just as the lead bullets lifted upward, so when they left their brass partners, they ripped across the thirty inches of empty space and punched into Jean LeClair's body. One rammed into his gut on the right side and drilled through his liver before exiting and burying itself in the wall. The second was just inches to the left and ripped into his abdomen just above his navel. It blew apart his abdominal aorta before smashing into his third lumbar vertebral body where it was stopped by the thick bone.

Rhody was stunned at the unexpected flash and loud reports as he watched the stranger simply drop face first onto his bed. He took two long strides and rolled him over to see if he was alive but knew it wasn't really necessary.

He left the room through the open door, closed it behind him then walked to the desk. No one was there when he arrived, but within two minutes, other guests began arriving in various night clothing. Soon, the owner of the hotel arrived from his private area and Rhody waved him over.

"Can you send someone to get the sheriff or one of his deputies?"

He nodded then pointed at one of the better dressed guests and said, "Go get Sheriff Matthews."

As the man ran from the hotel, Rhody said, "Some stranger had been following me all day, so I thought he might try to attack me tonight. I put my saddlebags under the blankets and my gunbelt on the pillow to make it look as if I was sleeping. I was in a chair waiting for him, and when he came in, I saw him lift his knife and when he tried to stab me, he must have hit the gunbelt's spare cartridges. I never even cocked my Colt's hammer."

"Let's wait for the sheriff to show up. It might be a while."

Rhody nodded then stepped to one of the lobby's chairs, sat down and laid his cold Colt on his lap.

Ten minutes later, the sheriff and the guest entered the lobby and Rhody rose from his chair.

"What happened?" Sheriff Matthews asked as he approached Rhody.

RHODY JONES

After Rhody repeated the same story he'd told the proprietor, they walked through the crowd of guests and down the hallway.

"Anybody been in here since you left?" the sheriff asked as he put his hand on the doorknob.

"No, sir."

The sheriff opened the door and saw Jean LeClair's body lying on his back while Rhody walked past him to light the lamp.

When he brought the lamp closer to the body, the sheriff said, "I've seen this feller walking around here the last few days. Do you know who he is?"

"No, sir. I seem to recall having seen him before, but it had to be at least five years ago."

"You said he used a knife, but I don't see one anywhere."

Rhody said, "I rolled him over to see if he was still alive, so it's probably beneath his body."

"Well, let's roll him back again and check."

Rhody set the lamp on the side table then he and the sheriff rolled Jean's body and the sheriff picked up the belaying stick and showed it to Rhody.

"This ain't a knife."

"No, sir. That's a belaying pin from a ship. It's a formidable weapon in a practiced hand. I think he did serious damage to my gunbelt with it, too."

The sheriff then lifted Rhody's half-ripped gunbelt from the pillow and whistled.

"Well, I'll be damned! I never saw anything like this before!"

The two empty brass cartridge cases were buried into the pillow, but the gunbelt loops that had held the cartridges long enough to release the lead were shredded and the leather belt itself was almost severed in half.

The sheriff then went through Jean's pockets and found some cash, but nothing else.

After pocketing the money, he turned to Rhody and asked, "Do you know why he tried to crush your skull?"

"I think it has something to do with my uncle. He's marrying a much younger woman up in Rhode Island and asked me to come to the wedding. It sounded to me like she was a gold digger. I think that she's planning on killing my uncle after they're married and if I wasn't alive,then she would inherit the shipping company."

"You were gonna inherit a shipping company?" he asked with wide eyes.

RHODY JONES

"I'd inherit his half of the company. I inherited my father's share when I was four."

"Why are you here? You've been around San Antone for years."

"I wanted to see the West and after five years of driving cattle to Kansas, I thought I'd head for California but had my journey interrupted by some Comanches. Now I need to get back to Rhode Island to see my uncle. I'd like to take the morning train to Galveston. Can I do that?"

"This isn't hard to figure out, so I don't see a problem. Can you give me a hand getting that body out of here?"

"Yes, sir."

Rhody picked up his damaged gunbelt, then slid his Colt into the undamaged holster and set it on the dresser before taking hold of Jean's arms while the sheriff grasped his ankles.

They slid the body from the bloody blankets and waddled it out of the room and down the hallway across the lobby then out the door and over the porch.

Once they reached the boardwalk they laid it down and the sheriff said, "I'll get the mortician to come and pick him up."

"Thanks, Sheriff."

"Hope things work out with your uncle and you might want to get a new gunbelt before you go."

"I hope so, too. I'll pick a new one up in Galveston because I don't think Mister Whitfield will have his shop open before I leave."

The sheriff glanced at the body then shook his head before looking at Rhody and saying, "You take care now," then he turned and walked away.

Rhody watched him leave then looked at the dead man's face and still couldn't recall where he'd seen him. He should ask the sheriff if he could go through the man's room to find out his name but decided it really didn't matter. Before they sailed, he'd ask Captain Randolph which one of his crew hadn't returned to the ship. He was already short on time as his train was leaving in just six hours.

He returned to his room and found the proprietor inside rolling up the blankets around the damaged pillow.

He looked at Rhody and asked, "Did you want a different room, Mister Jones?"

"No. I think I'll just get cleaned up and get ready to leave. I'm sorry for causing the commotion and I'll pay you for the damages."

"There's no need. We lose a lot of bedding to drunk cowpokes and at least this is a good story. I never saw a man shoot himself by hitting a gunbelt."

"I'd be surprised if either of us ever sees it again, either."

RHODY JONES

After the proprietor left the room, Rhody remembered that he already had a spare gunbelt. Folded in his spare britches was Jack's gunbelt that Emma had worn for the ride to Menardville.

He opened the saddlebag then pulled out the rolled britches and extracted the gunbelt. He was going to switch pistols but instead, he just rolled his own Colt and useless gunbelt into the pants and returned it to the saddlebag.

CHAPTER 10

Rhody left the hotel before sunrise with his two sets of heavy saddlebags over his shoulders and headed for the diner.

He had more than enough cash for his train ticket and realized that if he had given it to Emma, he would have had to delay his departure for another day to withdraw some more money from his bank account. Even if he had taken some more cash, he wasn't going to close his account with the Alamo State Bank because he was already planning for his return.

He wasn't surprised when his breakfast was interrupted by other patrons to ask about the bizarre shooting in the hotel, but he was able to enjoy his last meal in San Antonio in time to make his train.

———

By eight-thirty, San Antonio had faded into the distance as he sat near the window with his saddlebags taking the rest of the seat. The railroad's name was the Galveston & San Antonio Railway, which he thought was appropriate.

RHODY JONES

It was going to be ten-hour ride and he should have been sleepy by now, but he wasn't. He had too much on his mind including the early morning attack, his uncle's situation, and most importantly, Emma. He was happy for her knowing that she had reconciled with her father and that she'd be able to visit Willie and Marty, but that didn't detract from how much he already missed her.

Eventually, the rhythmic clicking of the steel wheels crossing the gaps between the rails and the rocking motion of swaying car had their effect and he drifted into sleep.

When the car lurched as it began to slow, his head snapped forward before his eyes opened and he wondered how long he'd slept. He assumed that the train was making its first stop, but he checked his watch anyway. He was surprised to find that it read 12:28, which meant he'd slept through at least three stops without waking.

He wasn't hungry, so he just stood and stretched before sitting back down. He was a bit disappointed that he'd slept through that first stop because it would have been Seguin. Maybe it was better this way because he might have been tempted to leave the train then rent a horse and ride to New Braunfels. Maybe he'd even walk because he had so much experience in ambulation lately.

After taking on water and coal in Columbus, the train began rolling southeast again.

Hours later, Rhody stepped onto the platform in Galveston, walked across the wide wooden space and headed for the docks. He was hungry but wanted to find the *Sweet Elizabeth* before he satisfied his stomach's demands. Aside from his need to speak to Captain Randolph, he was curious about the newest addition to their fleet.

A lot of advances had been made in ship design since he'd shifted to spending his time in the saddle rather than on the quarterdeck. Improved efficiency in steam engines were adding speed and endurance and some were already shedding their masts and sails, but they were mostly for short, coastal operations. The longer haul ships still sported sails.

He reached the docks and walked along the line of moored ships and quickly spotted the *Sweet Elizabeth*. Uncle Richard's fiancée may not deserve the adjective, but her floating namesake surely did.

He approached the gangplank then stopped to admire the new vessel. He wasn't sure that this was her maiden voyage, but it had to be one of the first two because his uncle had only met Elizabeth a few weeks ago.

Rhody hopped onto the gangplank and soon had the familiar feel of a wooden deck beneath his feet. He felt a bit out of character as he stood with his Stetson, gunbelt and cowboy boots, but at least he wasn't wearing chaps.

RHODY JONES

He was examining the rigging when a seaman approached him and asked, "You lost, cowboy?"

Rhody looked at him then smiled before he asked, "Is Captain Randolph aboard?"

"He's in the engine room. Why do you want to see him?"

"To tell him he can get underway as soon as the crew returns from shore leave."

"Who are you?"

"Rho…Roland Jones," he replied before leaving the astonished seaman and walked toward the doorway to the engine room.

Rhody still had his saddlebags over his shoulders as he climbed down the ladder and descended into the dark space.

He heard the captain talking to someone probably the engineer in the back of the engine room, so he headed that way.

When he passed the enormous boiler, he spotted the captain who was now listening to the engineer's explanation, so he waited until the engineer finished.

Before the captain could ask another question, Rhody said, "Myles! Could I talk to you?"

Captain Randolph turned his head to berate the crewman who had dared to address him using his Christian name and was taken aback to find a cowboy standing in front of him wearing a gun.

"Who are you?" he asked.

"I guess it's too dark down here, or your eyes are getting worse now. I'm here to let you know that you can cast off and head back to Providence for my uncle's wedding."

"Rollie!" he exclaimed as he stepped closer.

Rhody grinned at the captain's startled face and said, "For five years now, everyone has called me Rhody, and I'm fond of the nickname. But yes, I was called Rollie or Roland when I left the *Vivienne* in New Orleans."

The captain shook Rhody's hand and asked, "How have you been? You sure do look different from the last time I saw you."

"I'll tell you upstairs in your cabin, but can you send out word to the crew that you'll be sailing tomorrow?"

He turned to the engineer and said, "Go ashore and get a spare valve and let me know when it's ready and tell Oliver to get the crew back on board."

"Aye, aye, Captain," the engineer replied before passing the two men and climbing the ladder into the light.

RHODY JONES

"Let's get out of here. I never did get used to that damned machine."

Rhody snickered before he followed the captain up the ladder. Once on deck, they turned to the quarterdeck and soon entered the captain's cabin.

After setting down his saddlebags and removing his hat, he took a seat across from the captain's desk while Captain Randolph sat down in the leather chair behind the desk.

"Now you can tell me what you've been doing since you sailed aboard that poor excuse for a ship. I'll never understand why you did that, either."

"We'll have plenty of time to talk on the voyage, but right now, I'll tell you what happened last night."

Rhody then told the captain the story beginning with the first time Willie had spotted the rider trailing them on the way to New Braunfels and ended with the strange manner of the assassin's death.

When he finished, Captain Randolph had a lot more questions, but before he could even ask one, Rhody said, "I didn't recognize the man, but I must have seen his face in the past. He was a sailor, but I never got his name. I figure you'd be able to help when you found a missing crewmember."

"Why would he try to kill you?"

"I think he was trying to kill me so if Uncle Richard died after the wedding, his new bride would inherit the company. Do you know the woman at all?"

"No. I don't travel in your uncle's circles. I never met her, either. All I do know is that she's from Boston. You can imagine the rumors that are running around the crew about your uncle."

"I can imagine, so keep the story of what happened in San Antonio last night between us. I don't want to add more fuel to the gossip."

"I'll do that. What did this sailor look like?"

"Average height with dark hair and brown eyes. He wasn't really noticeable except for his thin moustache. Not too many sailors wear them that way because it takes too much work to keep them tidy."

"That doesn't sound like any of the crew. Are you sure he was a seaman from this ship?"

Rhody thought about it. He could have been sent by train or taken an earlier ship.

"Who dropped off the letter from my uncle?"

"I posted it here. There was no real reason to send a member of the crew all the way to San Antonio when the post gets there at the same time."

RHODY JONES

Rhody nodded but needed to rethink how the sailor had found him.

Captain Randolph then said, "I was going to go ashore in a little while for dinner. Will you join me?"

"I'd love to. My stomach's growling already after I skipped lunch. Do you have a spare cabin?"

"You can use the spare bunk in here so we can talk."

"I need to get caught up on everything, including this ship and I have a lot to tell you as well."

The captain grinned and asked, "You didn't go shooting any wild Indians, did you?"

Rhody grinned back and replied, "As a matter of fact…"

He began telling the captain about his first encounter with the Comanches as they crossed the main deck.

By the time they'd taken a seat at the closest restaurant, he'd reached the part where he'd shot the one warrior with his Sharps-Borshadt.

"Where is the gun now?"

"I had a friend store it for me with my Winchester and my two horses until I return."

"Return? You're not going to stay with your uncle?"

"I'm not planning on it. I need to return to San Antonio, or more accurately to New Braunfels, but I might go back to Rhode Island after that. Everything is still unpredictable right now."

"Let me guess. You met a girl, didn't you? Is it the girl you rescued from the Comanches?"

"I met a woman, Myles. I rescued her and the girl from the Comanches, but she's living with her parents now and the girl and her brother are living in the same town with their grandparents."

The waitress took their orders and Rhody continued his story.

When they returned to the ship an hour later, the sun was going down, and the members of the crew were already trickling aboard.

As they stepped across the gangplank, Rhody asked, "How many men do you have, Myles?"

"We have four able seamen, the engineer, a cook, a carpenter and four firemen for the boilers. The first mate is George Allen and the second mate is Leo Perot. I don't have any midshipmen on board, but I do have a cabin boy."

"How fast can she run on just steam?"

RHODY JONES

"We can hit fourteen knots, but it's a waste of coal. I normally keep her at around ten knots. If we have a good wind, I'll add the sails to save fuel. We only have enough coal to reach Charleston, so we'll have to fill the bunkers there."

"I know you're not fond of the steam engine, but she's still a pretty ship."

"Aye, I'll give you that."

―――

After a night spend sharing information, Rhody and the captain turned in. The captain had his ship ready to sail days earlier in anticipation of Rhody's arrival, so all that he needed to do in the morning was to notify the harbormaster that he was departing and wait for the tide. He did admit to the convenience of having the steam engine so he wouldn't have to wait for the wind.

―――

The next morning, the *Sweet Elizabeth* cast off her mooring lines and slowly left Galveston's docks with a pilot directing their way out of the harbor.

Rhody had left his gunbelt and Stetson in the captain's cabin rather than to risk losing his hat or letting the saltwater seriously damage the Colt.

Once free of the port, Captain Randolph ordered full speed into the gulf and Rhody felt the exhilaration of being on the deck of a ship again for the first time in almost five years. None of the sails were set because they were heading into the wind, but the new ship made good speed and because it didn't need to tack into the wind, the ten knots would cover greater distances than a sailing ship making the same speed unless she was sailing with the wind.

———

Over the next week that it took the *Sweet Elizabeth* to reach Charleston, Rhody spent time with the crew, renewing old acquaintances and making new ones as he answered their myriad questions. By the time the ship docked in the South Carolina capital to fill her coal bunkers and top off her ship's stores, he knew all of the new faces and each of them was in awe of the stories he told that had surpassed any of their tall old mariner tales.

The morning after their stop in Charleston, the steamer left the harbor and headed north for its last leg. Captain Randolph received Rhody's permission to be less concerned with the rate of coal consumption and let the *Sweet Elizabeth* have her head.

The ship was plowing through the Atlantic at fifteen knots in her last nine-hundred-mile sprint. A journey that would have taken two weeks or more on a sailing ship would take less than ten days for the latest steamship in their fleet.

RHODY JONES

Captain Randolph had to slow as he entered the busy traffic in Narragansett Bay but not by much.

Rhody stood on the foredeck watching the two halves of his home state pass by and smiled at the abundance of trees that covered the shores. Just a few weeks ago, he could scan the horizons and see one or two. The other big change was the air temperature. Even though it was July, it was noticeably cooler than it had been in west Texas, even during the night before the thunderstorm.

It was 10:35 in the morning on the tenth of July when Roland Horatio Jones set foot on the Providence docks that were just three blocks from his uncle's house. He'd donned his gunbelt and Stetson and had both of his saddlebags over his shoulders as the stepped across the gangplank and waved back to the crew who still had cargo to unload and perform other necessary jobs before they left the ship.

As he walked the Providence streets again for the first time in five years, he drew many curious glances from the city dwellers and he almost laughed as he recalled similar stares when he had first arrived in Texas and hadn't adopted Western attire.

He hadn't seen a single man with a sidearm and would have been shocked to see one wearing a Stetson, but as he strode along the sidewalk, he looked at the myriad of shops and saw them as he imagined Emma would see them. When he passed the fish market and saw the bushels of quahogs, he smiled and wished that Emma, Willie and Marty were with him to enjoy a clambake.

He soon turned onto Eddy Street and his focus shifted to his uncle's pending marriage. Uncle Richard had been forty-seven when he'd left, and Rhody doubted if he'd lost any weight or regained any hair, but his appearance didn't matter. He had missed his uncle and would be enormously happy to see him again despite the imminent danger he was probably facing if he continued with his plans to marry this gold digger.

Rhody had already built an imaginary picture of sweet Elizabeth. She'd be a blonde, but not like Emma's silvery blonde. Her hair would be a dark blonde and she'd have green eyes, not blue like Emma's. She'd be wearing a deeply cut dress to expose her impressive bosom that she had used to impress Uncle Richard and she'd have a phony smile. Her voice would be high pitched, and she'd giggle whenever his uncle paid her a compliment. He just hoped that she wouldn't be with his uncle when he arrived. It would be difficult for him to hide his disdain especially in light of the attempted assassination.

He turned down the long walkway to the familiar house and stepped onto the enormous wraparound porch. When he reached the double doors, he stopped and slid his saddlebags to the floor then hesitated while he collected his thoughts.

Finally, he lifted the heavy brass knocker that was shaped like an anchor and smacked it three times. He could have just entered, but he hoped to see his uncle alone first, assuming that sweet Elizabeth was probably in the house.

In the forty-two seconds that he waited for the door to open, he reviewed what he had to say if his uncle's betrothed was there. He wouldn't say anything about leaving San Antonio to ride to California. He'd only mention the assassination attempt and watch the woman's reaction. Only then would he be certain that she had sent the man to kill him and then he'd make her squirm when he elaborated more about that night in the hotel.

When the door swung wide, he smiled when he saw his uncle's face, but it looked quite different. It wasn't quite as round, and he wore a full beard, but it was definitely his Uncle Richard.

Richard had no problems identifying Rhody before he stepped out and embraced him in a massive hug.

"Roho! You made it! I thought you would be riding to California by now."

"I had to return to San Antonio where I found your letter, so here I am."

"Why didn't you wire me before you left Galveston?"

Rhody grinned before he replied, "I wanted to surprise you, Uncle. How are you doing? You've lost some weight. Are you all right?"

"Never better. After you left, I fell into a habit of overeating until I knew it was killing me, so I hired a cook and instructed her to only make light meals. It saved me a lot of money too, even after her pay because I'd been dining out all the time. You seem taller and more, um, seasoned. Needless to say, your mode of dress is a bit unusual as well."

Rhody laughed then said, "The height is mostly from my boots, but I'll admit that I drew some stares as I walked from the docks."

"Well, let's not spend the day talking out here. Come inside."

Rhody snatched his saddlebags and entered the home where he'd spend most of his childhood while his uncle closed the door.

Before he could ask, Richard said, "Your timing is excellent. I'd like to introduce you to my sweet Elizabeth. She's very anxious to meet you and was concerned that you might not make it."

"I'll bet she is," Rhody thought as he walked with his uncle out of the foyer into the large parlor.

Elizabeth had heard Richard greet his nephew, so when they entered, she was already standing.

When Rhody first set eyes on sweet Elizabeth, his imagined image of the woman vaporized. She wasn't blonde with green eyes, and her dress was quite conservative. But what struck him the most was her warm smile and her age. She was surely younger than his uncle, but he estimated her to be in her mid-thirties. She was a handsome woman with almost black hair and brown eyes, and her smile was hardly phony. As much as he wanted to revile the woman, he found it hard to even dislike her.

"Welcome home," she said in a melodious voice.

He still had his saddlebags in his hands, so he lowered them to the floor as he replied, "It's good to be back, and it's a pleasure to meet you, ma'am."

She laughed lightly as she stepped closer then shook his hand as she said, "Call me Bess."

He couldn't resist smiling at her as he removed his Stetson and said, "Call me Rhody, Bess. It's a nickname that the other cowboys hung on me and I've grown fond of it."

Elizabeth then said, "I imagine you have more than a few questions for me, Rhody."

He looked into her warm brown eyes and shook his head before replying, "Not very many, Bess. We can all talk over dinner after I get my things put away."

"It should be a very interesting conversation."

As he looked back at Elizabeth's smiling face, he wondered who had sent the assassin. He had dismissed her involvement in the scheme almost from the moment he'd seen her. *Who else would want him killed?* He simply couldn't see the motive anymore and began to wonder if the man was even a sailor. But he'd seen his face before and just wished he could make the connection.

After Rhody brought his things to his old room, he removed his gunbelt then returned to the first floor to join everyone in the dining room. He was almost disappointed when he was served roast beef rather than seafood, but the company made it less annoying.

Before he could ask any of his own questions, Rhody had to spend a long time telling his stories, which began with the hurricane. His uncle had been most interested in that topic as Rhody's letters had glossed over Captain Dent's performance. When he finished the story, Richard told him that the captain had simply disappeared after the *Vivienne* returned, and Rhody wondered if it had been the vindictive captain who had ordered his death. It made more sense than his previous theory.

When he reached the point in the tale where he was returning with Emma, Willie and Marty to New Braunfels, he finally mentioned the first time he spotted the stranger riding behind them. He didn't shy away from including the disappointment he felt when leaving the Ernst children with their grandparents, nor did he diminish his sense of loss when leaving Emma with her mother and dying father. He could see Elizabeth's compassionate eyes looking at him as he talked of their mutual forgiveness and wondered how he could ever have thought ill of her.

Then he reached his final night in San Antonio and the late-night assassination attempt. He described the extraordinarily bizarre way that the assassin died which seemed to impress his uncle even more than the fight with the Comanches which was nothing short of astounding.

Richard asked, "Do you still have that gunbelt, Rhody?"

"Yes, sir. It's upstairs. I still don't understand how the bullets had that much power. In a pistol, the chamber holds the brass in place, but all that was holding those cartridges was the leather loops. Those brass shells should have ripped right through the mattress and the bullets would have lost most of their power. As it was, the brass was buried in the pillow and the bullets had more than enough power to end the man's life."

"Can you get the gunbelt?"

"I'll be right back."

After he'd gone, Elizabeth looked at Richard and said, "He's in love with Emma, isn't he?"

"It's pretty obvious, even for me."

She smiled and replied, "You're doing pretty well, Richard."

"I was inspired, Elizabeth."

She then asked, "Is Rhody staying here or is he going back to Texas to save his damsel in distress again?"

"That's up to Rhody, sweetheart."

"I think he should sail back to Texas, tell her that he loves her and sweep her away. I'd really like to meet her."

"You've been reading too many fairytales, Elizabeth."

"Rhody's stories are better than any of the fantasies I've read because they really happened. And he surely looks like a knight on a white charger, but one who carries a pistol and wears a cowboy hat."

Richard laughed then said, "I have to admit, I think those five years he was in Texas were well spent."

Their conversation was interrupted when Rhody returned with his shredded gunbelt. He'd removed the pistol in his room and left it with the functional gunbelt.

He handed it to Richard who fingered the loops then tried to extract one of the other cartridges. It seemed stuck, so he pulled out his pocketknife and sliced the leather at the base of one of the loops as Rhody nervously watched, hoping that his uncle understood that those were rimfire cartridges.

RHODY JONES

Richard sliced through the hardened leather without setting off the cartridge then placed his pocketknife on the table before peeling the leather from the brass.

As he watched the cartridge fight to stay attached to the leather, Rhody said, "I wasn't able to oil the leather when I reached Menardville. I should have removed the cartridges and conditioned the leather but didn't have the time. It looks like the leather glued itself to the brass, but it wouldn't be enough to hold it against the power of the gunpowder. It was just the assassin's bad luck that he hit the gunbelt with his belaying pin."

Richard set the gunbelt down then slid his pocketknife back into his pocket as he asked, "And you still don't know this man's name?"

"No, sir, and it's been driving me to distraction since it happened. I wish I wasn't so anxious to get to Galveston and had asked the sheriff if I could check his room for his things to get an idea of who he was."

"What did he look like?"

After he described the man for his uncle, his mind flashed back to the shadowy figure as he swung his belaying pistol at the gunbelt and in that instant, his name erupted from his distant memory.

"Jean LeClair," he said quietly, "His name is Jean LeClair and I finally might understand why he tried to kill me."

"That name sounds familiar. Who was he?"

"We had just hired him as an able seaman on for a run to Charleston when I was first mate on the *Greenwich* in '72. On the second day out, I was on the quarterdeck when the cook emptied some garbage over the side. The wind caught some of it and it hit LeClair in the face. The cook apologized but was laughing when he did, and LeClair exploded.

"He pulled a belaying pin from the pinrail and struck the cook in the side of his chest. He was going to hit him again as he lay on the deck, but I jumped down from the quarterdeck, grabbed him then threw him to the deck and kicked the belaying pin from his hand. I had him put in chains and held in the anchor well until we reached Charleston. I put him ashore, but before I returned to the ship, he threatened to kill me."

"Why did he wait so long?" asked Elizabeth.

"I guess he floated around and wound up in Galveston. He probably heard some of the *Sweet Elizabeth's* crew talking about how they were going to bring me back from San Antonio. After all my theories of why he was sent to kill me, it all turned out to be nothing more than a coincidence."

Rhody felt like a fool for not making the connection earlier because he'd been so convinced that Elizabeth was behind it and hoped that she didn't realize that she had been one of the theories. She was a smart woman and she probably already knew that he had, so all he could hope was that she would forgive him.

They talked for another hour or so before Elizabeth had to return to her own house four blocks away, so after a cordial parting, Richard escorted her out of the house leaving Rhody alone. He hadn't really sorted his things in his room, so he returned to his upstairs bedroom and began to put his clothes into his dresser drawers. Now that he was back, he'd have to do some serious clothes shopping.

After he had moved his spare clothes into the drawers, he began emptying his other saddlebags. He set his telescope and compass on the dresser then his map case. When he pulled out his sextant's case, he held it in his hand and remembered seeing it beside Emma on the stagecoach and how she'd said that she'd taken it with her because she wanted something of his so she wouldn't forget him.

Now all she had was that one short, whisper of a kiss. He wished he hadn't been so stupidly convinced that he had to rush back to Rhode Island to save his uncle from a gold digger who was anything but that.

He set his sextant case on the dresser with the rest of his gear then left his room, trotted down the stairs and walked to the kitchen to get some coffee.

As he entered, he smiled at Susan, his father's cook and said, "How are you, ma'am? That was a very good dinner."

"Thank you, Mister Jones," she replied.

"Call me Rhody. I like it better than Roho or Roland."

"My name is Susan Donahue. Your uncle hired me three years ago."

"It's nice to meet you, Susan. I assume you'll be staying on after Bess moves in. Is that right?"

"Your uncle already said that I'll remained in his employ. Lilly will be staying as well."

"Who's Lilly?" he asked before blowing on his coffee.

"She's the new maid and housekeeper. She's at the market right now and should be back soon."

"What happened to Flora?"

"She married a sailor, if you can believe it."

"That is surprising. How long has Lilly worked for my uncle?"

"Just a few months, but I wouldn't be surprised if she married soon, either."

"Why is that?"

"You'll understand when you see her. She's a sweet young lady and quite attractive. She's helping her family right now because they need the money, but I imagine she'll find a beau as soon as her father gets back on his feet."

Rhody took a sip of coffee before he nodded.

Then Susan said, "I heard you tell the stories to your uncle and Miss Elizabeth. I can't imagine how horrifying that must have been for you."

"It wasn't bad at all for me because I could defend myself. The young lady and the girl that I had to help escape from the Comanches suffered much more terror than I ever did. I was simply astonished that they recovered so quickly. I guess it helped that neither of them had to see what I witnessed in the first ranch house, but they still suffered a full day of constant horror.

"Yet neither of them had nightmares or broke into panic when the Comanches chased after us. It's a hard life out there, Susan, and death is always lingering nearby. Knowing that hardens the heart and mind so when it does happen, it's almost accepted. At least that's the only reason I can come up with for their amazingly fast return to normal behavior."

He had taken his last sip when he heard the front door open and close, so he set the cup down then turned and walked down the hallway just as his uncle was hanging his hat on the coatrack.

Richard turned and said, "Sorry I took so long."

"I wasn't surprised, Uncle."

They walked into the parlor and sat down in the plush chairs before the quiet, cold fireplace.

Richard was smiling as he looked at his nephew and said, "I can't believe how fortunate I was to meet Elizabeth."

"Uncle Richard, while I'll admit that Bess seems to be a remarkable woman, don't go selling yourself short. You're an impressive man."

"Well, thank you, Roho, or should I call you Rhody now?"

"I'd prefer Rhody, if that's alright."

"I like it, to be honest. Can I tell you about Elizabeth?"

"I'd love to hear how this all happened so quickly."

"It was almost as if divine providence intervened on my behalf. Elizabeth has been a widow for six years and had just sold her husband's shipping business which was based in Boston. You've heard of Oakwood Shipping, haven't you?"

"Of course, I have, but you wrote that her last name was Wormwood."

"It is, but her husband's father, when he started the company, thought Wormwood would make his ships sound less than reliable, so he went with Oakwood."

Rhody snickered and said, "I'll admit that it does sound better."

"Anyway, the buyer was Claude Dupree and she was in Providence to sign the papers completing the deal and Claude brought her to the soiree where I met her. When she told me that she'd just sold the company to Claude, I was surprised that she hadn't even approached me for an offer, and she told me quietly that he had overpaid and that my reputation was too good to sully with lesser quality ships.

"After that confession, we spent the rest of the night together, much to Claude's chagrin. I believe that he thought once he made the deal, he'd be able to convince Elizabeth to marry him and join their assets. Essentially, he was hoping to have his cake and eat it too. Personally, I wouldn't have cared if she'd given it away. She is much more precious to me than an entire navy."

"She does seem to be a most impressive woman."

"She's much more than just beautiful. She's smart, witty and so very thoughtful. She knew that I didn't care about her money and I genuinely liked her from the very first. I was almost rocked on my heels when I found that she enjoyed being with me."

"You both seem to get along rather well, and I'm really happy for you, Uncle Richard."

He smiled as he said, "Now, tell me about Emma and the children you brought to New Braunfels."

"I already told you, Uncle."

"No. You told us how you found them and what happened until you left. Elizabeth told me after you went to get your damaged gunbelt that you seemed to be in love with Emma. Is that true?"

"It's as true as humanly possible. When I left New Braunfels, I didn't even tell her how I felt because I thought it was too soon after her husband died even though she told me she had an unhappy marriage that she hadn't wanted in the first place. I did kiss her before I left, but my lips barely brushed hers. Even then, I thought I was being too forward."

"You can write her a letter to let her know."

"No, that's the kind of thing that should be spoken when I'm looking into her eyes."

"What if she sends you a letter expressing her undying love?"

"I'd be surprised, but in that case, I suppose I'd have to include it in my reply."

"So, letter or not, are you leaving for Texas after the wedding?"

RHODY JONES

"After you and Elizabeth board my yawl for your honeymoon, I'll be on my way."

Richard smiled as he said, "I'm happy to hear that."

Rhody then said, "Speaking of the yawl, how far along is it on the overhaul?"

"It's still in drydock but it should be afloat in a week or so. Why?"

"I'm going to the ship registry's office and change the name to *Always Emma*. Can you notify the shipyard?"

"Of course. It's a good name. Maybe I shouldn't have used *Sweet Elizabeth* on a steamship that might be scrapped in a few years."

'You can always change it, Uncle."

"I can, but it can wait. She's a beautiful ship."

"She is and she made short work of the voyage from Galveston. I've got to do some clothes shopping tomorrow and pick up some other sundries. Do you need me to do anything else today?"

"You're on your own, Rhody. I've got to catch up on the books. I've been neglecting my duties since I met Elizabeth."

Rhody grinned then waved to his uncle before heading back up the stairs to his room. He wanted to write to Emma,

Willie and Marty, but decided to wait until he received mail from them. He had been disappointed that there wasn't an envelope waiting for him when he arrived.

It was too late in the day to do much of anything, so when he entered his room, he walked to the window and looked east across the bay. He watched the ships and boats plying the calm summer water and wished he could take the yawl out. He preferred the October winds and brisk temperatures when he sailed, but he felt the urge to be on the water again regardless of the season. They had a smaller sailboat, a catboat that they occasionally used to ferry passengers out to a ship that can't find a spot at the docks, so maybe he'd use it tomorrow after he did his shopping.

After watching for a few minutes, he turned and walked to his bed and sat down. He looked at the dresser and as he stared at the sextant case, he wondered what Emma was doing at that moment. He expected that she was careworn as she balanced ministering to her father's needs while keeping her mother from worrying excessively. He hoped that she had time to visit Willie and Marty because Marty was always such a comfort to her.

―――

Two thousand miles away, Emma sat in the parlor with her mother, her sister and her brother-in-law, Paul while their three children played a game of jacks on the floor.

RHODY JONES

Emma's father had passed away six days after Rhody had gone and after the funeral, Anna and Paul had spent the afternoon talking to her mother. It was obvious to Emma that Paul wanted to move into the big house and had suggested that his mother-in-law should sell the bakery and then he'd sell his shop and set up business in New Braunfels.

Anna was very pleased with the idea because with a new baby on the way, the extra room would be a godsend, not to mention the free nanny services that her mother and sister could provide.

"When do you want to move," Maria Ludden asked her older daughter.

Anna looked at her husband who replied, "I already have a buyer for my shop, so as soon as that's settled, we'll move. It should be less than a week."

Emma was watching her brother-in-law as he answered her mother and knew she would have to move out before he moved in. She had never told her sister or her mother what he had done to her and knew that he wanted to do much more.

It had been soon after Anna had given birth to little Elise and Emma had moved into their house as a temporary nanny. It was already a crowded house, so room was at a premium, but she hadn't had any warnings when he had cornered her in the kitchen while Anna was feeding her baby. She was kneading bread dough when he quietly walked behind her and placed his hand on her smooth backside. When she'd turned quickly to protest, he grabbed her then kissed her roughly as he squeezed her breast.

She had been too stunned to scream or even protest loudly but raced out of the kitchen with her flour-covered hands and locked herself in the small washroom. After washing and drying her hands, she unlocked the door and quickly left the house. She never asked Anna how Paul had explained her hasty departure and reluctance to return. She often wondered if Carl had described their liaison to Paul and that had made her fair game.

He never said anything about it but would always smile at her in a way that let her know that it wasn't going to be an isolated incident. After that scare, she always ensured that either her mother or Anna was in the room when Paul was visiting them in New Braunfels.

She discovered she was pregnant later that month and soon Paul was no longer the problem as Carl was forced to marry her and take her with him to his brothers' ranch.

Now the very real threat of having to live in the same house with Paul frightened her. What made it worse was that Rhody was so far away. If he'd been here, she could ask him to take her with him to Rhode Island or anywhere else. But he wasn't here, and she needed to find a sanctuary within a week.

After dinner, she left the house to visit Willie and Marty, as she'd been doing almost daily since Rhody left.

After she entered the house, she followed Mrs. Ernst into the parlor where Willie and Marty were waiting.

After they were joined by Gustav Ernst, Greta said, "We really appreciate your visits, Emma. We hate to admit that we're getting old and seemed to have forgotten how stressful it can be when raising children, even good grandchildren like ours."

"I understand, Mrs. Ernst. I might be able to help even more."

"That would be wonderful! The children adore you."

Emma smiled at Marty before saying, "My sister's family will soon be moving from Seguin and will be living with my mother. It's a big house, but they already have three young children and she's about to have a fourth. It's getting too crowded, and I was wondering if I could stay here with Willie and Marty."

Greta never so much as glanced at her husband before excitedly replying, "We'd love to have you in the house, Emma."

Emma smiled then said, "I'll even cook and help you with cleaning and your laundry."

"Now you're being too kind, Emma. We'd have to pay you for your work."

"That's not necessary, Mrs. Ernst. I'll be okay. Can I move in next week?"

"Anytime you'd like," she replied before she finally looked at Gustav.

He sighed then smiled at Emma as he said, "Thank you, Emma."

Emma felt incredibly relieved as she turned to Willie and Marty and said, "Let's go upstairs and I'll finish reading *Journey to the Center of the Earth*."

Willie jumped from his chair and said, "I hope there are a lot more of Mister Verne's books."

―――――

When she returned to her mother's house later that evening, she was more than annoyed to find that Anna's family was still there. They said they'd be leaving right after dinner and now it was too late for them to return to Seguin. She should have moved to the Ernsts' house right away but decided she could last one night. She didn't think that Paul would try to enter her room when she slept with her mother and Anna both in the house, but she wasn't about to give him any opportunities.

RHODY JONES

There wasn't a lock on her bedroom door, but she could put the chair against the door just to feel safe. She even thought about sleeping in her dress rather than change into her nightdress. But even as that almost extreme idea crept into her mind, she thought about the nightdress that she'd bought when she was with Rhody and that initiated more fantasies about him.

She sat down in the parlor across from her mother and said, "Mama, I just talked to Mister and Mrs. Ernst. They told me how they forgot how busy it was to take care of the children, so I offered to stay with them, and they were ecstatic with the idea. So, I'll be moving to their house before Anna moves here. You'll need every bit of space you can spare."

"Are you sure, Emma? This is a big house and if we let Peter and Freida share a room, then you can stay in yours."

"I'll just be in the way, Mama. Besides, you know how much I love Willie and Marty."

"Well, that's alright, I guess. When it gets close to Anna's time, can you stop by more often? I don't think it will be much longer."

"Of course, Mama," she replied as she watched Paul's reaction out of the corner of her eye.

Maria then asked, "Have you written a letter to Rhody yet? It's been almost two weeks, and I thought you were going to write it the day after he left."

She couldn't lie to her mother but didn't want to say why she hadn't written. It was for the most foolish of reasons imaginable. She had lost the small slip of paper that Rhody had given her with his address. She could have sent it to R. Jones Shipping Company but had decided to wait until she received a letter from him first. That way, she could gauge his feelings toward her more accurately. In the days after he'd gone, that one, faint kiss had convinced her that he loved her as much as she loved him, but after a few more days, she wondered if had meant anything more than friendly gesture.

She finally replied, "I've been too busy, Mama, just as you have."

"Yes, I'll admit that I've barely had time to think since you returned, but things are settling down now. You should write to him and let him know how you feel."

"I will, Mama."

―――

That night after dragging the straight-back chair to her bedroom door, she closed her drapes and changed into her nightdress before sliding beneath the covers. It was a pleasantly cool evening for a change, and she was grateful that she could keep her window closed.

As she lay in bed, she wished she still had Rhody's gunbelt. That would keep Paul at bay, and she wouldn't hesitate to use it either.

But after she closed her eyes, she whispered, "I wish you were here even without your guns, Rhody."

———

As he lay on the top of his quilts, Rhody had his bedroom window open and a nice breeze was blowing out of the bay bringing that unique smell that he'd missed for five years.

As much as he missed the smell, the ocean and even his uncle, he missed Emma so much more. August the first seemed like a year away, but all he could hope for was that she wouldn't meet some handsome unattached male who would win her heart before he could return.

Even if he left on the second of August, he couldn't reach New Braunfels before the middle of the month. Then he asked himself why he was limiting himself to travel by ship. If he took the train, he could get there in five or six days. It wasn't that much sooner in the big scheme of things, but his recent thought that Emma may be lost to him made those extra few days seem critical.

He made up his mind. On the second of August, he'd board a westbound train and spend almost a week of boring discomfort to reach Seguin as the railroad didn't go to New Braunfels. Maybe he should go all the way to San Antonio and pick up Jack and Morgana then just ride to New Braunfels. He'd have to go there sooner or later anyway.

Rhody had his eyes closed, pleased that his itinerary was set and now it was just a matter of waiting for the three weeks to pass. He was momentarily content when his eyes popped open. *It was twenty-one days before his uncle's wedding!* That was more than enough time to take the train to San Antonio and convince Emma to return with him.

He'd need a day to prepare for the long journey and he'd have to tell his uncle of his plans, but this could happen. He was suddenly too excited to sleep, so he hopped to his feet and began to pace as his mind went through the things he would need for the trip.

His uncle had some nice travel bags, so he didn't need to buy one. He did need more clothes and maybe he should pick out some gifts for Emma, Willie and Marty while he was shopping. At least he wouldn't need any food. He'd withdraw enough money to pay for the return trip, hopefully with Emma. He'd bring back Morgana and Jack, too.

He was pacing quickly while his mind raced as he exulted in his sudden change in plans.

CHAPTER 11

Rhody was out of his room shortly after sunrise and soon entered the kitchen where he found Susan as she was filling the coffeepot.

She turned and smiled before saying, "Good morning, Rhody."

"Good morning, Susan. How are you this fine July morning?"

"You seem very chipper."

"I am. I'll be doing some shopping today. Is my uncle still asleep?"

"Yes, but he'll be up soon. He seems a bit livelier these days for some reason," she replied with a smile.

"Good. I'll be back after I wash and shave."

"Didn't you want to say good morning to Lilly?"

Rhody saw the direction Susan was looking and turned to his right and spotted the new maid sitting at the table in the corner. She rose when he looked at her and immediately understood why Susan expected her to be married soon. She wasn't very tall, probably around five feet and three or four inches, but she was very pretty and still proportionally well-figured.

She smiled and said, "Good morning, Mister Jones. I'm sorry that I didn't get a chance to meet you yesterday."

Rhody returned her smile as he replied, "It's nice to meet you, Lilly. Please call me Rhody. Mister Jones is my uncle."

She laughed lightly before saying, "Thank you, Rhody."

Rhody had to admit that if he hadn't met Emma, he'd be at the head of the line to court Lilly, but he not only had met Emma, he was in love with her and it didn't matter how inspirational Lilly might be to other men. He'd learned that lesson years ago.

He then waved to both ladies and headed down the hallway to the washroom.

After he'd gone, Lilly walked close to Susan and said, "He's very handsome. I expected him to look something like his uncle."

"He's quite the catch for the young woman down in Texas. Mister Jones said that he'll be going back to see her after the wedding."

Lilly glanced down the hallway and said, "Really?"

RHODY JONES

Susan was shifting a skillet to the hot plate and didn't see the look in Lilly's eyes, or she may have warned her to remember her place.

Lilly was very aware how she drew men's attention and already had received several offers for marriage, but she'd had to postpone even allowing them to become too familiar because of her salary which helped to keep the family afloat. That handsome young man owned half of the shipping company and had a large bank account. *What if he got a better offer and didn't need to go all the way to Texas?*

Rhody didn't know that he had trouble brewing in the house, as he told his uncle of his plans to leave tomorrow morning on the train, but should be back four or five days before his wedding. Richard gave him his blessing and said that even if he missed the wedding, he understood his need for the hasty trip.

After leaving the house, Rhody took the carriage to The Arcade, which was a unique place for shopping. Even in the rain or heavy snow, the enclosed mall housed shops of all types and if a shopper couldn't find it at The Arcade, it was either alive, huge or both.

He parked the carriage in the large lot created for the customers and walked through the large columns to enter The Arcade.

He spent three hours in The Arcade buying some fashionable clothes and more work clothes for when he returned to Texas where fashionable meant work. He bought a very fancy pocketknife for Willie and a gold locket watch for Marty, but then spent almost another hour finding the right gift for Emma.

He didn't want to give her jewelry or clothing, mainly because he had poor taste in one and was lost in the other. Yet when he was in Farrah's Jewelry, where he'd found Marty's watch then bought a wedding band set just in case things worked out, that he found something she might like.

It wasn't fancy or glittery, but for some reason, he thought it would appeal to her. It was a boxed portable microscope set with slides. He had no idea why he believed she would like it, but he did. It was made in France and was elegant in addition to being useful.

He packed up all of his purchases and used a wheeled platform cart to move them out of The Arcade to the carriage. After loading everything into the boot, he left the cart in the area as was customary. The Arcade had staff to pick them up but more often, a customer who knew he was buying something bulky would bring it inside.

With his shopping done, he drove to the Providence Bank of Rhode Island and withdrew a thousand dollars before he drove back to the house and parked the carriage near the back porch. He unloaded everything onto the porch then drove the carriage back to the large carriage house and unharnessed the team. They were fine horses, but he missed his Morgans.

When he reached the porch, he carried the bag with the gifts and one of his clothing bags into the kitchen and smiled when he saw Susan and Lilly sitting at the table having tea.

Susan said, "Been shopping, I see."

"Yes, ma'am. I have another bag outside, too. I'll borrow a couple of Uncle Richard's travel bags when I come back down."

Lilly quickly said, "I'll get your other bag for you and follow you upstairs, Rhody."

"Thank you, Lilly," Rhody replied then waited for Lilly to retrieve the bag.

When she returned, he left the kitchen and walked down the long, dark hallway trying to think of anything he'd missed. He doubted it because he'd wandered the shops in The Arcade looking in the display windows and hadn't seen anything that he needed. What he had missed was Lilly's obvious intent.

He climbed the stairs to his room and hadn't paid any attention to Lilly as she followed two steps behind him.

Rhody reached his room then set down the bag of clothing and opened the door. After dropping the bag on his bed, he walked to the dresser and carefully set the gift bag onto the floor near his saddlebags. He'd see how much he could fit into his saddlebags before he decided if he needed one travel bag or two.

Lilly set the second bag of clothes on the bed then quietly closed the door. The only other person in the house was Susan, and she was busy in the kitchen.

When Rhody finally turned and saw the closed door, he finally had an inkling of why Lilly had shut it. She was an impressive young lady and Susan had said that she was only working to help her family, so she probably saw him as a way to help her family and herself at the same time.

He quickly said, "I've got to get a travel bag, Lilly," then took two long strides toward the door.

"Rhody, could I talk to you for a minute?" she asked.

"Of course, but you might want to open the door. I'm sure the breeze closed it, but it wouldn't be appropriate for us to be in my bedroom with the door closed."

"I don't mind," she said softly, confirming his suspicions.

"Well, I do. Lilly, I'm leaving in the morning to take a train to Texas. When I return for my uncle's wedding, I'll hopefully be with Emma. Now, I'll make a deal with you. If she turns me down, then when I come back, I'll gladly welcome you to my bed."

Lilly blinked and asked, "But what happens if you come back with her? Will I be fired?"

"No, you won't. We won't be living here, and I won't mention our arrangement to anyone. Okay?"

Lilly dropped her eyes to the floor as she said, "I'm sorry, Rhody, but I've been so lonely and frustrated. My father is ill, and we don't know when he'll get better. I thought that if I could convince you to stay here and marry me then I could help them."

He wasn't sure how sincere her apology was, but at least she hadn't tempted him by unbuttoning the first few buttons of her blouse. That would have made his refusal much more difficult, but he thought it wouldn't hurt to accept her excuse.

"I'll tell you what, Lilly. When I return, assuming that Emma is with me, you tell your parents that I said I'd give you a thousand-dollar dowry if you married. That way you won't have to work, and you can still help your family."

She looked up at him and asked, "Why would you help me after what I just tried to do?"

"Because I know what it's like to be lonely and frustrated, ma'am."

Lilly smiled and said, "Thank you, Rhody. I still hope you return alone, but if you don't, I'm sure that Emma will make you happy."

He reached past her, opened the door and replied, "She already has. Now, I need to make her happy."

Lilly nodded then floated past Rhody and down the hall before descending the stairs.

Rhody closed the door again and let out a long breath. That had been a lot closer than she realized. He hadn't been exaggerating when he said he'd been frustrated, and she only added to that sensation.

After arranging all of his new clothes and other necessities, he figured he could get his gifts and the rest into one of his uncle's large travel bags, so he left his room went to the end of the hallway to the last spare bedroom and found his uncles set of luggage.

He selected the right size then fifteen minutes later, he was fully packed and ready to leave for the station. His uncle said he'd drive him to the station in the morning, so he wouldn't have to lug everything the six blocks. He'd wear his Colt but leave the second pistol in the dresser. He had enough room left in the travel bag to add a couple of books, so he walked downstairs to the library and made his selections.

It was almost dinnertime when Richard returned with Elizabeth on his arm.

She smiled and said, "I hear you did the math and realized you could take the train to Texas and return in time for our wedding."

"Yes, ma'am. I'm all packed and my thoughtful uncle is driving me to the station in the morning."

Richard asked, "Did you get enough money for the trip?"

"More than enough to pay for everything and leave plenty of wiggle room. I'll use my money belt for most of it, but I'm not worried too much because I'll be wearing my Colt. I did borrow one of your travel bags."

"That's alright. We still have more than enough between us for the honeymoon."

"Just be kind to *Always Emma*."

Richard laughed then they walked into the parlor to wait for Susan to summon them for dinner.

———

After he'd undressed for bed, Rhody walked to the door and locked it. He didn't think that Lilly would sneak in while he slept, but he didn't want to risk the temptation to end his frustration. He only wanted Emma to permanently crush it into dust.

———

Emma was in her bed without the chair blocking the door. Paul had returned to Seguin with Anna and the children, so she was safe for a couple of days. Once she was living with Willie and Marty, she'd be able to sleep better and the only chance that Paul would have to fulfill his fantasies would be when she had to help her mother with Anna's delivery.

She was disappointed when she still hadn't received a letter from Rhody but thought he probably hadn't even reached Rhode Island yet and the mail could take another week to reach New Braunfels. She'd ask Willie to run over to her mother's house once a day to ask if she'd received any letters.

———

Just three days after arriving on the *Sweet Elizabeth,* Rhody was on a train heading back to Texas. There would be a layover in New York for three hours when he changed to a different railway. His ticket had been fairly reasonable, and he knew he'd have more than enough to pay for Emma's fare and transport for his Morgans. He had enough cash to bring a whole herd of horses back with him, not that he had any such desire. He would have spent even more if he could have bought tickets for Willie and Marty.

He'd clear out his San Antonio account after seeing Emma unless she wanted to live near her mother and sister. He wasn't sure it would be a bad idea himself because he missed Willie and Marty. He still had to keep his promise to Willie and was determined to teach him how to shoot a pistol. His hands weren't big enough yet, so he'd have to do some more growing first, and that meant he'd have to be there for a while.

He was traveling first class just because of the more comfortable seats and accommodations. He had his saddlebags on the seat and the travel bag in the overhead shelf as the train rolled across the heavily forested Rhode Island landscape. He couldn't see the bay as the train was rolling southwest, but he imagined he could still smell the ocean, which was technically from the shore that met the ocean.

Just over an hour after leaving the station, the train entered Connecticut and he smiled at the thought. It had taken his train almost ten hours to travel from San Antonio to Galveston. Even with stops, the train would reach New York in less than four hours. He'd send his telegram to Emma and get some lunch before the new train carried him through Pennsylvania and most of Ohio. Then he'd take a different railroad's train southwest and have to make two more changes until he reached Texas. Then it was one seriously long train ride across most of Texas to San Antonio.

Most travelers undertaking this lengthy journey would stop at the cities and towns where they would change trains to recover, but he intended to sleep on the trains and only use those stops for food and taking care of nature's needs. They had a washroom on the first-class coach, but he'd only use it to shave and clean up when it was stopped. Trying to shave with a straight razon so close to your throat on a rocking train was even more dangerous than trying it onboard a ship which is why very few sailors were clean shaven.

When he left the train in New York with his saddlebags over his shoulders and carrying his travel bag, he made his first stop at the Western Union office.

He wrote his message and hesitated when he thought about adding the words 'love' or 'marry' in the telegram. He wanted to look into her wondrous blue eyes when he said either.

Rhody paid for the telegram and then walked back to the row of ticket windows where he upgraded his ticket for eight dollars when he found that the second railroad had an express train leaving in an hour for Philadelphia. As he headed for the nearby railway diner, he began to recalculate his schedule.

There hadn't been an express train from Providence to New York, but after talking to the ticket agent, he learned that most lines did offer express runs. The express runs ran from major city to major city and only stopped for coal and water. They ran at a higher rate of speed as well, so he might be able to shave at least another twelve to sixteen hours off his journey, maybe even a full day.

He was in an even better state of mind when he left the ticket window to have his lunch. He was the only man wearing a sidearm when he entered, and his Stetson seemed a bit out of place as well.

When he placed his order, he refrained from ordering a coffee cabinet, but smiled when he remembered telling Emma that story.

An hour later, he was back aboard the express train and soon left the heavily populated city behind.

He soon drifted off to sleep before the train entered Pennsylvania.

———

By the time Rhody's third train, also an express, was halfway across the wide state, a messenger arrived at Maria Ludden's house and rapped on the open door.

Emma was doing the laundry, but was closer to the front door, so she stood dried her hands on her dress and walked to the foyer.

"Are you Emma Brandt?" he asked when she approached him.

"Yes. Do you have a telegram for me?"

"Yes, ma'am," he replied as he handed her the folded sheet.

She said, "Just a moment," then walked to the small desk and fished a nickel out of the small drawer then returned and handed it to him.

"Will you be sending a reply, ma'am?" he asked.

"I don't know," she replied as she opened the message.

She thought her heart had stopped beating as she read:

EMMA BRANDT 13 BISMARCK ST NEW BRAUNFELS TEX

LEAVING ON TRAIN FROM NEW YORK NOW
WILL ARRIVE IN FIVE DAYS
PLEASE WAIT FOR ME

RHODY JONES NEW YORK CITY

She looked at the boy and said, "No reply," then turned and clutched the short telegram to her chest as she walked to the kitchen.

Her mother looked at her and suspected that the telegram she hugged as if it was priceless had come from Rhody.

"Is it from Rhody?" she asked.

"Yes," she replied dreamily, "he'll be here in five days, Mama. He's taking a train."

"I thought he had to go to his uncle's wedding."

"I don't know if he's planning on taking the train back or something happened. His uncle was marrying a much younger woman and it sounded as if she was marrying him for his money. Rhody wanted to meet her and then talk to his uncle. Maybe he discovered her little plot and convinced his uncle to call it off."

"It doesn't matter, Mama. He'll be here in just a few days and he wrote 'please wait for me'. I'm going to finish the laundry then go and tell Willie and Marty that he's coming. They'll be very excited."

"You're a bit thrilled yourself, Emma."

"I am well past thrilled, Mama," she said as she closed her eyes and let out a long breath.

―――

An hour later, Emma arrived at the Ernst home and quickly found Willie and Marty.

She decided to give them the news as a surprise, so after they had taken their customary seats, she opened *The Adventures of Tom Sawyer* and said, "Okay, now where did I stop the story."

"When Tom went into the cave!" Marty exclaimed.

"Oh, yes. Here it is. Let me begin," she said with a slight smile.

She read the telegram verbatim and saw the confusion on their faces when she finished the first line then the clouds began to lift when she read the second and by the time she began reading the sender's line, they were primed to explode from their chairs.

When she closed the book, they may not have exploded but it was close as they bounced into the air and began to dance around the room shouting, "Rhody's coming! Rhody's coming!"

After their enthusiasm waned to just wide grins, Willie asked, "Is he gonna stay now?"

"I don't know, Willie. We'll just have to see what he says when he gets here."

"Will you be here when he does?" asked Marty.

"Yes, but I'll tell my mother to send him here."

They were all too excited to return to Tom Sawyer's adventures on the Mississippi but began to chat about what they would tell Rhody when he arrived.

As happy as she was knowing that Rhody was returning, she wished she didn't have to wait five more days. Now that she wasn't having to worry about Paul, she had been spending her nights fantasizing about Rhody and her frustration was growing to the point of distraction.

―

RHODY JONES

Two days later as travel weary Rhody's train was entering Texas, Emma completed her move to the Ernst home when a freight wagon arrived with Anna's family possessions that they were taking with them.

She was relieved to be out of the house before Paul arrived, but was much more than relieved knowing that Rhody would be there in three more days. She wished he'd added an explanation for his sudden return in the telegram or sent a second to let her know where he was, but she was grateful just knowing that he was enroute.

The next evening, Rhody's last train, the express from Dallas to San Antonio, had been on the rails for ten hours. He had a three-hour layover in Dallas, so he had taken the opportunity to get a hot bath, shave and a haircut. When he boarded that last leg of his journey, he felt invigorated and not just because he was clean. In twelve hours, he'd be in San Antonio, pick up his Morgans then make the ride to New Braunfels.

As he sat in his first-class seat watching the sun's rays cast a long shadow of the speeding train across the Texas landscape he felt as if he was going home, much more than he had when the *Sweet Elizabeth* plied up Narragansett Bay. It wasn't because Texas had been his more recent residence. It was because this was where his family lived.

It was just after nine o'clock the next morning when Rhody stepped onto the familiar platform in San Antonio. He took a deep breath, then stepped away quickly and headed to Hector's livery. He could reach New Braunfels shortly after noon if he hurried, but knew he'd probably spend some time talking to Hector.

When he neared the big barn, he was surprised that his Morgans weren't in the corral. Usually, long term boarded horses were kept in his corral rather than the limited number of stalls in his barn. But as soon as he cleared the opening to the livery, he spotted Morgana's rump and Jack's tail swishing in the next stall. He didn't see Hector anywhere, but as he was setting down the travel bag, Hector walked out of his small living area in back.

"Rhody!" he exclaimed as his face lit up.

Rhody grinned as he stepped closer to Hector with his hand extended and said, "It's good to be back, Hector!"

"How come you came back so soon? I figured you'd be gone a couple of months or so."

"It's a long story, and I'll start telling it to you if you can help me saddle Morgana and Jack. I need to ride to New Braunfels."

RHODY JONES

Hector smiled and said, "I reckoned you might be," then walked to Jack while Rhody headed for Morgana. Their tack was hung on the stall boards, so he didn't need to search for anything.

As they began to prepare the Morgans for the ride, Rhody explained what had happened since hastily leaving after the assassination attempt, which Hector told him had become legend already.

Both horses were saddled by the time Rhody was telling him about meeting sweet Elizabeth and that she was very worthy of the adjective and not the gold digger he'd expected.

Hector tied a trail rope to Jack and then strapped Rhody's travel bag onto the back of the saddle while Rhody went into Hector's private space to retrieve his guns and ammunition.

Once the long guns and the heavy saddlebags were in place, Rhody shook Hector's hand and told him he'd be back in a day or two then mounted Morgana and headed out of San Antonio to make the twenty-five-mile ride. He hadn't spent nearly as much time talking to Hector as he'd thought and knew that his Morgans needed to run, so he set them at a fast trot as soon as he reached the well-traveled road.

In New Braunfels, Emma was in her mother's house because Anna's water had broken late last night, and she was well along in her labor now. When Paul had shown up at the door of the Ernst home early that morning, she'd momentarily thought he had come for a 'private' meeting, but when he said that Anna was in labor, she was somewhat relieved. But as Paul stood waiting for her to accompany him, her concerns returned, so she'd asked Willie and Marty to come along so they could help, but really to act as chaperones.

For the past four hours, Emma and her mother had ministered to Anna's needs in the growing heat.

Willie and Marty were on the front porch with the door open working as nannies for Anna's two older children who were playing in the front yard while Paul was with their youngest child in the kitchen.

Anna's labor was nearing its end and didn't appear to have any complications, but Emma's biggest concern now was if her sister died in childbirth which was a very common occurrence. She was sure that her mother would back Paul's expected request to marry her and the thought gave her chills. When she'd gone to get more water in the kitchen, he still looked at her in that lascivious manner that let her know he appreciated what he saw even as he held his baby daughter in his arms.

It was just after Rhody had reached the halfway point that Anna delivered a healthy little boy, and Emma and her mother began the cleanup.

RHODY JONES

After the messier aspects of childbirth were out of the room, her mother took little Elise from his arms to let Paul enter while Emma took the refuse out the back door. When she was returning to the house, she swung around to the front of the house to tell Peter and Frieda that they had a new brother and that their mother was doing fine.

She and the four children then entered the house through the open front door and walked past the bedroom where she let Peter and Frieda enter while she continued to the kitchen with Willie and Marty trotting behind her.

When she saw her tired mother with Elise, she smiled and said, "You need some rest, Mama."

"I'll be all right, Emma, but I could use a cup of coffee. Unfortunately, I used the last of it last night. Would you be a dear and run over to Hoffman's and buy a couple of pounds?"

"Of course, Mama. I think you should let Elise crawl around before you drop her."

Maria smiled at her younger daughter and said, "I've never dropped one of my own, and I'm not about to start with my granddaughter."

She smiled then looked at Willie and Marty and asked, "Want to come along? I could bribe you with some penny candy."

"We'd come even if you don't buy us any candy," Willie replied.

Emma then said to her mother, "We'll be back in thirty minutes or so."

"I'll start a fire in the cookstove and have the coffeepot hot when you come back."

Emma nodded then stepped back down the hallway trailing Willie and Marty and as she passed Anna's room, she glanced inside and saw Paul sitting at the head of her bed talking to her sister. She wanted to scream at him for his duplicity but kept walking.

She soon reached the street and headed for Hoffman's General Store about a half a mile away.

———

As they left the house, Rhody was just three miles southwest and moving quickly. He was right in his horses' desire to run and neither showed any signs of fatigue yet as he saw the buildings of New Braunfels appear ahead of him.

He knew that the Ernst house was closer to the road, but wanted to see Emma's reaction when he saw her again a day ahead of his scheduled arrival, so after reaching the outskirts, he turned Morgana to the right and took a side street before turning left onto Bismarck Street.

RHODY JONES

It was difficult to restrain his excitement when he spotted the Ludden house and wondered if her father was still alive. *If he had passed, then would she be willing to leave her mother alone? Would her sister's family move into the much bigger house?*

There were so many questions that popped into his head during that last hundred yards that he finally decided not to even think about it. He'd be seeing Emma again in just minutes.

He pulled up in front of the house and quickly dropped to the ground. He tied off Morgana then swiftly stepped along the walkway. He soon hopped to the porch without using the steps and knocked loudly on the door jamb of the open door, expecting to see Emma's beautiful blue eyes in a few seconds.

When someone came to the door, it wasn't Emma, nor was it her mother. He had never met Anna's husband, but assumed that he was the man walking into the foyer.

Before Rhody could say a word, Paul quickly asked, "Who are you and what do you want?"

"I guess that you're Paul Schmidt, Anna's husband. I'm Rhody Jones and I was wondering if Emma was here."

"No, she left to buy some coffee at Hoffman's. She'll be back in a while."

Rhody may not have been able to understand women very well, but he could easily sense an underlying tone of dislike in Paul Schmidt's voice. He also noted the absence of an invitation to enter to wait for Emma's return.

"That's alright. I'll go find her."

Paul didn't reply but simply turned and left the foyer.

"Jerk," Rhody said under his breath then did an about face and trotted across the porch, leapt to the ground and walked quickly to his Morgans.

As he swung his leg over the back of Morgana's rump, he wondered why Paul would be so hostile to him.

He settled into the saddle, set Morgana at a slow trot toward the main street and decided it might be simple jealousy. He was sure that Emma had told her sister about him and her husband was annoyed knowing that Rhody was not only wealthy, but that Emma thought well of him.

How much she cared for him was his biggest question. He hoped that she loved him as much as he loved her, but he'd been gone for more than two weeks now and he was sure that other men in New Braunfels had noticed her return and may already have expressed an interest. She was a very attractive young woman and there was that other less attractive rumor that she'd left behind just a year ago when she'd married Carl Brandt and left the town, so there were probably other men around town that saw her in a different light.

RHODY JONES

He turned left onto main street and spotted Hoffman's on the left a few hundred yards away. His hands were already clammy despite the heat and he could feel sweat trickling down the back of his already damp shirt. He was glad that he'd had that bath in Dallas before he left, but there was nothing he could do about his shirt.

———

After he returned to the house, Paul took a seat in the parlor but didn't tell anyone that Rhody had returned. Everyone was still visiting Anna and their new baby, and he told himself that he just didn't want to bother anyone.

———

Rhody pulled up before the store and even as he dismounted, he could hear a commotion inside. He tied off Morgana then stepped onto the boardwalk and entered the open double doors.

The shouting match was in the back of the store and involved two women. He recognized one of the voices but wasn't sure about the other as he quickly strode past the counter and turned left down the last aisle.

He immediately spotted Willie and Marty as they huddled behind Emma who was facing a very large, stern woman he had already met and sincerely disliked. It was the frightening Mrs. Brandt and he didn't need to hear her words to know what had precipitated the argument.

No one noticed him as he passed other customers who were watching the war of words, and he soon was just a few feet Marty and Willie when the vocal argument shifted into the physical.

Olga Brandt spat, "Carl only died because you lured him away! You're nothing but a cheap whore!" then before Emma could even react, Olga whipped her heavy hand and slapped the left side of Emma's face hard, knocking her into a shelf of canned peas.

Her viscous attack had caught Rhody by surprise, but even as Olga was preparing to hit her again while Emma tried to regain her balance, Rhody had quickly pulled his Colt, stepped past a frozen Willie and Marty then shoved his pistol's muzzle into Mrs. Brandt's massive bosom.

He glared at her furious eyes and growled, "If you try that again, I'll put a .44 where your heart would have been if you had one!"

The Colt's hammer wasn't back, but Mrs. Brandt couldn't see the back of the revolver under her big shelf that blocked her vision.

"*Who the hell do you think you are?*" she snarled but lowered her hand as she did.

"I met you once before, sir, and I'm close to pulling this trigger, so you'd better change your attitude."

RHODY JONES

Olga could see the fury in the man's eyes and as much as she wanted to slap him the pressure of the pistol's muzzle changed her mind.

Emma had been expecting Mrs. Brandt to hit her again and was staring at her when she first saw a shadow appear on her left and then as a flash of steel crossed her vision, she heard Rhody's voice and instantly turned to look at him. She saw the same rage in his eyes that Olga did, but had a completely different reaction. She wanted to wrap him in her arms and tell him that she loved him, but he still had his pistol's barrel half-buried in Mrs. Brandt's chest and she knew he had other things on his mind.

Willie and Marty hadn't noticed Rhody's appearance until he growled his warning to Mrs. Brandt, and they looked at each other with wide eyes and big smiles. They had been on the verge of attacking the big woman but now Rhody was here to protect Aunt Emma.

Rhody's eyes were still boring into Olga Brandt's as he carefully said, "I want you to loudly apologize to Emma while all these people are here. Then if she's so inclined, you will stand there and let her slap that hideous face of yours. If you don't, then we'll walk down to the sheriff's office where I will press charges for assault."

"You wouldn't dare!"

"Mister Brandt, I would most certainly dare. I killed thirteen Comanche warriors to save and protect Emma, so marching you down to the sheriff's office would be a pleasure."

"Stop calling me 'sir' or 'mister'. I'm a woman!"

"I have no idea what you are, but the person you slapped is not only a woman, but a lady. She's the most woman and the finest lady I've ever met. Now I'd like to hear your apology."

She glared at Rhody then shifted her attention to Emma who was smiling, but looking at Rhody, not Olga.

"I'm sorry for hitting you," Olga said in a normal voice.

Rhody quickly said, "That wasn't enough. I want it louder and I want it for everything you said because they were all lies."

Olga almost slapped him despite his pistol but took a deep breath and announced loudly, "I'm sorry for what I did and what I said. I was just upset because I lost all my sons."

She then looked back at Rhody and snapped, "Is that good enough, mister?"

With his eyes focused on Olga he asked, "Do you want payback, Emma?"

Emma still didn't look at Mrs. Brandt as she replied, "No. I don't think she'd feel it anyway."

RHODY JONES

Rhody nodded then pulled his Colt back and said, "You may leave, and if you even think about bothering Emma again, I won't hesitate to beat you to a pulp."

Olga glared at him for another few seconds before whirling about and pushing her way through the small gaggle of shoppers and storming away.

Rhody quickly holstered his Colt then turned to Emma, saw the bright red blotch on her cheek and asked, "Are you all right, Emma?"

She was still smiling as she nodded then said, "How did you get here so soon? You weren't supposed to arrive until tomorrow."

"I took a few express trains," he replied then said, "We need to talk, so let's get what you need, and we can start the conversation on the way back to your mother's house."

"I only needed to buy some coffee, but when I saw her enter the store, I sort of hid in the back aisle hoping she wouldn't find me. You really weren't going to shoot her; were you?"

"No, ma'am. I didn't even cock the hammer. I'm a bit surprised she didn't take a whack at me anyway figuring the bullet wouldn't hit anything vital."

Emma laughed as Willie asked, "Are you gonna stay this time, Rhody?"

Rhody turned to him and said, "I need to talk to Emma about that, but let's get the coffee and walk back to her parents' house. Unless you and Marty would prefer riding Morgana and Jack."

Marty quickly exclaimed, "I call Morgana!"

Being with his adopted family again filled him with an effusive warmth as he walked with them to the aisle with the coffee and tea. The other customers had returned to shopping after Olga Brandt had marched out of the store, so they quickly made their way to the counter.

Rhody already had the thirty cents for the coffee in his hand and set it on the counter before Emma could even reach into her pocket.

After he turned toward the door, Emma slid her arm through his to let the other customers know that he wasn't some passing stranger. He was her man whether he knew it or not.

Her man already knew his status as they exited the store and he watched Willie help Marty into Morgana's saddle before managing to mount Jack despite the overly long stirrups.

As they began stepping along the boardwalk with Willie and Marty walking the Morgans behind them, Emma asked, "Why did you leave Rhode Island so quickly? Did your uncle call off the wedding?"

RHODY JONES

"Nope. I had it all wrong, Emma. Elizabeth is a wonderful woman and probably has more money than my uncle. It really was a love match, but I never had the chance to explain why I had to leave you so quickly."

"I thought you just needed to get to the ship before it left."

"No, I had plenty of time for that, but when I knew that you would have to stay with your mother to care for your father, I didn't want to get in the way."

"My father died just a few days after you left, and my mother invited my sister's family to move into the big house. She sold the bakery and my brother-in-law sold his shop and house in Seguin. He's still setting up his shop in New Braunfels."

"I met him when I stopped at your house. I may be wrong, but I don't think he likes me."

"I'm not surprised. I'll explain later."

"Okay, but not wanting to get in the way was only a secondary reason for my departure. Remember that stranger who was riding behind us on the way to New Braunfels? The one who Willie said was riding a horse that looked like Jack?"

"Yes."

"If you recall, I mentioned that after we left your sister's house, I spotted the horse in front of your brother-in-law's shop and it bothered me. Why would he take the same route to Seguin that we did when there was a more direct route? I did some checking when I returned to San Antonio and was sure that he was going to try to kill me."

Emma quickly looked at him with wide eyes as she asked, *"Did he try to kill you?"*

"He tried after midnight," he replied then began telling her the story.

After he finished the tale, he said, "I thought that he'd been sent by Elizabeth to try to get both halves of our company, but as soon as I met her, I knew she hadn't been responsible. I finally figured out that he was just a disgruntled sailor out for revenge and happened to be in Galveston when the *Sweet Elizabeth* docked and probably heard scuttlebutt from the crew."

"So, if the wedding is still on, then why did you come back? Aren't you going to miss the wedding?"

He stopped and waited until she was facing him before he said, "No, Emma, I'm planning on taking another train back to Rhode Island as soon as I can."

She was staring into his hazel eyes as she quietly asked, "Then why did you return at all?"

"You know why, Emma. I came back because I was afraid that if I waited until after the wedding that I may never get the opportunity to tell you how I feel. I couldn't lose you, Emma."

"You'll never lose me, Rhody."

He glanced at Willie and Marty as they sat on the motionless Morgans then turned his eyes back to Emma's warm blues.

"I was lonely without you, Emma."

"I was worried that something might happen to you that would keep you from returning."

"Well, I'm back now and we still need to have a long, private conversation."

"Yes, we do. I'm staying with the Ernsts now that my mother's house is so crowded. We can talk there after I bring her the coffee."

Rhody nodded then they resumed walking and didn't stop talking but left the serious discussion for when they were alone.

When they stopped in front of her mother's house, Rhody helped Marty down while Willie slid from Jack's saddle.

Rhody said, "Don't tell Emma's family about what happened in the store. Okay?"

"Yes, sir," Willie replied as Marty nodded.

Emma and Rhody stepped down the walkway with Willie and Marty following and soon entered the foyer.

Her mother was talking to Paul when she heard them enter and when she saw Rhody with Emma, she popped up from her chair and exclaimed, "Rhody! You're here already?"

He smiled at her and replied, "Yes, ma'am. I took advantage of some express trains."

"Was your uncle's wedding called off?"

"No, ma'am. I'll be heading back in a day or two. I have another ten days but should be back a couple of days before the wedding just to be polite."

Emma then said, "I have your coffee, Mama," and handed her the bag.

"Will you stay for some coffee, Rhody?" her mother asked.

"I appreciate it, Mrs. Ludden. I can't stay long because I need to take care of my horses before Emma and I have a long talk."

Maria smiled as she said, "I'm sure you do."

Emma then turned to Willie and Marty and said, "Why don't you entertain Peter and Frieda while we have our coffee."

RHODY JONES

Rhody watched the disappointment arrive on their faces as they agreed, so he said, "When we finish with our coffee, we need to take you back to your grandparents' house and I'll give you the presents I brought from Rhode Island."

"*You brought presents?*" Marty exclaimed.

"Now why would I tell you I brought presents if I didn't?" he asked with a grin.

The duration of their disappointment hadn't lasted three heartbeats before Rhody, Emma and her mother started walking to the kitchen.

Paul watched them leave and thought about following but decided that they wouldn't talk about anything noteworthy while he was there anyway. He doubted if Emma would tell Jones about him either. He knew her reputation and if she told him, he'd know what she was.

As they reached Anna's bedroom, Emma said, "Rhody, did you want to meet my brand-new nephew?"

"Let her know I'm here first. I don't want to make his mother uncomfortable."

Before Emma could reply, Anna said loudly, "It's safe to come in."

Rhody grinned but still waited until Emma and her mother entered before walking into the room.

Anna was still tired but happy with her new baby who was sleeping beside her.

Rhody stepped closer to the bed and smiled down at the peaceful newborn.

"He's a beautiful boy, Anna. He takes after his mother."

Anna smiled before she replied, "Thank you, Rhody. I heard you say you're leaving soon. Are you going alone?"

Rhody glanced at Emma as he answered, "No, ma'am."

Emma smiled when she heard his reply having her first unasked question answered. Now it was just a matter of the details.

Then Rhody burst her bubble when he said, "I'll be bringing my Morgans with me."

Anna and Emma were both confused, and Emma added a good dose of hurt before Rhody grinned and added, "I hope I'm not alone in the passenger car either."

Anna laughed, but even as Emma felt a warm rush replace her heartache she snapped, "That was a mean answer, Mister Jones! I have no intention of getting on a train with you."

Rhody was shocked and it showed on his face and was about to apologize when Emma smiled sweetly and added, "At least not today."

RHODY JONES

Anna laughed harder waking up her silent infant before Rhody said, "Very well played, ma'am. I have been had by a master."

Emma was still smiling as they left Anna's bedroom and walked to the kitchen where they had a seat at the table while Maria made the coffee.

After she joined them with her own coffee, she said, "I don't believe I can stay awake much longer. As you noticed, Anna is doing well and so is little Paul Junior. Emma, everything here is going well and even though I'll miss you, I think I'll be pretty busy helping Anna with her children."

"I'm happy that I arrived in time to see papa again, Mama."

"It made me even happier, Emma. Your father was a domineering, powerful man for his entire life, but when the doctor told him he was going to die, he had a metamorphosis. He suddenly realized what mattered most and he knew he had treated you poorly. He wasn't concerned about incurring God's wrath for his behavior, he simply wanted to make amends to you before he passed. You gave him the peace that he craved that no one else could have. I'll be forever grateful for those few days you were with him, Emma."

She smiled at Rhody and said, "I wouldn't have been able to make it if Rhody hadn't saved me. He didn't save me just once, he saved me three times and maybe four."

Maria looked at her daughter with raised eyebrows as she asked, "When was the fourth?"

"A few minutes ago, when we were in the store. I'm not sure that Mrs. Brandt would have gone so far as to kill me, but she did slap me hard across the face after calling me every foul name she could think of."

"That evil woman should burn in hell!" Maria snapped.

"She was preparing to slap me again when someone stuck his Colt into her chest and let her know that she was behaving improperly."

Maria looked at Rhody as Emma told the details of the confrontation including Rhody's part of the conversation almost verbatim.

Despite her anger, Maria found herself laughing when Emma repeated Rhody's insinuation that she was more of a man than a woman.

When Emma finished, she was smiling before she took a sip of her coffee.

Maria asked, "When does the train leave?"

"It leaves Seguin at 12:20, but if we return to San Antonio, then we can catch the express to Dallas at 7:40."

"So, are you leaving for San Antonio today?"

"I don't think I want to push my horses, so I'll stay tonight and leave the day after tomorrow. I still have some things I need to do in San Antonio."

"May I come with you to San Antonio? I'll take my buggy."

"Of course, you may. That's assuming that your daughter is coming along after all."

Emma said, "I'm not going to pretend to be anything but excited to be coming with you, Rhody."

Maria didn't ask the obvious question about them traveling without a chaperone because it really didn't matter to her. She could see the joy in her daughter's face and such societal niceties had no business interfering with their happiness.

As they finished their coffee, Rhody explained what had happened before he left to go to Galveston and the surprise when he met his uncle's fiancée.

When he finished, he said, "I think Willie and Marty are anxious to open gifts I have for them, so we should head over to their grandparents house."

Maria asked, "So, I'll see you tomorrow morning?"

"Yes, ma'am."

"I'll have Paul harness the buggy."

Emma kissed her mother goodbye then she and Rhody left the kitchen before they stopped in the parlor to collect Willie and Marty, who needed no incentive to leave Peter and Frieda's company.

As they headed for the foyer, Rhody glanced at Paul Schmidt and noticed the decidedly unfriendly look on his face before heading out of the room. He needed to ask Emma about that again when they had their private conversation. Of course, the heart of that conversation was already gone when Emma's mother had asked if he was going to return alone to Rhode Island, but there was still much more that he needed to tell her.

When they reached the Morgans, Willie and Marty said they'd walk, so Rhody untied their reins, handed Morgana's to Willie then they headed for the Ernst home.

Rhody was impressed that neither of them had asked about the presents again but as they walked, he could sense a subtle change in Emma. It wasn't much and he was surprised that he was able to spot it, but it was there.

He suspected that it had to do with Willie and Marty, especially Marty. She had been so close to the girl since they'd first been paired on that horse heading to the Comanche village, and the longer they were together, the stronger that bond had become. Now that she was living with them, he didn't doubt that she was more of a mother to Marty than an adopted aunt. Emma would be heartbroken to be separated from Marty and that created a problem if they were going to live in Rhode Island. Besides, he still had to keep his promise to Willie.

The long walk was mostly filled with chatter about what had happened while he was gone, so the time passed quickly.

When they arrived at the Ernst home, Willie said, "They have a small barn in back for their buggy and horse, Rhody. I'm sure you can put Jack and Morgana there."

"I'll do that after I ask your grandparents, Willie," he said as he tied them off at the hitchrail.

He followed Emma and the children into the house and was immediately greeted by Willie and Marty's grandfather, Franz.

"We heard you were coming back, Rhody," he said as he shook Rhody's hand.

Rhody smiled and replied, "My family was here, Mister Ernst."

Franz was confused and said, "I thought your family lived back East."

"My uncle lives in Rhode Island, but since that first day on the way to Menardville, I saw Emma, Willie and Marty as my family. It's why it was so important for me to protect them."

Franz's gray head bobbed as he said, "I understand. Let's go and see Greta. She's baking some strudel."

Willie and Marty both grinned and trotted down the hallway and were followed at a slower pace by the adults.

When Rhody and Emma entered the aromatic kitchen, Greta smiled at them and said, "I heard what you said, Rhody, and I was happy to hear you say that."

"It's just how I feel, ma'am."

"Well, have a seat and when the strudel has cooled, we can have some for dessert after supper."

"Thank you, Mrs. Ernst. I need to get my horses unsaddled. Do you mind if I leave them in your barn?"

"Not at all. When you return, we need to ask you something. When are you leaving?"

"Not until tomorrow morning. We'll be going to San Antonio for a day before leaving on the train the day after."

Greta smiled as she asked, "We?"

Rhody returned her smile and replied, "Yes, ma'am. I convinced Emma to come along."

"Why don't you stay here tonight, Rhody? We have plenty of room."

"Thank you again, ma'am. That makes things easier. I'll be back in a little while."

Then he turned to Emma and asked, "Could you help me with the horses, Emma?"

She nodded and replied, "Of course," understanding that she probably wasn't going to touch a saddle.

Willie quickly said, "I'll help, too."

"You stay here, young man. We need to talk to you and Marta," said Greta.

"Yes, ma'am."

Rhody and Emma then left the kitchen and soon stepped out of the house and approached Morgana and Jack.

"I think I know why Franz and Greta want to talk to Willie and Marty, or at least I hope so," she said as he untied the Morgans' reins.

After they started walking to the barn, Rhody asked, "What is it?"

"When I first started visiting Willie and Marty, they told me that they had forgotten how much time it took to raise children. After Anna's family moved into my mother's house, I became their nanny and they were very happy to have me there. I think that they're going to ask Willie and Marty if they wanted to come with us, so they could return to the peaceful life that they'd become accustomed to."

"Do you think that they'll want to leave with us?"

"I'm sure they will. You have to remember that Willie only had vague memories of his grandparents and Marty didn't know them at all. You know how much I love them, and I know that you do, too. Would it be alright if they came with us?"

Rhody could hear the hope in her voice when she'd asked, then replied, "If you must know, I was already trying to come up with some way of asking their grandparents if we could bring them with us."

"You were?" she quickly asked.

"Yes, ma'am," he answered as they reached the small barn.

He swung one of the doors open and led the Morgans inside as Emma trotted behind.

After he'd maneuvered Morgana and Jack into adjacent empty stalls, he let them drink at the long trough and turned toward Emma.

He stepped close to her and took her shoulders in his hands as he looked into those big blue eyes.

"Emma, we've been dancing around the single most important subject. You know why I returned and that we'll be leaving San Antonio in two days. And now, we know that we'll probably be bringing Willie and Marty with us. We've made all these plans and I have yet to say those critical three words to you, Emma."

RHODY JONES

Emma gazed into his hazel eyes as she placed her hands on his waist and quietly said, "I haven't told you either, Rhody."

"I love you, Emma. I've loved you almost from the start."

"I've loved you from the first day, Rhody, but I wasn't sure if it was out of gratitude because I've never experienced true love before. It didn't take me long to realize that I loved you with all my heart and soul. I thought you were going to tell me when you gave me that kiss that was barely a touch, but you didn't. Why?"

"I was worried, Emma. I'd only known you for a week or so, and I didn't want to hurt you if you didn't care for me in the same way. I even regretted that one kiss because I thought I'd gone too far."

"Can you kiss me again now that you've told me that you love me?"

Rhody gave his reply when he slid his hands from her shoulders, wrapped her in his arms and kissed her with all of the stored passion he'd been saving since that first whisper of a kiss.

Emma felt her knees weaken as she felt his love and soon added her own as they continued the kiss until they needed to breathe.

Rhody then looked into her yearning eyes and whispered, "I love you, Emma. Will you marry me?"

Emma's heart was thumping as she whispered back, "Yes, oh, yes. When?"

"When we get to Rhode Island. I want to have a double wedding with my uncle. Is that alright?"

"I don't care when or where it is, only that it happens. And I don't even care if it does, as long as you're with me."

He kissed her again then when their second real kiss ended, he slid his lips along her neck giving her goosebumps. She held his head close as she tilted her head to let him know she was enjoying his attentions.

Rhody knew he had to stop or there would be a long delay before they returned to the house and someone may come looking.

Emma's urges were exploding inside her and she wished they could continue, but even before Rhody stepped back, she had concluded the same thing.

"It's going to be a long train ride, Emma," Rhody said as he smiled at her.

"Yes," she replied hoarsely.

He kissed her once more before stepping awkwardly away to unsaddle the horses.

Emma was still flushed, so she sat down on an old barrel and asked, "Where will we live, Rhody?"

RHODY JONES

"That's an interesting question. My uncle and Elizabeth are planning on sailing to Newport for their honeymoon, so we can live in his house until they return. Elizabeth has her own house in Providence that she bought thinking she might just stay there after she sold the shipping company, so we could just move there until we build our own house."

"Do you want to live in a big city like Providence? San Antonio is the biggest city I've ever seen, and it only has about ten thousand people."

"No, I don't want to live in the city. In fact, a few years earlier, I bought forty acres of land about ten miles south of Providence, but I haven't done anything with it yet other than build a long wharf for my yawl."

"Why did you buy it?"

"Because I thought I was going to get married, but I told you how that turned out. So, we can build our house there and have a barn for our horses."

Emma was smiling as she asked, "What's it like?"

Rhody tossed Morgana's saddle onto the stall's sideboard, then replied, "It's a beautiful piece of land, Emma. It's in a town named Warwick and the land ends at a nice stretch of beach. There's lots of grass and trees, but what makes it special is the beach.

"There's a cove that's on the north side of the property that's usually dry. It looks like just a depression most of the time, but once a month when the moon is full, it transforms. It's what they call a moon tide. When the full moon exerts its pull during high tide, the seawater fills the lagoon. I don't know why, but it seems that every time I was there during that moon tide, the water was perfectly smooth and calm. There was no wind or waves, so the water simply flowed slowly into the cove. It's the most peaceful scene I've ever witnessed from mother nature."

"I can't wait to see it, Rhody."

"I have so many things I want to show you, Emma. I want to take you, Willie and Marty out on my yawl so you can feel the ocean's spray as the ship cuts through the waves."

"I can't swim, Rhody."

"I'll show you, but I'll give you each a life jacket, too."

Emma smiled as she asked, "Are you going to cook us some quahogs and lobstah?"

Rhody began unsaddling Jack as he laughed and replied, "Of course, I will. I don't know if I'll be able to convince Willie or Marty to try them once they see the what the lobster looks like, but I'll try."

Emma rocked back on the barrel slightly and watched as Rhody unsaddled Jack. She was happier than she'd ever been

RHODY JONES

and found it hard to imagine that just a month ago, she had been captured by Comanches and was terrified as she held onto Marty. Now the man who had rescued them both would be taking them to a totally different part of the country, and they'd experience things they could never have imagined. Much more importantly that incredible man loved her, and she now understood what genuine, unfettered love was.

When they left the barn, Rhody had his saddlebags hung over both shoulders and was carrying the gift-filled travel bag in his right hand and held Emma's hand in his left.

"May I ask what you bought for them?" she asked.

"You may ask, but I'm not going to tell you. You'll find out soon enough."

Emma smiled but didn't ask if he'd brought one for her because it didn't matter. He was the greatest gift she could have hoped to receive.

When they entered the house, they found Franz and Greta Ernst sitting on the couch in the parlor as Willie and Marty sat in chairs wearing big smiles. Rhody suspected it had nothing to do with the gifts in the travel bag.

"Have a seat, Emma and Rhody," said Franz, "and we'll tell you what we asked Wilhelm and Marta."

He glanced at Emma before they took seats facing the elderly couple and he placed his saddlebags and travel bag on the floor.

"When you returned our grandchildren to us, Rhody, we were very happy to see them again. But as much as we love them, we simply don't have the energy to keep up with them anymore. When you told us that you thought of Emma and the children as your family, Greta and I agreed that if Wilhelm and Marta wished to go with you, then it would be better for them. They did more than just agree. They were dancing when they said that they wanted to go with you. Our only question now is if you meant what you said."

"Mister Ernst, I've grown to love both of your grandchildren and would be honored to raise them as my own children. Emma has grown especially fond of Marty and I have a promise to keep to Willie."

He glanced over at Emma and even though she'd already expected it, the realization that she wouldn't be leaving Marty sent tears of joy sliding across her smiling face.

"Thank you, Rhody. I'm sure that you and Emma will raise them properly," Franz said as he smiled.

Greta then said, "I hope you'll write to us to let us know how they're doing."

"We will, and I'll send pictures as well, so you can watch them grow."

RHODY JONES

As Greta nodded, Rhody looked at Willie and Marty and could tell they were about ready to burst.

"I suppose my first job as your father-to-be is to spoil each of you with gifts as I promised."

Their dams ruptured and an avalanche of uninhibited elation erupted as Willie and Marty sprang from their seats and rushed across the parlor.

Emma hugged Marty while Willie stuck out his hand to Rhody.

Rhody wasn't about to let him get off so easily, so he rose and hugged Willie who didn't seem to object.

When the hugs ended, Rhody sat back down and set his travel bag on his lap. He pulled out the box for Marty and handed it to her.

Marty looked at Emma with her smile still growing, then opened the box and squealed.

"It's so pretty!" she exclaimed as she lifted the gold chain from the box which pulled the locket watch free.

Rhody said, "It's not just a pretty locket, Marty. See the little button on the side? Push that to open it."

Marty pressed the gold button and the locket case sprang open revealing the watch's face.

"It's a watch!" she exclaimed, "Thank you, Rhody!"

"I set the time to match my chronograph, Marty, but you need to wind that stem on top at least every other day. Okay?"

"I will. It's really pretty, too," she said before she stepped over to Emma to show her the watch.

He took out Willie's box and gave it to him.

"Thank you, Rhody," he said before he opened it.

When he pulled back the cover, he exclaimed, "Wow! It's a knife!" then carefully extracted the fancy pocketknife from its case.

"It's a very special knife, Willie. It has a four-inch blade and another four-inch blade that's really a saw. But what makes it even more special is what's stored on the other side."

Willie turned it over and saw a tab, so he pulled on it and a small magnifying glass slid out of its slot.

"I can use it to see things better!"

"But the main reason for it being there is so you can start a fire without a match. I'll show you how to do that later. Okay?"

"I can start a fire with it?" he asked as he focused it on the chair's upholstered arm.

"Only in the sunlight."

RHODY JONES

Willie slid the magnifying glass back into its slot then asked, "Did you bring something for Aunt Emma?"

Marty then asked, "Did you get her a pretty watch too?"

He looked at Emma, smiled and replied, "No, I didn't buy her a watch. I didn't buy her any pretty jewelry either because I didn't think that she wanted jewelry. I spent a long time deciding what to buy you, Emma, and I hope I didn't choose the wrong thing."

"I don't need a gift, Rhody. You are the most wonderful gift I will ever receive."

"You may believe that, but I still wanted to buy you something that at least lets you know that I'm beginning to understand you better."

He then slipped the polished cherry case from his travel bag and handed it to her.

She looked at him then turned her eyes to the case and released the two latches that held it closed before swinging open the lid.

She stared at its contents and asked, "Is it a sextant?"

Rhody laughed lightly before he replied, "No. It's a field microscope. See those glass slides on the side? You find something you want to examine closely, put it on the slide and then look at it through the lens. There are three other lenses of different magnification, so you can get up to a hundred times closer. You need to have enough light to bounce off the mirror on the bottom, but when you peer through that lens, a whole new world will become visible that you never knew existed."

Emma touched the polished brass tube then looked at Rhody and said, "It's perfect. How did you know that I'd like it so much?"

"You have a wonderful mind, Emma, and I thought you'd enjoy exploring the unknown more than wearing a fancy coat or gaudy jewelry."

She smiled as she said, "You're right, and I'll admit that I'm impressed that you seemed to understand me so well already."

"It's just the start, Emma. I'm not sure I'll ever understand you completely, but I'll spend the rest of my life trying."

Greta then turned to her husband and said, "Franz, can you show Rhody his room while Emma and I start preparing supper?"

"Yes, ma'am," he replied as he stood.

Rhody rose, hung his saddlebags over his shoulders, grabbed his travel bag and followed Franz up the stairs to the second floor.

RHODY JONES

After setting everything in the bedroom, he and Franz returned to the main floor where Willie was studying everything with his magnifying class. Marty had followed Emma and Greta into the kitchen.

While they waited, Rhody told Franz about the incident in the store and Franz told him he may want to clean his pistol.

After Willie and Marty had been put to bed and the Ernsts had turned in, Emma and Rhody were sitting on the couch in the parlor with a single lamp casting its orange light across the room.

With their travel plans set, Rhody finally asked his question about her brother-in-law.

"Emma, can you tell me now about Anna's husband? When I first met Paul, even though I'd never laid eyes on him before, he seemed unhappy to see me. It was even worse when we were leaving. I swear if he had a pistol, he would have plugged me in the back. Why is that?"

Emma was concerned about his reaction, especially after how he'd dealt with Olga Brandt, but couldn't cover for her brother-in-law.

"Before I had to marry Carl, I was helping Anna after she had Elise. He always seemed, um, interested in me and when Anna was feeding the baby, he snuck up behind me and touched me, then he kissed me hard and fondled me. I ran out of the house and have been nervous to be around him when I was alone ever since."

Rhody felt his anger already bubbling deep inside but calmly asked, "Why did he even do that with Anna so close? What about the other children?"

"They were too young, and Anna was still bedridden after giving birth. As to why, I never asked, but as I said, he always had that look in his eyes. I suspected that Carl might have been bragging about our liaison and he'd learned about it. I never told Anna or my mother, but that's the main reason I had to move out of my mother's house when he moved in."

Emma could see Rhody's fury building and was about to ask him not to do anything about it when he took in a deep breath.

"Emma, as much as I'd like to walk over there and beat him to a bloody pulp for what he did, I'm going to let it go because it's family business and I don't want to hurt Anna. Do you think she suspects anything?"

"No, but I wouldn't bet on it, but thank you, Rhody. I was worried that you might hurt Paul as much as he might deserve it. I just hope that Anna never finds out and he doesn't hurt her. I don't mean physically. I just hope he doesn't break her heart."

RHODY JONES

Rhody nodded then began thinking of some way to punish the bastard without upsetting the family. In the end, he decided that all he could do was to let it go.

After a relatively chaste kiss, they adjourned to their separate bedrooms for the night. Tomorrow they'd leave New Braunfels and Paul Schmidt behind them and then after a day in San Antonio, they'd be on their way to Rhode Island and the start of their new life together.

July 20, 1879

The express train pulled out of San Antonio on that already hot Texas day with Rhody and his new family sitting in their seats in the first-class passenger car. It had been a busy morning, but Morgana and Jack were in the stock car with his rifles and now it was just going to be a long four or five days on the rails.

After arriving in San Antonio yesterday afternoon with Emma's mother, Rowdy had closed his account with the Alamo State Bank and added most of the $821.20 to his money belt then they'd done some shopping, mainly for more clothes for Emma and the children. After her mother left for New Braunfels, he sent a long telegram to his uncle asking if a double wedding would be acceptable.

He'd received a reply later that afternoon from his very happy uncle and he assured Rhody that he and Elizabeth would have everything ready.

As the train raced across the Texas landscape, Willie and Marty were thrilled by the speed and spent the first few hours plastered to the windows chattering about everything that flew past.

That gave Rhody and Emma time to talk about the simple things in their lives that neither had much time to share before.

They weren't able to make all the express trains, and when they reached St. Louis which astounded Emma and the children, they decided to stay overnight before taking the next express train to Indianapolis. It would cost them a day, but Rhody thought it was worth it so Emma could enjoy a hot bath. She had been stunned when she found a full bathroom attached to her luxurious hotel room that she would share with Marty while Rhody and Willie used the adjoining room.

Without realizing it, Willie and Marty were acting as chaperones.

After the day in St. Louis, they continued their journey and even though Rhody had told her what to expect, she found the thick forests and pervasive green nothing short of miraculous. It seemed that towns were everywhere and while none were as big as St. Louis, they all seemed to be real cities.

RHODY JONES

As they left Pennsylvania two days later, Rhody said, "As big as St. Louis was, we'll soon be reaching New York. It's the most populous city in the country and to be honest, I like St. Louis better."

"Are we going to spend the night there, like we did in St. Louis? I don't want to meet your uncle and Elizabeth looking shabby."

Rhody laughed and replied, "You could never look shabby, Emma. But we can spend the night there so the train we take to Providence will arrive around noon."

"Thank you, Rhody. Can we find a hotel where they have baths like the one in St. Louis?"

"We can, and maybe when we build our house in Warwick, I'll have them put in a boiler so you can have hot baths anytime you'd like."

"You can do that?" she asked with arched eyebrows.

"Yes, ma'am. We can have steam heat, too."

Willie looked over from his seat across the aisle and asked, "When does it start snowing?"

"I've seen it as early as October, but it usually doesn't stay around very long until December."

"I've never seen snow before," Marty said as she knelt on the seat in front of them.

"Well, missy, you're going to see a lot of it from now on. You'll probably wish you were back in Texas by the time January arrives."

Marty giggled then plopped back down to her seat.

After the night's rest in a first-class hotel in New York, they were on the last leg of their journey by nine o'clock and just before noon the train crossed the Connecticut-Rhode Island border just three days before the wedding.

Without the two overnight stays, they would only have four days before the wedding, but the long journey had given Emma and Rhody plenty of time to get to know each other better and the explorations had only added to their shared love.

Emma's sharp wit had been unleashed while they were still in Texas and throughout the trip as she matched Rhody's dry humor. As they talked, she absorbed everything he could tell her about his uncle and Elizabeth so she would be ready when she met them. She felt somewhat intimidated despite Rhody's assurances as she'd never come close to mixing with the upper crust of society, even in Texas.

As the train pulled out of Kingston Station in southern Rhode Island, Emma asked, "Is there anything else I need to know before I meet your uncle?"

"No, ma'am. I think you know almost as much about him as I do now. But there is one more thing I need to tell you that I had totally forgotten about until we reached Rhode Island and I began to picture my uncle's house."

"And that is?"

"When I returned after five years, I met his new maid who he'd just hired. Her name is Lilly and she's a very attractive young lady."

Emma's eyebrows shot up as she suspected a confession was imminent.

"Well," Rhody continued, "shortly after meeting her, she followed me into my room and suggested that I didn't have to return to Texas and she was willing to ease my, um, frustrations."

"You didn't!"

"No, no, I didn't. But when I asked her why she hadn't married already because she was so attractive, she told me that she was only working because her family needed the money. So, I told her that when I returned with you, I'd give her a thousand dollars for a dowry so she could wed. I just didn't want you to believe I was giving her the money to keep her quiet or anything."

Emma stared at him for a good thirty seconds before she started laughing.

Rhody was befuddled by her reaction and asked, "Why are you laughing?"

"I don't know. After all you've done to bring me here, it sounded silly for you to think that you'd be paying her for her silence. I know you pretty well, Mister Jones, and I have no doubt that you would never have done anything shameful like that."

Rhody smiled at Emma's happy face and was pleased that he'd told her about it. He couldn't imagine having to explain it after the fact. He'd have to tell Uncle Richard about it, too.

―――

An hour later, the train pulled into the large station just outside of the northern tip of Narragansett Bay and the large port where the R. Jones Shipping Company's ships docked.

Rhody had already strapped his saddlebags onto Morgana and Jack, so as they exited the passenger car all he carried was his travel bag and another larger travel bag he'd bought in San Antonio. Willie and Marty carried small bags with their personal items while all Emma carried was her concerns.

Rhody let Willie take the lead as he bounced onto the platform followed by Marty. He left the car ahead of Emma and soon spotted his uncle and Elizabeth waiting nearby.

RHODY JONES

He set his bags down, waved then turned and took Emma's hand. He could tell she was still nervous but knew that would soon change.

Richard and Elizabeth strode across the platform and Bess approached Emma and smiled. Just as Rhody had instantly realized that she couldn't have been the gold digger he had expected, Emma quickly understood that Bess would become a friend.

"It's wonderful to meet you, Emma," Bess said as she took Emma's hands, "Rhody has told us so much about you that I feel as if I know you already."

"He told me as much about you. May I call you Bess? Rhody said that only his uncle seems to call you Elizabeth."

Bess laughed and replied, "Of course, you may. I think he still thinks I'm royalty. At least he doesn't bow when he sees me anymore."

Emma laughed lightly then turned to Rhody's uncle who was being introduced to Willie and Marty.

After shaking Willie's hand, he turned his eyes to Emma and said, "I can understand why you've won my nephew's heart, Emma. Let's all take the carriage to my house where we'll have lunch."

Rhody said, "Willie and I will ride my horses behind your carriage, Uncle."

"Oh, that's right. You said you were bringing your horses and guns with you. I want to see that Sharps-Borshadt, too."

Rhody smiled then turned to Emma and said, "We'll be right behind you."

Emma nodded as Marty looked at Richard and asked, "Are we having quahogs for lunch?"

Richard laughed as he looked down at the blonde-headed, blue-eyed little girl and said, "I'm sorry, Marty. We're having plain old roast turkey for lunch, but I'm sure that we can go to a seafood restaurant for supper and you can have whatever you want, even quahogs."

Marty grinned then took Emma's hand as they left the platform with Bess while Richard took Rhody's heavy travel bag.

Willie and Rhody headed for the stock corral and spotted Morgana and Jack being unloaded.

After claiming his horses, Willie mounted Jack and Rhody climbed aboard Morgana before they rode out of the corral and found his uncle's carriage waiting nearby.

When Richard saw them coming, he snapped the reins and the carriage rolled out of the large station with the two Morgans trotting behind.

RHODY JONES

Emma and Marty were no longer stunned by the size of the city after having seen St. Louis and New York, but after leaving the train station, they soon began seeing the large warehouses and the tips of the ships' masts of Providence's busy harbor.

Then Richard turned the carriage onto Eddy Street and Emma soon saw the rows of big houses that dwarfed any of the houses she'd thought were large back in Texas.

After swinging into the long drive, Richard pulled up near the front porch and set the handbrake before stepping down, then helping Marty to the ground. Emma and Bess both exited on their own as Rhody and Willie dismounted.

Forty minutes later, the Morgans were unsaddled and relieved to be free of their tack as they devoured oats in the large feed bins and the humans had moved their things into their assigned rooms. Marty and Willie were more than happy when they found that they each had a room to themselves.

The adults were in the dining room sharing coffee while Willie and Marty were given their first taste of chocolate milk.

Richard said, "Everything is set for the double wedding at St. George's on the first at ten o'clock. You'll need to stop by and see Reverend Potter to go over the paperwork tomorrow. We're still planning on taking your yawl to Newport for our honeymoon, so where will you go?"

Rhody glanced at Emma then replied, "We'll stay here, but haven't figured out the details yet."

Bess then said, "I think you can leave Willie and Marty with Susan and Lilly and use my house. It's just three blocks away."

Rhody then looked at Willie and asked, "Is that alright with you two?"

"Yes, sir."

Marty nodded then asked, "But you can come and see us too; can't you?"

"Of course, we will. We'd be terrible parents if we didn't."

Bess then shifted her eyes to Emma before saying, "Emma, you won't have to buy a dress for the wedding. I bought a second one similar to mine that I had adjusted to the description that Rhody gave me. You're taller than I am and a bit more…well, just more, so we'll probably just need to make a few small alterations."

Emma was surprised but blushed at Bess' comment about being 'more' as she replied, "Thank you, Bess. That was very thoughtful."

"We'll take care of that tomorrow afternoon after you return from your visit with Reverend Potter."

RHODY JONES

Emma smiled then looked at Rhody who didn't seem to be flustered at all about what Bess had said.

Rhody smiled back and said, "Well, at least I'm not marrying Olga Brandt. Then we'd have to use our sailmaker for her dress."

Emma burst into laughter at the mental image as Rhody described the vicious woman to his uncle and Bess. If she'd been a pleasant person, then her size wouldn't have mattered, but the combination of her spiteful personality with her aggressive nature deserved much more than insulting barbs.

After a supper at Shaughnessy's Seafood where the Emma and the children had their first experience with clams and lobster, which went better than Rhody had expected as he thought at least Marty would be offended by the lobster's insect-like appearance, they returned to Richard's house for more conversation.

When they turned in for the night, Rhody was somewhat surprised that Elizabeth stayed, although it was in a separate room from his uncle. That meant that Emma would stay in the house as well, and as much as he would like to have her join him in his room, he was concerned about the noise that they'd probably generate.

He still hadn't told his uncle about the arrangement he'd made with Lilly either and he hoped that she kept her side of the bargain. He hadn't talked to her since they'd returned, but he'd have to take care of that before the wedding, too.

When the sunlight bathed his bedroom the next morning, Rhody was well-rested and pleased that he'd awakened alone. He guessed that Emma had been too exhausted from the long journey and had fallen asleep as quickly as he had.

He quickly washed and shaved in the basin in his bedroom, then dressed and left the room and trotted downstairs to the kitchen.

He was somewhat surprised to find that Emma and the children weren't there yet, but not surprised that his uncle and Bess were still in bed. He just wondered if they were in the same bed or not.

Rhody entered the kitchen and Susan turned then smiled at him before saying, "Good morning, Rhody."

"Good morning, Susan," then he turned and found Libby smiling at him as she sipped her coffee.

"Good morning, Libby."

"Good morning, Rhody."

"Could I talk to you in the office for a minute, Libby?" he asked.

"Yes, sir," she replied before setting her cup down and standing.

She walked with him to the large office and library then took a seat before the desk.

Rhody remained standing, but leaned against the desk before saying, "I told Emma about our agreement and she thought it was a very nice thing to do. Now I have that much money with me, but I'll hold onto it until you find a beau. Is that alright?"

Libby smiled then replied, "I already have a beau, Rhody. Right after you left, I visited my parents and told them of your promise, so they freed me to choose my future husband. I had been ready to accept Teddy Finley before they told me I couldn't marry, so once they gave me permission, I let him know that I was available, and he proposed again. This time I was able to accept."

Rhody grinned then said, "That's wonderful, Lilly! It so happens that I still wear my money belt, so if you don't mind, I'll just turn around to extract your dowry."

Lilly giggled as Rhody turned his back to her, unbuttoned his shirt and unbuckled his money belt. He set it on the desk, opened it and counted out a thousand dollars before buttoning his shirt again.

He handed her the wad of bills which she quickly shoved into her dress' pocket before she put her arms around him and kissed him as if he was Teddy Finley.

It couldn't have been a worse time as Emma was passing the office on her way to the kitchen, looked through the open door an froze at the sight. She had seen Lilly and thought that she was prettier than she was but was confident in Rhody's devotion to her. She even wondered if Lilly had spent the night in Rhody's bed.

She didn't say a word as she stared at them from the doorway.

Rhody had been stunned and hadn't put his arms around her or even returned her kiss but finally, he put his hands on her shoulder and pushed her back. He didn't notice Emma in the doorway as he looked down at Libby.

"I appreciate that your grateful, Libby, but I think you went overboard."

"I'm sorry, Rhody, but you made me so happy."

"Well, I hope you can be as happy with Teddy as I am with my Emma."

Emma heard what Rhody had said and her flare of jealousy vanished as she understood that he had probably fulfilled his promise and given her the dowry.

RHODY JONES

She then cleared her throat, and Rhody looked at her while Lilly spun on her heels in horror knowing what it probably looked like to Emma.

Rhody stepped around Lilly and quickly said, "It's not as it appeared, Emma. You'll have to trust me!"

Emma glared at him as she asked, "When does the next train leave for Texas?"

Rhody strode closely to her then put his hands on her shoulders and begged, "Please don't leave me, Emma. I love you more than you can imagine. I had just given Lilly her dowry and she was happy. That's all!"

Emma locked onto his pleading hazel eyes and said, "I was just asking about a train schedule. Why would you think I was leaving for Texas?"

Rhody stared at her for a moment before she started laughing then threw her arms around him and kissed him much more passionately than Lilly had just done.

When they parted, Emma looked past Rhody's shoulder and said, "Congratulations, Lilly. Can I guess that Richard will be looking for a new maid pretty soon?"

Lilly relaxed before replying, "Yes, ma'am."

Emma took hold of Rhody's arm then escorted him out of the office while Lilly scurried to her room to pack. She'd give

Mister Jones her notice when he came downstairs and couldn't wait to tell Teddy.

By the time they reached the kitchen, Rhody was grateful that he hadn't done anything other than react as he did to Lilly's surprise kiss. He was still frustrated, and it was only his deep love for Emma that had kept his hands where they belonged.

Later that morning, they met with Reverend Juniper Potter which didn't take as long as they'd expected. Rhody figured that his uncle was a good patron of the church and his request was more than enough to grease the skids.

When they returned, Emma left with Bess to go to her house to have her wedding dress altered, which left Rhody time to talk to his uncle and explain what had happened before he came downstairs including Emma's horrifying yet hilariously funny response.

After they'd had lunch, he and Richard walked to the docks where he finally saw his overhauled yawl with gold lettered *Always Emma* painted in script on her transom.

"You've made some improvements on her, Uncle Richard," Rhody said as they boarded the boat.

"I had them extend the cabin by four feet and added some creature comforts inside including a sea stove in case you wanted to take her for longer trips. I may want to borrow her more often myself."

"I think you should buy your own and name her *Sweet Bess*."

Richard laughed then replied, "I may just do that, but I've got to improve my sailing prowess. Elizabeth is going to be doing most of it when we go to Newport."

"Why am I not surprised?" Rhody asked with a grin.

"When are you bringing Emma and the children to the docks to see her?"

"Tomorrow. We're pretty much all set for the wedding on Thursday."

"Do you have your wedding bands already?"

"I bought them before I left for San Antonio in case Emma didn't want to leave."

"Good, then you can give me yours and I'll give you ours. We're going to be each other's witnesses and the only others in the church will be the reverend, the organist, and Willie and Marty."

"Nothing like a private wedding."

Richard looked at him and said, "I'm happy that I waited, Rhody. I think I'll take that yardarm down from the house now because I won't be flying that pennant again."

"I hope not," Rhody replied with a chuckle before they left the *Always Emma* to return to the house.

―――

After breakfast the next morning, Rhody held Emma's hand as they walked to the docks with Willie and Marty trailing.

She was expecting him to show her his private boat, but still didn't know about the name change.

Willie and Marty were looking wide-eyed at the tall ships that were being loaded and unloaded at other docks and found them mesmerizing.

Emma was scanning the dock ahead looking for a small sailboat and was surprised when Rhody stopped and smiled at her.

He said, "There she is, Emma," as he pointed to his yawl.

She hadn't noticed the name on the transom yet but was gawking at the size of his boat.

"It's a lot bigger than I expected. I thought it was just fifteen or twenty feet."

RHODY JONES

"She's forty-six feet long and eighteen feet across her beam," he said but was surprised she hadn't commented about the new name.

She slowly stepped toward the yawl when Willie asked, "When did you name your boat, Rhody?"

Emma turned to look at Willie and then followed his eyes to the transom and understood why he had asked.

"When did you have that done, Rhody?" she asked quietly.

"Before I left for San Antonio. She was being overhauled for my uncle's honeymoon and I had him change the name. I had to register it with the new name, so that will be her name for the rest of her days."

Emma turned to him and asked, "What if I hadn't returned with you?"

"Then she would be the only Emma in my life, but she wouldn't come close to making me nearly as happy as the real Emma would."

Emma asked, "Are we going to look inside?"

"Of course. Let's go aboard."

Emma nodded then they stepped across the short gap onto the main deck of the *Always Emma*.

The tour of the yawl wasn't nearly as important to Emma as knowing that Rhody had christened his beloved ship with her name even before he knew she would return with him.

Willie and Marty explored every inch of the main deck and inside the expanded cabin asking questions constantly while Rhody and Emma strolled behind them.

After they returned to the dock and were heading back to the house, Emma asked, "Will you take us sailing after they return from their honeymoon?"

"That's what it's for, sweetheart."

———

After they returned to the house, Bess escorted Emma to her house where they would stay until their fiancés picked them up in the morning for the drive to St. George's.

Libby hadn't returned, so Susan helped them set out their suits and ties while they buffed their shoes.

She joined them and the children for supper and she introduced Willie and Marty to apple pandowdy for dessert. It was nothing more than an inch thick layer of apple pie ingredients across a deep pan then it was topped with an even thicker layer of sweetened dough which she coated with butter as it baked giving it a nice, brown crust. But to Willie and Marty, it was a new dining experience that was much better than lobster.

After the children were asleep in their rooms, Rhody and his uncle sat in the kitchen having coffee as they discussed Rhody's plans for building their house on his land in Warwick. He'd have to build it far enough from the beach to keep it safe when a nor'easter or a hurricane drove the water well beyond it would reach on normal high tides, but the land extended far enough up the rise away from the beach that it wasn't going to be an issue.

When Rhody finally turned in, he found it difficult to sleep. Tomorrow he would be marrying Emma and she would become his focus for the rest of his life. They already had two children and he hoped that by this time next year, they would have another. He'd need to have the adoption papers drawn up next week but knew that there wouldn't be a problem.

While he regretted not seeing the Grand Canyon or the Pacific Ocean, he was glad that he'd decided to make that ride across Texas because he'd found a treasure that was nothing less than priceless.

Friday, August 1, 1879

The double wedding day had arrived, and the Jones carriage was gleaming as the two couples climbed aboard with Willie and Marty.

Both Emma and Bess wore similar ivory silk dresses and veils, but neither bothered with a train. The only difference was the color of the sashes. Emma wore a dark blue and Bess had a deep red sash around her waist.

Rhody had been awed when he had first seen Emma in her wedding dress. He remembered how he'd first seen her and even after she'd worn a new dress, nothing could match how she looked on this day.

While he couldn't wear his Stetson with his new suit, he refused to wear a bowler hat like the one his uncle had atop his head. That was just going too far.

He stood with his uncle on the altar and both men looked down the aisle waiting for their brides.

Rhody felt his heart thumping against his ribs even though he'd already seen Emma in her dress.

In the back of the church, Bess smiled at Emma and quietly said, "I think our future husbands are waiting, Emma."

Emma smiled back then the two women left the back of the church and turned onto the aisle walking slowly toward the altar as the organist played the wedding march.

As she put one foot carefully before the other, Emma had her eyes focused on Rhody and found it hard to imagine the incredible changes that she'd experienced in such a short time. Two months ago, she was surviving a miserable marriage on a small cattle ranch in the middle of nowhere and her young life was empty and devoid of happiness.

RHODY JONES

Then the Comanches attacked, kidnapped her and Marty, and she knew she was about to die and maybe even deserved it. Then the man who was standing at the altar arrived to rescue them; a man who hadn't even known she existed until he'd seen her through his telescope.

Now she was going to marry him and already had a strong son and beautiful daughter who were sitting in the first pew. She had walked down the sidewalk of a big city and had eaten something she had never even heard of before Rhody had explained what a quahog was back in Texas.

She knew she was walking down the aisle in a church in Providence, Rhode Island, but felt that it was divine providence that had sent Rhody on that ride across West Texas and saved her in every way a man could save a woman.

EPILOGUE

May 11, 1882

The *Always Emma* tacked into the wind as it raced across Narragansett Bay on her way back to its home dock.

Willie was at the rudder while Rhody dropped the mainsail in preparation for docking. Emma sat in the small well near the cabin and watched her husband handle the sails as the bracing wind blew spray into her face. Her silvery blonde hair was tied with a blue ribbon to keep it in place, but she exulted in the sensation. Since that first trip down the coast to the site for their new home, she'd never tired of spending time on the water even when she was well along in her first pregnancy.

Their first born, six-month-old Russel James was in their house with his grand uncle Richard and Bess. Marty hadn't taken well to the sea and was happy to remain ashore.

They'd received a letter from Emma's mother just days earlier with the news that Anna had divorced Paul for adultery, and he'd left New Braunfels. Anna had remarried just two weeks later, and her new husband treated her like a queen. When he'd heard the news, Rhody was glad that it had worked out well for Anna without his intervention and wondered if Anna wasn't already familiar with her new husband before she had filed for divorce. It didn't matter because he still thought Paul was a jerk.

After the yawl slid next to the dock, Rhody hopped onto the wharf and looped the docking lines around its belaying pins to bring it to a stop.

He helped Emma onto the dock and after Willie was off the boat, they began walking to the beach.

When they spotted the rest of the family on the upper porch of their house a few hundred yards away, Rhody and Emma waved.

Emma had her arm locked on Rhody's as they crossed the sand as she said, "I never thought that I'd understand how you felt out there on the water, but I understood on that first short trip. Sometimes, I find it hard to remember what it was like living in west Texas. It seems like a whole different life to me now."

"It was a different life, Emma. This is your life now. My life has changed just as much, too. Now I have a family and we'll soon add our new child. But even more than having a family, Emma, I found you. And you are my life."

C.J. PETIT

Author's Note

I took a detour from the Evans family saga to write this standalone to be some form of tribute to my home state (and no, it wasn't Texas). I spent almost every day of my life in Rhode Island until I boarded a National Airlines Boeing 727 that took me to Lackland AFB outside of San Antonio for Air Force basic training.

Since then, I've probably spent fewer than thirty days in Rhode Island as my assignments took me to Texas, then a generous six-month tour in the panhandle of Florida before they honored me with a vacation assignment to Greenland. Then it was Andrews AFB in Maryland before a tour in Greece. When I returned to the States, I was sent to Missouri, then a few years in North Dakota before I returned to Missouri and finished in Nebraska, where I retired and still live in my man cave.

There are only five of the contiguous states that I've missed in my travels: Washington, Oregon, and probably most surprising, Maine, New Hampshire and Vermont.

Anyway, I'm going to edit all of the books before starting on the sixth Evans book. It'll be about Alwen and Garth, but I'm still not settled on a plot yet. I suppose I'll come up with something.

I do miss the ocean.

RHODY JONES

BOOK LIST

1	Rock Creek	12/26/2016
2	North of Denton	01/02/2017
3	Fort Selden	01/07/2017
4	Scotts Bluff	01/14/2017
5	South of Denver	01/22/2017
6	Miles City	01/28/2017
7	Hopewell	02/04/2017
8	Nueva Luz	02/12/2017
9	The Witch of Dakota	02/19/2017
10	Baker City	03/13/2017
11	The Gun Smith	03/21/2017
12	Gus	03/24/2017
13	Wilmore	04/06/2017
14	Mister Thor	04/20/2017
15	Nora	04/26/2017
16	Max	05/09/2017
17	Hunting Pearl	05/14/2017
18	Bessie	05/25/2017
19	The Last Four	05/29/2017
20	Zack	06/12/2017
21	Finding Bucky	06/21/2017
22	The Debt	06/30/2017
23	The Scalawags	07/11/2017
24	The Stampede	08/23/2019
25	The Wake of the Bertrand	07/31/2017
26	Cole	08/09/2017
27	Luke	09/05/2017
28	The Eclipse	09/21/2017
29	A.J. Smith	10/03/2017
30	Slow John	11/05/2017
31	The Second Star	11/15/2017
32	Tate	12/03/2017
33	Virgil's Herd	12/14/2017
34	Marsh's Valley	01/01/2018
35	Alex Paine	01/18/2018
36	Ben Gray	02/05/2018
37	War Adams	03/05/2018

#	Title	Date
38	Mac's Cabin	03/21/2018
39	Will Scott	04/13/2018
40	Sheriff Joe	04/22/2018
41	Chance	05/17/2018
42	Doc Holt	06/17/2018
43	Ted Shepard	07/16/2018
44	Haven	07/30/2018
45	Sam's County	08/19/2018
46	Matt Dunne	09/07/2018
47	Conn Jackson	10/06/2018
48	Gabe Owens	10/27/2018
49	Abandoned	11/18/2018
50	Retribution	12/21/2018
51	Inevitable	02/04/2019
52	Scandal in Topeka	03/18/2019
53	Return to Hardeman County	04/10/2019
54	Deception	06/02.2019
55	The Silver Widows	06/27/2019
56	Hitch	08/22/2018
57	Dylan's Journey	10/10/2019
58	Bryn's War	11/05/2019
59	Huw's Legacy	11/30/2019
60	Lynn's Search	12/24/2019
61	Bethan's Choice	02/12/2020
62	Rhody Jones	03/11/2020
63	Alwen's Dream	06/14/2020
64	The Nothing Man	06/30/2020
65	Cy Page	07/19/2020
66	Tabby Hayes	09/04/2020
67	Dylan's Memories	09/20/2020
68	Letter for Gene	09/09/2020
69	Grip Taylor	10/10/2020
70	Garrett's Duty	11/09/2020
71	East of the Cascades	12/02/2020
72	The Iron Wolfe	12/23/2020
73	Wade Rivers	01/09/2021
74	Ghost Train	01/27/2021
75	The Inheritance	02/26/2021
76	Cap Tyler	03/26/2021

RHODY JONES

77 The Photographer   04/10/2021
78 Jake   05/06/2021
79 Riding Shotgun   06/03/2021
80 The Saloon Lawyer   07/04/2021

Made in the USA
Middletown, DE
10 July 2022